WAKING THE WITCH

A GOTHIC MYSTERY

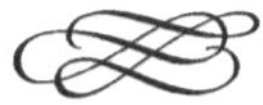

DAYLE A. DERMATIS

Waking the Witch
Dayle A. Dermatis

Print edition published 2018 by Soul's Road Press

ISBN-13: 978-1-946462-08-4
ISBN-10: 1-946462-08-X

Inquiries should be addressed to
Soul's Road Press
info@soulsroadpress.com
http://www.soulsroadpress.com

Cover art images © conrado, © Tonygers, and © dpaint, all via Bigstockphoto.com
Cover art and Soul's Road Press logo: Designs by Trapdoor

CHAPTER 1

*I*F SHE HADN'T been so exhausted by the red-eye from San Francisco to JFK, Rowan's psychic shields wouldn't have been down when Chloë met her at the train station in Poughkeepsie.

One minute she was stepping out of the station, juggling her bags and breathing in the crisp autumn air, and the next she was being swept up in a fierce hug.

"Oh God, Rowan, thank you for coming."

Normally she would never pry, never try to sense something personal without permission, but Chloë had caught her off guard. Rowan slammed the lid on her sixth sense and returned the hug.

"Of course. Anything for you. You said it's about Bryson?"

"Yes. God. I couldn't talk about it on the phone. Not here, either. Let's get your bags into the car."

Under other circumstances, Rowan would have been delighted to see Chloë. It had been nearly a year since they'd seen each other, when they'd been bridesmaids at the wedding of Amanda, the third member of their college suite. That celebration had taken place six months after Chloë had married David and moved to Duchess County, New York.

Rowan had been skeptical when Chloë first enthused about her new paramour. David was twenty years older than Chloë, a divorcé with a teenage son, and decidedly wealthy. Chloë wasn't the type to be swept off her feet by money, and Rowan couldn't quite understand what the attraction was; plus she and Amanda worried that David was merely looking for a trophy wife or a permanent nanny for his son.

At Amanda's wedding, though, Rowan had had to admit that she'd never seen Chloë happier. David had set up a sculpting studio for her and she was preparing for her first big show. They were obviously in love, always holding hands and exchanging kisses, both enthusiastic about trying to create a half-sibling for sixteen-year-old Bryson.

But now, sitting in the car on the way from the station, Rowan saw a huge change brought on by the strain of recent events. Pasty-skinned and hollow-eyed, Chloë looked as though she hadn't slept in days, which she probably hadn't. Was it possible to lose weight so quickly? Rowan wondered, looking at Chloë's hands as she deftly turned the steering wheel of her gleaming silver Saab turbo. The extravagant diamond-and-emerald engagement ring seemed to be sliding around on her thin finger.

"Thank you for coming, Rowan," Chloë said again. "I can't tell you how much it means to me."

"You know I'll always be there for you," Rowan said. "Just tell me what I can do."

Chloë flashed her a wan smile. "Just moral support right now, love. And a little stability in a world gone mad."

Then, as if granted a sudden surge of energy, she wrapped her fingers around Rowan's wrist, her grip as tight and as desperate as her hug had been. "I need you," she said, "to use your powers and find out if he really did kill someone."

"Isn't it a little early for drinks?" Rowan asked.

She'd indulged in a nap, needing to be at her best for what she guessed she had to do soon. Still, it was only early afternoon. The housekeeper had put together a seafood salad and left out crusty rolls, lettuce, and tomato, as well as apple crisp and fresh whipped cream, but they'd only nibbled. Chloë said she wasn't ready to talk just yet.

Now she was, with, apparently fortification.

"Yes," Chloë said. "But we'll need it. Scotch, still?"

The bar was behind the sofa, so Rowan murmured a response rather than nodding. She slipped off her shoes and tights, and stretched her bare feet towards the fire, her fuchsia-lacquered toenails shimmering in the light of the flames. From hidden speakers, Celtic New Age mood music provided a soothing backdrop.

The room's décor wasn't what she would have expected of Chloë, but she knew that Chloë had been loath to make major changes when she moved in, not wanting to disrupt David's or Bryson's home too much. Still, Rowan could see some touches that were definitely her friend's: the Waterhouse "Siren" print on the wall, the Salomé statue on the mantle.

Chloë handed her a cut-crystal glass of single-malt Talisker—just a finger—and settled on the burgundy leather sofa next to her with a white wine spritzer. And they finally talked about what had happened.

"A group of men gang-raped a girl and left her to die." Chloë said it all in a rush, as if needing to get it out before something choked her. She gulped at her drink and set down the glass. "The next morning, they all confessed. Only they weren't men—they were high school boys. Including Bryson."

She did crumble into tears then, and Rowan held her, murmuring words of strength and smelling the expensive shampoo in Chloë's silky hair. What must it be like, Rowan wondered, to have your son confess to rape? For Chloë had adopted Bryson and by all her accounts adored him, as he did her.

Chloë's sobs subsided. "I know things like this have happened before: upstanding, hard-working kids who nobody thought could do any wrong. Or the parents are too high-and-mighty to accept that their child could have done such a thing, or even if he did he must be protected at all costs." She shook her head. "I know I sound like one of those." Her red-rimmed eyes pleaded with Rowan. "But I swear, I *do* know Bryson! I *do* know he would never rape somebody! I mean, he's absolutely sick over what's happened."

"There is such a thing as mob mentality," Rowan said slowly, carefully. "Caught up in the heat of the moment, egged on by your peers…"

Chloë scraped back her blond hair. The short, classic cut was a far cry from the pink-and-blue spikes she had favored in college. "I know," she admitted, her voice tiny. She raised her glass to her mouth again, and Rowan did the same, feeling the burning of the Scotch chase its way down her chest. "But…it's the same thing with all the boys. I know them—maybe not well, but they've all been friends for years, and I do know their parents. They all seem…horrified—sickened, even—at what's happened. At what they've—they've—"

"At what they've done?" Rowan finished.

Her friend shook her head again, her green eyes suddenly stubborn. "At what they've *confessed to doing*," she rephrased firmly. "That's the strangest part, don't you see? They've confessed to raping this girl, but so far, none of the physical evidence incriminates them. In fact, so far it absolves each and every one of them."

"How so?"

"Nothing found at the scene links the boys to even being there. Not hair, nor clothing scraps, nothing. None of the boys had any unusual scratches or bruises that would indicate a struggle. Only one of them physically seemed to have, ah…" Chloë glanced towards the fire, obviously searching for the right word. "…seems to have been sexually active the night before, and as near as the doctor who examined him can tell, he wasn't…active with anyone else."

"Got it," Rowan murmured.

"Obviously, they could have showered afterwards, so that fact in and of itself doesn't say much," Chloë continued. "Meanwhile, none of the boys had ever shown a propensity towards anger or violence. Yes, two of them are on the football team, but nothing beyond just playing the game. Two of them have girlfriends, and both girls have gone on record saying the boys had never been abusive or rough with them."

Rowan let the last of her Scotch trickle down her throat. "What about alcohol or drugs? They can change a person, make them do things they normally wouldn't do."

"All the boys tested clean. Again, it was the next morning, and some or all of the effects could have worn off by then. I'll be honest with you, Rowan," Chloë said, looking at her. "Bryson does drink a little. I know he's underage, and we try to confine it to the home. We're trying to teach him that moderation is good, that alcohol can be part of the larger social milieu, and that getting plastered shouldn't be the end result."

"Hey, you won't get any criticism from me," Rowan replied. "You and I had to learn that the hard college way."

"We did let it rip a few times, didn't we?" Chloë agreed with a ghost of a smile.

"With varying results," Rowan said dryly. "I think we survived, though, and lived to enjoy another day. I'd love to take a wine-tasting course someday."

"If you have any questions, ask David. I'm honestly trying to get my head around everything in the wine cellar, but it's a slow process. On that note, would you like another Scotch?"

Rowan considered. "Sure, one more. Just another finger. I can get it."

"No, I'll do it. You're the guest." Chloë took Rowan's glass before she could protest.

Rowan folded her arms over the back of the sofa and rested her chin on them, watching Chloë at the bar. Her friend moved with a quick, precise, almost brittle rhythm, dropping ice cubes into the glass with silver tongs.

"I'm not sure if there's a polite way to ask this, but are you sure *you* should have another?" she asked.

An ice cube clattered on the sideboard and bounced onto the carpet.

Without turning, Chloë said, very quietly, "What do you mean?"

"I mean…in your condition."

Chloë finished fixing the drinks without speaking, although Rowan noticed that she'd changed her own selection to unadulterated sparkling water. Only after she came back around the sofa and gave Rowan her drink did she ask, "How long have you known?"

Not "how did you know?" Chloë was one of the few people who was privy to the knowledge of Rowan's ability.

"Since I hugged you at the station. I'm sorry, Chloë—I really didn't mean to pry. I was so tired that I let myself slip. The second I realized it, I shut it down."

Chloë took a deep breath. "It's okay, sweetie. I was planning on telling you, anyway. I'm barely three months along, and because of the miscarriage in May, I'm wary about announcing it too soon. David knows, of course, but we haven't told Bryson just yet. And now, with this other horrible mess…"

"I hope the stress won't cause problems with the baby," Rowan said, worried.

"So far, everything's okay," Chloë said. "I'm meditating every day, and drinking some herb tea that's supposed to help with relaxation. My doctor is wonderful for finding safe ways for me to deal with the stress, without resorting to drugs. Although he made it clear the occasional glass of wine is better than stress." She paused, biting her lip. "Could you…when you hugged me, could you tell if everything was okay?"

"I didn't sense anything wrong—although I wasn't looking for anything, and as soon as I realized you were pregnant, I backed off, because it was too personal. But no, nothing obvious leapt out at me. I could try again, if you'd like, but I don't know if I can actually suss out that sort of thing. Healing was Amanda's forte, not mine."

Chloë hesitated, and Rowan could tell she was trying to decide. Finally, Chloë said, "No, that's all right. If you didn't sense anything, then it's probably fine."

Rowan put her hand over Chloë's, sending some comforting energy and strength. Chloë closed her eyes, accepting the help. When they finished, she still looked wan, but re-invigorated.

"Thanks," Chloë said, smiling. "That felt good."

"I'm glad I could help."

Chloë's expression changed; now she looked intense again, and she gripped both of Rowan's hands. Her sculptor's fingers were long, supple, but cold and thin. "I'm not asking too much, am I? Asking you to help figure out what happened that night?"

"No, you're not." Rowan said, closing her eyes for a moment. "You wouldn't have asked me unless it was crucial. And I wouldn't be here if I didn't want to help."

"Thank you," Chloë whispered.

Rowan opened her eyes. "The thing is, I'm not entirely sure how I *can* help. I can't do anything that might interfere with the police investigation, and the only kid I'll definitely be able to talk to is Bryson—the other parents aren't going to appreciate some stranger bothering their kids."

"I've thought about it a bit," Chloë said. "First of all, the sheriff is a friend of the family's—hell, he's a friend of every family around here. He doesn't want to believe the boys did it, and although he's doing his job, I know he's going to be happier if it's proven that the boys didn't do it.

"The same goes for the other parents. I'm not sure if they'll all agree, but I'm pretty sure a couple of them will go along with it, if they think it might help prove their sons' innocence."

"I'm willing to do whatever I can, provided it's not breaking the law—too much," Rowan said.

Chloë smiled briefly. "Of course."

"Did you tell the sheriff about my ability?" Rowan asked.

"You said it would be okay, so I did."

"And?"

"He's skeptical. I'm sure he'll want to talk to you about it tomorrow."

Rowan sighed. "I can't say I'm looking forward to that, but if it'll help you and Bryson, it's worth it. Now, are you up to talking about the situation some more, or do you need a break?"

A burned-through log collapsed in the fireplace, sending a flurry of sparks up the chimney and the scent of burnt pine into the room.

Chloë shook her head. "Now that we're talking about it, I'd like to get it all out."

Rowan listened as her friend explained that the boys had been released on bail to the recognizance of their parents. The bail had been set at a moderate rate, she said, although Rowan realized it was actually quite high. High, at least, for those not of an upper-crust, upper-class background. David Waltham's family had invested in computers before computers were big, Rowan knew, but the money they'd invested had been old, family money. They'd already been well-off, and much the same was true of the other families in the community.

The four boys were confined to their homes unless accompanied by a parent or other adult authorized by the court. A tutor had been hired to continue their education so that they didn't fall behind in school, and all of them were regularly seeing a psychiatrist.

"That was part of the court arrangement, but we all would have insisted on it anyway," Chloë said. She picked up a baby pumpkin from the artistic autumn arrangement on the end table, and turned it over in her hands. "I just don't understand it, Rowan. If they didn't do it, why would they confess to it? Even the psychiatrist says their profiles don't fit that of a rapist or murderer. They're all completely torn up about this—shocked, upset."

"Repentant?" Rowan suggested.

"No." Chloë put the gourd down. "That's just it, Rowan. Like I said, they're absolutely horrified by it. But they don't seem remorseful. Oh, it's so hard to explain. Their reactions seem to be more like 'How could anybody do such a terrible thing?' rather than 'I did it, and I'm sorry.'"

"I don't know enough about psychology to comment on that one," Rowan said. "I'm sure the psychiatrist will make some headway there. Let's go back to the facts. So far, there's no physical evidence that puts them at the scene. What about witnesses? Did anyone see the crime? Do the boys have alibis for where they were supposed to be at the time?"

"Yes, that. Forensics placed the incident between 10:30 and 11:00 p.m. It was a school night, so all the boys should have been home or nearby. James was at Karl's, watching TV. Karl's father heard the TV on, but was in another part of the house and he can't swear they were home the whole time. Manny was at the gym swimming laps that evening, and the staff there said he left when the gym closed at 10:00. He said he then bicycled home as usual. No one remembers seeing him outside."

When Chloë didn't continue, Rowan prompted, "And Bryson?"

The gourd was in Chloë's hands again, turning over and over.

"David was away on a business trip that night," she said finally. "After dinner I went out to my studio—it's a converted guest house in the back—to work on some pieces for my show. Oh, I haven't told you about that. I will later. Anyway, I came down with a blinding headache all of a sudden, so I came back inside and decided to go to bed. Bryson was in his room, studying, I suppose. I called through the door that I was going to bed, and he commented that it was still early. I told him I wasn't feeling well, and he asked if there was anything he could do. I said no, and he said he hoped I felt better, and goodnight.

"There's a clock at the end of the hall, and I was looking straight as it while I was talking to Bryson. It was 10:45 p.m. There's no way he could have been gone and come back by that time, or that he could have left immediately afterwards and gotten to the woods in time.

"He was home, Rowan. I swear to you, he was home."

CHAPTER 2

*T*HE YOUNG WOMAN *had ceased to struggle. Her eyes, deep blue like a winter evening, stared sightlessly upward as the next man moved over her to violate her still body. Despite her lack of movement, two of the others pinned her arms against the frost-hard ground, just in case. She had fought like a wildcat earlier, and one of the men sported a puffy, purpling bruise around his eye, courtesy of her fist.*

He had answered in kind, breaking her nose in the process with a sickening crunch. She had cried out once, then almost choked on her breath and the flow of blood, black instead of red in the moonlight, sluggish in the late autumn chill.

Now even her whimpers had died away.

The man finished and, with a grunt, pulled away from her. Her skirt, roughly hiked above her waist, tore when he stepped on it.

He froze. "Why isn't she moving?" he demanded.

The others stared. "Shit," one of them barked. He nudged the girl with the toe of his boot. Her head flopped sideways with a rustle as the fall leaves caught in her tangled, dirty-blond hair.

"It doesn't matter—no one will miss her," said another. His breath, like all of theirs, stank of alcohol. "And if they did, who'd believe some whore over us?"

The first man was slowly buckling his belt. It was somehow obvious that he was trying to figure out if she'd been dead while he was raping her. Then he shook his head, turned, and followed his friends toward the path that led out of the woods.

Ghost-wisps of clouds began moving over the full moon. The wide blank eyes didn't see, and then it was dark.

~

Rowan jerked back, yanking her hands from beneath the crisp brown leaves. She rose and staggered a few steps to the nearest tree, then knelt behind it and threw up. When she was done, she still crouched there, gasping and spitting, unable to chase from her mind the vision of brutality.

Not just a vision. It might be a vision to her now, but it was something that had happened recently. A girl was dead.

Rowan moved to a sitting position, her back against the tree and her jean-clad legs folded against her body. She wrapped her arms around her knees and stared at the scuffle of leaves surrounded by the flapping remains of bright yellow police tape. If she squinted, she thought she could make out the imprint of the body that had lain there. But no—she closed her eyes momentarily, with a shudder—that wasn't possible. In the past few days, the wind had looped its customary trail through the trees, and the area contained a healthy scattering of newly dropped leaves in hues of scarlet and fire and rust.

Or blood.

"Stop it," Rowan said aloud. She fished in the pocket of her leather bomber jacket until she found the plastic bottle. She swallowed the pills dry, ignoring the heaving of her stomach, and shoved the bottle back into her pocket as she stood.

But still she didn't leave. She stood, staring at the leaves and the tape, ignoring the wisps of hair that the autumn wind dislodged and blew across her stinging cheeks.

She wished she hadn't needed to come here. It had been the best chance of finding a clue, of learning what had happened. As it turned out, she hadn't seen anything useful; all the men's faces had been shrouded in shadows, their clothing indistinct in the night's dark, their voices not something she was any good at remembering again. But even if she had seen some incriminating detail, the best she could have done was to try and prove it, or give the sheriff a tip on which to build solid facts and information. What *she* saw wouldn't be enough to convict anyone.

Rowan closed her eyes. Sometimes she hated her ability. At the very least she'd managed to keep it secret from everyone except a few close friends, knowing that otherwise she'd be ostracized as a loony or hounded by every desperate believer.

She started to walk away...then turned and looked back one last time. If she had in fact seen something useful, she wasn't sure she could have refused to help.

~

"Good lord, Rowan, you look terrible! Are you okay?"

"No," Rowan grunted. She had just returned from the crime scene; the vision of the rape still replayed itself in her head, a nightmarish video she couldn't turn off.

Chloë had opened the door just as Rowan pulled into the driveway. Because she'd had to stay home with Bryson, she'd told Rowan where the crime scene was, in a wooded glen less than half a mile from the village green. Rowan had borrowed one of the cars in the Waltham stable, a hunter green BMW. It had been Bryson's sixteenth birthday present.

It hadn't been an easy drive back.

"Is there anything I can do?" Chloë asked, unlocking the front door. Rowan stood on the brick porch, hunched over, waiting to be admitted.

"No," she said again. Feeling guilty, because it wasn't Chloë's fault, she added, "Need a shower. Talk soon."

The en suite bathroom contained some of the house's early charm, with a claw-footed bathtub that had been updated to include a shower fixture. With the shower curtain (decorated in a leafy pattern reminiscent of the bed frame) closed, Rowan was surrounded by a haze of steam. She scrubbed furiously, using the loofah like a scouring pad, as if she could scrape the vision from her mind by scraping off a layer of skin.

There were two problems with that, though: One, it wasn't going to work, and two, she needed to remember the vision. If only she could remove the feeling, the horror…

Eventually, the hot, soothing water and lavender-scented soap succeeded. The immediacy of the scene had faded, along with it the abhorrence that had consumed her. It was still appalling, but Rowan managed to deal with the emotions surrounding it, able to replay it like a real video rather than an experience.

She still wasn't ready to face it, or Chloë, just yet, so she took the time to properly unpack. The simple housekeeping task helped ground and center her.

A wrought iron four-poster bed dominated the guest room, its headboard and footboard each an artful swirl of leaves and vines. Filmy white fabric floated from the rail around the top. At the foot of the bed was a carved chest, upon which sat a stack of towels and a small basket of toiletries. A heavy rosewood armoire hulked in one corner, and the bedside table, of the same ironwork as the bed, held an Art Deco lamp with a glass dragonfly shade.

"I don't know—luxury like this and I might not want to leave," she'd said when Chloë first showed it to her.

Chloë had laughed. "We get enough visitors—relatives, colleagues of David's—that I try to make the guest rooms as appealing as possible." She gestured towards the roll-top desk, upon which leaf-shaped bookends supported a mix of paperbacks and hardcovers. "I put some books there that I thought you might like. I remember how you always liked to read before bed."

"It used to drive you and Amanda nuts, too," Rowan said.

"Some of us don't allow ourselves the decadence of what you call 'sleeping in a bit'," Chloë had retorted.

They'd talked downstairs, and then Rowan had investigated the crime scene.

Now, she dumped her suitcases on the bed. As usual, she'd brought too much. She didn't know how long she was going to stay here, so she'd tried to plan for every eventuality, including Indian summer and an early snowfall. The armoire was spacious, however, and scented with a clove-studded orange pomander. The long, flowing skirts that were the mainstay of her wardrobe went in there, along with the sapphire blue velvet dress (in case of an emergency party), a variety of silk blouses, jeans, and several pairs of shoes and boots. The matching dresser became home to knit shirts, sweaters, scarves, and jewelry.

She worked methodically, fighting against her usual impulse to fling everything inside and shut the door before anything tried to escape. Instead, she used the enforced neatness to compartmentalize the information she'd learned, putting a layer of dispassion between herself and the scene.

But she knew, even if she succeeded now, it was going to get worse before it got better. She just had to believe it *would* get better.

Sighing, Rowan reached for her computer bag and looked around for the best place to set up her laptop. She opened the rolltop desk. Other than some writing paper and envelopes tucked into its pigeon-holes, it was empty, and there was a convenient outlet nearby. Rowan placed her Apple laptop on the desk, and tucked the various files and papers and supply of Post-Its and pens in the drawers. At least her work was reasonably portable.

Then, finally ready to talk, she went to find Chloë.

"It was pretty wretched," she admitted to her friend. They curled up on Chloë's bed, Rowan still wrapped in a robe of thick peach terrycloth. The bedroom felt almost gothic in tone, with dark furniture and bedding, and fat candles squatting in shallow holders. But swags clutched open the heavy blue velvet draperies, admitting a broad beam of sunlight and exposing a view of a maple tree in full burgundy splendor. "I could feel the girl's terror, her pain." She shuddered. "And then I could feel her give in—I could tell she had abandoned all hope. In some ways, I felt her die."

Chloë slid a comforting arm around Rowan's shoulders. "I'm so sorry," she said. "I wish I'd never asked you to do this."

Rowan shook her head, her still-damp hair cool against her back. "You didn't ask me to do that; you just asked me to help. This is the only way I truly can. It's just…"

"What?" Chloë's query was gentle.

"Have I ever told you about when I got my ability?"

"No, you've always said you didn't want to talk about it."

I don't want to talk about it now, Rowan thought, fighting off panic. Aloud, she said, "I've only ever talked to one person about it—a healer. She suggested that the reason it manifested when it did was as a defense mechanism. It lay dormant until I needed it.

"It was in college, really early in freshman year, about six months before I met you guys. I was walking back from town, late at night, and a guy attacked me."

Chloë gasped. "Oh my God, Rowan!"

The arm around Rowan's shoulder's tightened. Rowan gladly accepted the energy from Chloë's touch.

"Nothing happened—he didn't rape me, I mean. I struggled, and someone heard me scream and came running. The guy took off. They never caught him." She kept her eyes fixed on her bare foot, watching the pulse just below the ankle bone. Steady, rhythmic. Life. Life went on. It had to. She'd learned to build a wall around the memory, around the fear. The vision this morning had shattered the wall, and although rebuilding it was much faster this time, she'd still been thrown off-kilter.

"I'm so sorry," Chloë said again. "Now I really know I shouldn't have asked you here."

"Stop it!" Rowan shrugged her arm away. "I'm here because I want to be; I'm doing this because I choose to." She took a deep breath, let it out slowly, through her nose. "I don't mean to snap at you. This isn't easy to tell, and there's more."

"Did they ever catch the guy?"

"No. It was dark, so I didn't get a good look at his face, and he ran off before anyone else saw him clearly.

"But I did see him again."

"What?" Chloë breathed.

"About a week later, in the student union. Like I said, I never got a good look at his face, so I wouldn't have recognized him. But I brushed against him, and when I did, I *knew* it was him. I saw the whole scene again, only through his eyes. He must have recognized me, because when I actually looked at him, he smiled. It was terrible. He knew, and I knew, but I'd already told the authorities I didn't see his face well enough to identify him, and he knew that. He knew he was safe." Rowan hadn't been aware that she was crying, but she brushed at her face and her hand came away wet. "I was helpless, and I hated that. The only thing that saved my sanity was that now that I knew who he was, I could be on guard against him—before, I had been jumping at every shadow, and couldn't stand to be alone.

"That, and my power."

Chloë was crying, too. "What happened to the bastard?"

Rowan shrugged again. "I don't know. I looked him up in the student roster online after I knew what his face looked like. I kept checking the computer, every few days. He was a jock; I don't think his grades were up to snuff, because eventually he left college." She clenched her hands, willing them to stop shaking. Steady pulse. Solid wall.

But the wall, no matter how shatterproof, was clear now.

"I'm here because I want to be; I'm here to help. You needed me to be here, Chloë, and of course I came here to support you. But there's more to it than that."

Chloë reached over to her night table, opened a drawer, and pulled out a box of tissues. She placed it on the bed between them. Rowan noticed Chloë waited until she had taken one before she pulled one out herself. A small, simple gesture that bespoke volumes.

Rowan blew her nose, using the brief time to ground herself.

"It's about feeling helpless," she continued. "When the guy jumped me, I fought back. I was reasonably fit. I screamed. I didn't have time to think about whether or not I had a chance. I didn't think about whether or not I was helpless.

"But when I saw him the next week, and he smiled, and we both knew there was nothing I could do—*then* I felt helpless. And I hated my powers. They'd started because of him, and they showed me who I was, so they always, always reminded me of him, and reminded me I was helpless.

"I finally realized that the powers, in some ways, made me *less* helpless. It took me a long time to come to terms with that. But maybe here, I can be helpful rather than helpless."

There was more, but she couldn't explain it to Chloë.

The girl in the woods had been helpless, too. Rowan couldn't do anything about her own attacker, but maybe she could do something about the guys who had attacked the girl.

She just prayed that one of them wasn't Bryson.

"I can understand that," Chloë was saying. "I won't say anything more about whether or not I should have asked you here. I just so appreciate it, Rowan. I think I'd fall apart—just shatter into little bits —if I didn't have your support. I wish Amanda could be here, too."

Amanda was in Scotland. Along with singing, she played the bodhran, uilean pipes, and pennywhistle; her husband played various types of fiddles. She was currently recording backup for a pop group whose name she wasn't yet allowed to reveal. "I know, sweetie. If it weren't for the limited studio time, she would be. She'll come as soon as she's free."

Chloë nodded, snuffling into a tissue.

For a while they were silent—each in her own private hell, Rowan thought pensively.

"Aren't you going to ask me what I saw today?" Rowan asked finally.

Like the bed in the guest room, this one was also four-poster, but was made of deep cherry, the posts reaching up to the ceiling like trees stretching toward the sky. Chloë lay back on the spread, which was midnight blue dotted with gold fleur-de-lys.

"I'm afraid to," she admitted softly.

"Because it might incriminate Bryson?"

"Yes."

A knock at the door interrupted Rowan's response. They both started; Chloë sitting up and automatically patting her hair as she called for the person to come in.

It was Bryson.

"Hi, Mom. Hello, Rowan."

Rowan accepted his proffered hand. "Hey, Bryson," she said. She felt suddenly vulnerable, and she didn't like it. She stood, making their heights closer to equal, adjusting her robe in case it was revealing anything.

"Are you okay?" Bryson had realized that Chloë had been crying.

"I'm fine, honey. Rowan and I were just talking about what had happened, and I got a little upset."

Bryson leaned his forehead against one of the bedposts at the foot of the bed. "I'm sorry," he said.

Rowan wondered if he had picked up the apology bug from Chloë, or vice-versa. Still discomfited, she took advantage of his stance to look at him carefully.

He was bigger than she remembered from a year ago. Taller, he'd also filled out a bit, his broad shoulders well-shaped; Rowan remembered Chloë saying he was on the football team. He was a few inches above Rowan's own five-foot-eight. He didn't look much like his father. In contrast to David's almost fey qualities, Bryson's face was fuller, his chin strong. His chestnut hair was thick and toying at being long in the back. To her surprise, she caught sight of a narrow gold hoop in his ear. They let prep school boys have piercings now? The earring was tiny, though, and noticeable primarily because the sun glinted off it.

Despite all her shields, Rowan found herself wondering: Was he a rapist? She felt immediately guilty, mortified at how Chloë would react to her thought. But she couldn't help it. She'd spent far too much of her life looking at every male with that question, and although she didn't react so strongly anymore, the situation had re-opened the proverbial wound.

"We're going to get this thing figured out," Chloë was saying firmly to him.

Anguish filled his hazel eyes. Rowan supposed it could be an act, but reading people's honesty wasn't her forte. Even if she touched him and tried, as she had with Chloë the day before, she might not be able to see past a well-placed façade.

But Chloë was briskly changing the subject, asking him what he wanted. It turned out he was checking in about dinner. Rowan suppressed a smile. No matter how bad the circumstances, a boy's gotta eat.

"Thanks for the reminder, honey," Chloë said. "Why don't you go down and see what Helen's putting together. I'm hungry, too."

Rowan realized she was, as well. Lunch seemed like a long time ago, and using her power always made her need extra fuel.

The door closed behind Bryson. Chloë didn't get up. Rowan waited, also making no move to leave.

"I need to know, Rowan," Chloë said. "I can't bear not knowing, even if it incriminates him."

"Then I'll start by saying it didn't." Rowan pressed her fingers against the bridge of her nose. "It didn't incriminate him, but it didn't rule anything out, either. Unfortunately, I don't think it did anything except make me ill."

"I'm sorry you had to go through it for nothing," Chloë said, standing and giving her a quick, fierce hug.

"When I can distance myself from it, I might be able to pick up something subtle. I couldn't see faces or clothes; nothing obvious like that."

Chloë let out a long breath. "I'm disappointed that it didn't help, but God, I'm so relieved."

"David's working late tonight, and Bryson's going to eat in his room so he can keep studying, so it'll be just the two of us," Chloë said. "We can eat in the kitchen."

The kitchen was larger than Rowan's living room. Gleaming white and chrome appliances ringed the walls, and brass pots dangled from a rack above them as they perched on bar stools at the long central island.

Their dinner conversation was light, confined to catching up on both their activities over the past year. Rowan guessed Chloë didn't want to spoil the meal by talking about upsetting things, and so she didn't press her. She didn't blame Chloë, either; she was exhausted from it all, too.

Instead, they ate salmon and rice pilaf and asparagus, and were finishing an exquisite chocolate mousse for dessert, and were chatting about the house when Chloë's husband arrived home.

"I'm sorry, sweetheart," he said, kissing Chloë. "I trust Rowan was a reasonable substitute for me?"

"I was glad for her company," Chloë replied. She squeezed his hand, and he held on to it as he turned to Rowan.

"Thank you for coming on such short notice, Rowan," he said. "I hope this isn't causing any difficulties with your work."

"They were pretty understanding," Rowan replied. "Of course, I'll have to keep working on the latest brochure while I'm here, but with e-mail and the Internet, it's not too hard to do it away from the office."

Chloë's husband was tall, with neat black hair that had begun a march backwards at his temples. Rowan had never been impressed by men in suits, but David seemed less severe than most. It was the shape of his face, she decided: narrow, with a pointed chin, it gave him an almost fey quality. His eyes, too, belied the rest of his appearance; warm and brown, they now looked rueful.

"I'm embarrassed to admit it, because I know Chloë's told me, but remind me what exactly it is that you do?"

Rowan smiled. "Don't be embarrassed—there are days when even I'm not sure what my job description is. I work for A Faire Day Out, a new Renaissance fair in central California. I worked a few different Ren fairs during college and just after, in different costumed roles. When A Faire Day was getting together, I hired on as a sort of media/marketing/advertising director. I design brochures and ads, and all the various flyers and stuff people pick up at the fair itself. I also handle a lot of the research to make sure we're re-creating things correctly. And occasionally, when the usual girl can't make it, I stand in as Queen Elizabeth."

"I can see why, with your coloring," Chloë said. "I've always envied you your hair."

Rowan lifted the heavy weight of red hair. "Hogwash. You know it's straight from the bottle, just like yours used to be."

"No, mine was usually from a spray can."

David wrinkled his nose. "I love you dearly, but I'm truly glad I didn't have to experience that phase of your life."

Rowan bit back a smile. Seeing Chloë now in her cream trousers and rust silk blouse, a single strand of pearls around her neck, she could understand why David would have a hard time accepting the previous incarnation of his wife, which had included a pierced nose and a propensity for tight leather pants.

David excused himself, taking a plate of food to his study with him.

"He's cramming in the hours now, in case he needs to take time off," Chloë explained as she put their dishes next to the sink.

She didn't need to explain why he might need to take time off. The dark thought hung in the air.

After lunch the next day, Rowan accompanied Chloë when she dropped Bryson off at Manny's house, where the boys were meeting for their tutoring session, and then Chloë drove her to the center of the village to meet with the sheriff.

"Are the police okay with the boys studying together?" Rowan asked when Chloë returned to the car after seeing Bryson to the door. "I mean, what about story corroboration and all that?"

Chloë shrugged. "What's to corroborate? They boys all admit they did it, and their statements to the police all match up. If they were suspects and were saying that they *didn't* do it, that would be different." She reached the road, checked both ways, then backed out, shifted into first, and headed off campus.

"I hadn't thought of that," Rowan admitted. Chloë sounded very circumspect, and Rowan felt bad for having asked the question.

Rowan hadn't been sure what was appropriate meet-with-the-sheriff clothing, and had finally decided on a long, flowing silk skirt of royal blue, a black silk turtleneck, low black boots, and silver Celtic knotwork earrings and necklace. Over it all she'd thrown a long black leather coat and burn-out velvet scarf. She'd thought she looked pulled together and elegant. But now, next to Chloë's plum knit skirt-and-top ensemble and small gold jewelry, she felt flamboyant, Californian (whatever that meant). Chloë, the artist, had always carried herself with a style that Rowan and Amanda had envied. Where Rowan felt her outfit was thrown together, Chloë's mishmash of styles had always seemed to somehow work. She was still getting used to this new, understated, preppy version of Chloë, but the clothes suited her slim frame well.

And it was too late now to change her own outfit.

Rowan had been in a police station only once in her life: when she worked in a small store that had been burgled, and the police needed all the employees' fingerprints to see if they could find any unfamiliar ones in the store. She felt unaccountably nervous as she paced the waiting room, examining the Wanted posters on the wall, as if she had done something wrong, or had something to hide. It didn't help that she was kept waiting for more than half an hour while the sheriff dealt with a "situation," as the desk clerk phrased it. She wasn't sure if he meant an incident involving the law or a personal problem.

She felt a little calmer when she entered his office, however. His desk had an air of familiar chaos that she could identify with.

Unfortunately, she shouldn't have relaxed.

"Sheriff Candusco," she said, shaking his hand. His grip was firm without being over-tight. Something tingled as he let go of her hand, but she couldn't quite identify what it was.

Chloë hadn't told her that he was so good looking. His smile was brief and polite, flashing a hint of a crooked incisor. His face was angular, his skin bearing the end of a summer tan. His black hair looked like it would have been curly if it weren't cut so short, and she wondered if he'd have grown it out if he weren't required to keep it close-cropped.

"Toby," he said, and she responded with the expected "Call me Rowan, please."

They had barely finished the greeting and seated themselves before he said, "I know about your past, Rowan."

She gaped at him, trying to maintain equilibrium as her stomach plummeted. Guilt surged in its place, even though she hadn't a clue what he was talking about.

"I know that you were attacked while in college. Your freshman year, wasn't it?"

It still took her a moment to speak. A mental picture of her attacker's mocking smile flashed into her brain, and she quickly locked it away again.

"Yes," she managed. "But how did you...? The case was closed because no one could identify the assailant."

"Local newspaper, university records."

"All right, then. You've done your homework." Rowan took a deep breath. "Is this important?"

"Maybe. Are you here to damn Caesar or to praise him?"

"I'm here to help my friend."

"Are you sure?"

They stared at each other. The sheriff didn't break the gaze, but some subtle shift told Rowan that part of the test was over.

"I'll be straight with you, Rowan," Toby said. "I know these boys; I know their families. I can't conceive of them actually raping and killing the girl. If you're honestly here to help the Walthams, then great. Maybe you can find something out that we haven't been able to. But if you're on a vendetta—"

"What kind of vendetta would that be, Toby?" Rowan asked, her tone icy to mask the wobble that might break through. He was closer to the truth than he realized, closer than she wanted to admit.

He picked up a black gel pen and flipped it between the fingers of his left hand, his eyes never leaving her face. "Against men, perhaps. Some women transfer their anger at their assailant towards men in general."

"I don't need your pop psychology diagnosis, thank you," Rowan snapped. "If you would prefer I not interfere with your investigation, so be it. Just tell me now if there's anywhere I shouldn't go or anyone I shouldn't talk to, so I don't step on any toes."

"Whoa, whoa," he said, putting down the pen. "I just wanted to get a feel for your motives."

"My motives aren't on trial; the boys are."

"Will be—maybe," Toby corrected. "There'll be a preliminary hearing to determine whether there's enough evidence for the case to go to trial. If not, then nothing will happen unless more evidence is found. Right now, there's nothing linking them to the crime except their confessions."

"So what's the next step?"

He leaned back in his chair; Rowan could hear the springs creak. He fiddled with the pen again. "Hard to say," he admitted. "We're waiting for the DNA tests; they could make or break this. In some ways, we're just looking for clues that would indicate that someone else did it."

Rowan sensed that she'd passed the final test; the sheriff was too canny to start chatting with her about the details if he didn't trust her to be an advocate for Bryson, if not the whole team of boys.

"Is there a chance that some of them did it, but not the whole group?"

He shrugged. "A slight chance, but unlikely. Why would they cross-check their own stories and all admit to it?"

"Peer pressure?"

"Now you're getting out of my grasp of pop psychology knowl-edge," he said. "Their psychiatrist might be able to explain that one, but I can't."

"I realize it sounds far-fetched," Rowan admitted with a small smile, acknowledging his gentle joke as a verbal olive branch. "What about the girl? Who was she?"

His chair came down with a gentle thump. "Her name was Mary Cooper, and she lived in the woods."

"In the *woods*?" Rowan had been expecting him to say she was a student at the all-girls' prep school, or perhaps a local girl who went to public school. Or even a college student home on break.

"There's very little information on her." Toby briefly shuffled through the papers on his desk, and found what he was looking for. "Apparently she and her mother were some sort of hippies. She didn't go to school, and they must have been pretty self-sufficient, because they only rarely came to town for supplies."

"Isn't a kid legally required to attend school?"

"Only until he or she is sixteen. We're not sure how old she was, but we're guessing about seventeen. If she ever attended school, it wasn't in Duchess County, but no one seems to have ever raised a protest in the past. Maybe she was home-schooled. A parent has to fill out paperwork and show test scores for that, but stuff like that can be lost."

"Is it just me, or is all this kind of weird?" Rowan asked.

"It's extremely weird," Toby agreed. "There's no evidence that the boys really even knew her. Her mother apparently passed away fairly recently; someone remembers Mary mentioning it when she came into town for supplies."

"Where were they getting money for supplies?" Rowan wondered aloud.

Again he shrugged. "Maybe they had some stashed away, buried in a coffee can or something. We're still trying to get more information on them both."

Rowan rubbed the bridge of her nose; a headache still hovered, despite the medication she'd taken earlier. "What about the alibis? Chloë said only Bryson has one."

Toby raised an eyebrow. "Provisionally."

"You mean because Chloë might be lying?" Rowan bristled.

"She might be—but I doubt it," the sheriff said quickly, before she could get angrier. "She might have only assumed she heard his voice, and heard a radio instead. She might have misread the clock. The clock time might have been tampered with."

Rowan had made a point of looking at it before she went to bed last night. The grandmother clock hung at the end of the upstairs hall. The face was reasonably big, with the hands visible from Bryson's doorway. The cover had been locked.

As if anticipating her next question, Toby said, "The housekeeper has the key to the clock, because she dusts and winds it every week. But she was out that night at a movie, and her ring of keys to various things in the house was in her room, which was unlocked. She doesn't think they were moved, but they could have been put back in the same place. The only prints on the clock were hers and Chloë's."

"It sounds like you've been doing a very thorough job," Rowan said. "I'm impressed."

"Thanks." He accepted the compliment gracefully, matter-of-factly without being egotistical. "I don't know what else to tell you, Rowan. If you're willing, then I appreciate the help. I'd suggest you talk to Bryson's lawyer as well, to make sure there's no legal thing about hindering an investigation or anything."

"What about the other boys' parents? Is it okay for me to talk to them?"

"As long as the boys' parents are willing, I don't know of any problems with that." Toby opened a drawer in his desk and pulled out a leather pen case. "There's one more thing we have to talk about," he said. "Your...special ability."

Rowan nodded. "Chloë said she'd talked to you about that."

"Did she tell you that I'm skeptical?"

"No, but I'm not surprised," Rowan said. Nor was she offended. She'd be suspicious if he didn't have some doubts. "There are a lot of quacks out there."

"And you're not one of them?" He said it with a smile, and she found herself distracted by the way his mouth moved. Where was *that* coming from?

"If I was, I'd be trying to make more money at it," she said easily.

"You've done your research on me, and you'd know if I'd been trying to scam people."

"I'd like to give you a little test, if you don't mind." He handed her the case, the type that usually housed expensive ballpoint, pencil, and fountain pen sets.

She snapped it open. Instead, it contained three Bic ballpoints, the clear ones with plastic caps that indicated ink color. These were blue, identical save for small white labels noting A, B, and C. Rowan looked at the sheriff for explanation.

"Exhibits?"

"Random samples," he replied. "Each pen has been handled by a different person. I want to see if you can tell me anything about the people."

"If they've simply been handled, I can't guarantee anything," Rowan said. "I realize that it's hard to explain, but essentially, I pick up visions from strong emotions. The object has to have been present during the strong emotions for me to see the vision."

His expression didn't change. "Duly noted."

Rowan wondered if that meant that the pens had been involved with strong emotions, but knew he was deliberately not telling her either way. Well, fine. She could play her part in this game, too.

Allowing her mind to still, she glanced over the three pens. The first looked fairly pristine, with most of the ink intact. The second had a chewed cap, the tab bent outwards, perhaps three-fourths of the ink gone, the remaining ink bubbled as these pens did when the ink got low. The third looked like the first—relatively untouched on the outside—but had a bit more ink missing.

She took a deep breath, grounding, then picked up the first pen and held in it a loose fist. She wasn't used to an audience when she did this. She was reasonably sure that she didn't have any strange physical reactions during the process—she didn't twitch or drool, or if she did, no one had seen fit to tell her—but being observed nonetheless made her feel self-conscious. She was going beyond, beneath the conscious level of things; to be judged by that scale made no sense.

So, it took her a moment to get focused, to block out the external reality and the force of the sheriff's gaze. Carefully, slowly, she brought her breathing to a slower ebb and her consciousness in, in, in to another level. No noise, no thought, only the feel of the pen in her hand and the weight on her mind of whatever might be revealed.

Rowan tapped at the pen with her mind, casting for sensations. None came. She frowned. In her memory, she recalled its shape and size—and the fact that it looked untouched, both because of its smooth cap and its relatively unused ink. Could it be a new pen? Although she tried to keep out the conscious, her mind intruded with a somewhat sarcastic comment that of course, the sheriff wouldn't be beyond trying to fool her.

She let out a slow breath, and opened her eyes. Refusing to look across the desk, she replaced the pen in the left-hand slot of the case, and picked up the middle pen. Another deep breath, and she found her balance again.

This pen was the most used, if the loss of ink was any indication. Rowan knew that looks could be deceiving. It always proved a difficult balance to make: On one hand, physical evidence, however minute or simple, could and often did prove relevant; on the other hand, what she experienced with her regular five senses could influence, possibly incorrectly, what she was to see with her deeper sense.

Rowan trusted her power, in that what images she received were usually strong and obvious. Even when influenced, her instincts almost always prevailed. She didn't take that fact for granted, though.

The first sense she got from the pen was innocence. Then, a hint of stress. She groped for the hint, feeling for where it was, and then latched onto it, like a hand around a banister.

"Jesus, I am so freaked about this test."

"Shit, me too. What if she won't let us use calculators? I'll be fucked."

Drawing back, Rowan saw that the first speaker was a young girl, perhaps ten or eleven, wearing braces and ponytailed blonde hair and a midnight blue cardigan. The scene shifted, and the girl sat in class, hunched over a math test. She brought the pen to her mouth, worrying at it.

Rowan gently pulled herself away from the vision. The prevalent emotion there was nerves about an upcoming test. She had the definite sense that the pen had been used for previous school assignments, with varying concern about the outcomes, depending on the subject involved.

She could sense Toby's gaze upon her. She hadn't heard him move during her examination so far, although she knew that when she was focused on an object, she often wasn't entirely aware of the physical world around her. Studiously ignoring his scrutiny, she set down the middle pen and picked up the final one.

There was a gun pointed at her, and she felt terror.

Rowan gasped, tried to back away. She hadn't expected something like that. A chair creaked; the sheriff had finally shifted. It was the last thing she noticed before she was sucked in, unprepared, no time to set up a wall to protect herself from the emotions that pinned her to the experience.

There was a gun pointed at her, and she felt terror.

Rowan let her view expand beyond the dark barrel of the gun, to what surrounded it. A gloved hand held the weapon; a ski-masked figure belonged to the hand. Around him, white metal shelves, harsh fluorescent lights, blurring of colors. A store of some sort, then; perhaps a Walmart or convenience store.

A flicker of movement: There was a woman in the store, near the person whose viewpoint Rowan was seeing through. A thin middle-aged woman, with a cap of platinum hair and dangling gold earrings. She looked terrified. Rowan didn't blame her.

The pen was probably in the viewpoint person's pocket, she realized, as the scene shifted back to the thief.

"Just open the fucking register—slowly! I don' want you trippin' any alarms," the man growled. Someone less familiar with weapons would have used the gun barrel to indicate what he wanted. This man obviously knew what he was doing.

Heart palpitations...hers or the clerks? Rowan could never tell where the vision's emotions ended and hers began. She could smell rank sweat. That would be the clerk's, as he stepped backwards and reached for the cash register. At least, that's what she assumed he was doing; she could see nothing but the black hole of the gun muzzle; the black ski mask behind which blazed black eyes.

Then something went horribly wrong.

Explosion, painfully loud, of both light and sound.

The woman screaming.

The slow, spreading stench of scarlet copper...

Rowan flung the pen away from her—its touch loathsome. Dimly she heard, "Are you all right?" It came through against a roar not unlike an angry ocean. She couldn't look up, couldn't speak. Could only swallow hard and repeatedly against the rising tide of bile and saliva.

"Are you okay?" the sheriff asked again.

Rowan opened her eyes and looked directly at him. "Bastard," she said. Her chair scraped like nails on a chalkboard as she pushed it back. She fled the room.

She made it to the bathroom before she was sick. She'd managed to ask where the room was, flee past the concerned glances, and get into the stall. Small successes.

Afterwards, she leaned her cheek against the cool porcelain and fleetingly wished for unconsciousness, because that was probably the only thing that would stop the bright sparkles of pain that burst like fireworks at the base of her skull. She hadn't brought her migraine medicine; hadn't thought she'd need it.

A low whoosh announced the opening of the bathroom door. A female voice asked hesitantly, "Excuse me? Sheriff Candusco asked me to check and see if you're okay."

Rowan thought of a few choice messages to have relayed back to the sheriff. But it wasn't this woman's fault. Instead, she swallowed several times, wincing at the taste of bile.

"I'll survive," she said. "I'd really love a glass of water, though."

"I'll get you one."

The door opened and closed, opened and closed again. A plastic cup appeared under the stall door.

"Can I get you anything else?"

"This is great, thanks," Rowan said. Her eyes were still teared up, coating her contacts, blurring her vision. She swished water in her mouth and spat into the toilet several times, then drank. The cool water was a balm against the vomit-scratch of her throat. Her head throbbed.

Her benefactor offered help if she needed it, and politely withdrew again.

Rowan lay her head back against the grey metal of the stall, and sat for ten minutes, eyes closed, willing the pain to subside. It didn't entirely—or maybe she got used to it enough to function again.

At the sink, she splashed her face with water and dried it with coarse paper towels that she pulled in a grasping handful from the dispenser. She examined her face in the mirror and winced at her red-rimmed, puffy eyes and, worse, the small red spots from the strain of throwing up. Her makeup was in her purse, which she'd left in the sheriff's office.

"Not a whole lot I can do about it, then," she said to her reflection. Her voice sounded nasal, and she blew her nose before she left.

A small consolation, but the sheriff did look contrite.

"I'm really sorry," he said. "Are you—are you okay?"

"Go on, say it," she urged. "I look terrible. Admit it." Even in her pain, she could make a joke. It had always confused her mother when they were in the emergency room after some childhood mishap.

"Can I get you anything?" he asked.

"First, an explanation. The third pen. There was a gunshot...blood. Did the clerk survive?"

His brown eyes widened; he'd obviously not fully believed in her powers. Rowan was in too much pain to gloat. Much.

"He did—although he's been paralyzed from the waist down. The doctors think there may still be a chance, with some tricky surgery. The shooter's behind bars, and will stay there for a long time."

"Who's the grade-school girl who owns pen B?"

Toby blinked. Now, Rowan thought, he was really convinced.

"My niece," he said.

"If you feel like tattling, tell her mom that she swears. I'm not even going to ask about the math test." Rowan took a deep breath, pressed her fingers to her temples, desperately wanting to be in a dark, quiet room. "Are you satisfied now? Have I passed *your* test?"

When she opened her eyes, she was gratified to see him looking down at his desk. "Yes," he said simply. "I'd like to know more about it —I can't say I'm not still skeptical—but there's no way you could have known those things."

"Let me tell you something about it, then," she said. "You didn't do your homework well enough. The more violent the image, the worse the backlash. If there's little emotion, or mild emotion, I might get a small headache. The stronger or more violent the emotion, the greater the headache. Thanks to you, I now have a full-blown migraine, and because I had no reason to expect this, my medication is back at Chloë's."

She rose, somewhat unsteadily from the fact that she couldn't entirely focus, and pulled her purse from the back of her chair. "Unless we have anything else to go over right now, I'd like to go home."

CHAPTER 3

*R*OWAN EXPLAINED what had happened, and her reaction to it, as Chloë drove home. Despite the chill, she cracked open the window, needing the cold, fresh air to keep her stomach calm. It wouldn't do to mess up Chloë's pristine Saab. Hell, she wouldn't have wanted to be sick in her own untidy Subaru back home. She held on to the handle above the door, too, as if it could give her strength.

"If I'd known Toby would do something like that—" Chloë began.

"No," Rowan said. "He had a right to be skeptical. I don't appreciate his methods, but I suppose I can understand them. This'll teach me to keep my meds with me all the time."

When they arrived home, she took the medication and managed to fall asleep for almost two hours. After she rose and knocked back some Pepsi, she felt well enough to finish out the day in a conscious state. She accepted the invitation to see Chloë's studio, grateful for the diversion.

As they walked, Chloë asked, "Other than making you sick, did Toby have anything helpful to say?"

The day had stayed bright, and the late afternoon sun slanted down the lawn behind Chloë's house. The gardener didn't come daily, and a flurry of scarlet and lemon leaves lay scattered on the short grass. Occasionally a gust of wind would gleefully repattern them, then die down to let the new arrangement lie for a while. Rowan scuffed her feet through the leaves as well, revealing the stepping stones laid into the gentle slope.

"More or less," she said. She related the basics of the conversation to Chloë, leaving out the accusation, and finishing with, "I think he's as stumped as everyone else. I appreciate him trusting me not to get in the way."

At the bottom of the lawn, they crossed over the hint of a stream on a charming white wooden bridge. Evergreens lined the lawn now, and the pine needles underfoot were startlingly silent after the rustle further up.

"This used to be a guest house, decades ago," Chloë said as they approached her studio. "It was empty when I married David, and he had it converted into a studio for me."

She unlocked the door and preceded Rowan into the dim room, which she transformed into a room bathed in light by flicking a switch that electronically drew back the floor-to-ceiling curtains.

"Oh, it's perfect!" Rowan cried.

The cottage had once been a series of rooms, but the walls had been knocked out to create a large studio area broken in a few places by sturdy wooden support beams. Art prints were tacked haphazardly on the walls, a contrast to the orderly artwork in the house. At the back of the room was a kitchenette with a big sink—"For washing up, and making frequent cups of tea," Chloë said—and a single door let to a tiny bathroom. Other than a sofa and bookcases bulging with art books, the only furniture was a custom-built chest designed to hold Chloë's sculpting tools.

"I'm sorry about the mess," Chloë apologized.

Also unlike the near-spotless house, the studio looked as though the demons of disarray had done a frenzied dance. A push broom sat against the wall next to a pile of marble dust, but the pile had been tracked through several times, now resembling a starburst. Drop cloths lived up to their name, apparently dropped at random throughout, except for those that were actually being used to cover some pieces huddled in one corner.

"I don't let Helen clean out here, and I was in the middle of finishing pieces for my show when all hell broke loose. I haven't had time to finish, much less clean up." She let out a long breath. "Then again, I don't know if I'll be able to do the show, now."

Had Chloë lived a hundred-and-fifty years earlier, she would have been firmly in with the Millais/Rosetti crowd. Her sculptures were lush, pre-Raphaelite; sensual and fantastic; evoking the Victorian vision of the medieval age. But where the previous artists had cast women as femme fatales and romantic symbols, Chloë subtly added a modern sensibility, making them heroines in their own right.

Valkyries. Warrior queens. Sorceresses.

"When does the show run?" Rowan asked, moving between the figures in the middle of the room, admiring the lines and curves and images.

"It's scheduled to open the fifteenth of November, but it will take at least three weeks to set up the place and transport the statues, and since I'm not finished with—*don't touch that!*"

Rowan froze, her hand in the air brushing against the sheet that covered one of Chloë's statues.

"I'm sorry," Chloë said hastily. She came beside Rowan and smoothed the drop cloth, even though Rowan hadn't actually touched it. "These pieces aren't finished yet. It's probably silly, but I don't like people seeing my works-in-progress. Superstitious, I guess."

"That's okay—I didn't mean to be nosy." Rowan couldn't remember Chloë ever having a problem with this before; their college suite common room always seemed to have a small, half-finished piece of something Chloë had been working on, in clay or papier-mâché or wood.

But that had been several years ago, and Chloë was working on more elaborate, professional stuff now—with the prospect of a show in NYC, even. And given her current stress over Bryson's potential rape trial, it was understandable that she would be acting oddly protective about things.

"I hope the show works out," Rowan said. She knew it was a lame comment, but she wanted to refocus Chloë.

"Me, too." Her friend seemed pale, almost shaken. "If we can't do it as scheduled, it could be up to a year or more—the gallery gets booked that far ahead. And if I back out, they might not give me another chance."

"Some of these are fantastic, though." Rowan moved back to the completed works. "Which ones are going to be part of the show?"

She successfully distracted Chloë for a few more minutes, before they closed the studio and headed up to the house. Round white lights, inset in the lawn along the stepping stones, had come on, timed with the encroaching dusk, and fairy lights glittered in the emptying branches of the birch trees.

Supper was in the dining room that night, because both David and Bryson were home, Bryson having been brought back by Manny's mother, who had delivered him into the care of Helen.

The main feature of the room was the table, a monstrous affair topped with black slate, which didn't seem to go with the rest of the décor of antiques in the house. David noticed Rowan frowning at it, running her thumbnail in the groove between the slate and the base of the table.

"My mother loved this table," he said. "She'd seen it somewhere, and spent ten years trying to find one. I was maybe thirteen when she succeeded. See this scar here?" He bent his head and drew some hair apart.

"Dad," Bryson said, shifting in his seat.

"Bryson hates it when I tell this story," David said with a grin. "Anyway, one day I came running around the corner, tripped, and skidded right into the table. I tried to duck, but didn't get far enough. I keep the table in honor of my mother's persistence and to remind me that when I duck, I need to *really* duck."

"To your mother and ducks," Rowan said, raising her wine glass.

Dinner consisted of thick, juicy pork chops, fresh applesauce from a local orchard, and new potatoes in garlic cream sauce, and even Chloë seemed to eat a reasonable amount of food. If Rowan hadn't known what was going on, she would have believed everything was normal in the family: the talk was of what Bryson was studying, and whether he could attend his school's football game that Saturday. The only difference was that, if things were normal, he would have been playing in the game.

Afterwards, David went to do some work in his study and Bryson helped Helen clear the table.

"He seems like such a good kid," Rowan commented to Chloë.

"That's just the thing—he *is*," Chloë replied, twisting her linen napkin between her fingers. "I know I've been here only a year and a half, Rowan, but still. He's friendly, helpful, and polite. I really hate that you insist he call you Rowan instead of Ms. Everly, but that's your fault, not his."

"Ms. Everly from someone ten years younger than me makes me feel ancient," Rowan complained. Chloë rolled her eyes and continued.

"He gets good grades and is considering an Ivy League college. He's athletic but not hyper-competitive. As far as I can tell, he's honest."

"A Stepford child," Rowan murmured.

Chloë laughed. "God, I do make him sound that way, don't I? Well, okay, he's not perfect. He likes his music at least as loud as we did, except half of it's rap. He's a slob; Helen refuses to clean his room anymore. He sulks with the best of them. He has an occasional drink, though I've never seen him drunk or sick. Oh, and once I found *Playboy*s under his bed."

"Ooh, what a rebel." Rowan laid a comforting hand on Chloë's, and she stopped her fidgeting. "Do you think I could talk to him?"

"Well, he knows you're here to help out, so I don't think it'll be a problem. Let me double-check that he's up to it." Chloë pushed her chair back across the black-and-white checked floor and stood. Before she could do anything else, the swinging door between the kitchen and dining room opened, and Bryson appeared. Chloë posed the question.

Bryson flicked a nervous glance at Rowan. She could see his Adam's apple bob as he swallowed.

"Yeah, sure, that would be okay," he said. "As long as it's all right with you and Dad," he added, glancing at Chloë.

She nodded. "We've already talked it over. Don't worry, Bryse, it's not going to be an inquisition, I promise."

"Definitely not," Rowan confirmed. "I just want to talk to you about what you remember from that night. No accusations, no pushing."

"Okay." He jammed his hands into the pockets of his navy Chinos.

"Tell you what," Rowan said. "Would you be more comfortable hanging out in your room?" He nodded. "I'll meet you up there in ten minutes, give you time to relax."

When she arrived at his room at the appointed time, she saw that Chloë was right in her estimation of Bryson's cleaning abilities. The room wasn't filthy, but it certainly wasn't neat. Clothes lived in piles on the floor, one side of the double bed, and on an easy chair; there was even a sock on the stereo. The desk was littered with papers and books and pens, which covered even the computer keyboard. There was little dust or dirt, so Rowan assumed Helen actually broke down and ventured in on occasion.

"Looks like my apartment," she commented as he dumped everything off the easy chair so she could sit.

He chuckled at that. "I clean sometimes," he defended himself mildly.

"Let me guess: Before a girl comes over?"

Bryson looked startled. "Yeah," he admitted.

Rowan nodded, smiling sagely. "Same here, when I have a date. Everything into the closets." She tucked her feet under her and gestured at him to sit, too. Nervous again, he sat on the edge of the bed, as if ready for flight. His hands dangled between his knees, and he looked at them, rather than Rowan, as he spoke.

"Look, I…I'm really not comfortable about talking about…*it*. The actual…incident, or why it happened. I know that's not really helpful, but I've already told the police and my lawyer and the shrink—"

"That's okay," Rowan said soothingly. "I just want to get some stuff clear in my mind. If I cross a boundary, you tell me, and I'll stop." He nodded, and she continued. "One thing that's got me confused is the timing. Do you remember your mom saying goodnight to you that night?"

"Yeah, I do. My window looks out on the back lawn, and I saw her come in from her studio. When she said goodnight, I was a little worried because she said she was sick, but she said she just wanted some sleep. I don't know what time that was."

"Did you touch the clock in the hall?"

"No!" His outburst startled both of them. "Sorry. No, I didn't."

"Okay, I believe you," Rowan said, and she did. "Do you remember how you got to the woods?"

"No."

"No?"

He looked at her, frowning. "No, I honestly don't. I don't remember why I left, or getting there, or even coming home afterwards. My shrink thinks it may be emotional amnesia, which is caused by trauma."

"I could use that, sometimes," Rowan said with a wry grin. "There are things in my life I'd rather not remember. Most of high school was pretty traumatic."

Bryson gave a small laugh. "Yeah."

"So, what are you studying now, anyway?" She got up and wandered over to his desk, glancing over the books and papers. He didn't jump up to hide anything, which was a good sign.

"Trig, English lit, programming...the usual stuff," he said.

"Your mom says you're getting pretty good grades," Rowan said, glancing at him.

He flushed. "I'm in the top ten in my class. I've started looking at college brochures, but I'm not sure where I want to go yet."

He sounded so calm and confident, as if there were nothing that could hinder his plans—like a prison sentence. Rowan wondered at the dichotomy. It was hard to match the alleged rapist with the boy she spoke to here, who seemed matter-of-fact yet not vain about being at the top of his prep school class; who, if things were different, would be headed off to an Ivy-League university in less than two years.

"Do you remember what you were studying that night?" she asked casually.

He thought. "I had an essay on Milton due the next day, so I finished typing that up and printed it out. I think I had trig homework, too, and some reading for science. I was kind of panicking, because I'd had football practice after school and so I got a later start on my homework."

"But you didn't notice what time it was when your mom came in."

He shook his head again. "I was sitting there—" he pointed at the chair she'd vacated "—and I didn't have my watch on. I was getting too stressed checking the time."

That, too, didn't match up. If he'd really been worried about finishing his schoolwork, why would he have gone out that night?

She noticed the phone on his desk. "Did you call anyone that night, or get any calls?"

Again, a negative answer. "The police have checked the phone and e-mail records, too. Nothing incriminating, my lawyer said."

"Sheriff Candusco sounds like a thorough man," Rowan said.

"I almost wish he *had* found something."

"What?" Rowan turned and stared at him. His head was down, his hands shaking imperceptibly. Was that it? Did the boys want attention? Teenage girls who felt out of control often became anorexic. Boys, on the other hand, acted out. But Chloë and David seemed like loving parents; they didn't seem to be pushing Bryson so much as encouraging him. Then again, maybe that's not how Bryson perceived it. Was he rebelling against being his parents' good boy?

"It would explain why." He looked up at her, and she saw tears brimming. "I know this sounds stupid, Rowan, but I don't know why I would do something like this. I almost feel like it was someone else, but I remember it. If the police found something incriminating, maybe it would explain how I could have done this."

Rowan sat next to him and put an arm around his shoulders.

"Don't worry; we'll figure something out." She sent soothing energy into him, and after a few moments, he calmed. Obviously embarrassed by her touch, he shifted away, and she helped by standing again. Surveying the room, she chewed on her lower lip.

"I don't suppose you have any of your clothes from that night, do you?"

"Nah, the police still have them. They're running tests on them, I guess."

Damn. She'd been hoping to be able to touch them, and see. There was no guarantee that she would see that night, but if Bryson had been one of the girl's assailants, and had been wearing those clothes at the time, then the clothes would have retained impressions of the attack.

She rubbed her forehead. The headache had never fully gone away.

"So, did you know Mary?"

Again, he frowned. Trying to remember or trying to come up with a story? Even as she thought it, she felt ashamed. He gave every indication of being confused and upset. She wanted to believe his innocence. But she wanted to know who had attacked an innocent girl.

"I'd seen her around town, a couple of times," Bryson said. "I don't...I don't think I ever spoke to her."

"Okay," Rowan said. "Well, I don't want to stress you out, so let's call it a night. I really appreciate your talking to me."

"No problem," he said, standing up as she approached the door. "Good night."

"Good night."

Rowan stood in the empty hallway. She thought about going downstairs and finding Chloë, but then she noticed the light beneath the master bedroom door, and heard murmured voices.

With her headache still niggling, it was probably better if she simply checked her e-mail and went to bed early. She started removing her jewelry as she headed for her own bedroom. Then she stopped.

Bryson answered the door promptly at her knock.

"I know this will sound like a strange question, but were you wearing your earring that night?"

His hand moved to the gold hoop. "Yeah, I only take it off when I'm playing football, because it gets caught in the helmet. I put it back in after practice that evening."

"Could I borrow it for tonight?"

"That was the strange question," he said. "But sure." He unhooked it and placed it in her hand.

Rowan shielded herself from the ring until she got back to her room and put it on the dresser. She didn't want to get random images; she wanted to be prepared and ready when she examined it.

In fact, she decided as she was brushing her teeth, she wasn't even going to try tonight. Twice in one day was far too much already—and even if this morning's horror seemed like long ago, it was still fresh in her mind, the awfulness still snarling in her soul. Better to sleep, get rid of the headache, and try tomorrow when she was refreshed.

She checked her e-mail and was relieved to find no panicked messages from work. Downing three Advil, she examined the books that Chloë had arranged on top of the desk. She selected a Sue Grafton mystery and climbed into bed. But although it was still early, the day's stresses and the headache soon sent her to sleep.

～

That night, she dreamed.

～

The woods were dark. The near-full moon cast enough light to navigate through the spare trees, but beyond its influence, the ink-dark night flowed like water, ever-moving, relentless, untamable. Rowan didn't like it. She never walked alone like this, in an unfamiliar, dark place, and she couldn't remember how she'd gotten there or, indeed, where she was going. Adrenaline-fear swirled in her veins, churned in her stomach, quickened her heart.

She walked quickly, trying to project confidence. Trying to get out of the forest, back to the safety of lights and cars and buildings.

The night hemmed in around her, and she resisted the urge to look over her shoulder. It would only slow her down. She could tell the time was early morning, the bleak silence before dawn, the most dangerous time. So quiet that her footsteps crunched on the frost-covered ground and her breath rasped, visible in the cold air. Bare birches thrust skyward to the edge of the moon's reach.

Her thoughts didn't seem to be her own, didn't seem to match up with her surroundings. I don't trust them, them from the town. Drunken bastards, all of them. My own fault for being nearby when they come out of the tavern.

Then, Curse them all. Curse them, their kith and kin, make them pay…

The snap of a twig, close by. So close and so quick that she gasped but had no time to turn before he grabbed her by the arm.

She struggled, trying to break his grip, but he kicked her legs out from under her and she fell heavily, painfully, the breath fleeing her lungs. By the time she snared it back he was on her, and he laughed at her struggles and screams. The dark, like an accomplice, hid his face from her.

The Rowan-part of her held knowledge that the other didn't, and she got an arm free and pressed a thumb into his eye. He jerked back. Something glinted. She flailed out with her other hand, hitting him on the side of the face. She grabbed for hair to pull, caught the glinting thing instead. He howled in pain as his earlobe tore, and fell away from her.

She used the opportunity to scramble to her feet. Her skirts tangled her and for a moment she thought she'd fall again, but then she was up, and running, running.

Ahead, she saw a light. No time to consider whether the person within offered safety: Anything was better than the grasping-dark woods. She ran to the light the way a deep-sea swimmer, down too long, rises to the surface for life-saving air.

Rowan didn't recognize the building until she'd stumbled through the unlocked door and slammed it shut behind her. Chloë's studio. Only a few spotlights were on, but she couldn't find the switches for more lamps. There seemed to be no one there. She locked the door behind her.

In the narrow light, the statues looked larger, menacing. The woman with the spear glared down, no longer a protector but a predator, Boudicca seeking retribution and not caring if the prey in her sights were guilty or innocent. The lovers embracing had exuded passion before, but now it seemed unhealthy, their embrace incestuous. Rowan shivered and turned away.

That put in front of her the cloth-draped work that Chloë hadn't wanted her to see. Unable to stop herself, Rowan moved towards it. The earring had grown warm in her hand—no, it was hot, burning. She looked at it, and saw that it had pierced her skin. With a cry, she threw it to the floor, where it skittered off along the slick, polished wood. She noticed that it hadn't been a hoop, but a small grey pearl, but that didn't seem to matter. What mattered were the statues before her.

As if belonging to someone else, her hand reached for the sheet. She bent and grasped the bottom edge, and in one sudden movement she jerked it up so that it flipped partially off the statue, catching on the top.

What she saw turned her bones to dust. She screamed.

CHAPTER 4

ROWAN FLEW AWAKE. For a moment she panted, disoriented; then, as her limbs agreed to move again, she switched on the bedside lamp. The action wasn't entirely necessary, for the window already admitted an early-morning glow. She was surprised to see that it was already six a.m.—it still seemed dim outside—but then she realized that the day would be an overcast one and the ashen clouds already smothered the sky.

With a groan she threw back the covers and padded to the bathroom, where she took more Advil, gulping water to alleviate her dream-dry mouth. Her face felt slick; she splashed water on it and avoided the mirror. Without her contacts, her image would only be a blur anyway.

Muttering to herself about hating mornings, she crawled back into bed and snugged the covers under her chin.

She wasn't sure what she thought of dreams. Some were obviously a case of neurons firing off extra bits of whatever neurons fire off. But she'd also had one or two dreams that had turned out to be premonitory, although not obviously so. Amanda had married a man with the same initials as the man Rowan had once dreamt of her marrying...

It was hard to say what this nightmare was, or meant, or would mean. She could easily trace back to the symbolic origin of the earring —it was sitting there on the dresser—but the fact that she had seen a different earring was…interesting. And the part about Chloë's statues…. Rowan shuddered. Either she'd woken before she truly saw what they were like, or her subconscious was being kind and blanking it out.

Probably the latter, Rowan decided. Chloë might be reticent about sharing her new work—much less exhibiting it—but given the strain she was under, a little unconventional behavior wasn't unexpected.

"Stress," she said aloud. This was a stressful time for everyone, including herself.

Well, it certainly wasn't going to help her stress level if she didn't get enough rest. Burrowing back under the covers, she performed a relaxation meditation until she slipped back into sleep.

The next time she awoke, she was blissfully unhindered by memories of dreams. Throwing on yesterday's jeans and sweater and pulling her hair back with a clip, she headed downstairs in search of breakfast.

In the kitchen she found a tall woman, her blunt-cut black hair streaked with white, washing dishes.

"You must be Helen," she said as the woman dried her hands on a white linen dish towel. "We seem to have missed each other up until now."

"It's good to meet you, Rowan," Helen said, gripping Rowan's hand with both of hers. "Thank you so much for coming here to help Bryson and the family. I've been just sick with worry."

Rowan settled on a bar stool at the island counter and watched while Helen efficiently moved around the kitchen, bringing her apple juice and toasting English muffins. The housekeeper worked as if she were totally at home in the kitchen. Rowan had somehow expected a matronly woman in a uniform, but Helen Krakowski wore faded denims and a black tank top under a white button-down shirt that hung open and loose.

"Chloë says you've been working for the family since before she came here."

Helen paused, squinting upwards. "Let's see, it'll be thirteen years in February. Bryson was just a toddler."

"Are you from this area?"

"Born and raised," Helen said. She opened the stainless steel refrigerator and extracted a jar of jam, seemingly without looking inside to find it. "My father was a drama teacher at the prep school, so I attended for free. I actually went on to train in dance, but my father passed on and I came back to town to help my mother, who had cancer. I cared for her until she died, and then came to work for the Walthams."

"No regrets on missing out on your career?" Rowan took a sip of juice; the fresh tartness sparkled on her tongue.

"Not really, no." Helen put the jam-spread muffins in front of her. "I didn't like the city; I missed Millburn. You know how they say that some people are born mothers? I guess I'm kind of that way, even though I never had kids of my own. In hindsight, I probably should have gone into nursing or something like that. I like taking care of people."

"So you were here when Mariette left." Bryson's parents had divorced four years before, and his mother had later died in a car accident.

"Well, somebody had to put dinner on the table," Helen said, her tone light. "It was a tough time for everyone, but we all knew—even Bryson—that it was for the best. David never said a bad word about Mariette, and I don't think Mariette ever said a thing against David. Mariette was a good friend, but she just didn't belong here—unlike me, she loved the city. She was a good mother to Bryson, even after she left. I was never the nanny while she was here, although I babysat a few times—she was a hands-on mother. My job has always been to handle the day-to-day running of the house."

She placed a cup of Earl Grey tea next to Rowan's plate, and Rowan picked it up gratefully, letting the bergamot steam drift across her face before she took a sip. "If you do all the shopping, you must have run into Mary once or twice."

"Mary, the girl who was killed?" Helen put down the rubber gloves she'd picked up to resume washing dishes, and came over and sat on a stool at the end of the island. She propped her elbows on the counter. "That's the strange thing, Rowan. I swear to you I've never seen her. I've asked a few other people I meet regularly in town, and they don't remember her, either."

Rowan frowned. "That *is* strange. What did the sheriff say about it?"

"You know, I never thought to mention it to him. Since other people said they saw her, I didn't think the fact that I hadn't had any bearing on the situation."

"You're right, it probably doesn't." Rowan nibbled on a muffin, washing it down with the pungent tea. "I'm sure the sheriff has already asked you all sorts of questions, but tell me: You know the family well. Any thought on what's going on?"

"Bryson didn't do it." Helen's tone was flat, matter-of-fact. "I'm sorry, but there's no way he could have. I honestly don't know what's possessed him to confess to it." She smiled briefly. "It almost sounds like a cliché, doesn't it? Everyone insists the boys are good, upstanding citizens…"

"It doesn't make a lot of sense," Rowan agreed. "None of this does. I really hope I can help out." She finished her muffin and tea, and thanked Helen for breakfast. She still wasn't used to the concept of someone doing all this for her, and tried to assuage her conscience by putting her dishes in the sink. "Is Chloë around?" she asked.

"She's out in her studio. Would you like to call her?" Helen explained that there was an intercom system set up between the house and outbuilding.

"No, that's okay. I have some work to do this morning, so if she comes back in, let her know I'll come find her when I'm done."

"Of course." Helen went back to the dishes, and Rowan headed back up to her room.

Once there, she smoothed the covers over the bed and sat cross-legged in the middle, the earring on the spread in front of her. She stared at it for a long time, dreading a repeat of yesterday's vision. She was inclined to want to trust Helen—she did seem to care about the family and have their best interests at heart. But that could also go too far, into protecting them. Rowan shook her head. Helen merely echoed what everyone else was saying. Unless there was some sort of town-wide conspiracy going on, there was no reason to disbelieve her.

She shook her head again. She was going to have to stop reading mysteries before bed.

Rowan pulled her hair back and braided it into a loose plait down her back. She took a deep breath, reaching down to the earth for contact, for energy. She became a conduit, seeking and finding the strength, the calm. Opening her eyes, she picked up the earring and cradled it in her palm.

A simple, small gold hoop. Seemingly innocuous, but potentially holding so much information.

Rowan closed her eyes again, dropped her shields, and opened herself to the information.

Images flowed through, and she saw them through Bryson's eyes. School, sports, girls, music, the Internet. Nothing was solid: It all shimmered and swirled, little taking hold for more than an instant. Rowan tried for more senses, and received the sounds of rap, of a movie, of laughter, of the shouting of people in a stadium. She tasted pumpkin pie and cheeseburgers, felt hot showers and the impact of a tackle. She smelled sweat and aftershave and a hint of a girl's shampoo.

Bryson was being a maddeningly normal teenager. Rowan pushed harder, looking for something with more emotion.

She saw Bryson pause on a wooden staircase and argue briefly with a blond boy. She couldn't hear the words, but saw the gestures, the scowls. He shifted his backpack from his shoulder to his hand and shoved a book inside. From the symbols on the cover, it looked like a chemistry text. More angry words, and they parted ways.

Subsequent scenes showed her stress over an exam, mild passion for Christina Aguilera, and adrenaline on the football field. Nothing violent, nothing cruel. Even the argument had seemed relatively mild.

Finally, exhausted, Rowan pulled back. She dropped the earring on the bed and stretched forward, feeling her spine pop and her shoulder muscles twinge from being tensed. For all the work involved, this had proved entirely useless.

The expenditure of energy had left her hungry, and the thought of more tea made life seem worth continuing. Since the emotions she'd received had been relatively mild, she'd be fine with a little caffeine and maybe an Advil. Downstairs, she heard the hum of a vacuum down the hall. When the kitchen door swung shut behind her, though, she was left in silence, save for the gentle hum of the refrigerator.

She was nursing a mug of tea and nibbling on the remains of a cream-cheese covered muffin when Chloë walked in.

"Oh, that looks exquisite," she said tiredly. Rowan found another mug and poured her some tea; she'd made a pot. Chloë rummaged in the fridge and found an orange. She sank onto a stool next to Rowan.

"How's the work going?" Rowan asked.

"Painfully slow." Chloë began tearing the peel. "No, slower than that. I don't think I accomplished a damn thing this morning. My doctor said I should try to focus on the show, in the hopes that it will take my mind away from everything else and relax me. I think it's adding *more* stress instead of relieving it. I'm so glad I have an appointment for a massage today."

"Now *that* sounds exquisite," Rowan said.

Chloë paused in the act of pouring milk into her tea. "Why don't you come along? I'm sure Constance can fit you in. It'll be good for both of us—a girls' afternoon out."

Rowan waited until Chloë had drunk some tea and eaten part of her orange before she related the events of her morning. When she said she'd borrowed Bryson's earring, Chloë grew still, her hands tight around her mug.

"Nothing," Rowan said. Chloë's knuckles faded from white to normal. "He seems like a perfectly normal kid. Unless, of course, he's a mutant and able to totally shield from me and create false memories for me to see."

"So that means he didn't do it," Chloë said. A statement, but Rowan knew better.

"Not necessarily," Rowan said. "First of all, for some reason the earring might not have picked up the emotional vibration. He said he was wearing it that night, but he might be mistaken. Or the earring could be too small or insignificant, or not touching him enough, or something else. I'm still learning about all this, and there aren't any manuals. Second, just because I didn't see anything, doesn't mean he definitely *wasn't* involved—it means that I didn't seen anything to prove that he was. And third, this isn't evidence I can go to the police with. It's not providing any clue for them to follow up on." She patted Chloë's hand. "But it could be a lot worse, so yes, this is a positive sign."

"So what's the next step?" Chloë asked.

Rowan blew out a breath. "If it's okay with you, I'd like to check out Bryson's room when he's not there. Not to snoop—I promise I won't move anything—but to see if I can 'feel' anything from some other object in the room. I'd like to talk to the other boys and their parents, if they're okay with that. Maybe I'll be able to examine their stuff, too. "Beyond that—" she shrugged "—when I come up with a plan, you'll be the first to know."

Rowan spent the rest of the morning and the beginning of the afternoon working on a brochure design, breaking for lunch with Chloë. At two they headed into town, only a ten-minute drive away, so Chloë could run a few errands before their spa appointment.

"The sheriff said that Mary came into town occasionally, to buy supplies and whatnot," Rowan said as they headed down the tree-lined road. The heavy branches bowed overhead, giving the impression that they drove through a tunnel. On a sunny day, the sun would dapple through here and there; today, the car was shrouded in gloom. "Where would she have shopped?"

Chloë pursed her lips. "The grocery, definitely. We have a small, family-owned one in town; for bulk purchases or more variety we go to a Costco in Poughkeepsie. Perhaps one of the specialty stores, for cheese or bread or—well, I suppose she wasn't buying expensive wine, so that's out. The drug store, for that sort of thing. The bank, perhaps? The Post Office?"

They emerged from the trees at the edge of town, and drove by closer-set homes and offices converted from older houses, until they reached the town center. Chloë maneuvered down a side street and into a parking lot. "I like the attention to history this town has," Chloë commented as they got out of the car. "They've tried to preserve the center of town with original buildings and the town green, even if there are some modern stores in the old buildings. I really appreciate not having a parking structure right in the middle of things."

Rowan zipped up her brown leather jacket in response to the chill air. "I'm all for that," she said. "How do they handle modern businesses, then?"

"Zoning laws." They walked down a wide alley as Chloë spoke. "Things like car dealerships and superstores can't be within a certain radius of the town center. Store fronts within the zone have to confirm to certain regulations about what they can change and display. I know it's tough on some of them, but in the end I prefer the quaint feel of the town."

They came out from the walkway onto the main street, and Rowan saw what Chloë was talking about.

The town square remained intact, a broad stretch of manicured lawn. At its center, a gazebo held court to a few massive old oaks and elms and the smattering of autumn leaves on the ground. The streets outlining the square had been converted to pedestrian-only walkways, although Rowan could imagine people astride horses or in carriages going about their business.

She might not have noticed it if Chloë hadn't mentioned it, but the lack of neon lights and garishly painted logos was obvious. In their place were tasteful, muted advertisements; hanging wooden signs; and an occasional A-frame message board. What struck Rowan most was the dearth of massive glass storefronts; even the Kinkos had no more than a small logo on its door and a larger sign that simply said, "Photocopies &tc."

"It's lovely," Rowan said.

Chloë smiled. "The plus is that it attracts tourists, so although that sometimes ups the prices on things, we get some nice stuff."

The Kinkos door opened and a woman hurried out, bumping into Rowan in her haste. Rowan began to apologize, but the woman bustled off, not looking at either of them. Used to the bustle of central California, Rowan shrugged at Chloë and let the incident pass.

"We have some time before the spa appointment, and I need to pick up some wine." Chloë gestured at the liquor store they'd just come abreast of.

Rowan followed her inside the specialty shop and browsed through the central display of mustards and chutneys and creative corkscrews and handmade wine bottle carriers. She soon realized, however, that Chloë would be awhile, chatting with the proprietor about vintages and wineries. Rowan knew little about wine; her only knowledge of liquor involved malt whiskey from obscure Scottish distilleries. "I'll be in the bookstore," she mouthed. Chloë nodded, and Rowan escaped.

Like the liquor store, the bookstore had made a successful attempt at ambiance. No plastic shelving or cardboard displays here; instead there was rich wood and comfortable chairs and a ladder on wheels that ran around the entire front room. Rowan looked at the map of the store and discovered that the owners had kept the building as a house rather than renovating it into an open plan. Cookbooks were in the kitchen, coffee table books in the living room, and gardening books in the sunroom at the back. She was checking to see what books were to be found in the bathroom when the conversation at the front desk caught her attention.

"I'm sorry, ma'am, but I don't think those would be appropriate to display in here."

"You have a community notice board." The woman speaking was the one who had bumped into Rowan upon exiting the copy shop. She wore a faded knit cap over her drab shoulder-length hair, which looked prematurely grey. She wore no makeup save for some pink lipstick that had sunk into the cracks in her lips. The skin pooched beneath her eyes.

"Yes ma'am, but that's for notices that are of specific interest to book lovers—" The clerk, a young man in his twenties, kept his voice patient and pleasant, but Rowan could see by his body language that he wasn't happy.

"This is of specific interest to the entire community," the woman insisted. She waved the sheaf of $8^1/_2$ x 11 posters she held, causing several to escape from her grasp.

"If you'd like, I could call the manager up front—"

"Oh, forget about it," the woman snapped. "We'll see how many customers you get when it's clear that this store doesn't care about what's happening in town." She slammed the door on the way out. The glass panes rattled, and both Rowan and the clerk winced.

Curious, Rowan picked up the papers from the floor. She handed the bulk of them to the clerk, glancing down at the last one as she did so.

What she saw chilled her.

Because it was a photocopy, the four photos on the paper were grainy and blurred, but it was nonetheless clear that one of them was Bryson. Across the top of the page, capital letters shouted, "We are not safe from these rapists." The rest of the text, at the bottom, ran along the lines of "These boys raped and murdered a girl, yet they are not in jail. This community is not safe. Your daughter's or wife's or sister's life may be at stake." There was more, but Rowan couldn't bear to read it.

With an sympathetic smile at the clerk, she stuffed the flyer in her pocket, hoping the woman hadn't headed in Chloë's direction.

She was too late.

Chloë had left the wine shop and was reading the poster that had been taped to the window outside. Before Rowan could reach her, she threw down her bags and stepped towards the woman who was ripping off a piece of duct tape to affix another poster to a telephone pole.

"Because no one is safe while these bastards are free," the woman was saying when Rowan caught up with them.

"But there's no proof that they did it," Chloë protested. "The sheriff and the D.A. are investigating."

With a snort, the woman said, "And while they're doing that, these bastards are free. *Someone* has to take action."

"They're under house arrest, under their parents' supervision. And this has all been reported in the papers. Action *is* being taken. What gives you the right to take the law into your own hands?"

Rowan could see Chloë shaking, and she reached out a hand to calm her. The woman's next words destroyed her efforts.

"Because my daughter was raped, too."

CHAPTER 5

A CHILL BREEZE snaked into their midst, swirling up around them and the telephone pole, its flicking tongue chilling each spot it touched.

"My son raped your daughter?" Chloë gaped at the woman, ashen, uncomprehending.

"No, but he as good as could have." The woman's voice chilled like the breeze. "Doesn't matter which one of your filthy rich kids did it—you all band together and close ranks and throw your money around. My daughter's rapist got no more than a slap on the wrist, thanks to his parents' pricey lawyer." She gave a bark of laughter. It wasn't a pleasant sound. "Imagine that. My daughter lives with nightmares for the rest of her life and he walks away with a few hours of 'community service' that he never probably did."

Rowan was growing increasingly alarmed at Chloë's color and the way she had begun shaking. "Look," she said to the woman, "we both sympathize with what your daughter—and you—have been through—"

The woman looked at her, apparently for the first time. "Who the hell are you?"

"I'm her friend," Rowan said firmly. "I love her much the way you love your daughter."

"Oh, I'm sure you do," the woman said, her voice deadly with sarcasm. "You rich bitches all stick together."

Rowan smiled gently. "If you saw my bank account, you'd know just how far from the truth you are. But that's not the point. We sympathize with what happened to your daughter, but that doesn't make my friend's son responsible for it, or any other crime."

"Rich or no, you're banding together, all right. You're protecting the rapist—"

"Look," Rowan repeated, but this time her voice held no pleasantness. She moved closer to the woman—just a step, but enough to make her point. "In this country, a person is innocent until proven guilty. This case has not yet gone to trial, and will only go to trial if the authorities believe there is enough evidence. Until that time, they are innocent. If you continue to harass my friend or any of the other families involved, they *will* use their money to sue you for libel and slander. And you know what? They'll win. Not because of their money, but because you will be proved guilty of both charges because of these very posters." Rowan ripped the poster off the telephone pole and shook it at the woman.

The woman stared at her for a moment, and Rowan stepped forward again, not too close, but within her comfort zone. Snatching the poster out of Rowan's hand, the woman turned away, muttering under her breath. But she didn't hang any more signs or go into any shops; instead, she disappeared down a side road.

Chloë was still shaking. Taking her by the arm, Rowan led her to a white-painted wooden bench, one of many that bordered the village green. Making sure Chloë was seated, Rowan went back to get the bag her friend had left outside the wine shop, then returned. By the time she did, a healthy flush had begun to replace the grey pallor of Chloë's cheeks.

The bench was cold, even through Rowan's jeans, and she knew Chloë must feel it even more clearly.

Chloë swore. "You even had me scared there."

"Remember when I said I did a little of everything for the Ren Fair? That includes the occasional role of bouncer," Rowan said. "Normally, you try to figure out what the other person wants, and if at all possible, supply that. But sometimes, as in this case, there's no goal, or no solution. Bottom line, she wants her daughter not to have been raped, or at least to see her attacker pay. She can't have that, so she's lashing out at the nearest thing like it. I wasn't lying—I *do* sympathize with her—and I do understand how parents will protect their children, just as her daughter's rapist's parents protected him. It's not always right, but the instinct is there."

"I know," Chloë said faintly. "I sometimes wonder, what if I knew Bryson had done it? I want to believe that I'd turn him in—not to punish him, but to get help for him. Psychiatric care, whatever. But I wonder...would I have the strength to do that? Or would my instinct be to destroy all evidence, lie, burn his clothes—whatever it took?"

Rowan slipped an arm over her shoulders. "I think you'd be tempted," she said. "But I think in the end you'd resist that temptation. At any rate, I was blowing a lot of that out my ass. I can never remember which one is libel and which one is slander, so I used both." To her relief, Chloë laughed. There was some shakiness in it, but it was heartfelt nonetheless.

"C'mon," Rowan said. "I think the need for massage has turned desperate."

They dropped the bags off at the car and then walked down a wide, tree-lined street to the spa, the entrance of which was tastefully shadowed beneath a pumpkin-colored awning. The receptionist led them through the hairdressing area to a locker room where they undressed and slipped on terrycloth robes. The wait for their masseuses was short, and they were led into separate small rooms.

Soothing New Age music, overlaid with sounds of the ocean, wafted through the room, and when Rowan requested a relaxing, rather than invigorating, massage, the masseuse lit lavender aromatherapy candles on the shelves. After a brief murmur about the knots in Rowan's shoulders, the masseuse fell blissfully silent, as if aware that Rowan didn't want conversation. With a sigh, Rowan drifted into the luxury.

When she felt ready, she let her mind drift back over the incident at the village center. She was used to dealing with belligerent people, and the woman's attitude hadn't upset her unduly. Rather, her words —and Chloë's subsequent comment—had struck Rowan, at a deeper level than she'd first realized.

The fight for survival was one of the strongest instincts in nature —even some plants had it. So too was the instinct for protection, especially towards protecting one's young. During a point in her life, shortly after her attack, Rowan had become somewhat obsessed with accounts of similar attacks. She'd even read some of the lurid true-crime books and a few tabloids. Her psychiatrist had said she was only going to succeed in re-living her experience, and advised her to stop. She'd stopped seeing him; she'd never been that comfortable with him anyway. Besides, the books and articles and court records weren't making her re-live what had happened to her. Whether or not she succeeded, what she was trying to do was find answers. Find a point of understanding about why this had happened to her, why someone would do what her attacker did; and even, to a degree, find out how other women had gone through similar experiences and come out the other side.

In many aspects, she'd succeeded. She'd learned a great deal. For a brief time she even toyed with majoring in psychology, before she realized that her interest wasn't scientific and she wouldn't be happy in a scientific field.

With strong fingers, the masseuse worked her way down Rowan's spine. The physical sensation felt glorious—and a little strange, counterpointed as it was to Rowan's dark thoughts.

Although she hadn't done a formal study, Rowan had seen a number of patterns in her research. What many said was true: Rape wasn't a crime of sex, but of violence. It was also, often, a case of the need for superiority. And one of the patterns she'd discovered echoed what the knit-hatted woman had said—that the children of wealthy families were too often involved in this kind of assault, and that the boys often did get off free, their families rallying around them to hide evidence and hire the best and most expensive, if not the most scrupulous, teams of attorneys.

Rowan sighed, half in happy response to the massage and half in frustration. She believed she knew Chloë well, from years of friendship, and she didn't believe that Chloë would close ranks like that. But she also knew that free-wheeling, dreaming Chloë had entered a unique and radically different segment of society upon her marriage to David. Rowan had read and re-read Chloë's e-mails and cards in search of signs that her friend was changing. She had, in subtle ways; ways that weren't unexpected. Of course she would begin to view money differently when she didn't have a fixed amount of student loan to live on for the next six months. Of course she would start dressing differently, have her hair done at pricey salons and no longer dye it the Hue of the Week. But no matter how hard Rowan searched Chloë's correspondence, she'd never seen a lessening or dimming of her friend's integrity, her values, or her hard-hitting view of life and love, and love of life.

Rowan didn't want to start questioning Chloë now. Didn't want to believe she'd changed so much that she'd shy from honesty, no matter how close a relative was involved. Nothing she'd seen or read or heard led her to believe that Chloë would do that.

But even though there was no physical evidence, one fact was clear: Chloë's stepson had confessed to rape and murder.

And whether or not he was guilty, Rowan wanted—needed—to find out who was responsible and bring them to justice.

She just didn't want to think of how it might destroy someone she loved.

Despite her tumultuous thoughts, Rowan emerged from her massage relaxed and refreshed, her muscles gently tingling and her body still smelling of tea tree oil.

"I could get used to this," she told Chloë, who looked similarly restored.

"I'm in luck: my doctor actually recommended regular massages," Chloë said with a laugh. "I really like this place, too; they have massages especially for pregnant women, with a massage table that has a space for one's growing belly."

"Almost enough to make me want to be pregnant. Not really," Rowan added before Chloë could make a sarcastic comment. She was known for her "never going to have children even though I like to play with other people's" declarations, even as Chloë had always expressed a desire for children and Amanda waffled between the two extremes.

"I thought I'd give Elizabeth Sinclair—Karl's mother—a call and see if she's free this afternoon," Chloë suggested. "When I talked to her earlier this week, she said she'd be home. I know you want to talk to her at some point."

"I'd like to talk to Karl, too, but maybe it would help to see his parents first," Rowan said.

Chloë flipped open her cell phone and dialed. Rowan moved discreetly away. Most people complained about the constant ringing of cell phones and the annoyance of people shouting into them at restaurants and other public places. Rowan hated that, but she also felt uncomfortable with the freeness with which people chatted into their cell phones, oblivious to whomever might be listening. At home or in the office, people tended to make phone calls quietly, in relative privacy. For some reason, cell phones made some people want to share their conversations with the world. Although Chloë was speaking in a normal tone of voice, and she had nothing to hide from her friend, Rowan still felt better being out of earshot.

"It's settled," Chloë announced, returning the phone to her purse.

The Sinclairs lived in the opposite direction of town from the Walthams. Chloë and David lived in the older section, their house among those built by the founding fathers of Millburn. Martin and Elizabeth Sinclair's home, on the other hand, was in a housing development that had grown up over the past fifteen years, and it couldn't have been more of a contrast.

The development was gated, but Chloë already knew the entry code. The metal door slid sideways with a clang that Rowan could hear even through the closed car window, and Chloë pulled through. Here, the trees were young and small compared to the towering elms and maples elsewhere. The landscaping was modern, with rock features and metal fountains and curiously out-of-place-looking tropical plants that reminded Rowan of California. Rowan wondered how they survived winter, getting a mental picture of them all being uprooted and stored in a greenhouse out back, to be replaced with pines for Christmas and cherry trees for the spring. The houses, too, were a curious mix of ultra-modern and retro; they passed one that looked like the Taj Mahal, and another that had a western ranch theme complete with a brand design in the wooden archway over the driveway entrance.

"Martin and Elizabeth used to live close to us, in his family's old home, but when this house here became available, they snapped it up," Chloë explained as she navigated the car over some speed bumps, faster than she should have. She seemed unperturbed by the car's rocking. "Sadly, it suits them. You're not going to believe it."

"Give me a hint."

"Think porn producer."

They turned between two sweeping stone pillars that flanked a long drive. A moment later Rowan murmured, "Dear God, I see what you mean."

The house was 1970s kitsch, apparently built to celebrate the recent nostalgia over that decade. Rowan hadn't realized the craze had extended beyond flared pants and platform shoes. "Either porn, or the Brady Bunch."

Chloë parked, and they walked up to the split-level ranch-style house on a graveled, needlessly curving sidewalk. A uniformed housekeeper (reminding Rowan of Alice from the same TV show, even though this woman was younger and rounder) led them to the living room. Rowan had just enough time to take in the massive slate fireplace and wet bar with a mirrored wall behind it before Elizabeth Sinclair entered.

"Darling," she said to Chloë, giving her stilted air kisses in the vicinity of each cheek. "You look divine. And this is the friend you told me about: Roxanne?"

"Rowan," Rowan said, shaking her hand. The skin felt slick, and she resisted the urge to wipe her own hand on her jeans.

"I knew it started with an R." Elizabeth fished an engraved silver cigarette holder from the pocket of her blazer and offered one to Chloë, then Rowan, both of whom shook their head. She lit one for herself, then moved swiftly to the bar.

"She always does that," Chloë whispered to Rowan. "She thinks everybody smokes because she does."

"Drink orders, please," Elizabeth chirped.

"Just Evian for me, please," Chloë said. Rowan asked for a Pepsi.

"You two are just no fun," their hostess complained, fixing herself a whiskey and soda.

"Social coke user, too," Chloë murmured in Rowan's ear. Rowan had no time to answer because Elizabeth was bearing down on them, all three glasses clutched in her hands. Chloë beamed at Elizabeth as she accepted her drink.

"Chloë tells me you're helping out with our little problem," Elizabeth said to Rowan once they were all seated on the cream brocade ensemble.

"I hope I can help," Rowan said, waiting for the inevitable question of what qualifications she had to assist in the investigation. It didn't come. Elizabeth either didn't care or hadn't thought things through that far.

"Well, we're anxious to get this behind us, so I'd be happy to answer any questions you have. Maybe you can speed things up so we can get on with our lives."

Rowan chose her next words carefully. "If I may be frank, Elizabeth, you don't seem too concerned about the fact that your son has confessed to a heinous crime."

The woman waved a hand, wafting a heavy perfume. "That's

because it's all ridiculous. Karl hasn't done anything, and Frank will see to that. I really can't understand why you won't hire Frank Manassan too, dear," she added to Chloë, naming one of the country's top attorneys.

"We're happy with our attorney, but thank you," Chloë said.

"I appreciate your willingness to answer some questions." Rowan attempted to bring the conversation to heel. "I understand that Karl said he was watching TV that night, and your husband heard the TV on but didn't see if Karl was there?"

"The door to the den wasn't open all the way. Marty basically walked by there a couple of times, but didn't go in. He doesn't watch much TV, except for the news."

"And where were you?"

"I spent most of the night upstairs. I took a nice long bath after supper and read before going to bed. I remember I was reading the latest Nora Roberts—I just love her, don't you?—and it was so good I stayed up late to finish it. I never went back downstairs."

"Did you see anything from your window, perhaps?"

Elizabeth considered. "Our room overlooks the pool. I never had a reason to look outside, dear."

Rowan sipped her soda. The ice jangled against the glass. She wasn't sure what else to ask. She was no PI; historic research didn't involve grilling people, and besides, Elizabeth Sinclair probably wouldn't have been much help even if she had been downstairs or seen something. Her only chance here was to find something she could examine with greater depth, although knowing her success with Bryson's things, she didn't have much hope. She suppressed a sigh. The mellow feeling left by the massage trickled away, to be replaced again by frustration.

"Why don't you show me around the house?" she suggested. "I'd like to see the TV room and Karl's room, if that would be possible."

"Oh, certainly." Elizabeth heaved herself off the sofa. "Just let me refresh my drink first."

Elizabeth led them down a paneled hall, pointing out Martin's study further down before opening a door. "Here's the den, darling."

The two-story room had a sloping ceiling, blonde furniture, and an entertainment center that covered an entire wall. The 50-inch HD TV faced an overstuffed, crescent-moon-shaped sofa in which a small tribe of pygmies could get lost.

There was little else to see. Rowan glanced through the magazines on the coffee table and thought about slipping one of the remote controls in her pocket and retreating to the bathroom. She might be able to see what was on TV the night of the murder, but that would prove only that the TV had been on, which they already knew. Karl easily could have left it on and left the house, knowing his parents were unlikely to come into the den during the evening.

Elizabeth then led them up an open spiral staircase to the second floor. As she opened the door to Karl's bedroom, a phone shrilled from somewhere else. She excused herself to answer it, and Rowan and Chloë entered the bedroom.

"At least you've taught Bryson to have some taste," Rowan murmured, looking at the poster of Britney Spears. The bare-bellied pop singer and auto racing seemed to be Karl's passions; a silk Indy 500 banner spread across the wall over his bed, and there were racecar figures on the shelves of his bookcase in front of books about drivers and cars.

In all, another typical teenage boy's bedroom: computer setup, stereo, bed. Karl made something of an effort to be neat; some of his dirty clothes dangled over the edge of an open wooden laundry hamper, the rest had been less-successful shots that now languished beside it. The same scenario had happened around his wastebasket.

"What do you think?" Chloë asked.

Rowan puffed out her cheeks and released the air in rhythmic pulses. "I don't exactly know," she admitted. "The police would have taken any evidence, same as with Bryson." She ran a hand over the quilted burgundy bedspread, then moved to glance out the window. Karl's room overlooked the side of the house. She could see the edge of the pool—probably kidney-shaped, to complement the house—and the cabana next to it. For a moment she thought she saw someone move, a flitting shadow behind the building. She blinked; nothing. Just a trick of the late-afternoon cloud-murked light.

"I'm so sorry, dears." Elizabeth joined them, dabbing her nose on a piece of toilet paper that she then stuck in her blazer pocket. Rowan glanced at Chloë, who studiously kept all expression from her face. "How are we doing in here?"

"Okay, I guess," Rowan said. "I think we're done, actually. Not a whole lot to report." She did one final slow turn to look at the room, not expecting to find anything. To her surprise, she did. "I see Karl has a cell phone," she said, indicating the empty charger on the desk.

"A Christmas present last year," Elizabeth explained. "Goodness, I always thought it was girls who liked to gossip, but it seems now every boy has to have his own phone, too. So when we bought one for Ashlyn, we bought one for Karl."

"Ashlyn is Karl's younger sister," Chloë said for Rowan's benefit. "She's—what, fourteen now, Elizabeth?"

Elizabeth nodded. Rowan asked how Ashlyn was dealing with the difficulties.

"Oh, she doesn't know about it," Elizabeth said, waving her hand. The last remaining slivers of ice swirled in her glass. "She's away at Brackenhurst in Vermont." She named a prestigious girls' prep school. "We didn't see the need to tell her—everything should be over and done with by the time she comes home for Thanksgiving."

Rowan wondered how sheltered Brackenhurst was from the national news, but said nothing. She didn't know much about prep schools, anyway, and maybe they did restrict the outside world. For Ashlyn's sake, she hoped so. *By the way, did you know your brother is a rapist?* The last thing she'd need was to hear it from a taunting peer.

Still, Rowan was amazed by Elizabeth's *laissez-faire* attitude about the whole ordeal. "Where's the phone now?"

"What? Oh, Karl's cell. Martin has it," Elizabeth said. "The police thought it best if Karl didn't use it, for some reason, so Martin took it. He wasn't too happy about it."

Martin, or Karl? Rowan again refrained from posing the question.

Between the alcohol and possible other substances in Elizabeth's system, she wasn't likely to make complete sense.

"Do you think I could borrow it for a few days?"

"Sure, dear, I don't think that'll be a problem. Let me go get it."

Chloë raised quizzical pale eyebrows as Elizabeth left again. "What are you going to do with a cell phone?"

Rowan shrugged. "It's a long shot, but if he had the phone with him that night, it would carry his emotions. Even if he didn't have it with him, if he used the phone right before or soon after, there might be some sort of imprint. It might show his state of mind, or his plans, or his memories. If he spoke to the other boys about it, I might be able to see that."

"Now, no calls to Japan," Elizabeth joked as she re-entered the room. "Can I offer you girls another drink?"

They both declined, Chloë saying that they had to get home to discuss dinner with Helen. "School trustee meeting tonight, so we have to eat early."

As the pulled out of the gate at the entrance to the housing estate, a steel-grey Cadillac was pulling though on the other side.

"That would be Martin, I think," Chloë said.

They were on the highway when Chloë's purse started to vibrate.

"Oh, damn, would you answer that?" she said. "I don't like to talk on the phone when I'm driving."

By the time Rowan found the cell phone and figured out where the *talk* button was, she was surprised the person at the other end of the line was still there. "Hello?"

"Darling, I'm so sorry, I forgot to tell you," Elizabeth's voice was as clear as if she'd been in the car with them.

"Hi, it's Rowan. Chloë's busy driving."

"Oh, Rowan dear, hello. Goodness, I'm such a scatterbrain today. You remember when the phone rang when you were here? It was Martin. I totally forgot to tell you that he was on his way home and wanted to see you two."

Rowan covered the phone with her fingers and relayed the message to Chloë. Her friend shook her head, eyes on the road.

"Tell her I'll call back tomorrow."

"She'll call back tomorrow," Rowan said into the phone.

"Hmmm. Well, he really did want to talk to you." Elizabeth's voice dropped to a conspiratorial whisper. "He's a little upset, you see. He didn't think I should have let you look around."

"I'm sorry," Rowan said.

"Don't you go apologizing, dear, it's not your fault. Whoops, here he comes. I'll tell him Chloë will call tomorrow." There was a click as the phone shut off at the other end.

CHAPTER 6

ROWAN REFILLED HER SCOTCH, adding the proper amount of bottled water and opting against an ice cube. She'd managed to relax in front of the TV for a while, but all the while, Karl's cell phone upstairs brushed at the edge of her thoughts, like a half-full pack of cigarettes whispering to someone who'd just quit. She'd already decided to wait until the morning to examine it— one item a day was enough—but that didn't stop her from being reminded of it. She knew it was partly because she was tired. It had been a long day. The alcohol—her second drink since dinner, at which she'd also had wine—helped press the shadows down.

She took the Scotch up to her room, sipping it as she undressed and drew on her peach robe. There were some e-mails from the office, relating to the work she had done earlier in the day, but nothing was problematical and she answered them quickly.

No, she decided; despite the Scotch, she wasn't tired, just mellow. Her brain still flitted from one idea to the next, searching for the missing puzzle piece that would cause everything to make sense. Personalities aside, there simply were things that didn't make sense.

For want of anything better to do, she opened a new Word file and began typing up what she knew so far.

Four teenage boys—by all accounts upstanding citizens and excellent students with great prospects ahead of them and no past criminal behavior—had confessed to rape and murder.

Playing devil's advocate…if they had actually committed the crimes, the scenario looked like this: They had snuck out of their respective houses and made their way to the woods by means other than their own or their parents' cars. They had found? met? the girl, attacked her, and in the process, killed her. They then returned home, slept in their own beds, got ready for school the next morning as if nothing had happened…and then, halfway to school, changed their route and turned themselves in at the local sheriff's office.

Add to that no physical evidence and the apparent horror felt by the boys, and the whole thing was an insane muddle.

Rowan tapped her fingernail on the side of the iBook, considering the words she'd typed. Try the opposite tack, then. Say they *were* truly innocent. What then? Why would they confess to something they hadn't done?

"Fear?" she typed. Fear of what? Had they been out on another errand of mischief, or worse, and come across the girl's body, or witnessed the attack? If so, why wait until morning? Even more important, why confess to it?

Back to the first scenario. The only way they could have completely destroyed evidence and had alibis was if all their parents were involved. Rowan thought of Elizabeth Sinclair's unconcerned, at least partly chemical-induced, breeziness, then of Chloë's thin hands and horrified expression and helpless tears. Maybe some of the parents could be accessories to the crime, but not all of them.

This was useless. Rowan saved the file and rose from the chair, stretching. Picking up her Scotch, she pulled aside the curtain and stared out into the darkness. Some of the day's cloud cover had dissipated; stars glittered around the slivered whiteness of the moon.

She started to drop the curtain, but then something caught her eye. A flicker of light. No, not light, exactly—more like the memory of movement, out across the lawn, near Chloë's studio.

Maybe Chloë and David had returned home, and Chloë had gone out to do some work?

But surely Chloë would have turned on the lights along the pathway?

Three options: Chloë (or another family member) was outside in the dark, there was an intruder, or Rowan was seeing things.

Sipping her drink, she watched carefully out the window, fully aware that she was visible. If someone was out there, they'd already seen her. Watched, waited. Nothing. Whomever she'd seen—if she'd seen anyone—had moved into the trees.

One choice of action: Check things out.

Bryson had watched some TV with her, then headed to his room perhaps half an hour before she'd come upstairs. She'd seen a light from beneath his door, heard a muffled bass beat from the stereo. She grimaced. There she was, assuming he was in the room just because of those clues. Chloë had actually talked to him, that night, when he allegedly was in the woods destroying a girl's life. Still, Rowan had no reason to assume he wasn't home; surely he wouldn't risk sneaking out now?

But, best to be sure. She crossed the hall and knocked on his door.

"Yeah?"

"It's just me, Rowan. I thought I saw a light outside, and wondered if it were you."

"No, I've been in here. Do you want me to check outside?"

Rowan was surprised at his offer to help. Politeness, or the desire to cover something up? "That's okay," she said. "I'm sure it's nothing. Maybe your folks just got home. Never mind."

The master bedroom door was half open, with no light showing within from the main room or the bath. Rowan headed downstairs; all was dark except for the front foyer and outside light, both left on in anticipation of the Walthams' return.

The housekeeper's apartment was located back on the second floor; or, more specifically, via a short stairway accessible from the second floor. The apartment itself was built over what was now the garage. There were two entrances, one in the house and one external, so Helen had some privacy when she came and went. Rowan ascended the stair from the hall.

Helen, dressed in leggings and a pale pink sweatshirt with "Maui" emblazoned across it in raised letters, answered her knock.

"Is everything all right?" she asked, taking in Rowan's nighttime attire.

"I think so, but I'm not sure," Rowan answered. "Chloë and David aren't back yet, are they?"

"No." Helen stepped back and let Rowan enter. "I can hear the garage door from here. Why?"

The apartment was small and neat, with homey touches such as the framed nature prints on the wall and the cranberry-red chenille throw over the back of an armchair.

"Maybe I'm overreacting, but I thought I saw a light near the studio. Could someone have broken in to it?"

"Not unless they were real experts—the studio is fully alarmed and the alarm is linked to the house system. If someone tried to get in the studio, we'd know about it."

Rowan nodded. "It was a will-o-the-wisp, probably. I'll pop my head out the back door and see what I can see."

"Do you want me to go with you?" Helen asked.

Over Helen's shoulder, Rowan could see the TV was on; Helen, still holding the remote control, had probably muted it before answering the door. "I don't want to keep you from your show," she said. "I'll be fine. Like I said, I'm sure it was nothing."

If it was nothing, then why are you checking? a little voice in Rowan's head asked as she headed back downstairs.

Peace of mind, she whispered back to it. Since her attack in college, she'd become just slightly paranoid about making sure doors and windows were locked, that everything was in its place. She knew people who went overboard, far more than she did, and in general, she'd become less obsessive about it with each passing year. But occasionally it flared up, and she wouldn't be able to sleep until she double-checked whatever her mind happened to have latched onto.

The TV room opened out onto a back porch, comprised of a railed redwood deck of several levels, one of which held a sunken hot tub surrounded by benches. The door had been locked, Rowan found with satisfaction. She unlocked it and stepped onto the porch, pulling the sliding glass door shut behind her. She spared a longing glance at the hot tub; Chloë had said she could use it anytime, but she'd pretty much forgotten about it until now. But now wasn't the right time.

Shivering, she pulled her robe more tightly around her. A chill breeze played tag around her ankles as she leaned on the railing and gazed across the back lawn. The night held the curious silence of autumn; birds had headed south, crickets had gone wherever crickets go when they ceased their summer chirping. The road that ran by the house was one that led only to more houses, and thus there was no sound of cars. Just the wind gently shaking the tree branches. The mostly denuded oaks and maples and birches clacked; the pines whispered secrets only the other trees could understand. Then a click and a faint hum: The Jacuzzi went into its heating cycle.

Across the lawn, whatever she had seen from upstairs was gone, or hidden, or never there in the first place. No light nor movement, no matter how hard she searched the darkness. Only the slightly less black forms of the stepping stones down the lawn, and the glow of the marble birdbath where the light from inside the house reached it.

The wind increased, cold fingers teasing the edges of her robe. Rowan turned to go in, but something stopped her. A sixth sense, perhaps. Not something seen, or even heard, but felt.

The draft teased at her hair, murmuring in a way that almost sounded like words, words she could almost understand.

Curse them all. Curse them, their kith and kin, make them pay...
Then,
You understand; I know you do. You remember, too...
Rowan knew her fear was irrational, but she really wanted to be back inside. Now. Before she could reach the door, there came a sudden frenetic scrabbling against the side of the deck. She yelped, half-turned back. Then the glass door rattled as if something violently slammed against it. She whirled back to it. Nothing there.

Sudden silence. Silent except for the throb of her veins, the buzz of adrenaline in her ears that made her momentarily light-headed and hypersensitized her at the same time.

Then the breeze picked up again. The scrabbling had been a swirl of dry fall leaves, she realized, and when she grasped the door handle she shook the door. It vibrated in its tracks. A sudden hard gust of wind would easily have made it sound like a bang against it.

Inside, Rowan clicked the lock with shaking hands and fumbled for the lines to close the drapes. As she turned off the light and left the room, she heard voices, and realized Chloë and David had returned home.

No way to get to the stairs before they saw her... Rowan re-tied the belt of her robe and greeted them as they emerged through the kitchen.

"Hi, Rowan," Chloë said. "I hope we didn't wake you."

"No, I'd come down to..." Rowan frantically searched for an excuse. She didn't want to tell them what she'd thought she'd seen—at least, she didn't want to tell David. She'd never discussed her power with him, although obviously he had to know about it via Chloë. This was something she didn't want to have to try to explain, didn't want David to think was nothing more that her overactive imagination.

She also didn't want to alarm Chloë, certainly didn't need something new to worry about right this second.

"I came down to make a sandwich," she finished, forcing her voice to be light. "I watched TV for a while and then went upstairs, but I had the munchies so I came down to scrounge for food. How was the meeting?" she finished, hoping to distract them from what she knew was babbling.

"The usual," David said, hanging his slate blue London Fog coat in the hall closet. "Too much debate about the finer points, not enough discussion on the overall issues."

"I've been to more productive meetings," Chloë admitted, handing him her own coat. She flicked off the kitchen light, which removed the backlighting and left them all in the single glow of the hall light. Rowan, standing where she was, fell in the spotlight.

"Rowan, are you sure you're all right?" Chloë put a hand to

Rowan's cheek. "You look terribly pale, and—dear lord, you're freezing!"

"I went out on the porch for some air, and stayed out too long," Rowan said, gently pulling Chloë's hand away and squeezing it reassuringly. "Really, I'm fine." As she spoke, she sent the same message over in another way, without words. *A strand of calmness, of everything-all-right. A brush of assurance, shade of faith.*

It was all she could do to keep the guilt out of it. She wasn't lying to Chloë, just not telling her everything yet.

The lines on Chloë's face smoothed. "Of course. It *is* nippy out tonight." Then she paused, and frowned again.

"What's wrong?" David asked.

"Oh, nothing." Chloë gave a brief laugh. "For a moment, I wanted to go out to the studio. But it's too late for that."

Her husband pressed his lips into her hair. "Yes, it is," he agreed. "It's the right time for us to go upstairs and snuggle."

They all ascended the stairs, and Chloë and David kissed Rowan goodnight before heading into their room. Rowan entered her own room. The remainder of her Scotch was a blessing. She tossed it back, relishing the burn down her gullet. Eyes watering, she flung herself backwards onto the bed. She took a deep breath, grounding and centering, and soon felt the tugging calm of the earth. Her face tingled with the warming whisky's touch. But though her body calmed and her heart slowed, her mind still raced.

Her rational mind wanted to explain everything—but Rowan knew her rational mind wasn't always right. Some espoused a theory that people's minds rationalized away things they saw or experienced that didn't fit into the "normal" realm of expectations. Rowan ascribed to that theory. She certainly experienced things that didn't fall under the category of "normal;" there were things out there that couldn't be explained as yet by science.

She rolled over on her stomach, shivering. *Curse them all...* Her rational mind hadn't come up with that one.

And, quite frankly, it terrified her.

～

Rowan dressed carefully for her lunch meeting with Toby. She knew exactly why. Armor. He'd shaken her, and she needed to regain control.

Jeans, always strong. Boots, for a little height and the sense of weight. A peach camisole of heavy silk under a chocolate-brown cashmere sweater: layers, for added protection. Her favorite gold hoop earrings and a necklace of enamel leaves in fall colors, because they made her happy, and she needed all the positive energy she could get.

The leather bomber jacket was obvious.

Toby hadn't arrived yet. Rowan told the waitress she was waiting for someone and ordered an iced tea. Too restless to read the menu, she scanned the mostly empty room. Toby had mentioned when they'd set the time that they'd have the place to themselves, and it looked like he was right.

The café, which specialized in health food and vegetarian fare, had a turtle theme. Cartoon turtles playing Big Band instruments were painted on the walls, the salt and pepper shakers were turtle-shaped, and a turtle fountain burbled in the center of the room. Instead of being kitschy, it somehow worked. Potted ferns and hanging plants muted and complemented the theme, as well as provided intimacy screens between the tables and booths. In contrast to the décor, early-80s pop music filtered quietly from discreet speakers throughout the room. Rowan wondered if that were because the manager was at the football game. At any rate, she preferred it to most other music.

In the end, it served to distract her. She refrained from commenting "I remember this one!" to the empty chair across from her, and was humming along to Duran Duran when the sheriff arrived.

"I hope you haven't been waiting long," he said as he tossed his black trench coat over the back of his chair. He looked casual in khakis and a red rugby shirt, but he was clearly agitated when he arrived; she could feel it pouring off him.

"You're right on time," Rowan said. "Thanks for meeting me on your day off."

He scraped back his chair. "I never really have a day off," he said. "I got a call on my cell just as I was leaving. We have a problem."

"What's wrong?" Rowan asked.

"This can't get out yet," he said, his voice low. "If the media gets wind of it... Hopefully it'll sort itself out first." He actually looked around to see if anyone was near before he continued. "They've lost Mary's body."

"What?" Whatever she'd been expecting, that wasn't it. It didn't even come close. "How is that possible?"

He shrugged. "It happens more than you'd like to think. I'm not saying it's often, but human error is what it is. A body gets mis-tagged at the morgue, or mis-tagged and taken to the wrong place... In this case, we saw her get loaded into the ambulance, but the county morgue has no record of her arriving. The ambulance driver is just plain confused."

"Where does that leave us, evidence-wise?" Rowan asked.

"The ME who examined the body at the scene has his preliminary report. He says he saw evidence of semen, but actual samples of that, along with nail scrapings and so on, would have been taken at the morgue. So, we know she's dead, we're pretty sure she died of head wounds, and we think she was raped. Or she could've had consensual sex before the probable beating—the closer examination would have shown whether—"

Rowan held up her hand. "I know what it would have shown; I don't need the graphic description over lunch."

"Sorry," Toby said. He rolled his head to relieve the pressure in his neck. Rowan wondered if she should suggest Chloë's masseuse. "I'm still processing it all myself."

"I understand, "Rowan said. "It's frustrating, I know. What might it mean for the case?"

"It depends, I suppose," he said. "I'm not a lawyer. If the boys plead guilty, then the evidence won't matter as much, I'd guess." He sighed. "I'm just hoping they find the body soon. If they do, it'll sort itself out.

In the meantime..." He picked up his menu. "Have you had a chance to decide what you want?"

"I've only glanced at it," Rowan said, opening the laminated pages. "Looks good, though."

She chose a whole-wheat pita stuffed with Swiss cheese, avocado, sprout, cucumber, and onion with chips on the side, and a refill on her tea. Toby ordered a tuna on pumpernickel, chocolate cake, and an iced tea. They chatted idly while waiting for their food, and turned to business only after they had eaten half of their meals.

"I'm going to be honest with you," the sheriff said abruptly, setting down his sandwich.

"I prefer it that way," Rowan replied, guarded.

"Okay. I was skeptical about your...powers, even after I'd talked to the cops you'd worked with. That whole California cereal thing."

"Filled with fruits and nuts," Rowan finished the saying. "In some ways, it's true. Even though I'm not originally from California, which you know from checking up on me."

He cleared his throat. "Yeah, well, anyway. What you did in my office —I can't find any other explanation for it. I'm the only one who knew about the pens, and which one was which. Even if you'd read about the 7-Eleven holdup, you wouldn't've known the pen had anything to do with it. So..." Toby looked away for a moment, then held her gaze. "So I want to apologize for doubting you about that. I can't claim to understand it, but it's obvious to me that it happens, and it works."

"Apology accepted." Rowan reached across the table, gave his hand one firm shake almost before he realized what she was doing.

"You might want to wait until I say the rest of it."

She drew her hand back, cautious again. "Oh?"

"The other thing we talked about: Your motives here. What I said stands: I don't trust you yet. I believe you're here to help figure out what happened, but I'm not convinced you're not out to prove the boys did it."

Rowan stared at him for a moment, and he returned her gaze unflinchingly. It was harder to be angry at him, she realized, when he wasn't in uniform. He looked so damned normal now. He'd probably become a cop because of that. The uniform and the authority counteracted the baby-faced image he'd no doubt had to fight since he reached maturity.

"Mary Cooper was probably raped," she said. "We're pretty sure about that, right?"

Toby nodded.

"And she was raped by a man—there was semen present."

He nodded again, a bit more slowly, obviously wondering where she was taking this.

"The other day, you suggested I had a vendetta against men. I don't, but I also don't care whether you believe that or not. Even if I did have a cause against the male of the species, why would I want to point the finger at the boys? Why should it matter to me *who* did it, as long as a man—any man—is punished for the crime?"

In truth, she wasn't sure about her own words. She thought she'd come to terms with what had happened with her, but this had brought back some of her fears, her mistrusts, her suspicion. She was afraid they were things that had been buried deep, even though she'd thought she'd purged them.

But she had to believe she could be impartial, that she could step away from her emotions. She had to try.

The sheriff leaned back in his chair and folded his arms across his chest, lips pursed, considering.

"Okay, I see your point," he said finally. "Maybe the particular man or men doesn't matter. But I can argue back at you: You were attacked in college, these boys are nearly college-aged. They represent your attacker. And they're already suspects, so they're easy targets. Or maybe, as you said, you don't care who gets punished, as long as some man does."

Rowan clamped down on her anger, knowing she felt it in part as a reaction to deeper emotions. "On the other hand, we're talking about the stepson of one of my oldest and dearest friends. Would I really want to see her devastated by this? Even if I didn't care who got punished, wouldn't I still have at least some interest in protecting her?"

Toby held his hands up, forestalling further words. "Okay, okay," he said. "I can see we could be going around and around about this for days. Can we agree to disagree?"

"How so?"

"The bottom line for me right now is, I could use your help on this." He sighed. "If we're going to work together, we can't be arguing all the time. I admit I'm not one-hundred-percent convinced of your motives, but—" he held up his hand again "—but I'm willing to reserve judgment until we've worked together more. I'll give you the benefit of the doubt, I won't keep bringing it up, and if I change my mind, I'll let you know."

He wasn't being any more difficult than the people who gave her grief about her psychic ability, Rowan realized. In fact, he seemed to be genuinely trying to meet halfway. It still galled her that he wouldn't believe her—it incensed her when anyone questioned her honesty or integrity—but, she decided, she would just have to prove him wrong. She made up her mind.

"I agree, on one condition," she said.

His eyebrows raised.

"You're buying lunch. In fact, I think you're buying all my lunches."

"I can live with that," he said, sounding relieved.

They shook hands again, and went back to their lunches for a while. Rowan felt herself slowly relaxing again, except for her right leg, which insisted on moving to the beat of "Blue Collar Man."

Eventually, the sheriff asked her about what she'd learned so far.

"I wish I had more to tell you," Rowan confessed. "I've spoken to Bryson and to Karl's parents, and I'll be meeting Manny and his family this afternoon. Karl's father was apparently reluctant to let me see him, which I didn't find out about until afterwards."

"Do you want me to talk to him?"

Rowan shook her head. "It's up to you, really. My guess is that he's just being protective of his son. I didn't get the sense that guilt was part of the issue...but you're the expert there. If everything else is a dead end, then maybe we can push it." She ate the last bite of her pita, wiped her fingers on her paper napkin. "Anyway, I've looked over Bryson's room but not closely. I didn't see anything useful."

"Is that 'see' in the conventional sense?" Toby had pushed back his plate and now watched her closely.

She tried not to flinch. She wasn't used to such close scrutiny.

"A little of both," she replied. "It takes some effort to 'look' deeper; I'm not able to just touch something, get an impression, and walk on. I plan to look at Bryson's room again, with his permission. Keep in mind I'm hampered by the fact that everything the boys were wearing that night was taken as evidence. I don't suppose you can get me any items of clothing?"

"Not easily, no, but it could be possible. Let's leave that in case of a dead end, too."

"Agreed." Rowan appreciated Toby's decisiveness, his ability to see through a muddled problem to its core. She could understand how this case frustrated him. "In lieu of clothing, I did spend some time with Bryson's earring."

The sheriff swallowed his iced tea and cocked his head, alert. "Yes?"

She sighed. "Nothing. I got only normal, everyday stuff. As I told Chloë, this isn't rocket science; I don't know why I have this ability or even how exactly it works. It could be that Bryson's strong enough to shield things from me, but honestly, I doubt that. I think there was nothing to see from his earring—although it could be that it's too small to be significant in this."

He echoed her sigh. "I'll have to take your word for it that this isn't something you can control, exactly. Is there anything at all you can tell me that I don't already know—anything that can make a difference in this?"

Rowan stifled a sarcastic reply, realizing she was reacting to his frustration. Seeking inner calm, she said, "I'm not sure if it'll help yet, but I went to where Mary's body was found, and picked up some images there." She saw that she had his attention again. "I hate to say it, I didn't see anything obvious, anything that either incriminates the kids or absolves them." The memory seeped around the barriers she'd constructed in her mind, and she swallowed against the nausea. "But there was a lot going on, so I'll keep working with it, see if there are any details I missed the first time around, anything that might provide a clue."

"That would be great." Toby signaled to the waitress for the check.

The first man was slowly buckling his belt.

Rowan took a long drink of her iced tea, struggling for control. Her words had been hollow; she hadn't wanted to re-experience the vision, hadn't want to re-explore its violent images and raw, painful emotions. But it rose, unbidden, in her sight, and she was forced to view it again, a helpless observer, an empathetic but useless champion.

"Rowan? Rowan, are you okay?"

The wide blank eyes didn't see, and then it was dark.

"Rowan?" He had her hand in his, and she found herself clinging to it, using it to pull herself back to the present.

"That's never happened before," she said. Her voice sounded thick, distant, but she recognized it as her own.

A good sign.

The sheriff swore. "What? What's never happened before?"

Rowan waved her other hand, signaling for him to stop. Blissfully, he did. She breathed slowly, deeply, grounding herself again. She felt the trembling slow, then cease. "Hold on a second," she managed. She heard Ultravox's "Dancing with Tears in my Eyes," and realized it was coming from the café's sound system. Another good sign. She rarely had visions repeat unbidden, and she was glad she was pulling herself out of this one.

She eased her hand away from his, lifted her tea and fumbled for the straw.

"Sorry," she said finally. "I was just... Basically, I saw everything again."

"What?" he pressed. "What did you see?"

"The rape, okay?" she snapped. She pressed her fingers to the bridge of her nose, feeling the inevitable buildup of pressure behind her left eye. "Sorry. It's just not a pleasant thing." He didn't say anything, and when she was ready, she looked him in the eye and said, "When I went to the site, I saw the whole rape. Just now, I was basically seeing the whole thing again. Seeing it again made me realize that something was different."

Her jacket was slung over the back of her chair. She found her medication in a pocket, took it with her soda.

"Different how?" His voice was quiet, but she heard the undercurrent of urgency, of eagerness to have another piece of the puzzle, even if it were just a scrap.

"Normally, I see from the viewpoint of the object. No, I realize that objects don't have viewpoints—they don't have sight. It's hard to explain. I see from wherever the object was during the situation. For example, if it's a pin a woman was wearing, I see things essentially from her viewpoint, because the pin was on her body; although I also get a sense of what she's feeling because she's wearing the pin."

Toby nodded. "Fair enough. Go on."

Rowan appreciated that he was taking this at face value. "I just realized, seeing it again, that this vision was different. It's as if I'm seeing it from two different perspectives. You know that there's nothing left there except a pile of leaves, and the ground. That's basically what I was touching to get the vision. So I ought to have only seen the viewpoint from the ground up—I should have seen only the men, not the woman."

"But you saw the woman."

Rowan nodded. "It was like…like I had two different points of view. Like a movie that flashes between the action from the outside and the action as the main character experiences it. I'm sorry that I can't explain it better—I'm trying to understand it myself. Unfortunately, I still can't pick out any details that help the case. I can't see the men clearly enough."

"Men," the sheriff repeated. "You said men, not boys."

Rowan frowned. "Somehow I do get the impression of men. But let's face it, a seventeen-year-old boy is pretty much a man in this day and age, isn't he?"

"Just pointing out your wording."

"I'm glad you did," she insisted. "Look, I'll tell you what. When I'm up for it, in the next day or two, I'll work on this again. I can't see much of the woman, either, and somehow I think that would be important. Mary is something of an enigma in this town, it seems."

"What do you mean?"

"Not everyone remembers seeing her."

Toby waved a hand. "So? Not everybody knows everybody."

"She just seems like someone people would remember, because she was different. She wasn't one of the rich folks, you know? Come on, wouldn't a woman who lives in the woods be a subject of curiosity?"

"Okay, I can see your point. I'll start asking around myself."

"Thanks," Rowan said. "But I'd like to go a step further." The thought hadn't struck her before; the idea had hit her as they were talking. She heard the click of something fitting into place. At Toby's queried look, she said, "I want to see where Mary lived. Will you take me there?"

CHAPTER 7

ROWAN HELD THE PHONE in her hand, feeling the size of it: light, small, rectangular. Cool plastic. Karl's phone.

No, just a phone. She had to divest herself of the owner, or at least what she knew of him. She was looking for information about him, about things he'd experienced, but she couldn't let her own knowledge or judgments about him cloud what she saw—she couldn't let it affect or change which images came to her.

She could, however, focus to roughly pinpoint the day and time of what she wanted to see. It wasn't an easy task, to focus on the innocuous facts of date and time and not think about what had happened on that very night. But she had to try.

Deep breaths, grounding, centering. Breathing slowing. Becoming one with her surroundings, then letting them slip out of her consciousness. Blocking her mind of all that had come before. Emotions a distant thing—not forgotten or ignored, but not valid here.

The phone. The day of the incident. Karl, innocent or not. She had to be open and accepting of all possibilities.

What she "saw" during her work varied, depending on the object and its relationship to its owner or those who came into contact with it. In this case, Karl's phone was often in his pocket, or clutched in his hand. Luckily, her ability included all senses—thus she could hear conversations he had on the phone as well.

Incidents cleared and faded, waxed and waned, as she sifted through them in an effort to find the time she sought. It was instinct, something unconscious, that allowed her to find that day. She brought a scene into focus, although "focus" was the wrong word, because the scene held only sound.

"I totally wiped on that geo exam," a voice said. Probably Karl; the intonation held the clarity of someone close to the object in question. "Was Mackie pulling those questions out of his butt? Tell me we didn't study all that."

An unfamiliar voice agreed, "Out of his butt."

"It was in the reading," a third voice said. Rowan could hear an accent, and pegged the speaker as Manny. "The hand-outs from two weeks ago, and a little of it from the book…"

"Roughly equivalent to coming out of his butt," the unfamiliar voice grumbled. "Look, it's over, we have to focus on other stuff. The paper on Milton is due tomorrow. You gotta help me."

Manny said, "Am I the only one who finds it ironic that the non-native American student is the one everyone comes to for help with their English essays?"

"No," came a voice Rowan recognized as Bryson's. "Because you actually know what 'ironic' means."

Manny, Karl, and the unidentified boy made plans to work during study hall. Rowan noticed Bryson didn't say he would join in. She remembered he had been working on the paper later that night; his comment about it seemed casual. Perhaps he hadn't wanted or needed Manny's help.

The boys parted ways, and Rowan "fast-forwarded" through aural scenes of schoolwork. She received a glimpse of the men's locker room when Karl answered the phone's ring after, she assumed, football practice.

"Mom, I told you I had practice tonight." Frustration increased the volume of his voice. "Mom, the schedule is on the fridge, okay? I'll be home in half an hour or so; just keep dinner warm for me."

It was the last call to or from the cell phone that night. Rowan found little to observe for a while; presumably Karl made his way home and ate supper. Once in his room, he changed his clothes, laying the phone on his desk. He clipped it to his belt, giving her a current view as he did some homework. After that, under the watchful eyes of Britney Spears, he extracted a plastic baggie from inside a model of Dario Franchitti's Indy car and rolled himself a joint. He opened his window—Rowan felt the chill air—and blew the smoke out into the darkness.

The scene ended shortly after that. He checked the TV listings on a computer website; then, with an audible *snick*, he unclipped the phone from his waist and tucked it in the recharging unit. A moment later, the scene went black as he turned off the light and left the room, closing the door behind him. After a moment, the connection between him and the phone was completely gone. The next thing Rowan saw was him tucking the phone in his pocked before leaving for school the next morning...an arrival that would be interrupted by a detour to the sheriff's office where all four boys confessed to the crime of rape and murder.

Rowan pulled out of the scene with some reluctance. Part of her wanted to continue on, to see what the boys said to each other when they met and decided to turn themselves in at the sheriff's office. She had no idea, she realized, how or when they met up; all she knew was that they had arrived on Sheriff Candusco's office steps together.

But no. She had spent long enough with the phone, as her twinging head reminded her. Using her power wasn't something she could do without paying a price. For small things, it drained her, and she came out of it needing food and/or sleep. For strong emotions, a migraine. Once she'd simply collapsed, later to be diagnosed as stressed, dehydrated, and suffering from low blood sugar.

This had been a long enough session to hint at a headache and definitely require sustenance. Lunch with Toby seemed like hours earlier. Rubbing her forehead, Rowan put the cell phone on the desk and went to raid the kitchen.

~

Manny Prabhakaran and his family lived on the Millburn campus. Manny's father, Jayadeep, was the head teacher of Chemistry, and his mother, Dhriti, was the school librarian, so Manny received free tuition at Millburn and his sisters went to the nearby girl's school equivalent, Wodesdown, under a reciprocal agreement.

Rowan admired the campus as they drove along the road that ran through it. Although it was situated just off the highway and had no gates or fences, the place felt separate, its own entity. Only a small, white, wooden sign announced the direction and entrance to the campus.

It was mid-afternoon, the football game and post-revels over, but a few lingering cars still passed them, heading away from the festivities. The Millburn Marauders had swept the game, despite the loss of team members Bryson and Trent, and spirits were high. The cars were all expensive models—Lotus, Cadillac, BMW—echoing the prep school concept. But the buildings they passed were hundred-year-old New England staples, large white-painted or brick structures that hinted at the echoing high-ceilinged, wood-floored rooms within.

"The stables are over there, behind those trees," Chloë, playing tour guide, said. "Some kids bring their own horses. Over there is the zoo—there's a zoo program on campus. The kids that do that each take care of a particular animal for the entire school year. Bryson was in charge of the platypus last year."

Rowan could hear the note of pride in her friend's voice. "I still can't handle anything but cats," she said. "Mostly because they can take care of themselves for a long weekend, if I leave out enough food and water and fresh litter. A friend's sitting for them while I'm gone now."

"How many do you have now?"

"Just two: Pyewacket and Grimoire. Small furry rampaging elephants."

Chloë snorted and turned the car into a short gravel driveway that arced in front of a two-story clapboard ex-farmhouse. Another car blocked their way: a silver-grey Lotus. "That's Martin's car," she said.

"Martin, as is Karl's father?"

"Yep. He did say he wanted to talk to me the other day, didn't he?"

"Well, Elizabeth said he said he wanted to talk to you…" Rowan remembered the phone conversation; Elizabeth hadn't sounded too concerned about the issue.

Before Chloë had even shut off the car, the other car's door opened and a man, whom Rowan assumed to be Martin, emerged and headed towards them. Something in his demeanor made Rowan get out of the car quickly.

"Martin, what a pleasant surprise," Chloë said, closing her door.

Rowan's gut instinct was reinforced by the scowl on his face and the angry tone of voice when he responded to Chloë's pleasant greeting:

"Who the hell gave you the right to interrogate my wife?"

Chloë was so startled that she took an involuntary step backwards.

"What are you talking about?" she asked. "We went to talk with Liz about what happened. We've talked about it before—you and I have talked about it, Martin," she continued. Rowan heard her voice gaining strength as she got over the surprise.

"That's not the way Elizabeth described it." His scowl remained, but he sounded less strident. "She said you brought over some private investigator or something."

"Rowan's a friend of mine; she offered to help out."

"'Help out'? In what way? What gives her the authority to talk to my wife? What are her credentials?"

Rowan's already-taut patience was reaching a breaking point. She hated being talked about as if she weren't there, and Martin Sinclair seemed to be oblivious to her presence, focusing solely on Chloë and his own anger. She stepped around the front of Chloë's car to his side.

"If you want information about my authority or credentials, I suggest you talk to Sheriff Candusco," she said. Martin swung around to look at her. He was a tall, broad-shouldered man, with the look of someone who'd played college football and never realized that his body had softened with age since. One of her suspicions about him was confirmed when he turned; she could smell the beer tang on his breath.

She was wary, but didn't let it show. He was a big man, and acted like a bully, but she'd taken self-defense classes. First, though, she'd try a different tack.

Before he could say anything, she held out her hand and smiled disarmingly. "I'm Rowan Everly, pleased to meet you. I'm sorry to cause such concern. Your wife seemed perfectly happy to have us over for drinks."

He recovered enough to remember not to accept her proffered hand. "Sheriff Candusco hired you?"

"*I* hired her, Martin," Chloë said. "She's my friend, and I thought she might be able to help clear the boys' names. The sheriff agreed and gave her the okay."

"I'm giving him regular reports," Rowan added. She hoped he wouldn't press for details about how she intended to be of help. People like Martin didn't take to the idea of psychics very well.

Luck was with her, because he didn't ask. He doggedly kept on with his rant, even though he was losing steam. He probably felt the need to save face, Rowan thought.

"Well," he said, "I'll be having a talk with the sheriff, let me tell you. Let me tell you," he repeated. "In the meantime, stay away from my wife."

"Martin," Chloë said, "Liz is my friend. How can I not see her? We have the school fundraising meeting on Thursdays."

"Well," he said again. "Well, I suppose I can see your point there. But if either of you—" and his pointed index finger jabbed at each woman in turn "—say anything to jeopardize Karl's case or harass Elizabeth, I'll slap a restraining order on you—"

"We know all about restraining orders, thanks," Rowan said dryly.

As he started to turn away, she added, "By the way, Elizabeth let me borrow Karl's phone so I could check something out. I wanted to make sure we were upfront about that. I'll drop it by tomorrow; is that okay?"

In answer, he slammed his car door. Gravel rainbowed behind him as he dropped the car into first and accelerated away.

"So, do you think he was waiting here for us?" Rowan asked, picking a splinter of rock out her hair.

"He must have been," Chloë said. "I'm guessing he called David and found out where we'd be."

They walked up the two wooden steps to the porch, and Chloë pressed the doorbell. After a moment, the door was opened by two grave-faced Indian girls with wide black eyes, who stepped back to admit them.

"Thank you," Chloë said. "Rowan, this is Mia and this is Sani, Manny's sisters."

Rowan greeted them. Mia looked to be about thirteen and Sani was probably a year older than Manny. They both wore jeans and sweaters, their glossy hair thick and straight; Mia's long, Sani's cut into a cute bob.

Inside was a direct, startling contrast to the New England farmhouse and its autumn setting. The walls were swathed in silken fabric, jewel tones shot through with gold and silver, dotted with sequins. Just inside the front door, a low teak table boasted a statue of Ganesh, the elephant-headed god, and a lacquered black bowl filled with flower petals. The memory of incense—sandalwood, Rowan thought —hung heavy in the air, twined with the faint twang of sitars.

Mia and Sani led the way down a short hallway that opened into the living room, then left through another doorway into the dining room. From the opposite doorway came a tiny Indian woman, no taller than Sani. She was wiping her hands on a half apron that looked incongruous over her turquoise sari and loose pants. Her hair was pulled back, thick and sable like her daughters', and she had a small red dot just above the space between her eyebrows. She and Chloë kissed each other on the cheek, and Rowan was startled to see how close Chloë seemed in size to Dhriti Prabhakaran. Chloë had always been the most petite of the three friends, but standing next to Dhriti highlighted her current gauntness.

In contrast to Martin Sinclair, Dhriti greeted Rowan warmly, thanking her for coming. She offered to make tea and they waited in the living room until she reappeared with a tray, china mugs and saucers, and a steaming pot, which she placed on the teak coffee table. She poured tea for all of them, then perched on the edge of the easy chair, balancing her cup on her knee.

"My family is grateful that you have come to help," she told Rowan. A brief smile flashed across her dark face. "I'm sure you've heard this before from the other families, but our son is not the type to commit such a crime. The very thought of it eats at him, like a wound that will not heal." She hesitated, glancing from one woman to the other. "Chloë, you have been a good friend to me and we have shared many things. When you told me that Rowan was coming, I sensed that…that she was someone who could help us.

"In India we believe in many things that here are ignored. We trust in our gods as you trust in yours, but we speak with them more regularly." She did smile fully at that, the skin around her eyes creasing into a grin as well. "We see things that you might call ghosts, keep faith in what you might call fate."

Something prickled down Rowan's spine, half-premonition, half-*déjà-vu*. "Some of us do see and hear similar things to what you describe."

Dhriti nodded and set her tea on the table. "I thought so," she said, and Rowan though she heard relief.

Rowan made a decision; surprisingly easy. If Toby could know about her power, with all his skepticism, then it was only right that she tell Dhriti, to explain why she was there and how she could possibly help.

As succinctly as possible, she explained her power to Dhriti; how she could hold an object and see events that had been imprinted upon it, meet someone and touch them and know something from their past. She didn't say how it had started, but mentioned that it first happened when she was in college, and that there had been a learning process to understand how to use this curse-gift. Dhriti listened gravely throughout, nodding slightly at times. Their tea was forgotten.

"I didn't know what exactly to expect, but this fits with what I sensed about you, even before I met you," Dhriti said when Rowan finished. She clasped her hands together, almost as if in prayer. "Thank you," she said, her voice fervent.

Rowan fought against a feeling of unworthiness, a flush of embarrassment at praise. She also had to tamp down an ember of guilt: Dhriti—and Chloë—believed her to be there to prove their sons' innocence, without hesitation or doubt, without looking any farther. Although that was the outcome Rowan prayed for, she accepted that it might not happen. And she worried about her own motives.

"So far, I haven't been able to tell anything from examining Bryson's or Karl's things," she said, not wanting to get Dhriti's hopes up. "I'm not sure what that means. It's good in that it doesn't obviously incriminate them, but it's bad because I don't know whether I'm not seeing anything because there's nothing to see, or because something's blocking me or causing me not to see or see wrongly—who knows?"

"I believe in being positive," Dhriti said. "What's the phrase? My glass is half-full."

"Good for you," Chloë said. "We could all do with a dose of your optimism."

They talked for a while with Rowan asking the usual questions about where everyone had been that night. Dhriti confirmed what Chloë had mentioned earlier: Manny had been at the gym in town swimming laps, leaving by the time the gym closed at ten. It was perhaps a twenty-minute bicycle ride back to their house. Sani, whose bedroom faced the front of the house, said she'd heard him arrive home at the expected time, but she hadn't looked out the window and couldn't say one hundred percent that the noises she'd heard were made by Manny and his bike. If he had returned home at that time, he couldn't have made it to the site where the woman was attacked, unless he'd been picked up by a car, and Sani hadn't heard a car. The house was on the school road, where for the most part the only cars that passed were those belonging to faculty. Certainly at 10:20 p.m. on a weeknight, it was unlikely that anyone else, even a parent, would be headed by. The school had asked all parents, and received a negative response. The sound of the car was rare enough that Sani probably would have noticed it.

"Is there any reason why Manny would say he did this? Any reason to confess to something he didn't do?"

"Not that I can think of," Dhriti said after a moment's consideration.

Rowan asked a few more questions about Manny's character, carefully phrasing them so as to not offend. The answers she received were similar to what Chloë and Elizabeth had told her about their own sons. Manny was a good student—top of the junior class, which was saying quite a bit at an elite prep school. He did well on the swim team, tutored children at the local school in computers during the summer, and wanted to study either cell biology or philosophy—or both—in college.

"You'll want to meet Manny," Dhriti said when Rowan ran out of questions. "I told him you were coming out this afternoon. He is willing to talk to you."

"I'd appreciate that," Rowan said. She hadn't been expecting that—assumed Manny had made himself scarce—probably because of her experiences with the Sinclairs.

"He's in his room—I'll go get him." Dhriti started to rise.

"Actually, I'd like to see his room, if that's okay with both of you." Rowan also stood.

"Oh. I don't think that will be a problem. Let's go see."

Dhriti led the two of them back out of the living room and into the front hallway, where a broad, straight wooden staircase led up to the second floor. The railing was decorated with dried boughs of eucalyptus.

Rowan noticed that, despite an undercurrent of tension no doubt from the current stressful situation, there was a strong sense of peace in the house. Most houses didn't have that, even happy ones.

People who were content and loving tended to have bright and loving homes in which newcomers felt happy. This peace was deeper, more fundamental. The Prabhakarans were at peace not only with each other, but with the world, with their gods. Rowan was sure there was a name for it, but she didn't even know how to phrase the question.

Dhriti knocked on Manny's door and then slipped inside, leaving it ajar. A murmured conversation, and then she opened the door and motioned for Rowan and Chloë to join her.

"Hello, Manny." Rowan shook the young man's hand. His eyes were solemn like his sisters'; his slim hand firmly grasped hers. Of the two boys she had met so far—three, if she counted "meeting" Karl via his cell phone—Manny was the first to whom Rowan had the immediate reaction that no, he couldn't have been involved.

Although he had the wiry-strong build of a swimmer, he was just Rowan's height. Still, there was something more…something she couldn't quite put a mental finger on. His demeanor, maybe, or his grace. Perhaps, although she hadn't been trying, she'd picked something up from their brief physical contact.

Manny's room also differed from the other boys'. His walls bore no posters of popular pastimes, although Rowan caught sight of *The Science of Star Wars* on his night table. For the most part, his room was devoted to academics and science. Dark bookshelves lined most of the walls: mostly nonfiction, but a few science fiction. A complex molecular model dangled from the ceiling in one corner. Schoolbooks were piled neatly on the desk beside his computer keyboard, and no stray clothes were to be seen.

"It might be easier if I talked to Ms. Everly alone," he said to his mother. "I think I'd be more comfortable."

A flicker of uncertainty, then Dhriti nodded and hugged him before exiting with Chloë.

"What can I help you with, Ms. Everly?" he asked after they sat, he on the edge of his bed and she on his desk chair. "I'm afraid there are gaps in my memory of that night."

She told him to use her first name, but with a small smile he shook his head, clinging to the formality. "Tell me what you *do* remember," she suggested.

"I took supper at the school, then studied at the library for a few hours. I rode into town, trained at the pool, and then rode back home."

"So you do remember coming home."

"Yes. I put my bike on the side porch and came inside…" He frowned, shaking his head. "I'm sure I came inside; it's what I always do. But I don't really remember exactly. Although I can remember the…incident, I don't clearly remember coming inside, and I don't remember anything afterwards, until the next morning."

His olive skin seemed jaundiced; his eyes never left hers, although he blinked frequently, almost as if too keep himself from looking away.

"That's pretty much what Bryson told me, too," she said, hoping to reassure him. "Your mother says that the only way you could have gotten to the woods would be if someone had picked you up in a car. Do you remember a car?"

"No, I'm afraid I don't. I've honestly tried to remember, to think back over each moment, but there's a point where it's just not clear anymore."

Rowan could hear the earnestness in his tone. *You speak to me in riddles, and I'll speak to you in rhymes.* Lord and lady, weren't any of them going to remember anything useful? She wondered if their psychiatrist had tried hypnosis, and filed that question away to ask the doctor.

She continued with much the same questions as she'd asked Bryson, and wasn't surprised to get much the same response. No, Manny hadn't known Maria personally, although he thought he'd seen her around town a few times. He hadn't made or received any calls that night that he remembered. He hadn't seen any of the other boys after school; because the rest of them lived off-campus, they didn't dine in the school cafeteria as he had.

"I'm sorry I can't be more help, Ms. Everly," Manny said, and again, Rowan heard the frustrated sincerity in his voice. "It's all so strange…

and so frightening." As with Bryson a few nights before, she could see that he was struggling against crying. "I have many plans—I want to study and learn and make the world better. And I don't want to disappoint my family." He closed his eyes for a moment, then looked at Rowan again. "It's so strange," he repeated. "Sometimes it's as if I'm seeing this through someone else's eyes."

CHAPTER 8

DINNER THAT NIGHT was a quiet affair. David and Bryson spoke enthusiastically about the football game, although Bryson was obviously disappointed not to have been allowed to play. They had met up with Martin and Karl Sinclair at the game, and David had been the one to tell Martin where Chloë would be that afternoon.

"I'm sorry, love," he said. He put down his fork and Rowan watched his hand clench into a fist. His brown eyes darkened. "If I'd known he was going to harass you—because that's what he *was* doing —I would never have told him where you'd be. I would've given him a piece of my mind, actually, and told him to stay away from you."

"You had no reason to think he had ulterior motives," Chloë soothed. "Besides, he'd been drinking; I'm sure that he would have been less direct otherwise."

Rowan doubted it. She'd met men like Martin Sinclair before, too many times, and she didn't like them.

Rowan listened to her laptop boot up with its melodic Macintosh chime as she undressed for bed. Wrapping her robe around her, she sat down at the desk and typed in the necessary information to check her e-mail.

From: Amanda Gordon-Davies, <agd@whisperwindmusic.com>
   To: Rowan Everly, <rowan@faireday.com>
   Subject: tallyho, pip pip

Hello there, sweet thing,

   Just checking in to see how you're doing. I haven't heard from Chloë in ages, 'though that doesn't surprise me, with what she's going through.

   How are you holding up? How's the investigation going? Any more run-ins with the sheriff? You =are= taking your migraine meds every-where now, right? Right?

   The recording here is going well – even better than expected, I think. I think it's the inspiration of the standing stones and sweeping mountains – what a magickal land this is! We're marginally ahead of schedule, and I'm pushing to get my parts done as expediently as I can. If I can get away early, I'm coming straight there, dearheart. If nothing else, maybe I can help Chloë.

   Ta, love!

   agd

Rowan smiled at Amanda's ability to combine exuberance with concern. It was probably her positive attitude that made her a good healer; she could take on the negative without being deeply affected by it.

She'd e-mailed Amanda a few days after she arrived, updating her with the details of the case so far. She hadn't mentioned Chloë's preg-nancy, because Chloë hadn't given her leave to do so, but she almost wondered if Amanda guessed somehow.

From: Rowan Everly, <rowan@faireday.com>
  To: Amanda Gordon-Davies, <agd@whisperwindmusic.com>
  Subject: re: tallyho, pip pip

Merry meet, Amanda!

Thanks for the note. Things are just...weird here. Hard to explain. Nothing makes sense. I don't feel like I'm getting any closer to answers. I've "checked" some of the boys' stuff, but no luck – and the boys themselves seem downright horrified by what happened. Maybe I'm a sucker, but I really have trouble believing they did it. But if they didn't, why would they say they did?

I had lunch with the sheriff today, and we've "agreed to disagree". He respects my ability, but isn't fully convinced of my "motives", as he says. *shrug* We're going out tomorrow to see the dead girl's house. Maybe I'll find something there that will give us a breakthrough.

Chloë's holding in there – David's been a rock. Even Bryson seems supportive (which seems odd, considering, but there you have it).

Raise some energy in those stones for us, dearheart – we can use all the help we can get.

Love,

Rowan

She couldn't tell Amanda the details of the case—at least, not through unsecure e-mail. But she knew Amanda cared most about her and Chloë, so she focused on that.

Rowan sent the message, then worked her way through several job-related ones. Sue could authorize the posters while she was gone. No, the printer could *not* raise his rates midway through the ticket printing. Her costume fitting would have to wait until she returned. Eddie would get her draft by Monday night.

She hit "send" again, and was surprised when the computer beeped to let her know another message had come in.

From: Amanda Gordon-Davies, <agd@whisperwindmusic.com>
  To: Rowan Everly, <rowan@faireday.com>

Subject: one thought

We have the night off and I'm about to pop down to the pub – we may do some pick-up work for fun. But before I go, this jumped out at me and I wanted to respond:

Maybe I'm a sucker, but I really have trouble believing they did it. But if they didn't, why would they say they did?

Guilt over something else? Blackmail?

Love, agd

Rowan dressed carefully again the next morning. Jeans and boots again, with a dark green camisole and mint green sweater with lace at the neckline and cuffs. She wore citrine for clarity and confidence, tanzanite for protection and to enhance her visions.

Waiting on Chloë's front porch, she tucked her hands deep into her jacket pockets and breathed in the fall air to calm herself. She paced.

She reminded herself that Toby Candusco was a law enforcement officer. That didn't mean there weren't corrupt and evil people in those jobs, but in a small town like this, surely the negative would have come to light. She reminded herself that he was a friend of the Walthams, and Chloë was damn good at reading people. She reminded herself that she knew self-defense.

All of that helped, but didn't take away the fact that she was going alone into the woods with a man who carried a gun.

Toby pulled up in a dark blue Blazer. He shut the vehicle off and got out before she could open the door on her side. Like her, he wore jeans, along with hiking boots and a fisherman's-knit sweater.

"I have something for you," he said. He handed her something.

She hefted the cylinder in her hand. "Mace?" she said. "Golly, Sheriff, you sure know how to woo a girl."

He chuckled. "Somehow, I thought you weren't the type to be swayed by flowers. Seriously, though: you're going out into the woods with a man you hardly know. I thought this might make you feel more secure."

She stared at him. "Are you a mind reader?" It really was a little creepy that he'd echoed the thoughts she'd just been having.

"Nah." He shook his head. "Call it an informed gut decision. If you're ready to go, I'll explain on the way."

She settled into the passenger's seat and fastened her seatbelt with a crisp *snick*.

"I have a sister, Tammy, who's five years older than me," he began. He set the car in reverse and draped an arm across the back of her seat so he could reverse the car out of the driveway. "She got married when I was a freshman in college. I was one of the groomsmen."

Rowan couldn't fathom where this was going, so she let him continue.

"When I came home the summer after my junior year, Tammy was there. Turned out her husband has been abusing her. She'd actually left him a couple of months earlier, but it hadn't been easy. When the rest of the family found out, they agreed not to tell me because they didn't want it to interfere with my studies. I was still ready to find the guy and, well, in all honesty, I wanted to kill him. Luckily my father and brother talked me out of it. My sister and my mom had had to talk *them* out of it."

"Blessed mother," Rowan said.

"Yeah," Toby said. He flexed his hands where they'd tightened on the steering wheel. "I was studying pre-law—I knew the statistics. But they seemed like that: just statistics. You don't think it will happen to someone you know. I was a *groomsman*, for chrissakes. How could I not have seen it? How could I not have known?

"Is that why you went into law enforcement?" Rowan asked.

He nodded. "I took criminal justice courses in my final year. I knew I could help the problem as a lawyer, but I wanted to be more hands-on."

"How's your sister?"

"She's married to a great guy, and they've got two fantastic kids." He grinned, and Rowan could sense his exuberance and pride. "Both boys. I'll show you pictures when we stop...if you want." Then he sobered again. "Thing is, she was skittish for a long time. It was hard for her to trust again. I know what happened to you was a few years ago, but it doesn't go away overnight. Hence the mace."

"Thank you," Rowan said. "I'll be honest with you: I was feeling conflicted. I didn't think you were dangerous, but you're right, it's a strange situation we're going into. I don't usually wander off into dark alleys or deep woods with men I barely know."

She also had to be honest with herself. She was touched that he'd thought of the mace, that he'd hoped it would ease her concerns.

Since that time in college, she'd met many wonderful men. Men who were horrified when she told them what had happened and understanding of her process in dealing with it. Gentle men, kind men.

Toby, though, was the first who'd taken the next step. He'd done something to empower her.

"I'm glad I guessed right, then," he said.

They fell silent for a moment. Then Rowan remembered something she'd wanted to bring up.

"I had another thought about the case." She didn't tell him that it wasn't really her thought; she knew he'd grill her about what she'd told Amanda, and he might not even believe that she hadn't revealed details about the case. "What about blackmail?"

"What about it?" Toby asked.

"I started thinking, if the boys didn't do it, why would they say they did it? What would compel them to admit to something like that? So, what if they're being blackmailed? If, for example, the person who actually attacked the girl caught them doing something bad, and convinced them to confess rather than have him expose them?"

Toby pursed his lips. "Now there's something we hadn't considered," he admitted. "Hm. It would explain some things, wouldn't it?"

He fell into a contemplative silence, and Rowan let him sink into it, recognizing his need to weave the implications, pursue threads, look for holes. Like Celtic knotwork, it was something that you couldn't see in its entirety until you'd followed the twining ideas back around to their beginning again.

"Here's the thing," Toby said suddenly. "Blackmail. Say they know who did it, but that person has something over them, and he convinces them to confess and cover for him. But what could they have been doing that's worse than rape and murder? Mass cheating on exams just doesn't cut it. They're facing spending most of their lives in prison—what could they have done that would give them a worse sentence?"

"That's exactly the question I can't answer, either." Rowan stared out her window, tapping her fingernail against the glass. "It's just so bizarre, though. They're all so horrified by what—by what's happened. It's hard to say 'by what they've done,' because they seem so horrified by the very act."

"The blackmail thing doesn't seem likely, but it's still an angle to explore," Toby said. "I'll put someone on it when I get back to the station."

"Are you dealing with any other unsolved rapes or murders?" Rowan suggested. "What about the daughter of the woman who confronted us in town the other day? Was her rape ever solved?" She'd told Toby about the encounter during their lunch meeting.

"Unfortunately, yes." He shook his head. "No, I mean, it was fortunate that we caught him, but unfortunate because it might have helped with this case. And before you ask, yes, we're sure we got the right guy. There was incontrovertible physical evidence."

Rowan shuddered.

They parked, and Toby grabbed a couple of bottles of water from the back of the Blazer. He tossed one to Rowan, and she tucked it in her jacket pocket.

They hiked down a closely wooded path, the ground a combination of grasses and rocky dirt. The path followed along a brook for a while, the water a dark blue-grey. Their feet scuffed through pine needles, and Rowan heard the call of a bird she couldn't identify.

The path gradually widened—still not cleared, but the trees spread farther apart, making the area more open. Rowan heard the brook again; looking to her right, she could see it just past the trees.

A blurred pain hit her eye: something under her contact lens, perhaps an eyelash or a microscopic bit of dust. Her eye watered, and she blinked furiously, trying to wash the offending scrap out. She found a tissue in her jeans pocket and blew her nose.

And nearly walked into the back of Toby, who'd stopped, just after stepping into the clearing.

"What the hell?" he said.

Rowan hurried to his side and followed his gaze.

The house—if that's what it could even be called—before them was derelict. There was no way someone could have been living there a scant month before. The reality was that nobody had lived there for at least fifty years.

The weathered boards had faded to a dull grey. Other than the sagging remains in one corner, there was no roof. No doors or shutters. Part of the back wall had collapsed, and Rowan could see through the doorless rectangle in the front wall straight through to the forest beyond.

"I don't understand it," Toby said. "We came out here right after the murder. It didn't look like this."

"Did we take a wrong turn somewhere?" Rowan suggested.

"Impossible. I remember the brook—that rock in it—the lightning-struck tree we passed..." He put a hand against the nearest birch, steadying himself.

"Are you okay?" Rowan asked, alarmed by his suddenly grey pallor.

He closed his eyes, shook his head, looked at the house again. "For a moment there, I saw..." He shook his head again. "Actually, I think I'd like to sit down."

Rowan took his arm. She didn't have the gift for healing that Amanda had, but she could help him ground, give him energy. It wasn't lost on her that she was doing for him what he'd done for her in the restaurant when the vision had come unbidden and tried to overwhelm her.

Ground. Center. Strength.

She guided him to a flat rock at the edge of the brook, brushing away leaves and moss before he sat. He gave a weak smile in thanks.

She looked back at the remains of the cottage, the dead emptiness of the clearing. Something wasn't right here. She couldn't put her finger on it yet, but it was there, tangible, a whiff of wrongness that teased at her nostrils.

"Do you mind if I look around?" she asked.

"Go right ahead," he answered. "It's not as if there's any evidence you could disturb."

Before she moved, Rowan glanced around the clearing. She could see no indication of a temporary structure, or furniture, much less a stove or even a firepit or ring of blackened stones. Toby was right: It made no sense.

Her contact was still bothering her. She squinted her right eye shut, then opened it and made slow, wide-eyed blinks. Both eyes teared up, and she delved for the tissue again. For a moment, as she looked through hazy sight, she could almost imagine the shack as it had been: Though unpainted and rough, with full walls and roof, the door open across a wooden step up to the threshold.

Then she blew her nose, and the vision departed. The hint of wrongness, however, remained.

She walked slowly to the remains of the structure, eyeing the ground beneath her feet as if expecting something obvious and helpful to leap up. It didn't.

Rowan peered through what had been the doorway. If the cottage had ever had a floor, the boards had long since rotted away. A slender sapling had pushed its way up in one corner, now starting to grow crooked at it leaned towards a light-giving gap that had once been a window.

She'd intended to go inside, but something kept her from putting her foot over the rotting piece of wood that had served as a threshold. Her sense of unease, of wrongness, intensified—she was loath to enter.

She shivered. Everything in her screamed to leave, *now*. She backed up a step. Nothing had ever given her this sensation, caused such a reaction before. Objects had shown her horrible things—scenes had unfolded that had made her cry or scream or vomit—but she'd never felt something push her away...urge her away.

The clearing remained silent. Too silent, she thought. No rustle of breeze through the remaining leaves, no trilling of birds or buzz-chirp of insects. She could barely hear the stream, only a short distance away. Reminded of Toby, she looked over her shoulder. He still sat on the rock, eyes closed, fingers against the bridge of his nose. The heel of one foot swung back to gently but rhythmically bump against the base of the stone.

Rowan looked back at the shell of the cottage. Dammit. What was going on? How had someone lived here less than a month ago, and left no trace? If Mary had lived somewhere else, why did everyone—including the local sheriff's office—believe she lived here? And if Mary hadn't lived here, why was Rowan experiencing these malevolent sensations, of the likes she'd never felt before and that made her want to bolt in the opposite direction?

She tried to pull her thoughts together, to focus. Maybe this wasn't where Mary had lived, in which case the morning was wasted. But while she was here, she might as well investigate all she could.

It took physical effort to step forward again. Stepping over the threshold was like pushing through a fog that had weight, mass. That didn't want her here.

The view wasn't much different—the place was a shell, and so decrepit that the shell would be gone soon as well. There was nothing inside worth touching to see if she could receive any images; she doubted if a rusty nail or worn board had much emotion imbued in them. She sighed. Still, she had to try.

Rowan turned and stood in the doorway again. With a deep breath, she placed her hand on the cool, rough wood.

And saw nothing.

Nothing, and almost disappointed, she started to pull away. The wood was, as she'd thought, too weather-stripped, the site too cold. If anything had happened here, it had nothing to do with Mary's murder.

But then a shadow flickered. Rowan locked her inner eye onto it, giving it room to coalesce.

The shadow solidified; the scene lightened. *A woman.* Rowan had the sense that the viewer—the person whose eyes she looked through—was male. At first she was surprised, but then she reminded herself that Mary had to have had a father. But still...

The images were hazy, distant, and she strained to see. The emotions weren't strong enough.

To the right, another figure emerged from behind a sheet or curtain that blocked off a section of the cottage. A girl, perhaps fifteen or sixteen, wearing a dark skirt and white blouse—of an era long past.

Dammit, Rowan mentally swore again. She was in the wrong time period completely. The young girl could be Mary's grandmother, if she saw the clothes correctly.

But something in the scene compelled her to keep watching...keep experiencing.

Rowan's sight, filtered through the man, fixed on the woman in the room. *She wore similar clothes to the girl's, but her hair was loose and her blouse unbuttoned at the top.* Trivial by modern standards, but Rowan understood the situation immediately. She winced, not wanting the girl to see what was to come next—or worse, see the girl be forced to participate.

To her surprise, she didn't have to. The scene blurred, then refocused, and she sensed that she was now seeing through the girl's perspective. *The woman's blouse was still partly undone, but instead of going to her, the man was reaching for a bottle of whiskey on a shelf.* Rowan couldn't see his face completely, but could tell by the cut of his wool suit that he was a visitor, not someone who lived in these shabby surroundings. So her instinct had been correct, at least in part.

The images swirled again, almost violently, refusing to coalesce completely. Rowan heard shouting, but couldn't make out the words. The mother looked pale and thin—too thin, and her lips were blue around the edges. The man threw the whiskey bottle, and it shattered violently against the rocks at the edge of the stream. Then Rowan was thrust out of the visions and back to reality so forcibly that she stumbled.

But not before she saw the girl standing by the brook, superimposed over Toby's seated figure. She looked directly at Rowan, and said, "They see what I want them to see."

And then she, too, was gone.

By all that was… Rowan pressed a hand to her chest, willing her frantically beating heart to slow.

She'd been out of the vision. She'd seen a girl who'd then disappeared.

Ground. Ground and center. She took a deep breath, smelling the loamy earth, the scents of autumn, the water of the brook.

She looked over at the sheriff. His head was still down.

Whatever she'd seen, it had been for her eyes alone.

Toby looked up as Rowan approached. "Damn, you look worse than I feel," he said.

"Flatterer."

"Did you find anything useful?"

She shook her head. "I saw a little bit, but nothing that related to Mary's attack. Everything seemed to be from about the turn of the last century—maybe her grandmother's time."

The sheriff made a noncommittal noise and stood carefully. "Ready to go, then?"

"With pleasure," she said. "This place feels—well, it just feels wrong to me." It did. Everything felt wrong.

"I can't argue with that," he said, and turned to go.

As he did, Rowan noticed that his foot had made a groove in the moist, mossy earth. Something glinted dully, and she picked it up. A shard of glass, filthy, its edges ground down and smooth from the running water before the layers of muck had built up over it.

She bit her lip, considering. Opened herself up, just a little bit, to it.

Sudden bright flash of a bottle shattering in the sunlight.

Rowan clamped her shields down tight. She started to toss the fragment away, but then, with a shrug, she pocketed it, and followed Toby out of the clearing.

They see what I want them to see. What the hell did that mean?

~

Helen had tomato soup simmering on the stove, and whipped up a grilled cheese sandwich as a late lunch for Rowan. The food before the guest, Helen quietly retreated, leaving Rowan and Chloë alone to discuss the morning.

Rowan was finding this one of the hardest things she'd ever had to do. In California when she worked on cases with the police, she never interacted with the victims' families, or with the public at all. That was the deal she'd struck with the law enforcement agencies. If information was required by the press, then the police would say they'd received an anonymous tip.

As it was, little of what she contributed could ever be used as evidence in court. She was more apt to "find" a kidnapped victim or provide details that helped the cops find a felon: physical description, clothes, car, whatever. If she gave them a license plate number, they could find the perp, but they needed hard evidence to convict him or her. And psychic mumbo jumbo rarely stood up in court.

That was part of the reason, really. Rowan accepted her talent—how could she not believe in psychic powers, when they were a part of her?—and she knew there had to be others out there with similar skills. But the vast majority of phone psychics, tarot card readers, and the like were fakes, plain and simple. Rowan had no interest in being lumped together with the charlatans and fame-seekers.

Nor did she want to be hounded day and night by desperate people who *did* believe and need her help. Sometimes she felt guilty about that decision—was it her right to turn away those in need?—but her sanity and privacy won out in the end. She was doing what she could in her work with the police, and that was all she was willing to sacrifice right now.

So she was unused to talking to anyone else about her visions or the case at hand, and even though Chloë was one of her closest and oldest friends, Rowan found herself weighing her words, choosing specific phrasings...even holding a little back.

She hated it.

"I'm really confused," Chloë said. "The house wasn't there?"

"Whatever was there wasn't where Mary lived," Rowan clarified. "Toby was just as confused, in fact. He said he'll go over the initial photos taken after Mary's body was found, and see how they match up to what we saw today. My guess is that it was her family's home, but her mother left and lived elsewhere well before Mary was born." She dunked her sandwich in the soup and took a large bite.

Chloë shook her head. "Such a private, secretive girl," she said. "I wish I'd known about her; surely there was something we—the community—could have done for her and her mother. The real tragedy is that we allowed people to live in poverty right under our noses and didn't notice."

Rowan rushed through her mouthful. "You didn't know *about* her, or you didn't know her?"

"I confess I didn't even know she existed until after...after her death," Chloë said. "Isn't that horrible? It's not like we're such a big community."

"Didn't you see her when you were shopping or anything?"

Again, Chloë shook her head. Her fine blonde hair, carefully styled, barely moved. "Helen does all the shopping and errands for the house. The places I go—the bookstore, the art shop, the restaurants— aren't places Mary would have frequented. Or maybe I did see her, and it was that easy for me to not notice her at all."

CHAPTER 9

C HLOË, DAVID, AND BRYSON were scheduled to visit David's grandmother that afternoon, at her apartment in a nearby retirement home. The plan worked well for Rowan, who had work to catch up on.

"Unlike other Ren faires, we do a Christmas show," she explained to Chloë. "I've got a bunch of updates to do to the website, and I need to go over the mock-ups for the new costumes, and—well, a bunch of stuff."

"Why don't you work in David's office?" Chloë suggested. "You can set up your laptop and spread out. Plus the desk and chair in there are ergonomic."

David's study was in an old section of the house. Natural wood beams, craggy and rough, stretched across the ceiling and sloped down to the floor, contrasting against the white walls. Two walls were lined with built-in bookshelves, nooks, and a writing area, although David's computer was on a wide cherrywood desk, the peripherals tucked in a cabinet to one side.

Her laptop set up, Rowan put on the headphones to her MP3 player, found the hard rock section—she worked best to Queensryche and Motley Crue—and set to work.

It was work she enjoyed, and she stayed engrossed for more than an hour, fiddling with details on the website, adding information that Eddie had sent, and writing new text. She did try to look up from the laptop's screen occasionally, trying to reduce eye strain by gazing into the relative distance of the far wall as her ophthalmologist had suggested. The far wall was too far for her to read any of the book titles, so she stared at the sloped wall instead, across which was spread a large topographical map of the area. Although she couldn't read the words on it, either, she could follow the sweep and flow of streams and forests, and the looping concentric lines of hills.

Still, she was startled by both the knock on the door and the realization that she hadn't left the chair in three hours. Helen entered, bearing a tray of a steaming tea pot and accessories and something that smelled divine.

"Lady Grey tea—I remembered you like it—and cinnamon toast," the housekeeper said, setting the tray down. "I hope I'm not interrupting."

"Helen, what is it going to take for me to convince you to come back to California with me?"

"More than you can afford," Helen said, but her words were tempered with a cheeky grin.

"How about cloning—haven't they perfected that yet?"

"It's illegal to clone humans for non-research purposes." The housekeeper poured tea, fragrant with bergamot, orange, and lemon, into a sturdy blue cup.

"Damn." Rowan added milk to the cup. "By the way," she added before Helen could leave, "you said you've never seen Mary downtown, right?"

"I've never seen her at all, as far as I can remember," Helen said.

"Chloë said the same thing, and you said before that you haven't talked to anyone who's met her. The more I think about it, the more it seems odd. I mean, she had to come into town for supplies."

"But other people have seen her," Helen pointed out.

"Who?"

Helen thought. "David. Logan Pritchard, the sheriff's deputy—he's the one who did the first report after the body was found; I remember that from the newspaper reports. Mr. Sinclair's mentioned her, I think." She tucked a lock of straight, chin-length hair behind her ear. "I'm sorry, that's all who comes to mind."

"Thanks—that helps," Rowan said, opening the Word file about the case and typing in what Helen had said. She'd talk to Toby again tomorrow and see if he thought this was odd. She sipped some tea. Maybe tomorrow would yield some answers, or at least some ideas. Usually she simply "read" an object, gave the police information, and was finished.

This just seemed to be getting more confusing.

Rowan fumbled for her glasses on the night table, squinting against the gleam of morning sunlight and her own nearsightedness. Her efforts succeeded in knocking not only the glasses onto the floor, but also the book beneath them that she'd been reading the night before. With a sigh, she reluctantly exited the warm, soft cocoon of blankets and groped around until she found both. Settling the glasses in place, she carefully picked up the book, which had fallen open, so as to not damage its spine.

Seeing the topo map yesterday had piqued her interest, and when she'd gone to bed she'd taken with her the local history from the selection of books in her room. The dry text and irritating typeface had soon impelled her to give up. Those, and an inability to concentrate. Her mind had still been whirling over the strange discovery—or lack thereof—in the woods. In the end, her sleep had been somewhat marred by snippets of confused dreams, with woods and destroyed cottages and Victorian dresses, Anne Boleyn and jousting and mutton, all superimposed with topo maps and HTML code.

But at least they hadn't been nightmares.

Rowan set the book on her knees. It had fallen open to an old map of the local area. Even though her interest in history was much earlier in time, Rowan found all old maps fascinating, be they a hundred years or a thousand years earlier. She loved to see how some parts of an area would change, and others would stay the same. How in Britain, major roads still followed the old Roman roads. How cities spread outward from a central core, a widening spider web of streets.

The book had been written in the late 1970s on the wave of the Bicentennial-inspired interest in local history. This particular map was reprinted from 1892, as close as the compiler could find to a centennial depiction of the surroundings. Rowan found the town center, with its central green and square ring of government buildings and stately homes. Spidery lines fanned out from the center, looping around estates and farms. If she had her directions correct… yes, there was a piece of land labeled "Waltham," and another, sort of kitty-corner, labeled "Sinclair." Rowan remembered Chloë telling her that the family had lived nearby before moving to the Brady Bunch house.

Rowan put in her contacts and took a quick, hot shower, then dressed in jeans and an emerald green, scoop-neck shirt patterned with gold fleur-de-lys. In her socks, she padded downstairs to the kitchen carrying the book. Helen greeted her.

"Good morning," Rowan answered. "Where is everybody?"

"David's gone to work and Bryson's at school—well, at James's house where the tutor is meeting them this week. I haven't seen—oh, good morning, Chloë."

Chloë, wan against her pink satin robe, gave a small smile.

"I've got pancakes warming in the oven; would you both like some?"

Rowan said yes, but Chloë shook her head. "Just tea, please. It's not being a good morning, tummy-wise."

"Chamomile, mint, or lemon infusion?"

"Chamomile. Thanks, Helen." Chloë crossed her arms on the counter and rested her head on them. "God, I miss caffeine," she said, the words muffled.

"Oh, sweetie." Rowan laid a hand on her shoulder, trying to send some healing and calming energy. After a moment, Chloë covered the hand with her own, giving a squeeze of thanks. Helen put a mug of tea in front of her, and she sipped it gratefully, the pinched lines between her brows smoothing away.

"I was wondering," Rowan said as the housekeeper handed her tea as well, "do you have a recent map of the area? A street map or something?"

"There's one in my car," Chloë said. "I'll get it for you."

"No, you stay there, I'll get it." Rowan took the keys Chloë indicated from the hook by the door and let herself into the garage. The chill from the bare cement seeped through her socks, and she minced as quickly as she could to the Saab and back. Chloë was gone.

"She couldn't handle the smell of the syrup, and went to lie back down," Helen said apologetically, handing Rowan a plate of pancakes, a pat of butter drooling down the sides. "She said to feel free to go up and see her after breakfast, though."

The housekeeper left then, and Rowan spread out the book and the road map in front of her as she ate. The street map, covering a larger area, showed less detail. She found the road that the Waltham's house was on, but the map didn't show the individual plots of land as the older map did. Also, the street had obviously been extended over the past hundred years, forest land cleared back to make room for more houses. Using the placement of cross streets, Rowan managed to correlate on the new map where the house was.

She savored another bite of pancakes (fresh local maple syrup, Helen had mentioned, and oh, it was good), then returned to the maps. With the other end of her fork, she traced the road that Toby had driven the day before, then followed across to where she thought Mary's house was, next to a blue ribbon that indicated water. As the crow flew, it wasn't really that far from the house; less than ten miles.

Rowan folded the street map and tucked it in the book to mark her place. She'd have to compare them to the topographical map later, just for fun. Resisting the urge to lick the remains of syrup off her plate, she put all her dishes in the sink, ran water over them, and went upstairs to knock on Chloë's bedroom door.

"Come in."

Chloë, still in her robe, was sitting up in bed, the covers tucked over her thighs. She had an aromatherapy pillow around her neck, and her large brocade Day Runner notebook planner open at her side.

"Feeling better?" Rowan asked.

"A little," Chloë said with a smile. "Although I'm going through this week's appointments and seeing which ones I can bow out of. I'm feeling the need to take it easy for a while—I know, I know, I should have been saying that all along. And I *have* cut back on some things; I did that as soon as I found out I was pregnant again. It's just hard to give up some things when I've made commitments. I don't like to let people down."

"But your health—and the wee one's—comes first," Rowan said.

Chloë smiled again. "Absolutely. Oh Rowan, I'm so glad you're here. I feel so much safer."

Rowan cocked her head. "Safer? That's an interesting choice of words."

"Did I say 'safer'?" Chloë asked hastily. "That's not exactly what I meant. I feel…more secure. Like you're helping take care of things."

"Well, I'm trying, but I don't think I'm getting very far." Rowan didn't entirely believe Chloë's explanation, but she let it pass. "Which reminds me: I'm supposed to meet with James' parents and the boys' psychiatrist today. You don't need to go with me; I can drive myself if you'll let me borrow a car again."

"I don't know…I remember from college just how you drive…"

Rowan glowered, and Chloë laughed. "Of course you can. Take Bryson's again. That way, if I do need to run an errand, I'll still have my car."

Rowan's interview with the final set of parents, Amelia and Colin Gottard, provided her with nothing new. Amelia spared her one long up-and-down glance that clearly dismissed Rowan as not worthy for her lack of designer labels, and would say nothing beyond firm statements that James had had nothing to do with the crime. He was, by Amelia's account, the epitome of perfection and destined for Very

Great Things; he could do no wrong in her eyes. James then spent the rest of the interview staring pointedly around their living room at various objects that testified to James's wonderfulness: an oil portrait of him above the fireplace, sports trophies (football, basketball, *and* track, Rowan noted), certificates in elaborate frames.

Colin began by questioning Rowan's right to ask questions, citing confidentiality and various legal terms he obviously didn't entirely grasp. She explained that she had the sheriff's blessing, and Colin promptly called the sheriff's office for confirmation. Thus mollified (although he pretended he wasn't), he responded to her questions with short answers, essentially echoing Amelia's estimation of their son's near-godlike stature.

Just before Rowan left, Amelia deigned to speak again, commenting that they were thinking of finding another psychiatrist for James. The current one, she said, didn't seem to be doing much to help James get over the horrifying incident he'd been through, being arbitrarily accused of a crime.

Rowan knew it would be useless to point out that James had confessed, or that being raped and murdered was generally considered to be more horrifying.

The psychiatrist's office was nothing like Rowan expected. Instead of stuffy, dark leather furniture and paneled walls, the area was light and airy. There wasn't even a desk; a section of the wall opened out to reveal a computer, but it was obvious that it was intended to be shut away during sessions. The cluster of comfortable, plump chairs and settees, covered with nubbly slate-blue-and-peach upholstery, could be easily moved into more intimate arrangements if necessary. The pale peach walls were covered with photos and paintings of serene forest, ocean, and desert scenes, as well as posters from all of the *Star Wars* movies.

Nor was Dr. Laverick what she expected. Only a couple of inches taller than she, he had a slight paunch, a slight overbite, and less-than-slight receding of his hairline. Despite that, the rest of his curly brown hair still somehow looked vaguely unruly. In a lavender dress shirt, crisp dark blue jeans, loafers without socks, and no tie, he looked entirely approachable.

Rowan's only experience with a therapist had been after her attack in college. While she hadn't been able or willing to tell the man about her new-found and unwanted psychic powers, she tried to explain to him her anxieties, particularly how they were affecting her school-work. She'd managed to get a peek at her files after about five or six sessions. In them, he'd commented that there seemed nothing to worry about because she wasn't failing.

To Rowan, usually an A or B student, getting Cs and Ds was tantamount to failing. She'd stopped seeing him soon thereafter.

"Pleased to meet you, Rowan." Dr. Laverick shook her hand, giving her a warm smile as he showed her to one of the plush seats. He sat nearby, at an angle to her chair. "Call me Ben, or Dr. Ben, by the way. I've asked the boys to do the same; it generally makes folks more comfortable."

"You know why I'm here, of course," Rowan said.

He nodded. "As I told Chloë, I'm afraid I won't be able to help you very much. I can't discuss with you anything any of the boys have shared with me during our sessions."

"I would never ask you to violate doctor/patient privileges," Rowan assured him. "I'm really looking more for your professional opinion. Things like: If the boys didn't commit the crime, why would they confess to it? If they did do it, why won't they show any proof, and why are they so horrified by it? And, if it's something you can comment on, I'm curious to know whether or not you think they did it."

Ben sat back, his hands dangling easily from the arms of his chair. Rowan recalled her own therapist, who'd often sat with his arms folded across his chest. Why hadn't her university hired someone like this?

"All very good questions," Ben said, "and all ones I've been trying to answer myself.

"One reason for their confession might be attention," he said. "They're at a difficult time in their lives, caught between childhood and adulthood. They've been big fishes in a small pond for some time: football stars, top of their class, popular. But now they're facing college: a new, unfamiliar place, with peers who don't already know and respect them. They'll have to reinvent themselves and re-establish their places in the pecking order. They might already been feeling pressure from the upcoming high school freshmen and sophomores, who are poised to take their places when they go."

"And that would make them confess to rape and murder?" Rowan couldn't wrap her head around that concept.

He spread his hands, then leaned forward, elbows on knees. "Theoretically, it could. Without evidence, they could expect to go free—but their reputations might precede them—people at college will already know who they are, and perhaps view them with a certain...a certain respect or awe that's given to celebrities, even those who have done something wrong."

"Do you think that's the case?" Rowan felt sickened by the idea that a reputation for rape would give someone respect.

Ben shook his head. "Remember, this is all my opinion. But no, I don't. The scenario I described would involve extremely insecure boys, and for the most part, these boys aren't terribly insecure. Oh, they have their moments—like I said, adolescence is a weird time of upheaval for everybody—but they don't have the deep-seated, unhealthy insecurity that would result in such a dramatic cry for attention."

"So, if they're not lying in an attempt to get attention, do you think they actually committed the crimes?"

Ben leaned back, looking thoughtful. "I don't mean to sound like I'm putting you off," he said finally, "but I'm not sure I can answer that question yet. The boys are troubled about something, and it's going to take some time to work out what." He paused again, one finger tapping against pursed lips. "If I had to fall on one side of the fence or the other, right now I'd say that I'm leaning toward them not having done it. It's hard to say why—call it gut instinct—but it's not ringing true with me. But as I said, we've got a lot more work to do."

"Building on the theory that they're innocent, are there any other reasons why they might confess?" Rowan asked. "Are they sublimating something? Feeling guilty about something else? Trying to sabotage themselves somehow?"

The psychiatrist laughed. "All excellent questions, Rowan. You've taken some psychology courses, haven't you? I mean that in a complimentary way—you're using what you've learned to ask the right questions. Of those questions, the only one I can really touch on is whether they're feeling guilty about something else. That's a possibility, but I haven't gotten any impression about what that other thing might be."

"I asked the sheriff this, and he considered it: Are they being blackmailed somehow? If so, what threat would be worse than conviction and imprisonment?"

"If they thought they'd go free because of lack of evidence, perhaps," Ben said. "An interesting twist. I can't say much more than that...client confidentiality..."

"I understand." There wasn't anything else to go over. Rowan stood, and they shook hands warmly. Ben offered to answer more questions if she came up with any, and let her know if he thought of anything else that might help.

His phone rang. "Excuse me."

"I'll let myself out." Rowan tiptoed to the door and closed it gently behind her, cutting off Ben's greeting into the phone.

His secretary, however, motioned to her. "Hold on a sec," she said. "He might want to talk to you again."

Puzzled, Rowan complied. She picked up a current *People* magazine and started to leaf through it, but barely had time to read anything before the door to Ben's office opened.

"Rowan," he said. "We'd better get to Millburn. Karl Sinclair has committed suicide."

CHAPTER 10

ROWAN, USING THE DRIVING SKILLS that Chloë remembered from their college days, beat Dr. Laverick to the Sinclair's house by several minutes.

Chloë's Saab was outside, so she rang the doorbell. The plump maid led her to the living room, which was filled with people: neighbors, police. Martin Sinclair saw her and glared. Elizabeth Sinclair, drink in hand, started to move towards her, but stopped when her husband put a hand on her arm. Chloë, however, flew into her arms, buried her face in Rowan's shoulder.

Rowan led her out into the arching hallway. "Talk to me, honey."

"It's terrible," Chloë sobbed. "The boys were all here for tutoring, but Karl hadn't come down yet. Elizabeth said he'd said he hadn't been feeling well this morning, that he hadn't slept well. The tutor went up to find out if he was coming down for class, and found him. He'd taken pills and alcohol—Elizabeth's sleeping pills and something from the bar, it seems. God, it's horrible."

"How are the other boys doing?"

"They've all gone home. David took Bryson; I thought I'd stay to give some support to Elizabeth and Martin."

"Did Karl leave a note?"

Chloë shook her head. "I don't think so. It's pretty obvious what he was upset about, isn't it?"

"That's true." Rowan hugged her again, not voicing her thoughts. They'd only upset Chloë more.

Was this an admission of guilt? Had Karl finally buckled under the pressure of the knowledge of what he'd done?

Or had he been unable to keep whatever secret they were all hiding?

"Look, it's awkward for me to be here; I'm not a friend of the Sinclairs," she said. "Unless you want me to stay with you, I think it would be best if I headed out. Do you want to stay, or come home?"

Chloë fished a tissue from her pocket and blew her nose. "I should stay, I think," she said. "Elizabeth's a friend, even if we have nothing in common. I'll be all right, though, so you go on."

She headed to the bathroom to freshen up, and Rowan let herself out the front door. For a few minutes she sat behind the wheel of the car, fingernails tapping thoughtfully against the steering wheel. She felt restless, not willing to return to the Waltham house. But she didn't know what to do next, either. She'd talked to everybody, examined objects, and nothing seemed to be bringing her any closer to an answer.

Eventually she started the car, and, without really thinking about where she wanted to go, drove to the park on the edge of town. From there, she walked back to the spot where Mary had been found. The overcast sky pressed heavily down; the radio had said there'd be a storm that night.

Hands shoved deep in her jacket pockets, she stood across from the site. A week later, and there was definitely nothing to show what had happened. Leaves had scattered; new ones had fallen. The broad-limbed maple tree and the cold, hard ground, the only witnesses, protected their secrets with silence.

Toby had said there was no evidence that Mary had been brought from elsewhere—this was, they were sure, where the incident had taken place. It was potentially close enough to the nearest houses for someone to have heard her scream, but the night had been blustery, the wind raucous. Odd that they had chosen a spot so close to the edge of the park—unless, as the theory was, the attack hadn't been planned. But if the boys hadn't planned it, then why had they all snuck out of their homes and met here? Or, the same nagging question: If they didn't do it, who did, and why convince them to lie?

Everyone she'd spoken to had described Mary as an almost fey creature, rarely seen in town (if she'd been seen at all, according to Chloë and Helen), keeping to herself, never mingling or socializing. What would have been her connection to the boys? They swore they'd only seen her a few times, at a distance, when she came into town on an errand. Had she hung around the prep school, perhaps? Rowan made a mental note to ask Toby if the faculty or other staff there had seen her.

She stepped forward into the center of the wide avenue of trees and looked both ways: back towards the park, then up the other way, where it led into the woods. This had obviously been a walking area for a long time. It led to the park, beyond which was the town—but from where?

Rowan looked back at the site. The wind was picking up; a tendril snaked down her neck under her jacket, and she shivered. Playing about in old maps wasn't going to help solve the puzzle she'd been brought here to help with. Given what had happened to Karl, she wondered if time was starting to run out, sooner than anyone had expected.

Back at the house, she paced, restless. Bryson and David were in the living room, and she didn't want to disturb them. She checked e-mail. Checked it again. Tried to do some work, but couldn't concentrate.

Rowan got up from her seat before the rolltop desk and paced through the room again. The rising wind slapped against the window. On the top of her dresser was a clutter of jewelry, her airplane boarding stub, loose change, an empty glass from several days before, hair clips. She opened the top drawer of the dresser and swept all of it in, except for the glass, which she moved to her night table. Then, on the cleared surface, she placed Bryson's earring, Karl's cell phone, the fragment of glass from Mary's house, and a couple of crumbling leaves that she'd taken from the site of Mary's murder the first time she'd been there. After a moment, she rearranged the items. It looked like some ghoulish shrine to the dead girl.

It revealed no answers.

Leaving the items there, she flopped onto the bed and picked up the police report, which she'd picked up from the sheriff's station that morning; Toby had finally gotten permission to release a copy to her.

Strangely, there were no photographs of Mary. Those taken at the murder site hadn't come out; something wrong with the camera, Toby had said. There were several sketches of her, done by a police artist from descriptions given by some of the locals. Rowan took one and propped it up at the back of the dresser, behind the assortment, and stared at it.

Mary's likeness stared gravely back. She had dark hair, pulled back almost severely from her thin face save for a curling tendril on each side. Her dark eyes dominated the fragile bone structure around them. She wasn't smiling. Rowan thought she saw a familiarity between that picture and the woman and girl she'd seen with her vision at the river, but she couldn't be sure. The sketch was, well, sketchy, as it had to be. Without an actual photo, or the subject herself, the artist had to be vague rather than to add details that might be wrong.

Rowan went back to the report.

She skimmed through the boys' statements, seeing no new information from what they'd already told her. The same was true of the parents' statements. As she'd noted, the only clear photos of the crime scene were ones without Mary's body. Between piles of crushed and disturbed leaves, the green grass was gouged from the struggle; dark, damp earth had been furrowed up.

She read the ME's report, however. Rowan knew little about the subject and she struggled over much of the terminology, settling for having a basic grasp for what was being said rather than a clear understanding. For much of it, she wasn't even sure if the details were important or not. But some...the presence of semen, the blow that had probably been the cause of death... She closed her eyes, seeing again what she'd envisioned at the site. The violent attack. The men. The sightless black eyes. She shivered, breaking away from the scene again. She knew she'd have to review it again, look for more details that might help. But not now.

When she looked back at the coroner's report, a paragraph she hadn't noticed before jumped out at her.

"Lacerations in earlobes...gouges, really. It looks as though she had been wearing earrings and they were torn or ripped out of her ears. It happened very close to the time of death, because there was some bleeding, but it's unclear whether it was right before or right after."

Earrings? Rowan remembered her dream. Oddly, then she had been the one to rip the earring out her attacker's ear. Did it mean anything? Sometimes, after she'd used her power, her visions bled over into her dreams. But dreams were capricious, just neurons firing off random information that was in your brain: memories, experiences, stresses of the previous day or two. They weren't meant to make sense. But they could bring an otherwise minor detail into the spotlight.

It had been...a small grey pearl on a delicate gold wire. Rowan remembered wondering why the earring had looked like that, rather than a simple gold hoop like Bryson's. She wondered again, now, what had prompted her to see a unique pearl. She couldn't recall ever seeing an earring like it.

She flipped through the rest of the file. There was nothing indicating that earrings had been found at the scene. That seemed to imply that during the attack, one of the men had ripped the earrings out of her ears and pocketed them; they hadn't caught on something while she struggled. She saw nothing else in the file that mentioned earrings at all.

Rowan went down to David's study, report and iBook in hand, and dialed the sheriff's office.

"Jesus, Rowan, have you heard what happened to Karl Sinclair?"

"I have," Rowan said, cradling the phone between her head and shoulder and using her free hands to ruffle the pages of the report. The house seemed very quiet. She hadn't heard Chloë come back, and although she assumed David and Bryson were still around somewhere, she hadn't seen them. Helen would probably be starting dinner. "How come you're not at the Sinclair's house?"

"Local cops have jurisdiction in something like this," he said. "Although our phones have been ringing off the hooks. How are you holding up?"

"Fine," she said. "It's Chloë I'm worried about—but she wants to stay with the Sinclairs for a while. Listen, I've been flipping through the report you left for me, and I have a question."

"Fire away."

"Did you find Mary's earrings?"

Silence. "What earrings? Wait, hold on a minute."

Rowan plugged the laptop in and connected it to the Internet, listening to an incredibly bad instrumental of "Greensleeves" before the sheriff returned to the phone.

"Okay, I've got the report in front of me," he said. "What earrings?"

Rowan explained about the coroner's report. "I'm assuming that one of the perpetrators took the earrings. I was just wondering if one had been found at the scene, or whatever."

"Not that I know of," he admitted. "None were found, that's for sure. I don't even think we could start checking pawn shops and that avenue, because we don't even know what the earrings look like."

It was Rowan's turn to be silent. She stared across the room at the topo map on the far wall. "I might be able to find out," she said finally.

"What? How?"

"You know how I've been to the scene and essentially seen what happened?" She heard Toby's assent, but it wasn't easy to continue. It never was. "If I try, I can keep calling up the incident, the vision. That day at the café, I did it spontaneously, which has never happened before. Usually I can do it with control, and sometimes, I can see more details. Kind of like watching a movie again—the first time, you see the plot; the second time, you see what's going on in the background, or catch subtleties, or whatever."

"You can do that?" He sounded impressed.

"Sometimes. I can't guarantee it, but I can try." Rowan thought about telling him about her dream, about the grey freshwater pearls, but she didn't. It was probably more than he could handle right then, and it still sounded absurd even to her.

"I'd appreciate that. Just…don't hurt yourself in the process. Do you want me to come over?"

She was surprised, and touched, by his offer. "No, that's okay. I'll be fine. I'll let you know what happens."

Rowan hung up the phone and sat for a moment, bending the corner of the report folder back and forth. She really didn't feel ready for this. Instead, she turned on the computer, logged in, and found the local newspaper's website. A few keystrokes later, and she was searching their archives for articles about the murder.

They, too, had no photos on file. No school photos seemed to exist for Mary, much less school records, medical records, a Social Security number, a birth certificate, or anything else. One article noted that the police were unsure whether they should extend their search outside Duchess County, since it was common knowledge that Mary and her mother had always lived on the outskirts of Milburn.

None of the articles mentioned anything about earrings, nor, indeed, revealed anything new. For some reason, not all of the articles had been archived, but from the headlines, it didn't look as though they'd say anything new. Rowan knew how frustrated reporters could get when there was no new information on a case; she'd watched the cops in California deal with them.

Yet another good reason not to let anyone else know about her powers.

She read through the report again, just in case she'd missed anything about the earrings the first time around, but found nothing. Frustrated, she typed up a few notes on what she'd learned, then spent a couple of hours working on the Faire Day website. At least it was something she felt as though she could accomplish, that didn't present more questions and confusion and pain. Plus, she still wasn't ready to face what she'd offered to do.

Finally, though, she had to. She took her laptop and files back to her room, reviewing the past week as she went.

The last time she'd used the vision had been Sunday at Mary's house, two days ago. Before that...Rowan thought for a moment. The day before that she'd checked the cell phone, and the day before that she'd examined Bryson's earring. She shook her head. Luckily, none of those had given her any scenes with strong emotion, save for the smashing bottle at Mary's house. The stronger the emotions, the stronger her physical reaction afterwards. So far, though, she'd used it five times in six days—two of them violent—plus had one very strange flashback. Her usual practice was to not use the vision more than once or twice per week—certainly her migraine medication wasn't supposed to be taken more frequently than that. Her work with the police in California usually didn't require so much work: She'd examine the object, see what there was to see, and they would take the information and piece together all the clues on their own.

Here, though, she was more deeply involved in the situation. There were no easy explanations as to what was going on, and most of what she'd seen so far hadn't produced any more information than what the sheriff's department already had.

She sighed. She probably shouldn't try again so soon, but she had to. For Chloë's sake. For Mary's sake. For her own sake. Maybe even for Bryson's sake.

Rowan stretched out on the bed and did some deep breathing exercises, clearing her mind of reports and web sites, clearing her body of tension. She reminded herself to distance from the scene she was about to see, to keep herself and her emotions out of it, to watch it as if it were a movie. She already knew what violence was going to happen, and she hoped she could shield herself from it.

~

The young woman had ceased to struggle. Her eyes, deep blue like a winter evening, stared sightlessly upward as the next man moved over her to violate her again. Rowan swallowed, reminding herself about the shields, and tried to move her sight closer, to focus on Mary's face rather than on the man violating her or the two holding her down.

Dark blood moved sluggishly from her shattered nose. Rowan didn't want to look, but she forced herself to. Unfortunately, despite the full moon and the lone lantern sitting a few feet away, the night hid what she was trying to see.

The man finished and pulled away. "Why isn't she moving?" he demanded.

The others stared. "Shit," one of them barked. He nudged the girl with the toe of his boot. Her head flopped sideways with a rustle as the fall leaves caught in her tangled brown hair.

Like a camera lens, Rowan's vision zoomed closer. Yes! There it was, something at her ear, glinting in the moonlight. One of the men picked up the lantern, and the added light brought the earring into clearer focus.

It was the grey pearl she had seen in her dream.

The three men started to walk away. Then the man who'd sworn turned back. He knelt, one knee near the girl's shoulder, and reached to her head. One sharp pull, then another, and he'd torn the earrings off her, slicing through her lobes. "No sense wasting these, or leaving them as a mark," he said to no one. Then he rose and followed his friends, making no hurry to catch up. As he went, he reached into his pocket and pulled out a flask; took a swig.

Ghost-wisps of clouds began moving over the full moon. The girl's wide blank eyes didn't see, and then it was dark.

Rowan opened her eyes and stared at the ceiling. She felt vaguely nauseous, but nowhere near the way she'd felt before. A headache was forming behind her eyes. In a moment she'd get her medication and a glass of water. First she needed a moment to rest and re-orient and think.

She'd proven there'd been earrings, and she'd managed to see what they were. That they were the ones from her dream didn't mean she'd projected them into the vision—rather, she was sure that they'd been in her subconscious since the first time she'd seen the rape, and they'd first broken through into her consciousness by way of the dream. Occasionally that happened: details that had seemed inconsequential or even gone unnoticed had risen to the forefront later and proved to be important.

What was also interesting is that one of the men had pocketed the earrings, not only because they were obviously valuable, but because he thought they were a "mark." What did that mean? Did they mark who Mary was—had he thought it would be harder to identify her body without them? None of the people who'd said they'd seen or met Mary had mentioned earrings. Still, it was odd that a young woman who was essentially destitute (if not homeless, given the state of her "house") owned and wore costly jewelry.

It was odd, Rowan reflected as she got up and headed for the bathroom, that during her vision, she thought of the attackers as men, not boys. She hadn't noticed anything distinguishing their ages, and Bryson and his friends, in their late teens, were nearly the shape and size they'd be as adults.

She was in the dining room nursing the remains of a cup of tea when she heard Chloë come home, and went out to meet her. Her friend looked haggard; Rowan thought she saw her hands shake as she hung up her navy wool coat.

"They'll get through," she said. "Elizabeth's soused to the gills, but if that's her way of dealing, so be it. I can't say I'd do different if the circumstances were the same. Martin…well, he's Martin."

Chloë went to find David and Bryson. At a loss again, Rowan looked at the grandfather clock in the lower hall. It would be at least an hour until dinner. Although the day was still grey, the rain hadn't started. Although her headache wasn't bad, and was muted further by the medicine, fresh air would also help, and might help cure her restlessness and give her more time to think. She put on her boots and shrugged into her bomber jacket, told Helen where she was going, and headed around to the back of the house.

The house was bordered by woods in the back, beyond the studio. The delineation between the property and the forest was obvious; the manicured lawn stopped cleanly at the wall of trees. This was new forest, though, reclaimed former farmland, and so lacked tangled undergrowth. Some of it had even been planted as a Christmas tree farm in the late 1960s or early 1970s, but the industrious businessman had gone off to war and the trees had grown up without him. Together, they made for a simple woodland walk, rather than a cross-country fight through underbrush.

Rowan had walked for only about fifteen minutes when she came up, suddenly and surprisingly, against a tall, chain-link fence topped with a rolled strand of barbed wire. A yellow metal sign was attached to the fence a short way to her left. Underneath the warning symbol and the usual "trespassers will be prosecuted" line, it proclaimed "Property of New York State Electric and Gas." She could see another sign farther away on the right; they no doubt appeared at regular intervals. The warning was clear, and the way was impassable.

Just to check, she walked for about ten minutes in one direction, then fifteen or twenty in the other. The fence stretched on. Going beyond wasn't an easy option.

The light had mostly faded by the time she arrived at the bottom end of the property. Ahead, she could see lights on in Chloë's studio, seeping around the closed blinds. Her sculpting had always been a method of relaxation, of escape for her. Rowan rounded the building, intending to knock on the door and see how Chloë was holding up.

Just as she got around, however, the lights in the studio went black, all at once. Rowan expected to see Chloë emerge, but then she realized that all of the inlaid lights along the path leading to the house had also suddenly winked out.

A power outage? She turned and looked up at the house. The deck light was on, and the glow through the closed blinds across the glass door attested to electricity being on within. There was just enough glow to faintly illuminate the way back up the slope, even without the inlaid lights.

Puzzled, Rowan turned back to look at the studio again.

And stifled a scream, because someone was standing right behind her.

She opened her mouth to say that she hadn't heard her walk up, but then she realized it wasn't Chloë.

It took her a moment more, in the dim light, to realize that the person standing there was Mary Cooper.

CHAPTER 11

ROWAN'S STOMACH DROPPED in the direction of her feet. For a moment, her heart did stop, just like they always described, and her brain refused to function, refused to release any coherent thought. It was trapped in the instinctive mode of fight-or-flight, although her body wasn't doing a good job of responding to either command.

She'd seen a young woman—Mary—when she and Toby were leaving the clearing, a woman who had looked at her and spoken. Up until this moment, she'd convinced herself to believe that what she'd seen then was simply another part of a vision, a fragmented continuance from the scene in the cottage. She'd pushed aside and locked away all quiet suggestions that it had been anything else.

That she had seen a ghost.

She couldn't push away the thought now.

"They need to be punished, you see," Mary said, as if continuing a conversation they'd already started. "Punished for what was done to me."

"Even if they weren't the ones who did it?" Rowan wasn't sure why that was the question that came out of her mouth.

Mary's eyes narrowed dangerously. Then her brows twisted

upwards, sardonic. "Does it matter, as long as someone is punished?" she asked.

And then she was gone again.

Rowan didn't need a second thought. She turned and bolted up the low slope to the house. She was tired after her hike, but panic drove her on. The muted light from the house allowed her to dimly see the path, but she tripped anyway, yelping as her left ankle twisted. She thought she heard laughter behind her: a woman's laughter, tumbling over her shoulder as if someone followed her, pacing her, head just behind her ear. Her boots thudded on the wooden porch stairs as she ran up them. Her fingers fumbled with the door latch; she prayed it wasn't locked from the inside. It wasn't, and she fell inside. Without paused, she turned and slammed the heavy door shut and flipped the latch.

She turned, sweating and gasping, to see that nobody was in the room.

Something banged against the glass door and she whirled. She swept the long drapery aside. The light inside mirrored the glass and she saw her own disheveled, panicked self. Nothing beyond.

Rowan let the curtain fall.

Then a hand landed on her shoulder. She screamed.

"Good God, Rowan! What is it?"

It was Chloë, looking pale and frightened, her eyes wide and smudged below with exhaustion. This time it was Rowan's turn to need a hug, although she made sure, even as the adrenaline made its last pass through her system, that she didn't burden Chloë further by taking energy.

"You're trembling," Chloë said as Rowan pulled away. "What happened? Wait, let me get you a drink."

Chloë pushed her towards the sofa and grabbed a crystal glass and a bottle of Scotch from the bar. She poured a finger of the whiskey and Rowan knocked it back, shuddering as the heat chased the dissipating adrenaline. Her hearing, which had made everything distant and surreal for a moment, normalized. She held out the glass and Chloë poured more, then got her a tall glass of water from the bar before sitting on the sofa herself. Unable to relax yet, Rowan perched on the arm, trying to slow her breathing. Chloë set the water and Scotch bottle on the table.

Rowan stared. "Why does that look familiar?"

"That?" Chloë asked. "Because we drank it the other night?"

Rowan shook her head. "I've seen it somewhere else recently, I'm sure of it." The Dhà Sionnach bottle had a unique shape, almost hexagonal. A double-headed fox leered from the label, tongue out, eyes wicked. It certainly wasn't your average Johnny Walker or Dewar's.

"Oh," Chloë said, understanding. "You probably saw it at the Sinclairs. Apparently Martin's grandfather or great-grandfather was an aficionado of it, and had it ordered specially from Scotland, and the tradition got passed down. They always give us a bottle every Christmas."

"That must have been it," Rowan agreed slowly. She wasn't convinced, but her brain wouldn't focus to pinpoint the information yet. Her hands still shook; her panic still flared.

"Jesus, Rowan, you look like you've seen a ghost. What happened out there?"

Rowan gave a weak smile. "Actually, I think you've hit the nail on the head. As near as I can tell, I *have* seen a ghost." She glanced over her shoulder at the porch door, shrouded by curtain. No banging. She shivered.

She told Chloë about her walk, about seeing the lights in the studio and assuming Chloë was inside, about the lights in the studio and on the path going out.

"And I turned around, and she was standing there. Mary. I recognized her from the police sketch."

"Are you sure?"

Rowan gave her friend a look.

"Right. Sorry. You're sure." Chloë ran her fingers through her hair. "Okay. Damn, all of my questions are probably things you can't answer: How? Why?"

Rowan poured herself another finger of Scotch, drank it, chased it with water. She was finally beginning to feel rational again. "You know the theories as well as I do, dearheart. Ghosts are dead people who haven't moved on to the next plane, usually because of some trauma or unfinished business hanging over from their lives. In this case, it's sort of obvious, isn't it? Mary was brutally attacked and killed. She can't rest until her attackers are taken care of, until she sees justice done. In effect, that's what she said."

"She said what, exactly?"

"That they needed to be punished for what they did to me," Rowan said slowly.

"Who?" Urgency threaded through Chloë's voice. "Who needs to be punished? Did she say?"

Rowan slid down onto the sofa, shaking her head. "No, she didn't."

She hesitated, unwilling to reveal the rest of the conversation to Chloë. It came to close to the heart of what she was feeling, to the crux of what she'd felt deep down and guiltily since her own attack. "Should the wrong people be punished?" she'd asked Mary. "Does it matter?" Mary had shot back. That question rocked Rowan to the core. Did it matter? Sometimes, she wasn't sure. After the attack, she'd gone through a period of hating men, of being frightened of them. She'd gotten better, but she was still, often, wary, as she had been with Toby before they'd gone into the woods.

On one hand, she felt guilty about being suspicious of someone just because he had particular plumbing. On the other, every day she could open a newspaper and read about a rapist, a wife-beater, a child molester. Travesties were also committed by women—she acknowledged that—but the statistics clearly showed that men beat women hands down in the violence game.

So she struggled. Logically she knew that not all men were violent, not all men were misogynistic. But, sometimes, it was hard to believe that, to feel that, deep down in her gut. If the wrong man were convicted of a crime, what was the likelihood that he wasn't guilty of some other crime? Mary had been attacked, and believed someone should pay. In some regards, that wasn't an unreasonable desire.

"Rowan, are you okay?"

Chloë's voice interrupted her reverie, and she realized she'd been silent for too long. Rowan took a deep breath, pulling herself and her thoughts back into the conversation.

"Mary didn't identify who attacked her," she clarified. "I really didn't get time to ask her. I admit it—I panicked. I was scared out of my tree."

"I know, honey." It was Chloë's turn to hesitate. "I mean, I really might know." Rowan stared at her, and she ducked her head, her honey-blonde hair swinging to partially obscure her. Finally, she said, "It's not the same as what you're describing, so maybe I'm off-base here. I've been putting it down to nerves, to stress, and I'm not sure if that's still correct. It's just…there are times when I'm in the studio and it's…it's like…it's as if someone's there with me. Not someone I can see, though, like you saw Mary. And I've dreamed about her, I think. I can't really remember the dreams when I wake up, but somehow I know she's been in them."

Rowan remembered her own dream, when she'd been chased in the woods. Dreams never made sense—had she been chased, or had she been Mary being chased? In the end, it probably didn't matter.

"I wonder what it is about the studio that attracts her," she mused.

"What?" Chloë's head shot up.

"A few days ago I saw a light in the studio, but Helen said the place was alarmed, and when I looked again, it was dark. I figured I'd misseen it. I thought I heard someone speaking, but, well, I wanted to write it off. I didn't want to alarm you if it was nothing, and I was scared to admit it was something. Then, today, the same thing: The lights were on, then they went off right before I saw her. And you say you sense someone, probably Mary, when you're in there."

"It's probably just a coincidence," Chloë said quickly. "Maybe she can't come into the house because she hasn't been invited."

"That's vampires," Rowan said. "Is something drawing her to the studio? Is there a clue there?"

"You sound like a bad 'Scooby Doo' episode," Chloë said, breaking into her pondering. "I'm going to go check on supper."

She left the room. Rowan sat for a moment, thinking about the studio. But nothing, she decided, was going to make her look out the back door at it again tonight.

~

Dinner that night was a somber, mostly silent affair. Helen had made chicken cordon bleu and pasta in a creamy cheese sauce, with steamed broccoli and cauliflower. It smelled delicious, and, Rowan reflected, it probably tasted delicious. However, she wouldn't have been surprised if everyone else's taste buds were as numbed as her own, leaving the food bland on her tongue. Only Bryson cleaned his plate, but it seemed reluctant, as if he fought his young body's need for energy and sustenance.

For Rowan, it was awkward. For the first time, she felt like an intruder in the midst. This should have been a family time, a time for Bryson's parents to be there when he had questions about suicide, a time for Chloë and David to be close to their son and believe that they could prevent him from following his friend's path. Had she been alone with Chloë, Rowan would have known what to say. She didn't know David or Bryson well enough, though, and so she fell into uncomfortable silence, wracking her brain for an opening line or an appropriate subject, and finding none.

Unsurprisingly, they all retired early as well. It became apparent to Rowan almost immediately that she wasn't going to get much sleep that night. Turning off the light was simply not something she wanted to do. She felt like a little kid scared of monsters under the bed—but so be it. She'd seen a ghost. She was allowed to feel like a little kid.

She checked e-mail, watched TV for a while, checked e-mail again. Finally she picked up the book on local history, tucked herself under the leaf-colored covers with two pillows behind her back, and read.

The book talked about the Revolutionary and Civil wars and how Millburn had played a part in each (of course). It covered the completion of the rail line that brought trains to the area, the majesty of old theatres, and the creation of the prep school. Prominent townspeople —Rowan saw the Walthams, Sinclairs, and Gottards all listed, but unsurprisingly, no Coopers—and visiting celebrities. The sensational trials of the man who had murdered his wife and buried her body in the basement with a good helping of lye, and of the embezzler who'd squeezed a local bank nearly dry of money before he was caught. The effects of the stock market crash and Prohibition on the town.

Prohibition. Rowan glanced up at the fragment of glass on her dresser. Was it from a bottle of Scotch, like the one the Sinclairs favored? Or just a random piece of glass from a canning jar or soda bottle? She wasn't going to find out tonight—it was too soon, and besides, what good could it do? It was from another era.

Thinking about the whiskey made her review the events of the evening. She was glad for the glow of the dragonfly lamp as she did; shivering, she missed the warmth and comfort of her cats, who spent evenings like this purr-curled at her side. *Does it matter, as long as someone is punished?* The question still disturbed her. It felt as though Mary had seen into Rowan's soul, reached in and bare-fisted wrenched out the very heart of the matter.

She forced herself to move beyond that, refusing to consider it now, aware that she was cringing away from it like a coward and yet willing to retreat. She'd have to face it at some point. Just not now.

Rowan thought about the fact that Chloë had sensed, if not seen, Mary's presence in the studio. No wonder her friend looked so drawn. How could you handle the potentiality that your stepson was a rapist and murderer if you were being haunted by the ghost of the woman he may have attacked? On the other hand, Chloë hadn't said she'd seen Mary, just that she'd sensed a presence. It could, possibly, be in her head, be because of the stress of Bryson's confession and Chloë's pregnancy and even the upcoming art show.

Gack, now she was sounding like a late-night made-for-TV movie starring Tori Spelling, in which no one would believe that the heroine (who'd suffered some trauma like miscarriage) saw what she actually did see. "You need help, dear," the concerned husband would say as the white-coated guys were carting her off. Bah.

If Mary was back as a ghost—which seemed to be a pretty reasonable statement given what Rowan had experienced—then there was no reason to disbelieve that Chloë had seen or sensed her, too.

And yet...

Yet even Chloë had tried to brush it off. She'd made the "Scooby Doo" comment and rushed off to see about dinner. Actually, now that Rowan thought about it, it hadn't been the presence (or non-presence) of Mary that Chloë had rebuffed—it was the idea that Mary was somehow drawn to the studio.

Rowan picked up the book on her lap and flipped back to the early map of Millburn. She found the Waltham's property, with a big rectangle for the house. There was no corresponding building. Next door (if you could call it that—the estates were big), the Sinclair's property had a big rectangle and three small rectangles. She searched through the book for corresponding comments, and found one about the Sinclair's "vast" and "modern" estate with its house, horse stable, cow barn, and servant's cottage.

She looked back at the map, the tip of her tongue tucked beneath her upper lip. Maybe the Waltham's servant's cottage had been too small. Still, something didn't line up quite right. Reluctantly, she crawled out from underneath the covers and found the street map. Again, it didn't show individual plots of land, but it did show a big blank area marked "NYSEG" that corresponded with one side of the chain-link, barbed-wire-topped fence she'd found earlier that night. On the other side of that, several miles away, was where she pegged the location of Mary's house.

Rowan took a piece of paper and laid it out on the street map, lining up the ends with where she guestimated the Waltham's house was and where Mary's cottage ruins lay.

In the center, almost exactly, was the skewed angle off the park where Mary's body had been found.

She picked up the historic map and tried to line it up the same way.

Also along the line, unless she'd messed up the directions somehow, was the Sinclair's servants' building. It lined up from the

Waltham's house through the servants' building, through to Mary's supposed abode.

CHAPTER 12

T HE NEXT DAY, Rowan called Toby and told him about the earring, describing it as best she could. He faxed over an artist's sketch, which she approved, and he said he'd get it on the various computer searches available.

And then she had nothing to do. She couldn't really continue interviewing parents or asking for their boys' things in the wake of Karl's suicide. She'd been over the police report again and again, and she had no items or objects to examine. For a while, anyway, she wasn't needed. She thought about flying home for a few days, but the cost seemed exorbitant, and she didn't want to abandon Chloë.

They went for massages the day after that, and afterwards, when Chloë went to buy a dress suitable for the funeral—her bump had gotten just large enough to make all her others too tight—Rowan wandered into the liquor store and asked about Dhà Sionnach.

The clerk was a pretty woman with brown hair French-braided to her shoulder blades, wearing gold-wire-rimmed glasses and a rose-colored sweater-and-skirt set.

"Oh yes, Dhà Sionnach," she said. "I recognize the name because it's so unique. The Sinclairs order it frequently."

"What about the Coopers?" Rowan asked. "Did they order it as well, or just buy extra bottles?"

"The Coopers?" The woman frowned. "I don't think I know them."

"Mary Cooper, the girl who was killed recently?"

"Oh!" Her face cleared. "No, she never came in here while I was working. I've never met her at all."

It was Rowan's turn to frown. "Did you ever see her, on the street, maybe?"

The clerk shook her head again. "I'm afraid not."

Rowan thanked her absently and left. Yet another person who'd never met or seen Mary. How reclusive had the young woman been?

She asked the same question in the local grocery store. The place was small enough and the clientele known well enough that the store still often operated on a credit system where regular shoppers paid up at the end of the month. Rowan doubted someone like Mary would have been trusted with this system, but she had to have shopped somewhere.

Two check-out clerks were working that day, a middle-aged woman with greying hair flattened under a net and a girl who looked as though she'd just graduated from high school that spring. They shared one bagger between them, a young man a few years older than the girl—no doubt someone for whom college wasn't an option for whatever reason. He still had traces of acne, especially high on his forehead where his hair touched his face.

The older woman responded negatively to Rowan's question. "No, I've never been working when she came in. Janey?"

The girl popped her gum between a small gap in her front teeth. "Nope."

"How many other clerks work here?" Rowan asked. "Mary must have come in during their shifts."

"There's just us and Carole," Janey supplied. "Well, and I replaced Margaret, who retired in May. Sometimes Mr. Mackey—he's the manager—helps out if we're busy."

"I remember her," the bagger boy interjected. "I've helped her with her groceries."

"Who rang them up for her, then?" Rowan asked.

They all stared blankly at her. A customer came to Janey's register, balancing a toddler with a red knit cap on one hip and settling her carry basket on the rolling belt. Janey turned to help her, and the bagger followed.

"It seems odd, doesn't it?" Rowan said. "She had to have been buying groceries somewhere."

"It's very odd," the older woman agreed. "Maybe Mr. Mackey can help out; I'll go get him."

Store manager Mackey, it turned out, could indeed help a little. He remembered Mary, had been at the checkout a few times when she shopped here. He didn't remember if she wore earrings; in fact, he didn't really remember what she wore at all. But he was sure he'd seen her.

Rowan thanked them all, bought some apples, and went to sit outside and wait for Chloë. She was glad she'd worn leggings and a tank top under her oversized sweater; the autumn chill would have been unbearable otherwise. Poor Mary, she reflected as she bit into one of the crisp apples, the tartness twitching on her tongue. How had she survived the chill, much less the bitter cold and snow of winter, in that ruined hovel or wherever she'd lived? How must she have felt, skulking around in a town where the well-off barely ever noticed her? Typical, wasn't it, that men could bring her to mind; no doubt they'd had a few lecherous thoughts about…

Rowan swore she felt her mind click. She closed her eyes and thought. The people who remembered Mary were Bryson, David, Toby, the bagger, and Mr. Mackey. The people who hadn't ever seen her were Chloë, Helen, the liquor store clerk, and the two grocery clerks.

There was a completely clear line separating the people by gender. Too delineating for Rowan to pass it off as men's lechery.

But why? It didn't make any sense.

Then, unbidden, she heard Mary's voice in her mind, repeating what she'd said by the river: "They see what I want them to see."

Now, *there* was something. Rowan sat back suddenly, considering.

Did Mary have some sort of paranormal hold on people? Had she been able to make herself invisible only to women? It sounded absurd, but Rowan couldn't discount psychic ability when she had a form of it herself.

But why women? And why was she appearing now, after her death, to Chloë and Rowan herself? She didn't seem to be appealing to them for help.

"Goodness, you're lost in thought." Chloë sat down heavily beside her, sounding out of breath. She had a shopping bag with the maternity boutique's logo on it, though, so Rowan assumed her quest had been successful.

"Thinking about weird stuff, I'll admit," Rowan said. She told Chloë about the gender separation between who remembered Mary and who didn't, about it possibly being a form of telepathy.

"Do you think...?" Chloë hesitated. She was sitting forward, upright, tense. Almost expectant, but also frightened, as if what she anticipated wasn't something she looked forward to.

"What?" The wind kicked up; Rowan's leggings and sweater were no longer adequate and the cold sliced her.

"Is it possible—if Mary can make people see stuff, could she be making the boys *think* they attacked her when they didn't?"

Rowan stared at her. "Chloë...I don't know. It's possible, I suppose. She obviously wants somebody punished. If she *is* doing that, though, it doesn't give us anything to go on. It doesn't help tell us who did do it. And who's going to believe a coerced confession via telepathy?"

"We could ask her who did it," Chloë said tightly.

"Does it matter, as long as someone is punished?" Rowan remembered Mary's words, the ones she hadn't repeated to Chloë. They could ask, but Mary might not care to answer.

"I suppose we could," she said carefully. "Provided Mary wanted to talk to us. Provided she actually knows who did it. Provided she'd want to tell us."

"You're right, it's an insane idea." Chloë ran her hands through her fine hair. "Right now, it all feels pretty insane. The doctor says I should avoid stress, but how can I? My stepson is confessing to a heinous crime, one of his best friends has just committed suicide, and we're being haunted by the victim who might be psychically manipulating everyone!"

Rowan hugged her. "Let's keep taking everything one step at a time. A lot of this is supposition. The important thing is to keep trying to figure out who actually did it." For Chloë's sake, she didn't add that they also should keep in mind that maybe Bryson and his friends *were* guilty.

They went into a coffee shop to warm up. Rowan ordered tea; Chloë a hot chocolate.

"Let's change the subject for a sec, okay?" Rowan said. "Has the studio always been on David's family's property? Do you know when it was built?"

"I haven't a clue. Good non sequitur, though. I'm impressed." A grin broke through Chloë's clouded face. "Why do you ask?"

"Oh, I don't know. I'm still wondering why Mary seems to like the studio so much, and I noticed on an old map that the building lines up with the edge of the town through to where Mary's house was."

"Bizarre," Chloë said. "But I don't know what that means."

"Probably nothing," Rowan admitted. "I noticed it in part because even with all the driving, I didn't think we'd gone that far away to see where Mary lived. And when I went for a walk the other night, I hit up against the power station fence. I matched stuff up, and realized that if Bryson had been…at the scene of the crime, he couldn't've walked there, because there wasn't time to walk all the way around the power station perimeter."

"Somebody would have heard his car," Chloë said, a stubborn jut to her jaw.

"I know," Rowan said. "And that's a big point in his favor—it would be hard to prove how he got out and back. Anyway," she added, trying to change back to a more neutral subject, "I'd be curious to see the old property records. Wanna come to the town hall with me?"

Chloë looked down at the narrow watch that hung loosely on her fragile-looking wrist. "Oh hell, look at the time! No, I can't—I've got to get home and change before the viewing this afternoon. We promised Liz and Martin that we'd come early and help out. Neither of them is going to be in good shape."

Rowan had already decided not to go to the viewing; she didn't know the family well enough and her presence would only be a painful reminder of the situation leading up to Karl's suicide. She didn't relish the idea of sitting around in the near-empty house while Chloë and David were at the viewing and Bryson was at the Gottards'.

"You get going," she said. "I'll get a taxi home later. I'm not quite ready to let this property question go yet."

Rowan paid the taxi driver and let herself into the house with the key that Chloë had given her. Other than a light in the kitchen, the house was dark. But the family should be home reasonably soon; the viewing was supposed to go until 4 p.m. Unless they stayed later to help the Sinclairs, they'd be home in half an hour or so.

She went up to her room and put the small stack of photocopies on the desk next to her laptop. Her research had proved successful. Thanks to a very helpful clerk at the town hall, she'd gotten her hands on the files she needed, and from there it was just the tedious paging-through until she found the information. The Walthams' studio, once servants' quarters, had originally been the servants' quarters on the Sinclairs' property. David's father had bought the chunk of land and the building in 1959, just before David was born. It made sense because it smoothed out the line between the two properties. Trees were cut down and others planted, landscaping had been altered, so by this time, there were no obvious visual clues that the studio didn't belong squarely behind the Waltham's house.

The information also meant that the line between the studio, the murder site, and Mary's house was a straight one, but one that crashed into the old Sinclair property rather than the Waltham one.

Which, unfortunately, didn't mean much of anything. It didn't explain Mary's apparent interest in the building—and it wasn't even certain that Mary even had an interest in it. Just because Rowan had seen the lights on, unexplained, in the studio twice, and one of those times Mary appeared, wasn't much of a scientific subsample.

Rowan reached for the curtain, but she didn't pull it back right away. The memory of yesterday evening was still too strong. She felt a little silly, now, in the daylight, but not so silly that she could throw back the curtain without thinking about the fact that, last night, she'd met with a ghost. After a moment, she took a deep breath, leaned forward, and looked down the lawn at the small building.

Just a building, though, she saw with relief, letting her breath back out. The last of the day's light didn't quite reach it there, squatting beneath the trees. Chloë said the place got a decent amount of light in the summer, because the evergreen needles didn't block sunlight the way deciduous leaves did, but that in the winter it was gloomy. They'd have to cut down all of the tress to solve the problem, Chloë had said, and she wasn't willing to have perfectly good trees cut down because of a little sunlight.

She was about to move back from the window when she saw the flicker of movement. Something fluttered in the pit of her stomach; her muscles tensed. *You're being ridiculous*, she thought, but it didn't make her feel any less nauseous, and it didn't change what she saw.

Mary beckoned to her.

Rowan realized that she was silhouetted against the window-square of light from her room. She wanted to duck inside, to hide. To pull the covers over her head and deny that anything was out there. It took everything she had to remain standing, one hand holding back the brocade curtain, and face the figure across the lawn.

Mary beckoned again; the gesture was clear. Rowan had no clue why Mary would want to talk to her again. She didn't *want* Mary to want to talk to her, dammit. She didn't even want Mary to be there, impossibly, as a ghost.

But she wanted to find out who had raped and murdered Mary, and Mary seemed to want to be involved in that process. Rowan closed her eyes, commanding back tears of fright and frustration. She had to do this.

She opened her eyes and waved down at the figure, indicating her intentions. It took her only a few moments to retrieve her Reeboks and lace them on, and head out of the house towards the studio. Before she did, she made sure the lights that illuminated the path were on. She wanted to be able to find her way back in the darkness. Even if the moon had been more than a crescent, the clouds scudding across the sky would have blotted it out.

The lights were off in the studio, but there was enough light for Rowan to see Mary standing in front of the building as she got close.

"You rang?" she said as she got near, knowing she was using humor as a defense.

Mary cocked her head. "Perhaps. Or did you call to me? We are alike, you and I. I sense that. We have both suffered atrocities at the hands of men, and we both seek revenge."

"I don't know about that," Rowan said. She struggled with the concept of who—what—she was talking to. She felt a curious light-headedness, like an adrenaline rush just after a near-miss car accident. "Yes, we were both attacked, though yours was far worse. But I don't seek revenge on the man who did it to me. He's gone."

"Is it the man, or men?" Mary challenged. "Aren't there others who should pay?"

Rowan still felt sick to her stomach. "There are other men who've attacked woman and committed atrocities," she said. "I agree that they should be punished. I don't see it as revenge, though."

"Are you sure?"

"Yes," Rowan said firmly. "With them it's not personal, so it's not revenge."

Mary nodded. "Fine, then, I've used the wrong words. But you and I agree that men should be punished."

Rowan shivered. Mary was echoing her deepest thoughts, the ones she kept hidden—the ones she didn't want to face and ascertain, once and for all, whether they were what she truly believed.

"Men who attack women should be punished," she said. She struggled to move away from her own experiences, towards the current situation. "If the boys—Bryson, Karl, Manny, James—if they're the ones who attacked you, then they should be punished. But if they're not the ones, then they shouldn't."

"Are you sure?" Mary asked again, in a tone that made it sound as though she were sneering. "They could go on to be cruel to our kind. Might we not be doing a favor to our sisters to stop them now?"

"If we knew they would do something in the future, then I'd say yes," Rowan answered. She wrapped her bomber jacket more tightly around her. "But I don't have the ability to see into the future. Do you?" She meant the question honestly. Did spirits know what was to come?

"It doesn't matter." Mary dismissed the question, and Rowan found fury building within herself.

"Yes, it does matter!" she said. "If these kids attacked you, then they should be punished. If they didn't, then they shouldn't be punished. If they do something in the future, then that's the time to punish them. I don't think it's fair that they should suffer for something that they didn't do."

Mary's form seemed to shimmer. For a moment, Rowan thought she could see through her to the white wooden slats of the studio siding.

"If that is the lie you wish to believe about yourself, then so be it," Mary said. "Perhaps someday you'll come to accept the truth about what you really believe, deep inside. A pity for now, because I thought you could be my ally in this fight."

The sound in the ghost's voice chilled Rowan to the core. She seemed, almost, to desire something more than revenge.

"What did you expect me to do?" Rowan asked.

A shrug. "Help seek revenge. Help settle the score. Help punish men who would force themselves on women."

"*Did* the boys do this to you?" Rowan asked the question quickly, desperately, afraid that Mary would deem further talk unnecessary and end the conversation before Rowan got more information.

Mary cocked an appraising eyebrow. "If I answer you true and straight, there won't be a challenge," she said finally. "You won't help me, so I won't help you. I'll say this, though: They deserve to be punished."

"If they didn't do it, then who did?" Rowan demanded, not expecting a straight answer but willing to try.

Mary smiled. It wasn't a pretty smile, nor a pleasant one. "If you really want the answer, look close to home," she said, and then vanished. But not before she raised a hand, seemingly to indicate the studio behind her.

A sudden gust of wind blew up a swirl of dry leaves. Rowan swore. The adrenaline still pumped through her system, and she felt a mix of emotions—anger, fear, frustration. If Mary truly wanted her attackers brought to justice, why was she being so evasive, so obtuse?

Rowan had never said she wouldn't help, but Mary had apparently found something lacking in her. Emotions swirled with the leaves, guilt adding to the mix. She didn't want to go there; didn't want to probe and pick and see if Mary's accusations had any truth.

So she turned her attention to the studio, and Mary's final words. "Look close to home," she'd said. That might actually indicate that the boys—or at least Bryson—had been involved. Mary had seemed to indicate the outbuilding. Rowan assumed it would be locked and the alarm set, but given that Mary seemed to have the ability to turn the lights inside on and off, perhaps she'd been so kind as to release the catch.

She had. Either that or Chloë had forgotten to lock it up, but Rowan doubted that. Chloë was methodical about things like that, and she obviously cared a great deal about her work, both what Rowan had seen and what—at Chloë's frantic request—she hadn't.

Rowan opened the door slowly, half-expecting Mary to be inside. But the closed curtains blocked out any fragment of waning evening light, and she could see almost nothing. It seemed preternaturally still. For a moment, she wondered if Mary had lain some sort of trap. She tucked her hair behind her ears and groped for the light switch, which she assumed would be on the wall near the door. If there was something waiting, she wanted to meet it with the lights on.

She found the switch, and the room blazed into light. For a

moment, blinded and disoriented, she could only blink and brace herself for something to take advantage. Nothing did, and slowly she relaxed, her vision settling.

The large, open room was as she remembered it. Dust still tracked across the oak floor, drop cloths still scattered like a giant's discarded napkins after a good meal. The Arthurian fantasy-esque statues regarded her as she stepped into the center of the room and turned slowly. Nothing seemed obviously out of place, nothing looked damaged or broken. Overhead, the fluorescent lights hummed, a murmuring commentary understood by no one else.

Rowan walked around the room. The former servants' quarters had been completely converted; she couldn't really imagine how it must have looked before. Probably divided into small rooms, with the same above—a second story rather than the current open space to the vaulted ceiling. She hadn't a clue what the walls would have looked like, or if the windows were in the same place, or what might have been in the kitchen. The best she could guess is that the toilet had been outside.

It didn't make a lot of sense. David had probably had the place gutted in order to convert it into his sculptor-wife's dream studio, and the work had been done well before Mary's attack. Why was Mary so attached to the place? Rowan did some mental arithmetic. Had Mary's grandmother lived here? She remembered Chloë saying that it had been used as a guest house when David was growing up. In that case, had Mary's mother stayed here? But nobody seemed to really remember Mary's mother, much less Mary herself, and the family had been poor, not the type to be invited guests of one of the founding town families.

Rowan remembered the remains of Mary's cottage, much smaller and cruder than this building. It occurred to her that at some point, this building had fallen into disuse, and guests had begun staying in the house. At that point, she wondered, could Mary and her mother have taken it over? Lived here in secret because in comparison to their own shack, it was a mansion? Before it had been converted, Chloë said, the windows had been small and the underbrush and trees had made the place shadowed and gloomy. By the same token, they would have served to screen a squatter's presence from the notice of those in the house above.

It seemed far-fetched, but it was the best Rowan had come up with so far. She made a mental note to ask David about how long the building had been empty and unused.

She continued her slow walk around the inside of the studio. Chloë had hung prints of famous sculptures on the white-painted walls, but otherwise, the only decoration was her own work scattered throughout the room. Rowan paused to look at the shelves full of art books, still unsure what she was looking for. As she turned away from the bookcase, something skittered across the floor.

There was another pile of swept-up dust here. Chloë had obviously gone into a fit of cleaning one day, but lost interest when her Muse called, and had never gotten around to finding the dust pan. Rowan had stepped in it and kicked something across the room.

Assuming it was a piece of stone or clay, she only idly glanced in the direction it had gone, not intending to chase it. But something glinted by the baseboard, and curious, she walked over and picked it up.

A grey pearl earring, like the one she'd seen in her dream.

Laughter rippled through the room, sweeping over Rowan and raising the hair on the back of her neck as it brushed by. She jerked upright, searching for the source of the laughter, which she somehow knew to be Mary's. There was no one she could see, even though she had to dodge between statues to check. She chased the sound to the corner near the covered statues.

Whereupon it faded out.

She looked down at the earring in her hand.

And watched as it, too, faded from sight.

CHAPTER 13

*S*ONOVABITCH!"

The laughter again. This time, it took the form of a breeze, rustling the edge of the drop cloth over the statues.

"Mary, what are you telling me?" No response. "Are you trying to tell me to look at those statues? Chloë asked me not to. I don't like lying to one of my best friends."

Again the edge of heavy cloth raised, as if caught by an unnaturally strong breeze, then it fluttered back down. The laughter swelled, diminished into silence.

Rowan swore again. Mary—who was a ghost, for crying out loud! —was toying with her. She'd said she wouldn't make it easy, and it wasn't. She was challenging Rowan, but to what end, Rowan didn't know.

Chewing her lower lip, she regarded the muted statues. She'd meant what she'd said: She didn't want to go against what she'd said to Chloë. The fact that she'd never "promised" not to look at the statues meant nothing; she didn't care about semantics. Chloë had asked her not to look at them, and friends honored such requests, regardless of whether the honoring was sworn aloud or not.

On the other hand, she was concerned—about Chloë, about

Chloë's intense personal reaction to Rowan potentially viewing the statues, and about Bryson and the whole horrible mess of Mary's attack. She didn't know whether the hidden artwork was related, or whether Mary was trying to distract her.

She couldn't imagine what had Chloë so frantic about the statues. Did she think they were so bad that they couldn't be seen by anyone else? A ridiculous thought. Chloë had always laughed at her failures (which had always looked like perfectly good pieces to Rowan), and in college the three of them would save them for smashing to bits when they were in a bad mood.

Maybe Chloë wanted to use them in her show, and didn't want anyone to see them ahead of time. That made a bit more sense, but only a bit. Even if Chloë didn't want art critics or the viewing public to see them too soon, there was no reason why Rowan would be denied access. And Chloë's reaction had been too emotional for a simple concern for pre-show secrecy.

The studio was utterly, completely silent. The laughter was gone, and with it, any hint of Mary's presence. Rowan was alone. Mary wouldn't know if she looked at the statues or not.

Then again, neither would Chloë.

Rowan rejected the underhanded approach. This was silly. She'd look at the statues, see if they had anything to do with anything, and later, she'd confess to Chloë what she'd done and apologize. They'd laugh about it and move on.

She grasped the edge of the drop cloth and pulled.

She had somehow forgotten about the end of her dream, the one in which she'd seen the earring. When she revealed the statues, she remembered.

In the dream, she'd pulled back the cloth, and then woken in fear.

Now she saw what her subconscious had suspected, and denied her.

The first word that came to Rowan's mind was *evil*.

The grouping of statues seemed to emanate evil, in a way she couldn't put into words. They portrayed the attack. Three figures loomed over a fallen fourth, whose face was fraught with fear. One man was reaching down to pin her arms.

It was their faces that did her in. Leering, laughing—they saw this as a sport, and the woman wasn't even a player, just an object, a goal. Their features were just indistinct enough that Rowan couldn't recognize any of them; not obviously the boys, not obviously any of them men she'd met in Millburn. Yet somehow, they seemed familiar.

"Who's in there?"

Rowan bit back a scream of pure terror. All of the adrenaline rushed through her again, slamming together in her stomach and creating a fireball that exploded back outwards through her system. She whirled, recognizing even in those few seconds that the voice was Chloë's.

"Rowan? What are you—oh my God, Rowan, no!"

Chloë came through the door and saw her. She flushed, then all the color dropped out of her face in a single rush.

"Chloë, I'm so sorry." Rowan ran to her side. "I can explain—it was Mary—I saw her again... Are you okay?"

"Dizzy," Chloë said, her voice faint. Her eyes seemed unfocussed.

"Let me help you to the sofa." Rowan put her arm around Chloë to help prop her up. Which was a good thing, because before they even took a step, her friend went limp and it took all Rowan's strength to keep her from dropping to the floor.

Rowan laid her down and rested fingers against her neck for a pulse. She had one, and she was breathing.

Helen had said there was an intercom... Yes, there, over the custom-made chest for Chloë's sculpting tools. Rowan ran to it and slapped the button.

"Helen, it's Rowan, in the studio. Call 911. Chloë's fainted."

Rowan had never liked hospitals—not that she'd ever met anyone who did. Not even the people who worked in them seemed to honestly like them. She'd known doctors and nurses who cared immensely for their professions and their patients, but actually being in the hospital served to wear them down, inexorably, day after day. It was always worse for the patients themselves being there, and for the family and friends who waited for news.

David looked haggard. Rowan didn't blame him, given everything that had been going on. In some ways, she expected him to be worse off than Chloë. Bryson flipped through a tattered issue of *Newsweek*, his face inscrutable. He was a teenaged boy; they didn't show emotion.

At least, not until the doctor walked in. Then Bryson glanced up quickly, his eyes gleaming with expectation and hope, but tinged with worry.

Chloë's obstetrician, Dr. Bridget Melora, had long, thick, greying brown hair plaited down her back, and the usual stethoscope dangling around her neck over her baggy scrubs. She was smiling. Rowan felt a certain tension leave her shoulders.

"She's fine, and the baby's fine," the doctor said, sitting down next to Rowan, across from David and Bryson. Her smile faded slightly. "She's weak, though, and low in nutrients and fluids. I know you've all been under a lot of stress, and I'm afraid it's taking its toll on Chloë. Because of all that, I'd like to keep her here for a few days. Get some food and fluids into her, and keep an eye on things. And give her a chance to relax."

"Whatever you think is best, doctor," David said. "I know she'd like to attend Karl Sinclair's funeral on Sunday, if at all possible. But only if you think she's healthy enough, of course."

"Three days from now?" Dr. Melora nodded. "She should be back up to speed then. If she's not, but doing better, she can go to the services for a few hours and then come back here."

"Is there anything we can do for her in the meantime?" Rowan asked.

Dr. Melora turned to her. "She's lucky to have family and friends so close by. Short visits, as long as she's not reminded of stressful things, would do her good. Books, plants—whatever you know makes her comfortable."

"I'll pack a bag and bring it in tonight," David said, rising.

"I'll let her know," the doctor said. "As for you, try not to worry about her. We'll do everything we can to return her and the wee one to you, safe and sound."

~

Helen had kept warm a meal of beef stroganoff, noodles, steamed broccoli, and blueberry cobbler, which the three picked at, sitting at the kitchen island counter.

"Mom's going to be okay, isn't she?" Bryson asked at one point.

"Yes. Yes, she is," David replied firmly.

Rowan cringed deeper inside herself.

Afterwards, Bryson headed to bed and David to his office, explaining that he was going to cancel his appointments for the next few days and defer any business he could. Rowan made herself a drink and retreated to the TV room, a small room at the front of the house with shelves filled with videos, DVDs, and movie guides. The white-painted TV center, shelves, and walls, made the room feel bigger than it was, even with the squishy, cranberry-colored sofa.

With the tinkling Scotch-and-ice glass in one hand, she flipped through channel after channel. The History Channel was doing a special on the Crusades, so she stopped and let it play. She couldn't call it "watching"; her mind was elsewhere.

With Chloë. In the studio. Awash with guilt.

She could understand why Chloë didn't want those sculptures viewed; she could understand why they were hid. What she couldn't understand was what dark Muse had compelled her to create them.

The twisted faces of the men leered at Rowan in her imagination, in her memory. She shuddered, sipped her drink. She hadn't had the opportunity to truly apologies to Chloë, much less ask her about the statues, which would only serve to cause stress for her friend.

The TV narrator droned on about Saladin, with Chris de Burgh's "Crusader" playing as counterpoint.

Rowan rolled the Scotch on her tongue. It reminded her of the first time she'd met Mary: Chloë had given her a drink and she'd recognized the bottle. Mary, in turn, had led her to the statues. Why? What were they supposed to influence? Frustrated, she picked at the nubble on the couch. The faces didn't resemble anyone she recognized, so she didn't understand Mary's insistence that she see them. The only thing Mary had managed to do was drive a wedge between Rowan and Chloë.

She felt so alone now, with Chloë in the hospital. She barely knew David; Bryson not at all. Amanda was in England and the rest of her friends were in California.

There was no question about leaving, of course. More than ever, she was determined to track down Mary's killers. Dr. Melora had said that Chloë and the baby would be all right, but that stress was bad for them both. The ongoing *not knowing* was probably causing the most stress of all. Chloë needed closure, not day-in, day-out wondering. Unless one of the attackers did turn out to be Bryson, the truth would be a relief.

And if it did turn out to be Bryson…well, at least they'd know for sure. Rowan hoped Chloë's stepson wasn't involved, more for Chloë's sake than anything. But if he was, this thing had to get settled.

Was Mary right? Was she lying to herself?

Despite all of the positive encounters she'd had with men through the years, both before and after her attack, she still approached each one with a degree of mistrust. Toby had recognized it for what it was and had taken steps to preempt it. He'd been the first to acknowledge it in those terms. Not "trust me," but "protect yourself to feel safe."

The evil that lurks in the hearts of men. Mary assumed they were all capable of evil, and so, Rowan thought miserably, did she. The only difference was that even though she assumed the worst of them before she got to know them, she didn't think all men were bad.

It was a short, slippery slope from there to how Mary felt.

None of it, though, helped the current situation. Anger surged inside her. She was sick of this game. If Mary wanted Rowan to help bring her attackers to justice, then she'd damn well better start giving her straight information, not wild clues and coy hints.

Maybe Mary had provoked them, or agreed to sex that had then gotten out of hand. Rowan dismissed the idea even as it came to her. It was too easy to blame the victim; the courts still struggled to cast out evidence of provocative clothing or behavior. The bottom line was, no matter what the woman said or did or how she dressed, she still had the right to say no, at any time. The same right that a man had.

Rowan couldn't fathom any other motive for Mary's unwillingness to provide straight answers. Unless... She sat up straight, taking a thoughtful swallow of smooth, peaty liquor as the idea coalesced in her mind. Maybe Mary didn't know who her attackers had been. It had been dark; if they'd jumped her, she might not have had much opportunity to see their faces full-on and clear. And she didn't spend much time in town, so she may not have encountered the men frequently enough to put names to faces, or even to recognize them. They could have been tourists, even, or non-local businessmen. In her anger, in her need for retribution, Mary might simply be latching on to convenient people to blame.

But that didn't explain why Bryson and the others would confess to the crime if they hadn't committed it. Rowan slumped back onto the sofa and drained her glass. With all the curiosity around Mary, she'd let that point slip to the back of her mind.

The show on the Crusades ended, replaced by one about the bombing of Pearl Harbor. Rowan idly scanned through channels again. A VH1 special on Styx held her attention for half an hour, but when it was over, she gave up and went up to her room.

She'd sent an e-mail to Amanda before dinner, letting her know about Chloë's collapse and that she was essentially okay, but resting in the hospital. Not expecting a response, she checked her e-mail anyway, too restless yet to retire.

From: Amanda Gordon-Davies, <agd@whisperwindmusic.com>
   To: Rowan Everly, <rowan@faireday.com>
   Subject: Re: urgent update

Sweetie, I am doing everything I possibly can to wrap up my parts of this recording as quickly as possible, so I can fly over there. I don't mean to imply that you can't handle this on your own, but if nothing else, I can be there for support for you and Chloë.

Please give her my love and many kisses. And TAKE CARE OF YOURSELF. I'm liking all this less and less. Mary sounds (sounded?) like a seriously f*cked up chick, and I don't trust her. Take what she says with a grain of salt. And please remember that I love you.

agd

Rowan had to grin at Amanda's description of Mary. Their former roommate had never been one to pull any punches. She pulled the peach terrycloth robe tighter around her and re-scanned the message on the screen. Despite the blinking cursor and cold text, the e-mail had made her feel better. She was lucky—she and Chloë were both lucky—to have such a good friend.

Had Mary had any friends? she wondered. Any close, female friends? Anyone at all with whom she had bonded?

There was always her mother, Rowan supposed. But not all daughters got along with their mothers.

And, for that matter, why hadn't Mary's mother come forward? Rowan remembered the woman who'd accosted Chloë, who'd put up posters against Bryson and the others. Her daughter had been raped, by another prep-school student, and she'd railed against it. Mary's mother, one supposed, would do the same.

That is, if she knew what had happened. If she was even still around. If she was even alive.

Rowan visited Chloë late the next morning. She brought with her the latest *People* magazine, a sketchbook and drawing pencils, "Scooby Doo" socks, and a six-pack of Evian. Chloë still looked too thin, but there was color in her cheeks again.

"I'm very lucky to have such good friends," Chloë said after surveying the loot and hearing Amanda's message. It was odd to hear her echo Rowan's thoughts from the night before. "I've got friends here, you know?—several have already stopped in—but they're not the same. I still feel like an outsider sometimes."

"I'll bet Mary felt like an outsider, too," Rowan mused. "I know I'm not supposed to talk to you about it; you can tell me to shut up anytime."

"No, that's okay." Chloë popped open one of the water bottles and drank deeply. "Believe me, it's something I've thought about more than once over the past few weeks. I wonder if she realizes just how much effort is being made on her behalf right now."

"She doesn't seem to care," Rowan muttered.

"Maybe it's come too late," Chloë said. She twined the plastic from the edge of the cap around her finger. "Nobody seemed to care much about her when she was alive, when it was really important."

"Do you know anything about her mother?"

Chloë's eyebrows knit. "No, actually. I remember hearing that she and her mother lived outside of town, but like with Mary herself, I never met her."

"I'm going to try to track more information down about them today," Rowan said. "Right now I'm kind of at a loss to do anything else. In the meantime, you are *not* to think about it at all, okay?"

Chloë rested a splayed-fingered hand on her abdomen. "Okay," she said softly. "I'll try not to."

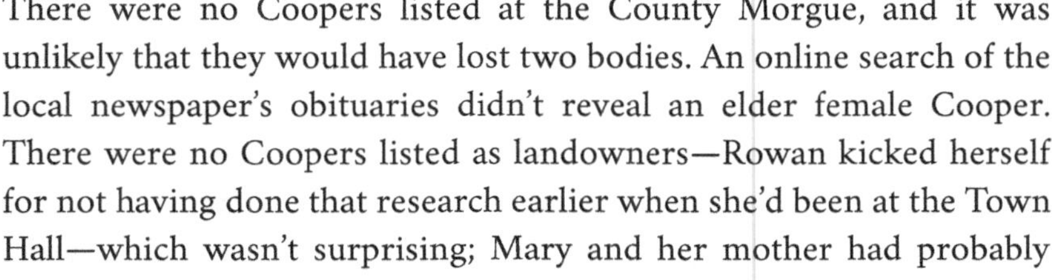

There were no Coopers listed at the County Morgue, and it was unlikely that they would have lost two bodies. An online search of the local newspaper's obituaries didn't reveal an elder female Cooper. There were no Coopers listed as landowners—Rowan kicked herself for not having done that research earlier when she'd been at the Town Hall—which wasn't surprising; Mary and her mother had probably been squatting on the land for years, wherever they'd lived.

She tried different avenues for the rest of the week, with no results. Rowan tried to throw herself into her work, but eventually ran out of things she could do from this distance.

Late Saturday morning, though, Toby called.

"You're not going to believe this," he said. "Someone's recognized the earring."

With Rowan's help, a sketch of the earring had been completed and submitted to the local paper. It had been in Thursday's edition, and when they hadn't heard anything by Friday, they assumed nobody had recognized it.

"He says he was so busy this week that he didn't catch up on all his newspapers until today," Toby said. "Can you meet me downtown in half an hour?"

Rowan looked down at her faded jeans and thought about her unwashed hair. "Of course," she replied.

Toby and the man in question, Arthur Hayes, were waiting for her outside the local museum when she screeched into the closest parking space she could find. She'd showered without washing her hair, thrown on a skirt, and jammed a green velvet scrunchy hat on her head.

It was good to see Toby again, she realized. For all her feelings of being alone, he was one of the few people she could talk to about the crime and investigation. Like her, he was emotionally involved, but not to the level of the family members.

When he smiled at her, flashing that crooked incisor, she felt curiously comforted.

She had an ally.

The museum was housed in a small brick building. Arthur, the curator, unlocked the door with one of several large brass keys on a ring and turned on the lights before letting them in. The fluorescent bulbs hummed and flickered before finally coming completely to life.

"This used to be the old hospital, if you can believe it," he said conversationally, leading them down the hallway and into the main exhibit room. The lights there followed the same pattern and were just as dim, barely picking out the water-stained white walls and the exhibits, whose glass cases had been recently cleaned, judging from the smell of Windex. Despite the obvious care taken, the place was in desperate need of funding. Rowan was surprised that it wasn't open on a Saturday, and voiced the thought.

"There's not nearly enough interest to make that cost-efficient, dear," Arthur said. Perhaps in his seventies, he hadn't been a big man to begin with, and age was already bowing his shoulders and adding liver spots to his skin. His tan cardigan was mended in the back, but it seemed to be more a case of frugality than neediness. "Nothing terribly exciting happened here in Millburn, so we just don't get a lot of visitors. Now, Tamarack, the next town over—they had a family who helped with the Underground Railroad, and the secret passage in the house still exists. They get the tourism, what there is of it."

Rowan got the distinct impression that Toby was fidgeting because he'd never actually been to the museum himself. She could imagine bored schoolchildren shuffling through, looking at the bits of farm equipment and fading sepia photographs, and anticipating the lunch at McDonald's that would follow on the field trip.

"You said you recognized the picture of the earring we ran in the paper?" the sheriff said.

"Yes, that's right," Arthur said. "I'm sorry I didn't call sooner. I didn't have the chance to read Friday's paper until this morning. I was quite astonished when I saw the sketch."

"Where have you seen the earring?" Rowan asked, eager to hear the response.

"Why, right here, dear," the curator said, walking to one of the display cases. "It's been here all along."

CHAPTER 14

O HER AMAZEMENT, the earring was indeed the one Rowan had seen. The yellowed, typewritten card said that it dated from about 1910 and the donor in 1958 had been anonymous.

"What I'm really curious to know," Arthur said, "is where you saw the other one. It would be incredible to have the pair on display."

Rowan stuttered, not wanting to tell him about her vision.

"It was possibly seen being worn by the victim, Mary Cooper," Toby said. "Have you ever met her?"

The curator squinted, his eyes almost lost beneath the wrinkles created by the action. "Can't say that I have, no," he said finally. "I'm sure I would have noticed her wearing the earring, though. It's an antique."

"Is it possible she could be wearing a copy?" Rowan asked.

"Certainly. The partner to the one here has never turned up. According to the files, the person who donated it did so in part because he couldn't find its mate."

"It was a 'he'?" Toby asked.

"I'm afraid I said that rather sexist, didn't I?" Arthur shook his head. "The donation was anonymous. A box of things showed up with a note saying that these were the person's grandparents' effects. They were obviously things the donor simply didn't want anymore; there was little of any real value or use. A moth-eaten mink stole, jewelry with missing stones or, like this, missing its pair, that sort of thing. I'm surprised the earring was included, because the pearl could be of some value. But obviously the donor either didn't know that, or it wasn't worth enough to him—or her."

"Mr. Hayes, thank you for your time," Toby said, shaking his hand. "You've been quite a help. If we come across the earring's mate, we may have to borrow this one to match them up, but otherwise, you keep it safe here."

"Not a problem." Arthur beamed. "It was my pleasure. Always nice when someone takes interest in our little museum."

"Coffee?" Toby said to Rowan after they'd made their goodbyes to Arthur Hayes and the curator had driven away.

"Make it tea and you've got a deal."

They walked across the green to a coffee shop, found a table in the corner after ordering their drinks.

"Well, what do you think?" Toby asked, sipping his coffee. "How did one earring get donated to the museum in 1958 while the other ended up with our murder victim?"

"Arthur said the earring was donated with a bunch of stuff, someone's grandparent's effects," Rowan said. "The other earring must have been lost before the stuff was donated. I can't imagine how we'd track down how it wandered through time to Mary. We know her family wasn't well off—someone might have been working for the family that owned the earrings, and stole it, or found it, or was given it after they realized it didn't have a match anymore. Any chance we can find out who donated the one to the museum?"

Toby shook his head. "We could ask, but it's been fifty years. The person could have moved out of the area, passed away... And if they wanted to be anonymous then, they probably still do now."

"Another dead end," Rowan said.

Across the small room, the barista laughed at something another customer said. Rowan glanced over at the noise. The barista had a nose ring—which Rowan had noticed because it stood out as unusual in this town—and several piercings in each ear.

Each ear. *One sharp pull, then another, and he'd torn the earrings off her...*

"I think the earring really is a dead end," she said to Toby. "I must have seen something wrong in my vision, because in it, the man ripped earrings out of both of Mary's ears. And she couldn't have been wearing a pair if one of them was in the museum."

"Could she have been wearing a different one in the other ear?" he suggested.

"I doubt it. What are the chances that she'd be wearing several expensive earrings?"

"True." Toby went back to his coffee.

Rowan brooded into her tea. The earring *had* to mean something; that's what was so frustrating. It had to, or it wouldn't have appeared in the studio just after she'd met Mary.

What was Mary trying to tell her?

The following afternoon was Karl's funeral. The typical mid-state New York autumn day couldn't decide whether to be sunny or overcast; the pressing grey flatness tried to obscure the sun, which occasionally broke through, highlighting the leaves and grass with a beauty that seemed inappropriate under the circumstances.

Chloë had been released from the hospital that morning, under strict orders to take it easy and keep her stress level as low as possible. Dr. Melora said she could go to the funeral and wake, but that if she started to feel the least bit unwell, she was to go home. For that reason, they took two cars; if Chloë needed to leave, Rowan could take her, leaving David and Bryson to grieve and support the Sinclairs. Helen would also drive on her own, because after the services, she would head back to the Sinclair's house to help prepare the buffet.

Rowan hadn't thought to pack for a funeral when she'd left California, but the blue velvet dress she'd bought, although perhaps a little too party-like, would do. She pulled back her hair with a silver clip and wore silver Celtic-knotwork earrings.

Chloë was in an all-black wool suit, which made her look even more wan. David and Bryson, in nearly matching black suits of their own, looked so alike in form and expression that Rowan felt her heart twist. They shouldn't be made to face this, with all their other troubles.

And odd thought, given what Bryson had confessed to doing.

Rowan was surprised at the number of people who crowded into the white clapboard church on the school campus. She realized that she shouldn't be. The Sinclair family had been in Millburn for generations, and Karl had obviously been popular on campus, given the number of students who stood along the back wall or sat on the floor down the sides. A huge banner behind the coffin proclaimed "We'll Miss You, Karl," and seemed to be signed by hundreds of people.

The service itself was long but not unusual. Many had asked or been asked to speak: the headmaster of the school; various teachers; the other boys and several other students, both male and female; family friends. All of them said essentially the same thing: Karl had been a good student, good athlete, good friend. His future had been bright. He had been loved. Rowan didn't disbelieve any of it, although wondered if some wasn't more intense than it needed to be. A girl, weeping, read Robert Frost's "Miles to Go." James Gottard read the lyrics to "Enter Sandman." Rowan glanced at his parents; they looked mildly bewildered.

The eulogies were interspersed with hymns for the congregation and songs by the school chorale, all dressed in purple robes, each with a white lily pinned to his or her breast. They were proficient on both "Let It Be" and the school song, on which they were joined by all of the other students and many of the adults, which ended the service.

Afterwards, the banner was folded by some of the students with all of the reverence of soldiers folding an American flag, and it was draped over the coffin. Bryson, James, Manny, Martin Sinclair, Colin Gottard, and the headmaster carried the coffin out to the waiting hearse. The rest of the congregation shuffled out of the church, through leaves covering the sidewalk, through the green yard, and down the road to their cars. They murmured to each other; no one seemed to want to speak too loudly. A girl's shrill giggle rose above the murmur, to be quickly and efficiently shushed.

Rowan slipped behind the wheel of Bryson's BMW and pulled out behind the car containing the Walthams. The drive to the local cemetery wasn't a long one, but it took time, first with all the cars jockeying for position in the procession, then as they drove about twenty-five miles per hour through town, lights flashing. Driving left-handed and keeping her eyes on the road, Rowan fished in her purse for a tin of Altoids. The sharp mint made her sneeze.

At the cemetery, the people ranged in concentric rings around the gravesite, waiting for the minister's final words. Elizabeth Sinclair sat in a folding chair, its left front leg starting to sink into the soft ground. She sobbed silently into a handkerchief, and wore sunglasses even on the variably shady day. Beside her, Martin was expressionless, gripping her knee with a white-knuckled hand, in a gesture unclear whether it was for her comfort or his own control. A girl in her early teens sat beside them—Ashlyn, Rowan remembered her name. Ashlyn's blonde hair had been bleached blonder, and her black dress was accentuated by heavy kohl eyeliner and bright red lipstick, behind which peeked incongruous braces. She didn't look overly upset. Rowan wondered if her mother's drug use, whether alcohol or something stronger, had been passed on to the child.

From where she sat, she could see all the boys with their families. Bryson was two seats down from her, between Chloë and David. Manny was a bit farther down, surrounded by his parents and sisters. James, apparently an only child, sat almost directly across from her, flanked by his mother and father.

The sun was winning in its fight with the clouds, and had broken through in several places. Nonetheless, the day was still chilly. Rowan pulled on black stretch-velvet gloves, set her purse back down at her feet.

Something didn't feel right. She straightened, looked around.

Nothing seemed out of the ordinary. A few people were still arriving; the minister was consulting and rearranging several cards of notes. The day seemed darker, colder, but the clouds hadn't totally obscured the sun. A breeze rifled through, and she shivered.

And then she was aware of a presence. Of Mary.

A low, vicious chuckle—was it in her ear, or in her mind? She couldn't see the girl anywhere, but then again, she didn't know what exactly ghosts were capable of; this was new territory for her. The breeze, or perhaps Mary, sped away, and Rowan thought she could relax.

Then she saw the boys' faces. To a person, they'd gone grey, horror etched on their features. Not that they were seeing something outside, not that Mary had just appeared to them—but that they were seeing something inside.

Like reliving the attack.

Manny looked like he was going to bolt. James's lips were pressed tight, as if he desperately tried to keep from being ill. Closer by, Bryson had his eyes closed; his breath was shallow.

Rowan glanced around the crowd. No one else seemed to be affected. Then again, everyone seemed uncomfortable. That could be because they were at a funeral, or because the funeral was for a teenage boy who'd killed himself after confessing to rape and murder. Or it could be because there was a malevolent feel swirling around the cemetery, a feeling of anger, resentment, pain. Rowan was glad for the cold metal chair in which she sat; she wasn't sure her suddenly weakened legs would support her. It was as if her energy was being drained from her.

Rowan looked around the people gathered in the cemetery and sighed. She was probably making all of this up. If she wasn't hallucinating and Mary was really a ghost, then she might as well accept that she was out of her league. She knew how to point the finger at a criminal for the police, but she had no experience in dealing with spirits. Besides, so far her work here had been for naught. The boys had confessed; there was no point in trying to prove them wrong.

She might as well just go back to California and forget about it.

No! The thought snapped her alert again. What was she thinking?

The feeling swirled around again, more angry this time. A chill cat-paw pranced down Rowan's spine.

Was Mary doing this? Even as she wondered, she knew, with all certainty, that it was true.

Mary was here, draining their energy, drawing off everyone's sadness and pain. She was getting stronger, and angrier, while the mourners were becoming weaker. Not physically, really, except for being tired. More of an emotional drain, a feeling of *why bother?*

Rowan looked at the boys again. Mary was certainly getting to them: That was evident on their faces.

Go away, she thought fiercely.

Is that fair? the response came, silky in her mind. *No one came to my funeral.*

Not even your mother?

Long dead. The words spat out, as if they'd been bitter on Mary's tongue. *And it was not my lot to have the townsfolk rally around me. I didn't have the fortunes of birth as these children did.*

Rowan bit back any social commentary on how even kids from poor families can do well in school and get scholarships, and said-thought instead, *I'm sorry for that, but nothing can change it now. Would you begrudge these parents the chance to mourn? Good or bad, innocent or guilty, Karl's parents loved him and will miss him.*

Whose side are you on? Mary demanded.

Before Rowan could stop it, she responded, *Truth, justice, and the Amer—.*

If Mary had been corporeal, the sensation would have been a direct slap on Rowan's cheek. Instead, it was impossible to describe how Mary lashed out—but Rowan felt it nonetheless.

Justice! I wasn't shown justice!

Give us a chance, then, Rowan replied. *Help us find your attackers instead of leading us on a wild goose chase. Don't punish the innocent—Karl's already dead, and even if he was guilty, his parents aren't. Leave them in peace!*

She thought the last line with as much strength and force as she could muster, mentally shoving Mary away, driving her out of Rowan's brain and away from the funeral.

"Rowan?"

Chloë's voice drowned out Mary's parting comment. Rowan could tell, though, that the girl was gone.

"I'm sorry, what?"

"Can I ask you a favor?" Chloë said. "Dr. Laverick wants to talk to us, and technically we're supposed to keep an eye on Bryson. He's right over there with the other boys. Can you just keep him in your sights? You won't be really responsible; just let us know if any of them leave."

"Sure, no problem." Disoriented, Rowan watched Chloë and her husband walk away. Other people were standing up, milling about, clumping in small groups and murmuring again, or walking slowly to their cars. Slowly she realized that while she'd been "talking" to Mary, the graveside service had come and gone.

Bryson and James had gone to sit next to Manny, so all she had to do was adjust her chair slightly to the right to keep them directly in her line of vision. She turned her head to watch the three boys' parents standing with Dr. Laverick. They all looked somber. She wasn't surprised.

She took a deep breath, grounding and centering, finding her equilibrium again now that Mary was gone from her mind and, apparently, from the funeral.

Martin and Elizabeth Sinclair stood a few feet away from the coffin, on which were scattered lilies and white roses. Elizabeth, sobbing, was being comforted by an older woman with similar features; her mother, Rowan guessed. Martin was half-turned away from them and she couldn't see his face. From his pocket he pulled what seemed to be a small bottle, which he brought up in front of himself before putting it away again. The gesture reminded Rowan of something, but she couldn't place what it was.

She glanced back at the boys. They had pulled their chairs in a tight circle and were talking.

"How's it going?" Toby Candusco turned around the chair next to her and straddled it.

"As well as can be expected, I suppose," she replied. "Funerals aren't my favorite form of entertainment. But Chloë's feeling better, and barring any stress this afternoon, she's home for good. Yourself?"

He shrugged. "About the same. Nothing new to report."

"It's just so frustrating," Rowan said. Even as she did, she knew she was stating the obvious.

She wasn't being fully honest with Toby; she knew that. She'd gone over and over in her mind, debating back and forth about whether to tell him about her encounters with Mary. He'd grudgingly accepted Rowan's psychic powers, but hauntings were something else entirely.

By the same token, she also wasn't prepared to tell him about Chloë's sculptures. Right now, that remained Chloë's secret. Rowan hadn't had a chance to talk to talk to her friend about it, what with her being in the hospital and as removed from stress as possible, and she wasn't sure when they'd have the opportunity. She hoped Chloë would choose to broach the subject.

The sculptures weren't things Rowan could tell the sheriff. She didn't think she was withholding evidence; after all, there was no reason to believe the sculptures *were* evidence of anything. They were just another strangely shaped piece in a puzzle that seemed to have no edges.

When she'd met Toby at the museum, she'd felt like she had an ally. They were both working on the same puzzle, both trying to fit the pieces together. If she didn't share the pieces she had, he'd be more in the dark than she.

Being an ally went two ways.

He probably wouldn't believe her, but that's what trust was all about. Taking the chance.

Are you mad? Mary's voice in her head was incredulous. *Trust him?*

Lord and Lady, Rowan thought. Was Mary really a ghost, or was she hearing her own subconscious.

She'd regained enough strength after Mary's attack that when she mentally shoved again—*go away*—Mary did.

"Rowan?" Toby's hand was warm through her velvet glove.

She didn't pull away.

"If I say something that sounds insane, will you at least try to understand? Keep an open mind?"

He squeezed her fingers. "You've already shown me there's more possible than I ever expected. I'll do my best."

So she told him. About meeting Mary, about the young woman's barely contained rage, her fury at all men. About Mary here, stalking the funeral, feeding on grief and twisting to her own needs, gathering strength from those at their weakest.

Toby watched her the entire time, his eyes giving away nothing of what he was thinking. When she finished, he was silent at first. Frowning, brow furrowed.

See? He didn't believe her.

Rowan wasn't sure if that was her thought or Mary's.

"A little earlier," Toby said, "I was sitting here, thinking it was all hopeless. The evidence is scanty at best. We're not getting anywhere. The boys confessed, and now one has committed suicide, which to a lot of people is tantamount to confessing his guilt even more solidly. I thought, what was the use of struggling to find out whether they're innocent?"

He looked away, looked back again. "You're telling me that might not have been my own fears. That might have been Mary, deliberately crushing my spirit?"

"It might have been," Rowan said. "I can't speak to how you honestly feel, but I wouldn't be surprised if Mary didn't capitalize on your concerns about the case, magnify them, use them against you."

"I don't like being fucked with," Toby said. "And I don't like the idea that someone—something—could get inside my head and fuck with me."

"The first time I saw Mary," Rowan said slowly, "was at her house."

"I felt pretty awful there, too," he said. "Jesus."

"So you believe that it's possible?" Rowan was astonished that he'd consider it.

"I'm not in the habit of feeling so despairing," he said. "I've dealt with some pretty awful things, and I've gotten upset and frustrated and even a little depressed. But I've never felt like so hopeless before. I suppose, in a way, I'm relieved it might not have been real.

"I'm not sure what I believe. It's still a lot to take in. But I believe it's possible. I believe you wouldn't lie to me, or make things up.

"So, what does she want?"

"Revenge," Rowan said. "Any way she can get it."

Rowan looked at the boys, huddled together, shoulders bowed in grief. They'd lost one of their own. It could very well have been the first time they'd been faced with the concept of their mortality.

And then there were three...

"That's odd," she said aloud.

"What?" Toby asked.

"In my vision of Mary's attack, there were three attackers. I've gone over it several times, and I'm sure of it: There were only three."

Toby shook his head, not getting what she was on about.

"If only three people attacked her, why did four boys confess?"

CHAPTER 15

*B*Y THE TIME they got to the Sinclairs' house, the wake was in full swing. Perhaps not the best way to define it, Rowan reflected as she handed her coat to one of the uniformed maids, but it really did look more like a party than a continuation of a funeral. At the bar, Rowan asked for a glass of white wine. The bartender, a man about her age with brown hair and a sleek moustache, rattled off the names of four or five different vineyards. Rowan didn't know wine well enough to know the difference, but did know enough to recognize the names as top-quality.

"Something dry," she requested with a smile. She watched him slice the foil and deftly twist the corkscrew in, while via the mirror behind him she watched the guests fill the room. Accepting the chilled glass, she made her way across to Chloë and David, careful to dodge the waiters and waitresses who crisscrossed the room with trays of hors d'oeuvres.

"Yeesh," she said under her breath to Chloë. Her friend nodded.

Every flat surface in the room now displayed some picture or portrait of Karl: class portraits, sports photos, framed news clippings, trophies. It looked more like James's house than Karl's. And it looked more like a graduation party than a wake.

"Everyone mourns in their own way," David said quietly. "I don't agree with this, either, but if it brings Martin and Liz some sort of comfort or closure, then it's what they should do."

They chatted for a few moments. Then, Chloë stiffened.

"David, where's Bryson?"

"He went to the den to watch TV with the others." He touched her arm. "I'll go check on them."

Chloë's shoulders relaxed as he walked away.

"You okay?" Rowan asked.

"I will be when all of this is over." Chloë squeezed her eyes shut for a moment. "Dr. Laverick's concerned about the boys. He said we should keep an eye on them, especially now, for any signs of suicidal thoughts or plans or activities. A suicide watch, he called it. They're all vulnerable right now, more so because of Karl…"

"Darlings!" Elizabeth swept up to them in a haze of perfumed cigarette smoke, the older woman in tow. She kissed the air in the vicinity of Chloë's cheek. "Thank you so much for coming; you've been such a comfort." Her eyes were unnaturally bright. "This is my mother. Mum, this is my dear friend Chloë, and this is her friend Rosanna—"

"Rowan," Rowan said pleasantly, shaking the older woman's hand.

"I'm so sorry, darling. I knew it started with an R. She's out from Los Angeles," Elizabeth added proudly.

"Monterey, actually," Rowan murmured, but they had already gone on to the next victim.

"Someday, probably soon, that woman is going to explode," Chloë said under her breath. "She can't keep medicating herself into oblivion like that."

"You'd be surprised," Rowan said. "Everyone has some way of channeling their pain. Elizabeth and Martin run away from it. Mary turns it into anger and a need for revenge. You and I tend to internalize it and turn it into stress." She took another sip of the very nice wine.

"Begs the question of which one of us deals with it the healthiest," Chloë said.

"A question for Dr. Laverick, I suppose." Rowan set down the glass and hugged her friend. "Don't you worry about Bryson. We'll all keep any eye on him. This will be over soon."

As if in response, she heard Martin's voice saying, "Don't be ridiculous. The boys will get off scot-free, and my son's name will be cleared. All of them will."

He was standing at the bar with Colin Gottard, James's father. The bartender turned and began wiping glasses with a white terrycloth towel, studiously ignoring them as per bartending protocol.

"You sound very sure," Colin said.

"Of course I'm sure. I'm right! Look, you've got Frank Manassan on the case! If he can get that baseball player off, he can get anybody off." Martin nudged Colin, expensive suit against expensive suit. "Besides, c'mon! It was a prank that got out of hand. Boys will be boys, right? They were just having some fun. The girl probably had a weak heart or something."

The room had fallen silent, but neither man seemed to notice. Rowan noticed with relief that Elizabeth and her mother had left, probably to greet guests in the other rooms.

"Look, there's no law that says the boys can't be sexually active—they *should* be at that age," Martin continued, with another nudge at Colin. This time, the nudge was a little too forceful, and James's father had to steady himself with a hand on the bar. "It's just too bad Karl was too much of a wuss to ride it out." Martin's voice softened towards the end; he sounded less strident, less sure, as if finally remembering he was talking about his own beloved son. His dead son. "Hand me that bottle of Scotch," he said to the bartender. "No, the other one." He fished in his suit jacket pocket and removed the small bottle-like object Rowan had seen earlier, set it on the bar in front of him. Rowan leaned to one side, trying to see better. Conversation started throughout the room again, first soft, but gaining momentum.

Martin unscrewed the cap on the bottle that the bartender handed him, and began pouring. Rowan leaned farther. She couldn't see directly, but could see a reflection in the mirror behind the bar. It wasn't entirely clear because the mirror was threaded with gold, but he was pouring into what seemed to be a metal flask. He wasn't doing a great job of getting the alcohol into it, and she saw the bartender discreetly pick up a cloth in preparation for cleaning up the damage. With a pat on Chloë's arm, Rowan headed across the room.

"Hello, Martin," she said, handing her empty glass to the bartender and nodding at his unspoken query. Karl's father looked at her blankly. They'd met only twice: once outside Manny's house, and once earlier that day, one in a long line of people giving the Sinclair's their condolences. "Rowan—Chloë's friend," she said. Before he could process his previous memories of her, and remember he didn't like her, she added, "I was just admiring that flask. Is it silver?"

"Yes, it is." Martin actually handed it to her. It was wet with Scotch. "It was my great-grandfather's. He passed it to my grandfather, who gave it to me on my sixteenth birthday."

Rowan knew she had to be careful. She couldn't get too deep into the vision; she had only a moment, and she couldn't afford to make Martin or anyone else think she was having a seizure or something.

The man rose and followed his friends, making no hurry to catch up. As he went, he reached into his pocket and pulled out a flask; took a swig.

Ghost-wisps of clouds began moving over the full moon. The girl's wide blank eyes didn't see, and then it was dark.

Rowan took a deep breath. "It's lovely," she said, shoving the flask back into Martin's hands. "Thank you." She fled to the nearest bathroom.

She wasn't feeling sick exactly, although the burnt orange and olive green décor didn't help. It was the same vision that she'd seen several times already, and on that level she'd been prepared for it. She hadn't been looking for something new, but rather, a confirmation of what she suspected.

Rowan turned on the tap and let cold water run over her wrists. So, it was the same flask. She wondered if there was some polite way she could ask Martin if Karl ever borrowed it—which could be tricky if, say, Karl hadn't asked permission first—or whether it would be better to share the information with Toby and let him follow up.

Either way, the information was circumstantial and didn't reveal much of anything. All they knew now, that they hadn't known before, was that Martin's whisky flask had been at the scene, probably carried by Karl.

Or what if it wasn't? Rowan paused in the act of patting some water on the back of her neck. In the mirror over the sink, her cheeks looked fever-flushed, her eyes deep and hollow as they stared back at her.

All this time, they'd been operating under the assumption that the boys, having confessed, were the prime suspects. But what if their *fathers* had been involved?

Too many thoughts and pictures flashed in Rowan's mind, and she sat on the closed toilet seat, setting her arm on the counter and resting her head on the crook of her elbow. In some ways, it could make sense. If they boys were being blackmailed or otherwise felt like they had to lie to protect someone, who more obvious than their own fathers? And in at least one situation, the father was the alibi: Martin hearing Karl and James watching TV.

But in other ways... Now Rowan did feel ill. Chloë felt traumatized enough at the thought of her stepson being involved. If it was her husband... Rowan barely knew David, but she still couldn't imagine him committing the violent deeds. Nor could she imagine slender, soft-spoken Jayadeep Prabakharan being involved. Martin seemed a likely enough candidate, though, and Colin Gottard was an unknown entity.

What about *their* alibis? Rowan tried to remember. Elizabeth Sinclair had taken a bath and gone to bed, leaving Martin, Karl, and James downstairs. Colin Gottard, she had no idea. She was pretty sure the entire Prabhakaran family had been home.

But David—Chloë had said that David had been away on a business trip. Had he really? Did he have associates to back that up? Rowan groaned softly.

A polite rattle of the locked doorknob reminded her that other guests might need the facilities. "I'll be right out," she called. She found lipstick and powder in her purse and applied them quickly.

Outside the bathroom, she skirted the waiting woman, someone she didn't recognize, with a small smile of apology, and made her way back through the crowd. Not quite yet willing to face Chloë, she turned down the hall and went into the den.

The boys were in there, grouped at one end of the crescent sofa. Bryson raised a hand, and she waved back. Dhriti and Jayadeep were conversing in another corner; Rowan realized they must be on Watch Duty. At the other end of the sofa, a few other young men were eyeing the wide-screen TV. The sound had been turned off, but the motorcycle races still drew their attention.

She was about to go over and talk to the Prabhakarans when David entered the room and headed straight for her. She couldn't quell the small but sharp leap of panic, a holdover from her recent thoughts. She just hoped it hadn't shown on her face.

"Everything okay?" he asked. "Chloë said you bolted out of the living room after talking to Martin."

"Emergency trip to the bathroom, but I'm fine," she said, forcing a wry smile. "Then I wasn't quite ready to face the crush of people in the living room, so I've been wandering a bit. I didn't mean to worry her. I'll head back now." Was she babbling? Was it obvious?

"Rowan."

She had started to walk away when he spoke her name. Startled, she looked back at him.

"Take care of her," he said, and there was pleading in his eyes. "I love her, and I'm doing everything I can, but you've known her longer, and I respect that. I know there are things between you two, and Amanda, that I can't share. I can't tell you how much better it's been with you here."

"I love her, too," Rowan said. "I'll do everything I can."

She left the room then, guilt nipping at her heels. He did seem sincerely worried about Chloë, sincerely believing in Rowan's influence. It was so hard for her to wrap her brain around the concept that he might have been directly involved with Mary's attack.

On the other hand, was he using Rowan as smoke-and-mirror—could her being a buffer mean that Chloë was less likely to guess the truth? Even as she thought it, she had to shake her head. She had to be reading too much into this. The heightened emotions of the day were taking their toll on her.

But before she entered the living room, another memory struck her: the statues in Chloë's studio, the horrible likeness Chloë had created of the violent, deadly assault. If David *had* been involved, maybe Chloë knew or guessed the truth. Maybe this was her way of crying out.

At some point, as soon as she believed Chloë was strong enough to deal with it, Rowan was going to have to ask her about the statues. It was a conversation she wanted to run screaming away from, even though she knew it had to be done.

"I'm fine," she told Chloë when her friend asked, and gave her the same explanation she'd given David. "It's been a long day."

"I know," Chloë said. "In fact, I'm seriously considering heading home. I hate to abandon Liz like this, but after several days in a hospital bed, I'm finding it hard to be moving around and sociable for so long."

"You wait here; I'll get your coat and tell David," Rowan said, relieved for the excuse to leave as well.

She wanted to do some more thinking about what she'd just learned.

And then, tomorrow, she'd call Toby.

Despite the high emotions and stresses of the day, everyone seemed to sleep well that night. The next morning, the circles under Chloë's eyes had lessened, and David seemed fine when he left for work. As for Rowan, her sleep had been dreamless. Right now, she couldn't ask for more than that.

It was the Waltham's turn to host the boys' tutoring session, so Manny and James showed up that morning. James's father dropped him off and didn't come inside, but Dhriti Prabhakaran came to the door and Chloë invited her in for tea and the Eggs Benedict left over from breakfast. Dhriti bartered for coffee and won. A few minutes later, Dr. Laverick showed up and accepted tea before going to meet with the boys for a counseling session before the tutoring session started.

"Grand Central Station," Chloë pronounced as the housekeeper went to answer the doorbell for yet another time. "I'm glad Helen's dealing with a lot of it."

"You know you can count on me as well to field stuff for you," Rowan said.

Helen entered the kitchen with the tutor in tow.

"Coffee?" the slender, dark-haired man said hopefully. "You promised coffee?"

He introduced himself as Ivan Novikov and gratefully accepted a steaming mug of French roast. While waiting for Ben to finish with the boys, he entertained them with stories of his world travels, which had begun when he was small and his parents had left the then USSR. Between high school and college, he'd backpacked through Europe, and he spent his summers exploring various countries by motorcycle.

"I didn't take up teaching in order to have the summers free," he said, "but it's certainly proved useful."

"He doesn't look old enough to be teaching them," Rowan commented after he left.

"Believe it or not, he's our age," Chloë said. "Apparently on one of his trips he found Ponce de León's Fountain of Youth. He's also a highly sought-after teacher. He'd been working at Milburn but was on sabbatical this year; he agreed to come back to work with the boys. He's writing a book on his various travels, I think."

The traffic had through the house had slowed by then, and Helen had gone to do laundry. Rowan, Chloë, and Dhriti freshened their mugs and went to the TV room, since the boys were in the den.

"I have been thinking," Dhriti said. "You may think I am crazy, but I want to mention this." She set her mug down in a decided gesture. "I sensed you, Rowan, would understand, or at least accept, what I want to say. This is a strange thing that's happened, and as I have said, it is nothing like Manny—the opposite. I believe that perhaps more is involved. I felt it very strongly at the funeral yesterday, at the gravesite. It's hard to put into words…"

Rowan took a chance. "Something supernatural?"

"Wait a minute," Chloë interrupted. "You know I believe in a lot of stuff—I know about—" she broke off, and Rowan guessed she'd been about to mention Mary. "I've seen and experienced unnatural things, if you will. But how could this be something supernatural? Were the boys possessed by demons or something?"

"Perhaps," Dhriti said, a second before Rowan's "I hadn't thought of that."

"I wouldn't say 'demons', exactly," Rowan said. She looked at Chloë, who nodded slightly, giving her the okay to continue. "I remember you saying that your culture believes in ghosts. Well, Chloë and I have both…experienced something, which seems to be Mary Cooper's ghost. She seems intent on revenge, and she isn't clear on whether the boys actually committed the crimes or whether she's viewing them as convenient scapegoats."

Dhriti's dark eyes widened. "The ghosts we believe in are benevolent," she said. "Movies like *Poltergeist* are not the same."

Rowan readjusted the clip holding back her hair, capturing loose strands. "I think we're talking about similar, but not the same, things," she said. "Mary's definitely not feeling benevolent, and I can't say that I blame her."

"Was she at the funeral?" Dhriti whispered.

Rowan knew Chloë was staring at her. "Yes," she said. "I talked to her—well, it wasn't talking, but it was a conversation. It's hard to explain. She was angry. No one came to *her* funeral…"

"Yes, they did," Chloë said. She frowned, a crease appearing between her eyebrows. "I'll grant you that it was small, and there was no actual coffin, but Reverend Shaw said that there were four or five people there."

"A piddling amount compared to yesterday," Rowan said. "So few people even knew who she was. And, as near as I've been able to find out, only men remember her."

"What?" Chloë and Dhriti said simultaneously.

"Of all the people I've talked to, the only ones who honestly remember seeing or meeting her are male. No female thus far has any actual memory of her."

Both women were staring at her. "Don't you think that's weird?" Chloë asked.

"Of course I do," Rowan replied. "I wouldn't've mentioned it otherwise. But I don't have an explanation for it, and I don't see how it helps figure out what happened."

"I did not know it was Mary at the funeral," Dhriti said. "But I thought I felt something, and now I believe I truly did. As you said, she must be angry. I felt anger. I felt...as if something had drained me."

"So did I," Chloë said. "I just assumed I was tired, what with everything going on."

"I think Mary was feeding off people's energies," Rowan said. "I couldn't get her to admit it, but I felt it, too. She was angry at everyone, and she may have lashed out accordingly."

Dhriti shuddered. She picked up her mug and wrapped her fingers around it, seeking warmth. "Has she been doing that to our sons?"

"I think she may have been doing that to all of us," Rowan said, thinking of Chloë's sculptures. "We just haven't realized it. We've passed it off as stress, depression, anxiety. I don't know if Mary is targeting any particular people, although at the funeral, I sensed she wasn't. But we should all stay aware."

"This is really bizarre," Chloë blurted. "I don't understand how she could be...feeding off of us without our knowledge."

Rowan didn't bring up Chloë's sculpture out of deference to her friend; she knew Chloë would want Dhriti to know about it. But now she wondered: had Chloë made it because of Mary's influence, or because of David's?

"Yes, it is bizarre," Rowan said. "As for how..." She threw up her hands. "We can cite any psychic mumbo-jumbo we want to. We're out of the realm of science here. I can't explain it any more than I can explain my own power."

"The important thing is that we try to be aware of when it happens, and stop it," Dhriti said quietly. "And to pay attention to our sons. She is affecting them. Even Dr. Laverick has warned us to watch over them."

"You're right," Chloë said. "If Mary's 'possessing' the boys or whatever, we have to do everything we can to stop her."

"I think we should remain aware, but not go overboard at this point," Rowan added. "We don't know exactly what Mary's doing. The main thing, I think, is to keep an eye on the boys, as Dr. Laverick said. Try to keep their spirits up." On top of figuring out if they're the ones who did it, she added mentally.

Dhriti left a little while later, citing errands to run. Chloë went to the study to pay some bills, and Rowan took the opportunity to call Toby.

"I'm positive it's the same flask as in my dream," she said. "However, since Martin's been carrying it around and using it—not to mention spilling alcohol all over it—there wouldn't be any of Karl's fingerprints left to find, would there?"

"No, which is too bad," Toby replied. "But thanks for the tip. If I get the opportunity, I'll ask Martin about it. I don't see the need to formally interview him again, and I'd prefer to avoid bothering him right now; he's not going through an easy time."

"Agreed," Rowan said. "Anything else come up on your end?"

"Not a thing. Yours?"

"Not recently. I'm fresh out of ideas."

"Okay, then. Take care of yourself," Toby said.

She hung up the phone. Fresh out of ideas and solutions—and, she was starting to worry, soon to be out of time.

That evening, after dinner, as she was helping Bryson clear the table, she asked him if he'd ever seen Karl with his father's silver flask.

Bryson frowned, thinking. "You mean the one that's his great-great-grandfather's?" he asked. "I know he's shown it to me. His dad's really proud of it." He paused, set the dishes on the counter next to the sink, and turned to her. "You're not trying to trick me into admitting we've indulged in underage drinking, are you?"

Rowan grinned. "Can't miss a trick with you, boy-o. Seriously, though. I'm not trying to get information about you guys drinking. If you have been, that's another matter. I'm honestly just curious about the flask itself."

He dried his hands on a white linen dishtowel. "I only remember him showing it to me once, at their house. I don't remember him taking it anywhere or using it."

"Fair enough," Rowan said. "So how're you doing?"

"Okay, I guess." He frowned again. "I've got homework to do."

Rowan watched him go. Ah, men and their inability to show emotion.

Rowan curled up in bed with a glass of wine and the book on local history. The evening had been quiet so far. David was at a meeting, expected to be out until late. Chloë had retired to a warm bath and an early evening. Bryson was doing homework, and Helen, Rowan assumed, had been given the opportunity to relax.

For her part, Rowan refused to look out the window at the studio. She wanted nothing to do with Mary right now.

The history book wasn't making her sleepy; in fact, its dodgy writing and bad print seemed to be making her more restless. Rowan got up, wrapped her robe around her, and grabbed her purse for her contact lens case.

It wasn't there. Rowan held the purse upside-down and shook it. A disgusting plethora of stuff emerged: a tin of Altoids (and a few loose ones), pens, scraps of paper, an amethyst crystal, used tissues, a ring she'd thought she'd lost, loose change, a hair tie, her wallet, a small flashlight, receipts and coupons, a comb, lipstick and gloss and powder and eyeliner. But no lens case.

She sighed. Getting up again, she ransacked the rolltop desk where she'd put her laptop and various supplies. No luck.

Hands on hips, she surveyed the room. Where could it have gone? Then she remembered upending her purse in the car yesterday. She thought she'd gathered up all of her stuff, but the case could have slipped between the seats.

Rowan padded her way downstairs, flicking on lights as needed and then turning them off at the other end. The house seemed silent, and she didn't want to disturb anybody. In the kitchen, she snagged the keys to Bryson's BMW off the hook, and opened the door that led to the garage.

The smell of gas and the rumble of an engine told her instantly that something was wrong.

CHAPTER 16

ROWAN FELT ALONG THE WALL for the light switch. The long fluorescent bulbs on the ceiling flickered, warming up far too slowly. "Come on," she urged, and then the garage was lit.

Bryson's hunter green BMW was on. Rowan had to edge around the front of the silver Saab to get to it. The smell of gas was almost overpowering, and she was already feeling light-headed. As she feared, there was a rubber tube leading from the back of the car into the almost-closed driver's side window. And a body was slumped over the steering wheel.

Cursing her own stupidity, she squeezed back past the Mercedes and slammed her hand down on the button next to the light switch. The electric garage door started its grinding upwards motion, again painfully unhurried. The cement was cold beneath her bare feet, the chill rising into her legs. Rowan hurried back to the BMW, praying she wasn't too late. She yanked on the door handle.

The car was locked. She fumbled on the key ring for the remote control, but in her haste, dropped the whole set. The car blocked some of the light; the cement below was in shadow. She dropped to the rough floor and scrabbled around until she found the keys again. The cement grazed her toes and she hissed in pain. Rising to her knees, she found the remote. Which button was it? She twisted so she could see the tiny symbols. The one on the left. She pressed it. The car lights flashed and all the doors thunked as the locks gave way. Rowan yanked the door open.

Waves of fumes engulfed her, rolling out from the car, and she choked back bile. Blackness crept around the edges of her sight, and she had to pull back, gasp relatively cleaner air. Holding her breath, she leaned back into the car and grabbed Bryson. He was limp, heavy —heavier than she could manage.

Then the visions hit her.

She was in the mind of a man raping Mary. *He was uncaring, vicious, only interested in driving closer to his own release. He sneered at her struggling; her squirms only excited him more. And her fear...that was an aphrodisiac as well. She wasn't a person—she was just a lowly woman, and a poor, classless one at that.*

Dear Lord and Lady, she was seeing the attack through Bryon's eyes. Rowan's stomach heaved, and she swallowed repeatedly, willing herself not to throw up.

There was something else, too—something else she was feeling or sensing—but she didn't have time to consider it.

"Bryson!" she shouted, shaking his sagging form. She managed to pull him into a more upright position. His head flopped against the backrest. "Bryson, wake up!" He was still breathing, but shallowly. "Hey!" she yelled, pushing against his shoulder.

His eyelids fluttered. "Wha—?"

"You have to get out of this car." Rowan reached across him and fought with the key in the ignition. Where had he gotten another set from? He was supposed to have turned his over to his parents.

They'd probably thrown them in a drawer; after all, the set Rowan was using always hung by the garage door, where she'd found them mere moments ago.

She managed to turn the car off. "Come on, Bryson, I can't do this alone. You have to help." Rowan tugged at him.

"Huh? Rowan? Leave me alone." His words were slurred, and he tried to push back at her, but his hand waved uselessly.

"No, I will not leave you alone," she said firmly, putting as much authority as she could sum up into her voice. She pulled on his arm, and this time he responded, although it seemed to be more out of confusion than anything else. She helped him extricate one leg, then the other, from the car. Putting her hands under his arms, she lifted. She knew she couldn't pull him to his feet on his own, but hoped the motion would encourage him to stand.

"You're doing great, Bryson. You're doing just fine." She kept up a running encouragement as he rose, unsteadily, bracing himself on the open door. "Now, let's get out of the garage. Put your arm over my shoulder...there you go."

Rowan took a step backwards, away from the car, to give him room to turn. But her feet hit the tubing that was still stretched between the door and the car's exhaust pipe, and she tumbled backwards. She hit the garage wall hard and dropped to the floor, her feet shooting out from under her. Something came down and hit her on the head, before she had time to flinch or block. Then Bryson, who had been leaning on her, lost his balance and landed on top of her.

The wind was knocked out of her, and Rowan struggled to take in a full breath. The sharp pain in her temple help drive back the encroaching darkness, but the room still spun and she needed air...

"Get up," she managed to gasp. It took effort, but she dragged more air into her lungs and continued. "Bryson. Get off me."

The air in the garage was clearing thanks to the open door, and it seemed to be affecting Bryson positively as well. Although he moved slowly, he apparently understood her words and her distress, and pulled himself up and into a sitting position, leaning against the car.

For a moment, all Rowan could do was suck in full breaths of air. Although clearer, it still stank of carbon monoxide, and she craved fresh, untainted oxygen. She pulled herself up, moved aside the rake next to her—fuzzily, she realized that must have been what fell on her head—and struggled to a standing position.

"C'mon," she said, holding out a hand to Bryson. Together, they managed to stagger out of the garage and off the side of the driveway, where they both collapsed again.

The grass was cold, wet, and the ground was hard, although not as hard as the cement garage floor or the tarmac driveway. Her terrycloth robe did little to keep out the chill, and the dampness was even more shocking to her bare feet than the cement had been.

The shock woke her out of the cloud from the gas fumes and the blow to the head, and she realized what she'd sensed in the garage was still present.

Mary. An enraged swirl of energy.

Rowan knew how to shield herself when she used her power, to keep herself from falling too deeply into her visions. She used the same principle now to fight off Mary, before she realized that it wasn't really even her that the spirit was after. Rowan had never thought about shielding someone else, but now she had to try, to help Bryson.

Whatever she did, it seemed to work. Mary coalesced, her face dark with fury.

"How dare you interfere?" she hissed.

"How dare you attack this boy's mind?" Rowan shot back. "How dare you attack any of them? If they did it—and that's *if*, because you won't tell the truth—if they did it, then they deserve to be punished, but not to be mentally tortured until they take their own lives!"

She braced herself for the attack that came. The buffeting anger nearly knocked her over. Beside her, prone, Bryson groaned. But at least he was alive.

Gritting her teeth, willing herself not to pass out, Rowan added, "And for that matter, all of the boys couldn't have done it. At least one of them has to be innocent. Only three attacked you, not four. Why are four confessing?"

Mary pulled back, so abruptly that Rowan's defenses almost toppled her in the opposite direction. The effort of fighting the spirit had sapped the last of her strength. Her temple throbbed. She put her hand up. In the light spilling from the garage, she saw dark wetness.

"They were all friends; so close that it wasn't worth culling one out. It was easier to...affect all of them."

Rowan, dizzy, almost missed Mary's quiet reply.

"Well, stop it," she answered, and then the blackness won.

She was only unconscious for a minute or two, because the next thing she knew Helen was calling her name.

"I'm okay," she said, managing to sit up again. "Bryson...breathed in a lot of carbon monoxide; I don't know if he needs a doctor or not."

"I'll get the others," Helen said.

Toby showed up on the heels of the paramedics, his car's red emergency lights mixing with the ambulance's blue ones as he parked.

"What happened?" he demanded. "Rowan, are you okay? You're bleeding. Hey, Bob," he said to the paramedic who was leading her towards the back of the ambulance.

"I'll be fine," she said. She let Bob guide her down to sit, pressing the gauze he'd given her to her forehead. "I inhaled a little carbon monoxide, that's all."

"Fresh air is probably all you need." Bob shone a narrow flashlight beam into both her eyes. "Contact lenses?" he said. She nodded. To Toby, he said, "Hey, Sheriff. She'll be fine." He eased the gauze away from her head. "Won't even need stitches. I'll just clean this up..."

"Give us a minute, would you?" Toby said.

Bob nodded and went over to where two paramedics were examining Bryson, who was sitting up and seemed to be reasonably coherent.

"What happened?" Toby asked. He sat down next to her and took her hand in his. There was, she thought, a certain comfort to that. The contact was nice, and she didn't want to pull away.

"Mary tried to get Bryson to kill himself," she said. "I came down to get something out of the car and found him. She tried to stop me, but I pushed her back."

"She hit you?" Toby indicated the gauze.

Rowan laughed. "Hardly. A rake fell off the wall when I bumped into it."

David's car screeched into the driveway then. He jumped out and, barely sparing a glance at Rowan and Toby, ran to his wife and son.

"So, she wasn't able to physically hurt you?" Toby asked.

"Not exactly." Rowan tried to remember, but the carbon monoxide had made things fuzzy. She was clear-headed now, but recent events were blurred. "It was more like a storm of rage. She was furious that I stopped Bryson—that I stopped her."

She shivered, remembering. It might not have been physical, but it had been fierce and violent.

Toby tucked the ambulance blanket more securely around her shoulders. "That took a lot of courage," he said. "She attacked you, but you fought her off. Well done."

Rowan blinked. She hadn't thought of it that way. Hadn't thought of it at all, really. She'd been so focused on saving Bryson and protecting herself that she'd simply done what was needed.

"Thank you," she said. She wanted to protest that it had just been against a girl, and an insubstantial one at that. But she didn't. She appreciated Toby's words.

Bob came back over and shooed the sheriff away. Toby went to talk to Bryson and Chloë and David while Bob cleaned and bandaged the scrape on Rowan's forehead.

"Good as new," he said. "Sorry, but I'm fresh out of lollipops."

"Ah, they'll rot your teeth," Rowan said. "Thanks for the blanket."

"Go inside and get warm," Bob said.

She saluted him and turned to go. They'd put Bryson on a stretcher.

"Is there anything you need?" Toby asked her.

"Just some warm clothes and a hot toddy," she said.

He reached out a hand as if it touch her face, but then he just laid a hand on her shoulder briefly. "I'll call you tomorrow," he said. Then he added, more quietly, "I knew you were strong. I'm glad you're okay."

～

"Tell me again," Chloë said. "I want to hear it again."

Rowan sighed, stretching her feet towards the fire. She was in leggings, a sweater, and thick socks, but she still appreciated the heat radiating from the flames.

Bryson was in no danger, but the paramedics thought he should be kept at least overnight; David went with Bryson in the ambulance, insisting that Chloë stay behind and try to relax. She'd already called Dr. Laverick and he was going to meet them at the hospital.

"I couldn't find my contacts case, and realized it must have dropped out of my purse in Bryson's car," she said. "So I went down to get it. I saw what he was doing, and managed to get the car open and him out of the garage. It's as simple as that."

"But it's not!" Chloë hugged her again. "You saved his life. If you hadn't gone down there, he'd be dead."

Rowan couldn't argue with that. "I know," she said. "And I'm grateful that I was there at the right time. He's going to be okay, you know. He's messed up right now, but he's alive and the paramedics said there shouldn't be any permanent damage."

"I just can't believe he would do something like that."

"Chloë, honey. The important thing is that he's going to be okay. It's not going to help to re-hash it and get ourselves more upset. We need to let it go, for our sakes as well as Bryson's and David's."

Chloë drew her knees up under her chin and pulled her oversized sweater over her knees to mid-calf. She looked so small, so dainty, so fragile. "I know you're right," she said. "I'm just...overwhelmed, really."

"Me, too," Rowan said. She set down her mug, swirling with the remains of mint leaves, on the coffee table. "It's been a long couple of days."

"Hasn't it? And yet, it seems like time is flying by. We were supposed to visit David's grandmother yesterday, but couldn't because of the funeral. We didn't tell her the truth about why we had to reschedule, either." Chloë sighed. "We're supposed to see her tomorrow evening, but now I don't know. I don't want her to get upset about what's going on."

"Does she know anything?"

"She has a TV in her apartment—the retirement community she's in has small apartments for the residents, but the nurses have access twenty-four hours a day. It's a good compromise for people who don't like the idea of leaving their homes and being dependent. The phrase 'nursing home' has such negative connotations nowadays. Anyway, she has a bedroom, living room, and bathroom, and the meals are communal. Like I said, she has a TV, and people do talk—but the staff has been asked to try and minimize the gossip. We've told her that Bryson is innocent and it'll blow over. I hate to say it, but it's almost fortunate she's in the beginning stages of Alzheimer's; her short-term memory is terrible and it seems like she doesn't remember the initial news reports."

"I understand," Rowan said. "But don't stress about going, okay? David can always go alone, can't he?"

Chloë nodded. "Cecilia loves to see Bryson, of course, but we'll see how he's feeling and play it by ear."

"That's the best way to deal with all of this." Rowan gingerly touched the sterile dressing on her head. "I think I need some Advil."

They went to bed soon after that, after Rowan convinced Chloë not to wait up for David, that she needed her rest more than anything right now. As she climbed between the sheets, she realized she'd never retrieved her contact lens case. But now she was too tired to care.

Her last thought, as she drifted off, were Toby's words: *I knew you were strong.* Was she?

She wanted to be…

The persistent ring of the phone in the hallway dragged Rowan from groggy unconsciousness. She hadn't slept well. The memories of finding Bryson in the car and getting him out of the garage kept re-playing in her mind, with all the related issues and fears and emotions —not to mention the taint of conversing with Mary again. Because that's what it felt like, more and more each time she'd encountered the spirit: like a slimy stain that she couldn't wash off her psyche. Plus, her head ached, and every time she rolled over, the pressure of the pillow against the bandage caused a fresh stab of pain that jolted her awake again. She knew she'd finally slept only because the jangling phone had awakened her.

The noise halted in mid-ring, indicating that someone had answered. Rowan burrowed deeper under the covers, hoping to regain blissful darkness.

It wasn't to be. A knock on her door pulled her firmly back. Reluctantly she called out for the person to come in.

"Is everything okay?" she asked quickly when she saw Chloë. "Bryson's okay, right?"

Chloë nodded, sitting down on the edge of the bed next to her. "He's fine. David's gone to the hospital to pick him up. I'm not sure what's going on, though. That was Dhriti Prabhakaran on the phone. She says Manny's recanted—he swears he didn't have anything to do with Mary's death after all."

"Excuse me? Rowan stared at her. "He just woke up and decided he didn't do it?"

"Apparently so. Well, either he didn't do it and was lying about participating, or he did do it and is pleading innocent now, or... Dammit, Rowan, I don't know!" Chloë put her head in her hands. "I feel totally defeated; I don't know if I can take much more of this. If the boys didn't do it, why did Bryson try to kill himself, and why did Karl commit suicide, too? What the hell is going on?"

Rowan disentangled her legs from beneath the covers so she could reach out and hold Chloë. "I don't know, sweetie, any more than you do. But we're going to get this whole thing sorted and figured out." She let the news tumble around in her brain, trying to figure out how to deal with it. "Has Manny told the sheriff yet?"

Chloë helped herself to a tissue from the box on the night table.

"No, not yet. Dhriti called me first, because of our conversation yesterday."

"She thinks Mary had something to do with this." Rowan's eyes widened as she felt an audible click in her brain. "Oh shit."

"What is it?" Chloë asked sharply.

"At the funeral, I realized that four boys had confessed even though there were only three attackers according to my visions. I mentioned it to Toby, in fact. Then last night, when I pulled Bryson from the car, Mary was there, and I asked her about it. She said..." Rowan paused, trying to remember the words. "She said that they were all such close friends that it wasn't worth separating them, or differentiating. That it was easier to just affect all of them."

"So she admitted to—to brainwashing them?" Chloë's voice rose to a near-hysterical level. Rowan put a gentle hand on her thigh, projecting calm.

"I can't remember a hundred percent what she said," she answered. "I'd inhaled some fumes as well, plus I'd been whacked on the head with your attack rake. I could have misunderstood, or not be remembering part of the conversation. I think we're where we were yesterday: We're pretty sure she's affecting a lot of people."

Possibly including you. Rowan thought of the sculptures. She wished she felt safe to ask Chloë about them, but with her friend so stressed, with potential ill effect to her unborn baby, she didn't feel she could in good conscience bring up the subject.

Chloë nodded, visibly becoming more relaxed.

"I think we should talk to Dhriti," Chloë said, "and maybe Manny if he's willing. If they want to go to the sheriff first, that's fine, but I'd like to find out first-hand why he's recanted."

"Isn't he coming over for tutoring today?"

"We cancelled classes because of...because of what happened with Bryson."

That made sense. Rowan left her hand on Chloë's leg, not feeling at all guilty about soothing her.

～

By the time Rowan had showered and dressed in jeans and a turtleneck covered with green leaves and purple flowers, David and Bryson had returned from the hospital. Bryson sought out Rowan in the living room, where she and Chloë were finishing their breakfast tea. He hugged Chloë, then turned to Rowan.

"I wanted to thank you. For saving my life." He sat down on one of the recliners, leaning forward to her on the sofa. He was still wearing the pale blue plastic patient bracelet, and he twisted it between the fingers of his other hand.

"I don't think you really wanted to die," Rowan said softly. "I think you were pushed to the edge, by your own emotions and perhaps by other influences, and you saw this as the only way out. But I don't think you really wanted to die."

"I don't know what I wanted, or what I was thinking," he admitted. "I felt…out of control, kind of. Like I couldn't stop what was happening, even though I was the one doing it."

"I think I know what you mean," Rowan said. As she had earlier with Chloë, she tried to project safety, tranquility. Bryson didn't know her that well; knew her only as his fairly new stepmother's best friend. He'd been friendly and respectful so far, but he'd soon hit a point where he wasn't comfortable confiding in a near-stranger—not to mention discussing things he might not have revealed to Chloë. "When I pulled you out of the car, I sensed something. Have you been seeing the attack in your mind? As if you're reliving it?"

He looked both startled and relieved. "Yeah!" he said. "It's like being unable to turn off the TV—and it's worse when I close my eyes. But it's more than that, too. I don't just see it: I feel it."

Rowan nodded. "That's pretty intense. I think that's what pushed you so close to the edge." She paused, considering how to phrase her next words. Chloë was watching both of them, understanding the need not to intervene. "Does it feel like a memory?"

"Of course—I mean, I did it, so I remember it." He cocked his head; the gold hoop earring flashed. "What else could it be? What do you mean?"

"I'm not yet sure what I mean," Rowan said with a quick grin. But the smile faded at the look on his face. "What is it?"

He looked away, at the now-cold ashes in the fireplace, apparently formulating his next words. "This probably sounds crazy, but... It kinds of relates to what you're asking. Sometimes it feels like—like someone's putting the pictures in my head. Dr. Ben has suggested meditation, relaxation techniques, that sort of thing, for taking our minds off what happened. But even when I try those things, even when I try *not* to think about it, it's still there. Like it's being forced on me."

"For what it's worth, Bryson, it doesn't sound crazy to me," Rowan said. "I think I understand what you're saying. When I pulled you out of the car, I seemed to see and feel what you were seeing and feeling. It didn't feel like it was coming from you, but from outside of you. I don't know what it means yet, but I'm trying to find out. But you've got to trust me with this—can you do that?"

He looked at Chloë, then back at Rowan. After a moment's hesitation, he nodded. "Chloë trusts you," he said. "She's been good to me since she and Dad got married. If she trusts you, I trust you, too."

She couldn't meet Chloë's eye. Trust. It all came down to that. And Rowan wasn't sure if she could trust Bryson. She honestly didn't know if he was guilty or not. And she honestly didn't want to know if she agreed with Mary's assessment that it didn't matter either way.

Manny Prabhakaran and his mother came out in early afternoon. He'd already been to see the sheriff, with his lawyer present, and he looked a combination of shaken and relieved.

They sat with Rowan and Chloë in the living room. Bryson and his father were outside raking leaves. Rowan assumed they normally hired a gardener to do the work, but that it was something to keep Bryson occupied. In some ways, she envied them in the fresh air, getting physical rather than mental exercise.

"I must apologies to you, to both of you," Manny said. "I have been instrumental in making things worse by my earlier confession."

Rowan shook her head. "Don't blame yourself, Manny," she said. "There's a lot more going on here than just that."

"Absolutely," Chloë agreed. "No matter what, you've been a good friend to Bryson, and he needs you more than anything right now."

"Manny," his mother said, "why don't you explain what you told me, and told the sheriff. About what changed."

The slender Indian boy took a deep breath. "Before, it was a memory—something I remembered doing. Now it seems like something I saw in a movie or on TV. It's still very vivid, but it's not something that actually happened to me."

"What changed?" Rowan asked. "I mean, what's different today from yesterday?"

He shook his head. "I'm not sure," he admitted. "I don't remember dreaming last night. I only remember waking up, and knowing that I hadn't been a part of what happened."

"This isn't going to be an easy question, but I have to ask," Chloë said. Her voice was gentle, but her body was tense. "Did any of the other boys put you up to it in the beginning? Did they make you say you'd been a part of it, when you weren't?"

"Oh, no, Mrs. Waltham," he said emphatically. "They didn't pressure me into anything. Whatever...whatever it was that made me believe that I had done it, it wasn't them. I don't know what it was. I don't know why it's stopped, although I'm very relieved."

"Do you have any idea, or any thoughts, on what was making you believe that you had done it?" Rowan asked.

Again he shook his head. "It was as if someone was...putting the memories in my head," he said. "But as to how or why, I don't know."

The words were similar to the ones Bryson had used to describe how he felt. Rowan shivered. It was becoming more and more clear that Mary was influencing their memories. But was she enhancing what they already had, or adding new information?

Dhriti met her gaze over Manny's head. "Do you think it's what we talked about yesterday?"

"Probably," Rowan said. "And I think I know why this new development has happened."

They asked Manny to go outside and say hello to Bryson. He was obviously not happy about it, but he complied.

"Last night, before I passed out, I asked Mary why four people had confessed when only three had attacked her," Rowan said. "I think I told her to stop—affecting the fourth, or something. It's really hazy, unfortunately. But I'm wondering if she didn't do it after all."

"You mean, she stopped affecting the innocent one?" Dhriti suggested.

"Something like that."

"Does that mean the other three boys are guilty?" Chloë whispered.

"I don't know," Rowan said slowly. "It would seem to imply that, but I couldn't say one hundred percent. Maybe she got scared that nobody would believe four were involved." She looked at Chloë. "I promise, I'll do whatever it takes to find out."

It wasn't until Dhriti and Manny had left that Chloë turned to Rowan. For the first time, Rowan realized how pale she was.

"Ask David to come inside, please," Chloë said.

"Why—"

"I've been cramping and spotting. I need to go to the hospital. I'm afraid I'm going to lose the baby."

CHAPTER 17

*J*THOUGHT I SAID I didn't want to see you back here," Dr. Melora chided Chloë, her tone gentle and laced with teasing, before she whisked the pregnant woman into the examining room. David went with them; Rowan and Bryson were consigned to waiting. Rowan flipped through a *People* magazine for a full minute before she realized it was the same one she'd looked at the last time they were in the waiting room. Bryson was staring around the room with an expression she finally interpreted as familiarity; after all, he'd left here only this morning.

Thankfully, the wait wasn't long, and David's face showed only slight concern when he reappeared.

"The baby's fine, and so's Chloë," he said immediately, allaying their fears. "The spotting isn't uncommon, but given the previous problems, Bridget wants to keep her in again, just to make sure and to give her more time to rest and relax.

"She'll need some time to get settled, so let's go to the retirement home, grab a bite to eat, and come back for evening visiting hours."

Rowan felt a little awkward interfering in family time, but it made much more sense to have her come along than to be dropped off at home, only to be picked up again when they came back to the hospital.

David put an arm around Bryson's shoulders as they walked out. Rowan followed, chewing her lip. Nothing seemed safe anymore; nothing seemed certain. She felt like she was on one of those tilt-a-whirl fair rides, which spun until the centrifugal force pushed you back against the wall, and then the floor dropped out. Watching David and Bryson, she couldn't imagine either of them being violent. She knew looks could be deceiving, but she also knew Chloë, and Chloë would never stay with someone who wasn't respectful of women.

And yet, and yet...

Rowan let Bryson take the front seat, and slid into the back. The drive to the retirement community was conducted mostly in silence.

Cecilia Waltham's small apartment was cozy and tastefully decorated; Rowan thought she could even see a few of Chloë's touches, including a small statue of an enchanting faun. A grouping of silver-framed photographs on the antique highboy included her late husband's picture; wedding portraits of Chloë and David, and David's sister and brother-in-law; and Bryson's latest school photo. Cecilia insisted on making them tea with the hotpot in the kitchenette and put out a variety of Pepperidge Farm cookies, reminding Rowan of her own grandmother's food-supply habits. A TV murmured in the corner, turned down to low for words to be clear.

Rowan could see traces of David and Bryson in Cecilia's sturdy frame and strong features. Her pure white hair was still thick, pulled back in a braid. She must have someone help her with it; her fingers were gnarled with arthritis.

The conversation was light, pleasant, with no mention of murders or attacks, no thoughts of suicide or ghosts. The hot tea and chocolate cookies were almost enough to raise Rowan's spirits. Of Chloë, David explained simply that the doctor wanted to keep her in for observation because the pregnancy was delicate.

"In fact," he said, as they were starting to gather up their things to leave, "why don't you come out to dinner with us and then visit Chloë in the hospital? I know she'd love to see you."

"Hospital?" Cecilia asked. "Oh dear, what's wrong?"

David explained again about Chloë.

"Yes, of course," the elderly woman said. "I'm sorry. It's my memory again. Of course, I'd love to go."

Bryson went with David to sign Cecilia out and let the staff know she wouldn't be eating in the dining hall tonight. At a loss, Rowan asked Cecilia about some of the pictures on her dresser, and Cecilia pointed out a variety of family members, although a moment after explaining that one sepia-toned one showed her brother Michael, she referred to Bryson as Michael.

As they settled back on the sofa, the TV flashed the evening news logo. "You don't mind if I turn this up, do you?" Cecilia said. "I may not remember it tomorrow, but I do like to keep up with what's going on in the world."

Rowan told her to go ahead. To her dismay, though, the headline story was about Manny recanting his story. Desperately, she cast about for something to do. It was lame, but all she came up with was knocking over the dregs of her tea.

"I'm so sorry!" she said, leaping up. "I'll clean it up."

"No problem, love," Cecilia said. "It'll be faster if I do—despite how slow I creep around. I know where everything is." She carefully rose from the armchair and made the few steps to the kitchenette, where she produced paper towels. Together, they mopped up the tea and righted the cups, and Rowan carried the tray to the counter.

Unfortunately, it wasn't enough of a delay. As Cecilia settled back down, the news anchor said,

"That's the only new development in the rape and murder of Mary Cooper, and it doesn't bring authorities any closer to the answers. Coming up next, sports and weather."

"I just don't understand it," Cecilia said, muting the TV with the remote control.

"What's that?" Rowan asked, hoping against hope that the anchor's last words meant nothing to the older woman.

"Why they're bringing up that old case again," she said, shaking her head. "Especially if they have no new information."

"I'm sorry," Rowan said slowly. "I don't understand." She knew she shouldn't continue the discussion, shouldn't risk the chance of upsetting Bryson's great-grandmother. But while Cecilia's words made no sense, something about them sparked a light. A little more, and Rowan felt as though it would illuminate something important.

"Mary Cooper's murder, dear." Cecilia waved a dismissive hand. "I don't understand why they're bringing it up again after all these years if there isn't anything new to say. Isn't there any recent news they can talk about? This town isn't *that* boring."

Rowan stared at her. "After all these years?"

"Young lady, if I were you, I'd see a doctor," Cecilia said with a warm chuckle. "You sound worse than I do. I remember when Mary's body was found, because they came and told my father. He didn't realize I was in the room. When I asked him about it later, he paddled my bottom and told me never to bring it up again. Goodness, I wasn't much more than ten years old. But I remember not understanding why I never heard anything about it after that—they hushed it right up. Until now, of course."

"I'm sorry if I sound a bit confused," Rowan said. Her brain whirled. "Mary Cooper was killed when you were ten years old?"

"Right about then. Nine or ten, I'd say." The elderly woman hummed softly for a moment. "Years later, when I worked as a secretary at the Milburn *Post*, I went back through the old newspapers to read about it. Not much after the first report. Someone hushed it right up."

Before Rowan could ask another question, David and Bryson returned. "All set to go?" David asked. "Grandmother, bring your umbrella; it's started to rain."

As the others turned towards the door, Rowan plucked a photo of Cecilia and her father off the dresser and tucked it into her pocket.

By the time they got in the car, Rowan's brain had stopped dipping and diving like a seabird and she'd managed to come up with a vague idea of what to do next. She asked David to drop her off at home, claiming she'd remembered some work she needed to do tonight for A Faire Day Out. She promised to try and catch up with them at the hospital, but if she didn't, she asked if they'd tell Chloë that she promised to visit tomorrow.

The rain had gone from a light patter to an insistent fall by the time they arrived at the house. Rowan ran for the door, head ducked, fumbling for her borrowed set of keys.

She replaced her damp shirt with a different one, threw the iBook and peripherals into the laptop case, grabbed her leather jacket, and went to find Helen. The housekeeper was in her apartment, dressing to go out.

"I hate to leave with Chloë back in the hospital," the angular woman said. "I'd planned this evening with friends a while ago, but I'm willing to cancel. David says it's all right for me to go; what do you think?"

"I don't there's much you can do tonight," Rowan said honestly. "It could get crazy around here in the next few days if Chloë has to stay in, so I think you should enjoy your evening."

Helen smiled, though the gesture was wan. "Part of me feels like I should stay, but I can't explain why," she said. "Just upset, I guess. You've been a good friend to her," she added, reaching for her raincoat. "It's good to see that."

Rowan followed Helen down to the kitchen, leaving her there to wait for her ride. As she slid into the driver's seat of Bryson's BMW, she thought of Helen's words, a repeat of what others had said. Was she really that good a friend? She backed out of the garage and pressed the remote control for the door. They, along with Amanda, had been best friends since college. But Rowan wasn't sure if keeping things from Chloë fit the description of being a "good" friend.

She drove slowly, cautious because of the rainy darkness. Helen had said the library was open until 9 p.m., which should be enough time for her to find what she was looking for. It had never occurred to her that Mary would be so angry because the same thing had happened to her grandmother.

Cecilia remembered being nine or ten years old when the incident occurred. Rowan banged the heel of her hand against the steering wheel. Dammit! She hadn't thought to ask how old Cecilia was.

At the library, she dumped her coat and laptop on a desk and tried calling David's cell phone. She got a recorded message that service was down in the area. Probably because of the storm, she guessed.

The librarian was a young man, perhaps a few years shy of Rowan's age, with a blond ponytail and goatee.

"No problem," he said when Rowan thanked him for helping her find the town genealogy records. "It gives me something to do. It's slow tonight—not many people like to be out on a night like this. In fact, I think you're the only person here right now. Here you go." He pointed at the shelves she needed, then went back to his desk.

Because the Walthams had lived in Millburn since time began (or so it seemed), they were mentioned in several local history tomes. Rowan found mentions of Cecilia, but nothing specific. Reviewing the shelves again, she found what she really needed: local church records. From there, it was a simple matter to find that Cecilia had been baptized on January 12, 1908. If she was born in 1908, Rowan mentally calculated, she'd've been nine in 1917 and ten in 1918.

The microfiche and microfilm machines were in the basement, which, despite being paneled and carpeted, was still ten degrees cooler. Rowan flipped through the small file drawers to extract the microfilms for the Millburn *Post*, October 1915 and October 1916.

The snapping of the roll counterpointed the underlying satisfied hum of the machine as Rowan hurried it through the first nine months of the year. She couldn't remember the exact date of Mary's murder, but knew it had been in October and about three weeks ago, which put it about the 28th of October. Slowing the film at the beginning of the month, she stopped at the 20th and read through until 31st. No mention of Mary Cooper. She rewound that tape first with one hand, then the other, tucking the free hand between her knees to warm it up.

She repeated the process.

There were a grand total of two articles about the death of Mary

Cooper in 1918. The first stated that the body of a young girl, "ill-treated," had been found at the spot that seemed to be described as the same place this Mary had been found, by Rowan's reckoning. The second article said that the body had been identified as that of Mary Cooper, the daughter of Agnes Cooper, a woman of "questionable finances and morals." They lived outside of town and were little known by the community. Well, Rowan thought, that sounded familiar, except for the "questionable morals" part.

The newspaper reports stopped there. Cecilia had said there was little printed, and Rowan guessed that because Mary wasn't of good town stock, the newspaper's editor hadn't considered her more newsworthy.

Rowan double-checked to see if her obituary appeared, but it didn't in either October or November. There was a one-sentence notice of a burial, with no services.

Rowan felt the dizzying light-headedness of adrenaline pumping through her body. It was too much of a coincidence that two related Mary Coopers would have been raped and murdered in the same place and on the same date, nearly a hundred years apart.

While she'd considered the fact that Mary might be accusing the wrong people of attacking her and might even be influencing the boys to *believe* they had done it, it had never occurred to her that Mary's true attackers might have lived several generations ago—and that Mary herself had died more than ninety years past.

The only thing that didn't fit was the body. How could Mary's body have been found now if she died in 1918?

Rowan shuffled through the files from her laptop case until she found the medical examiner's report. As she'd remembered, it was brief, just enough that had to be done at the scene. He'd noted that she'd worn a simple black skirt and white top, no details.

The body had disappeared on the way to the morgue. What if Mary had enough supernatural strength to make her body *appear* real long enough for the ME to examine her and put her in the ambulance?

The lights flickered, and with no sound, went out, plunging her into blackness.

Involuntarily, Rowan screamed. Immediately embarrassed, she shrank back in the chair, waiting for her heart to stop pounding. She had a flashlight in her purse…which she hadn't brought with her; she'd simply tossed her wallet into the laptop bag. She pulled her trembling hands back, straining to see in the blackness. The basement had no windows, although she thought she could see a faint less-blackness behind her that might indicate where the stairs were. She remembered, though, that there were tables and desks between where she was and the exit. She took a deep breath. It wouldn't be easy; she'd have to move carefully.

Then she remembered the librarian. She was in the library with a strange man, and according to him, they were alone.

Rowan's breath caught in her throat. Alone. With a strange man. She'd done everything in her power over the past eight years to never let that happen. She cursed herself; she hadn't even thought about it tonight. She'd let herself slip. No excuse that she'd been intent on solving the mystery of Mary's death. How stupid that she'd let herself slip.

The mace was upstairs, in her jacket pocket.

Her heart thudded, hurting her ribs. Stupid, stupid, stupid. Now he was going to come downstairs…

The night she'd been attacked, the lights had gone out on campus. There were something akin to streetlights along the concrete path that meandered along the river behind the dorms, allowing back access to the buildings. Normally the lights were motion-activated, so when you walked near them, they came on. But that night, there'd been a power outage, and Rowan hadn't realized that until she was halfway home. She certainly couldn't have predicted that someone would take advantage of the situation…or should she have?

It was a question she'd asked a thousand times. Walking along a dark path—just like Mary had—was it asking for trouble? Shouldn't a woman have a right to walk along a dark path alone? Or was it sheer stupidity, sheer blindness?

She had to get out of here. Rowan automatically grabbed her things—either remembering where she'd put them or groping for them in the dark—and shoved them in the case. The car keys she shoved in her jeans pocket, within easy reach. The case had double straps, and she pulled it on like a backpack.

Something thudded above her, and her breath caught. He was going to come down... She felt along the table again and found a microfilm roll. It wasn't much, but if she hit him with it, it would distract him, or she could throw it in the dark and make him think she was somewhere else. Gripping the roll, Rowan edged in the direction of the stairway, her other hand extended to check for obstacles and give her an idea of where she was.

The faintly lighter area by the stairway grew brighter.

"Hello? Hello, ma'am, are you okay?" The librarian's voice floated down.

Rowan whimpered, clamping the sound in her throat so it wouldn't carry.

"Ma'am?" A light flashed down the stairs, and footsteps clumped down. "Are you okay?" The beam flashed across her eyes, and she winced. She started to raise the roll to throw.

"I'm so sorry about this," the librarian said. "The power's been knocked out by the storm. I swear there's something wrong with the fuse box in this place—although the electrician swears there's nothing wrong." He was close enough now that she could see him in the glow of the huge mag flashlight (which was much more of a weapon than the flimsy plastic roll, she noted). He looked worried, although his face cleared somewhat when he got a good look at her.

He let out a breath. "I was afraid you'd walk into something or trip before I got down here," he said. "I'm glad you're all right. Have you got all your stuff? Good—I'll lead you out."

"Thanks," Rowan said, the adrenaline and fear leaving her in a rush. Her legs felt rubbery and she had to force them to move.

"I'm glad you're the only person here; it would have been a nightmare to round lots of folks up in the dark," he added over his shoulder as he started up the stairs. "Besides," and his laugh was embarrassed,

"I'm also glad I wasn't entirely alone. Scared the shit—excuse me, the bejeezus out of me at first."

I'm an idiot. Rowan shoved her shaking hands in the pockets of her jeans. *I assumed he was out to get me, and here he's just as jumpy as I am. Maybe I* am *too paranoid about men.*

He could have been lying, of course. There was a time when she would have assumed his admission of nerves was a ruse to distract her, to throw her off guard, then led her willingly into another part of the basement.

But she didn't presume that now. Her initial fears had been automatic, but reason had taken over, faster and stronger than in the past.

They were passing the stacks where the local histories were held when some other portion of Rowan's brain—the one still working on the mystery of Mary—kicked in again. "Wait," she said. "I need to look something up."

The librarian stared at her. "Lady, no offence, but are you crazy? You can come back tomorrow."

"I really need to find out tonight." The urgency mounted in her head, her heart. "Can I check out the book?"

"The books in the reference section can't be taken out of the library."

"Hold on." Rowan found her wallet, held it in the beam of the flashlight to see what she was doing. "Here's my credit card. Keep it until I bring the book back, okay? I swear it'll be tomorrow, or the next day at the latest. I'm staying with Chloë and David Waltham. You *really* don't want to wait for me to go through it, I promise you."

He stared at the Mastercard that she'd pressed into his hand. "You *are* crazy," he said. "Maybe I'm crazy, too, but you're right, I don't want to wait around." He handed her the flashlight and she quickly found the parish records. She tucked the volume deep into her bag so it wouldn't get wet.

"Thank you," she said, meaning it.

He made sure she was in the car and the car had started before he drove off in his VW Beetle, waving as he went. Rowan appreciated that, even if she did wait another few minutes with the defroster on high so she could see out the windows. The rain, if possible, was coming down even harder. Rowan put the wipers on maximum speed, and they still did little to clear the sluice of water on the windshield. She put the flashers on and drove slowly, hoping she didn't hit anyone and that nobody hit her.

But even as she concentrated on the road, that other part of her brain kept working. If she disregarded the weirdness of the body, everything else snicked into place, pointing directly at the idea that Mary had actually died in 1918. She'd accepted that Mary was a ghost —there was little reason not to accept that she'd been a ghost for eighty-plus years.

And if she had been dead that long, then Bryson, Karl, James, and Manny had had nothing to do with it.

The problem was, the question still remained: Who did? Because until she answered that, Mary would keep hounding Bryson and James until they, too, killed themselves.

She almost missed the corner for the road the house was on, and without thinking, slammed on the brakes. The car fishtailed in the flooded street, and she skimmed the steering wheel one way, then the other, trying to pull out of the skid.

The back corner of the car thudded against a tree. The sudden halt jerked Rowan against the seatbelt, and for a moment, paralyzed, all she could do was stare out the window, listening her own panting and the rain pelting, the sound hard and metallic, against the roof.

"Okay," she said finally. "Okayokayokay. You're okay. You're fine. Car's still running. Just put it in gear, move forward." Speaking the instructions aloud helped somehow, and she shifted the car carefully into first. It hesitated at first, then something gave at the back end, and it lurched forward.

"Goodgoodgood," Rowan said. She was facing the way she'd come, but on the right side of the road. A few yards ahead was the street she needed, and she turned carefully onto it. Only a minute or two later— even with the creeping speed she'd adopted—she was at the house.

The front light was on, and the garage door opened when she pressed the button. She sighed with relief; the electricity hadn't been knocked out here yet. Chloë's was the only other car in the garage, meaning that David and Bryson weren't back yet. She doubted Helen was, either, although she called out when she entered the kitchen. Unless their plans were rained out, Helen and her friends probably didn't plan to be back until late.

Rowan tossed her jacket over a barstool, put her laptop case on the butcher block island, and turned on the kettle for tea. While it heated, she pulled out the parish records, turned twenty years earlier than Cecilia Waltham's baptism, and started searching for any mention of Mary Cooper.

CHAPTER 18

*B*Y THE TIME SHE'D BREWED and drunk one very strong and very hot cup of Earl Grey, Rowan had found what she was looking for.

A Mary Cooper had, in fact, been baptized, in 1903. Which would have made her fifteen at the time of her death.

Rowan carefully shut the old book. She stared at the cover, unseeing.

Another figure emerged from behind a sheet or curtain that blocked off a section of the cottage. A girl, perhaps fifteen or sixteen, wearing a dark skirt and white blouse—of an era long past.

More clicked into place. Of course Mary's cottage was derelict— she hadn't been there for more than eighty years. And the girl she'd seen in her vision there hadn't been an ancestor; it had been Mary herself.

A crack of thunder made her jump. She wished fervently that someone else was home. She wasn't superstitious per se, had never been afraid of storms, and didn't think Mary was going to appear and attack her in the bathroom. But too much had happened in too short a time, and Mary *did* have a strong influence.

Now that she had more information, Rowan realized she had no idea what to do next. She'd call Toby in the morning, or better yet, go down to the sheriff's office and show him what she'd found. She could try him tonight, but the phone lines were either down or would be busy, and she was sure he had emergencies to deal with in the storm.

She'd also visit Chloë tomorrow and tell her as well. It wasn't any more stressful than what she already knew, and maybe she'd have a few ideas.

She had a plan for tomorrow. The next step was getting through this night. There wasn't, she told herself, anything she could do now.

Some TV, she decided, to distract her. Some TV, a bit of Scotch, and then David and Bryson would be home, with Helen sometime after that. Yes, she liked that plan.

Lightning flashed, followed almost immediately by another shatter of thunder. Okay, Rowan thought, it's a good plan until the power goes out.

Just in case, she rooted around in the kitchen drawers until she found a flashlight, bigger and sturdier than the small one she kept in her purse. She also made note of the emergency candles in the pantry. Gathering up her case, coat, book, and the flashlight, she headed out of the kitchen towards the stairs.

She was passing by the front door when the doorbell rang.

The unexpectedness of it made her scream. For a moment, all she could do was stare at it, gasping for breath, heart racing once again. Muttering an invective against things that startled her, Rowan shifted her burdens to one arm and opened the door.

The wind snatched the door from her hand and banged it against the wall. Rain and wind filled her face, and she got only the impression of a tall, wild-haired figure at the door. Swiping the hair out of her own eyes, Rowan gaped.

"What? *What?* Are you going to let me in? I've been through the seventh layer of hell trying to drive here from the airport—with lousy directions, I might add. Anyone who says British weather is bad should visit here. Bloody hell!"

"Amanda!"

Rowan had stepped aside during the diatribe, allowing her friend to enter. At six feet tall, Amanda Gordon-Davies was an imposing woman, although she could in no way be called overweight. Her presence and her spirit filled a room, with the help of her waist-length, curly brown hair and singer's voice. Now that the door was struggled shut and the wind no longer a factor, her hair dripped down her back. Rowan dropped her own things on a nearby table and hugged her anyway.

"It's been a very strange and awful day," she said.

"That sounds like the beginning of a children's book," Amanda commented. "What's up?"

Rowan held her hand out for Amanda's coat. "Not yet," she said. "Come in, have a drink, and I'll tell you."

After Rowan finished, Amanda stared at her. The explanation of all that had happened—told as Rowan remembered it, and in her present state of mind that didn't mean a linear order—had taken the better part of an hour. Amanda had interjected questions when something wasn't clear, but had otherwise kept quiet, hadn't commented.

"Wow," she said finally.

"You believe me?" Rowan asked. Even as she'd told the story, she'd heard how amazing it sounded.

"I've got no reason not to, pet," her friend said. "There's no reason you'd be making any of this up."

Rowan still felt a twinge of guilt. Her suspicions about the boys, the fathers, and men in general gave her every reason to make things up.

"I still feel bad about looking at Chloë's sculpture when she asked me not to," she admitted.

"Of course you do," Amanda said promptly. "Maybe you shouldn't have. That's water under the bridge right now. If you have to work it out with her, you will. What's important now is what you saw and what they represent."

"Why do you think she made it?" Rowan voiced the question she hadn't yet been able to ask Chloë.

Amanda shrugged. "If Mary can influence the boys, there's no reason why she shouldn't be able to influence Chloë. Chloë's energies are in flux right now because of her pregnancy. On one hand, they're stronger, to give more protection as her body is less able to protect her and the unborn child. But on the other hand, most women don't know how to handle that increase of energy, and it goes all over the place in the form of those raging emotions pregnant women always complain about. That energy could have attracted Mary—perhaps she's feeding off of it. And it could be leaving Chloë open psychically; she's both stronger and more vulnerable by being pregnant, and she doesn't know how to use that strength."

"Well, hopefully she's safer in the hospital—hopefully that's far enough away from Mary's influence." Rowan shivered.

"I hope so, too."

The phone shrilled. Rowan would have spilled her drink if there'd been anything but a few drops in the glass. "Damn, I can't stop jumping," she said as she got up to answer it.

It was David. "Roads are flooding left and right," he said. "Bryson and I are going to stay at a motel near the retirement home. Will you be okay there?"

Rowan assured him that she would, reminding him that Helen was out.

"She'll probably end up staying with a friend," David said. "I'm sure she'll call—if she can get through. It took me several tries."

"By the way, you'll never guess who showed up: Amanda Gordon-Davies, our other college crony."

"Really? That's wonderful." She heard warmth in David's voice. "We'll definitely have to bring her to see Chloë tomorrow—she'll be thrilled. Make her feel at home, would you?"

"Not a problem," Rowan said. "We'll take it easy tonight, and touch base with you in the morning."

As she hung up, she got the fleeting image of David and Bryson guiltily fleeing town. She chuckled. Now she was *really* overreacting.

Amanda had poured them each another finger of Scotch in her absence, and was looking out the back window when she returned. Rowan relayed the updates to her, sipping her drink.

"Okay," Amanda said absently. "Rowan, you said nobody goes in the studio usually but Chloë?"

Rowan froze. "Yes."

"The light's on down there."

Her gut lurched downwards. The roar in her ears she quickly realized was heightened hearing. She set the glass down, not even trying to fight the trembling of her hand.

"It's Mary," she said.

"Are you sure?" Amanda asked. "I don't see anyone there. Holy mother of destiny, woman!" She'd turned and seen Rowan. "You're white as a sheet. Are you going to faint?"

Rowan took a shaky breath. "No," she said. She walked to Amanda's side and grabbed her hand. "I'm glad you're here, though."

Amanda squeezed. "What should we do?"

"Go down there," Rowan said. She didn't want to, but she knew, without question, that it was what they had to do. "She wants a confrontation. We'll give it to her."

They gathered flashlights, candles, and matches, in case the power went out; they put lavender and mugwort in their pockets for protection at Amanda's suggestion. She'd had them in her suitcase. She also grabbed some acorns from the autumn arrangement in the living room.

"Ready?" Amanda asked.

"No," Rowan answered. She flicked on the path lights. "But don't let that stop us."

A boom of thunder heralded their exit from the house. The rain pounded steadily on their hats as they made their way down the slippery grass.

"Any last words of advice before I meet this demon-chick?" Amanda shouted over the downpour.

"She hates men," Rowan shouted back. "She doesn't care who pays, as long as somebody does."

"Charming," Amanda returned. "I won't ask her about her sex life."

They paused under the eaves before the door. Amanda took her hand, and Rowan opened the door.

But it wasn't Mary they found inside.

It was Chloë.

"What are you doing here?" Rowan demanded, even as Amanda was gasping Chloë's name.

Their friend looked at them, eyes glazed.

"I'm not sure," she said. "I just knew I had to come."

"How did you get here?" Rowan asked.

"I checked myself out."

"Let me guess," Amanda said. "You called a taxi. I passed one just before I got here."

Rowan, muttering expletives under her breath, found a reasonably clean drop cloth and draped it over Chloë's shoulders. Chloë wore the clothes she'd had on when she went to the hospital, but apparently hadn't grabbed her jacket; her shirt was damp and she shivered uncontrollably.

"I'm calling the hospital," Rowan said, turning for the door.

"No!" Chloë's voice, the urgency laced in it, stopped her. "I've stopped spotting; Bridget gave me some medication for that. I need to be here. I don't know why, but I have to."

"Did Mary call you here?" Amanda asked, crouching next to her.

Chloë's pale brows dipped. "I...I'm not sure," she said. "Something did, I guess."

"Bryson didn't do it," Rowan told her, the first thing that came into her head. "Mary's been dead eighty years. I don't know why she targeted the boys, except that she wants revenge and doesn't really care who pays as long as somebody does. I found the records that this happened eighty years ago. Cecilia remembers it." She realized she was babbling.

Chloë raised her head, the gesture seeming to take most of the energy she had. "Then what do we do?"

"In most ghost stories, it's a case of laying the past to rest," Amanda said thoughtfully. "You know, like finding the body or proving the dead person is innocent. In this case, I'd say it would be to expose who was guilty."

"But how do we do that?" Rowan asked. "They're probably all really old, if they're not dead already."

The lights went out, then came back on again almost before they could react.

"They are," said a new voice. Mary's voice, flat and cold. "They're all dead. They lived out their lives happy and prosperous and never giving me another thought."

She stood next to the grouping of statues that Chloë had done, which showed the very act that killed her.

"But you couldn't be happy, could you?" Amanda said softly, rising to her feet. "And, in fact, that meant you couldn't die in peace. Instead of moving on, you've been stuck here."

To Rowan, it really did sound like the plot of a bad TV movie. *Go toward the light, Mary.* Yeesh.

"No, I'm not happy!" Mary snapped. A swirl of chill air licked around them. "*She* understands," she added, pointing at Rowan.

Everyone looked at Rowan. Did she understand? she wondered. Was she any different from Mary?

Yes, she was.

"I do understand," she admitted. "I understand how you feel: Your rage, your frustration at being helpless and powerless. I was, too, for a long time. Like you, I didn't have the opportunity to confront my attacker or get revenge—even if all I wanted as revenge was for him to pay with jail time.

"But the fact is, I've been able to come to peace with that. There was nothing I could do, and that angered and frustrated me for a long time, but I managed to move beyond it. It's more important now for me to make sure it doesn't happen again, and do whatever I can to make sure it doesn't happen to other women." She took a deep breath.

"So yes, I understand how you feel; I understand that you're not happy. But that doesn't mean I agree with how you're choosing to deal with it."

Mary's face uglied into a scowl. She started to respond, but Chloë's voice, weak and wan, floated over from the sofa.

"Tell us what really happened, Mary," she said. "We don't want to cause you more pain, but we'd like to know what happened. You have nothing to fear from us—in fact, you'll get our commiseration, our sympathy."

"I think I know some of it," Rowan said, as Mary pressed her lips together, considering. "It happened in 1918, when you were fifteen. You probably don't know this, but there were two newspaper articles about it. Then they stopped, probably because someone hushed the incident up. You lived out by the brook with your mother, didn't you? And there was a man out there..."

"Oh, very good," Mary said, but admiration was mixed in with her sarcasm. "Fine, then. I said I wouldn't answer your questions because it wouldn't be a challenge, but I suppose you've risen to that challenge. Fair's fair. I'll tell you.

"Yes, we lived out by Cooper's Brook—does the name surprise you? My grandfather build that house, and it wasn't our fault he was cheated out of the rest of the money, or that I was born out of wedlock from a man who would never have married my mother. I'm not sure if my mother would have married him, anyway; she'd learned not to trust men. It was ironic, I later realized, that the only way we survived was by her interaction with them."

The woman wore similar clothes to the girl's, but her hair was loose and her blouse unbuttoned at the top. Rowan remembered the scene clearly, and she'd deduced it then. Chloë and Amanda were nodding; they understood as well.

"I was probably ten years old when my mother's best client asked for me. She refused, because, she finally told him, he was my father. You might recognize the name: Edward Sinclair."

"Sinclair?" Chloë gasped. "Martin's...grandfather?"

"Great-grandfather, I believe I learned," Mary said. "Are you starting to understand? They were all involved. Sinclair, Gottard—and Waltham."

Chloë shrank back against the sofa cushions, eyes wide in her pale face.

"So that's what you've been doing: making their descendants pay," Rowan said.

Mary didn't spare her a look; she was too involved with her story. "From that point, we survived on my mother's business, but we were better off because now that Edward knew, he was afraid my mother would tell—and she did nothing to dissuade him of the idea. He began paying us to keep us quiet. When my mother grew ill and he stopped visiting, it was my job to go to him and collect the money." She waved a hand to indicate the studio. "As you might expect, I couldn't go to the house, so we met here."

"In the servant's quarters," Rowan supplied, understanding. "That's why you're here so much. I knew the place had been owned by the Sinclairs by then, but hadn't realized you'd been here."

Mary acknowledged her this time by nodding.

"On top of that, I was old enough to know my own mind then, and was willing to get more money out of him. My mother was sick; we needed it."

Rowan winced. The daughter prostituting herself to the father. Worse, the father agreeing, probably instigating it.

"The last time I came here, he didn't have enough money to pay me," Mary continued her story. "His wife was pregnant—imagine that! —and needed expensive care. He gave me a pair of earrings instead. We both knew, I think, that they were worthless to me. I couldn't sell them, because I'd be questioned where I got such costly jewelry. For all my years, though, I was young." Her face grew stony. "I'd never had a father. I wanted his love, I suppose. I saw the earrings as a gift, something special from him. Something I could keep to remember him by.

"That was the night he killed me."

CHAPTER 19

ROWAN SHIFTED, UNCOMFORTABLE. She'd seen Mary's attack, witnessed it more than once in her own mind. She didn't want to hear it from Mary's point of view; didn't want to hear the description from the woman who'd experienced it. But she knew she had to, and she would, and she would do whatever she could to use that information to stop Mary's vendetta against the remaining boys.

It was too late for Karl, and Mary had released her hold on Manny. But Bryson and James were still at risk.

"I don't know if he ever meant for me to have the earrings." Mary's voice was bitter. "He was drunk that night—he often was, sipping from that silver flask of his. Maybe he used that to make it seem as though it was happenstance rather than a planned attack, in case anyone found out. In case anyone cared, which they didn't.

"They caught me on my way home, he and his friends. You know what happened then—you've seen it," she said to Rowan. "One too many blows when I struggled, and they killed me."

"I don't think they planned to kill you," Rowan said, remembering the scene.

Mary's eyes were dark, fierce. "Does it matter? They did. And then he ripped the earrings out of my ears before my body was cold. His own daughter."

Chloë hugged herself, her hands crossed low across her belly where the life inside of her was barely big enough to make her bulge. Rowan prayed she wasn't miscarrying; that the doctor's prescription would carry her through this stress unharmed.

For the first time, she wondered about the gender of the child, and of the one Chloë had lost before.

She sensed Mary's anger building as the young woman had relived her tale during its telling. She glanced at Amanda, who nodded slightly; she'd noticed it, too. They had to keep Mary calm.

"That's one thing I haven't been able to figure out," Rowan said carefully, knowing she was going off on a tangent. Mary could find the tangent insulting, taking away from the story of what had happened to her. "Only one earring is in the local museum. What happened to the other one?"

The smile that grew on Mary's face chilled her. The spirit held out her hand and uncurled her fingers. On her palm lay a pearl earring, the match to the one in the museum.

"He dropped it that very night, the stupid man," she said. "I followed them, and I found it. It was my link, all these years. The earring, this place—" she indicated the studio "—the whiskey that burned on his breath and his children's breath. These things gave me strength, fuelled my need for revenge. At first I had very little energy; I could barely stay awake, barely move from the place where I lay. But over the years, I gained more and more. I saved it, I savored it. And I hoarded it, until I had enough to do what I needed to do."

"What did you need to do, Mary?" Amanda asked. Her voice was low, calm, and Rowan sensed a hint of calming power in it. Whether that would work on Mary, she didn't know.

Mary turned to stare at her as if she were mad. "Have you not been listening?" she demanded. "I waited all these years until I was strong enough to make them pay."

"But the boys aren't the ones who have to pay," Amanda said before Rowan could tell her the argument was useless.

"It doesn't matter!" Mary screamed. Whether because of her fury or because of the storm, the lights flickered and the windows rattled.

"You're right, it probably doesn't," Amanda said, again with the soothing power in her tone. She'd moved, Rowan realized, partway around the room during the time they'd been talking. As if circling Mary. Making a circle around her. Rowan shifted her stance, making it look as though she were just getting comfortable, but taking a few steps in the same direction Amanda had moved in.

Amanda continued, "What have you been able to do, once your power was strong enough?"

"Let me guess," Rowan said. "I want to see if I've lived up to your challenge." At Mary's nod, she began ticking things off on her fingers. "You were able to manifest your body at the site again, so that there was evidence in the present time just long enough to prove a crime had happened. You got into the boys' heads and made them remember committing the crime, even though they didn't do it. You pushed them hard enough that Karl committed suicide and Bryson tried, too."

She took a deep breath and looked over at Chloë. Although her friend's eyes were closed, she was obviously still awake. She seemed tiny, huddled on the sofa with her arms around her knees. "What I don't know," Rowan continued, "is whether you had anything to do with these sculptures."

Chloë's eyes flew open. She opened her mouth to speak, but no words emerged.

Mary's laugh made Rowan shiver.

"Oh yes, that," the spirit said. The glance she cast at the sculptures was almost fond. "Well, of course I did. Her creative energy was at a peak, especially once she was with child. I tapped into it to increase my own energy. I wasn't trying to give her the memories like I did with the boys, but she picked up on them anyway."

"So you've been feeding off Chloë's energy," Amanda said.

"It was available," Mary said, shrugging. "Why not?"

"Because you're hurting her," Rowan said. "And you attacked me when I tried to help Bryson, and you also tried to feed off my energy, didn't you, when I first got here? You got into my dreams."

"You were harder to take from," Mary said. "It wasn't worth it to keep trying."

"So you've been hurting Chloë, and you've tried to hurt Rowan more than once," Amanda pressed the issue.

"So?"

"So you said your vengeance was at the boys—the young men who were convenient to your need for revenge. You're angry at men; you've made that clear. But is it also okay to hurt women?"

Mary seemed taken aback by the question. Rowan used the moment to slide further left.

"It doesn't matter," Mary said defensively, almost sulkily.

"Of course it matters," Rowan took up the argument. "You told me before that even if the boys weren't guilty now, they might be guilty of something in the future. If you've got a vendetta against men, that's one thing. But in doing so, you're saying that you're protecting women from future attacks by men. How can you justify hurting women? We've done nothing to harm you. No woman attacked you, raped you, killed you."

"I don't care," Mary snarled, whirling on her. "She—" and she pointed at Chloë "—married one of them, is bringing up one of them. You keep trying to stop me from getting my revenge. I thought you would help me, but no. You're just as bad if you're protecting them. I won't let you stand in my way any longer."

"The problem is," Amanda said, gaining Mary's attention, "we're not very inclined to let you have your way and hurt innocent people any longer. Rowan, come here and help me."

Rowan complied, unsure what Amanda was planning. At her friend's request, she took one of Chloë's hands, and Amanda took the other. Amanda then joined hands with Rowan, completing a circle.

"First of all," Amanda said, "we need to help Chloë build a barrier so Mary can't keep drawing energy off of her."

The words were barely out of her mouth when Rowan felt buffeted by a mental wind, so hard it made her physically stagger. She didn't know if it was the same thing, but she threw up the wall she used when she was getting visions from objects, the one to keep her from getting too involved in the scene the object showed her.

Apparently it *was* the same type of thing, because the constant shoving against her mind stopped as abruptly as it started.

"Good, you already know how to do it," Amanda approved. "Now, draw up some energy and send it towards Chloë, through the link with your hands. Don't give her all of it and drain yourself, though. Feed it slowly and steadily. Be a conduit from the earth to Chloë. Be strong; don't let Mary affect you."

Amanda's words took on a hypnotic cast, which helped Rowan do as she instructed.

Ground and center. Draw energy from the earth, direct it where it needed to be.

"Good, good," Amanda said.

Rowan opened her eyes and saw that Chloë's pallor had improved. That definitely *was* good.

"Rowan, imagine some of that energy you're drawing up is making a cone or a dome around Chloë. Light or color: Whatever works best for you. Chloë, you imagine the same thing. I'm feeding energy towards it as well."

Closing her eyes again, Rowan did what Amanda said. The area around Chloë became a web, as if she were surrounded by a net. The strands glowed and pulsed a warm orange-red. From Amanda came more strands, midnight blue; they intertwined with Rowan's, tightening the web. From inside, from Chloë herself, came a pale green that seemed to coat the inside of the net. The three colors drew closer, tighter, until they formed a smooth barrier. At Amanda's suggestion, they all imagined the barrier drawing closer to Chloë and molding to her body, so she was completely covered in an invisible shield.

"Chloë, energy can flow out of the shield only if *you* want it to," Amanda said. "Remember that, and strengthen the shield whenever possible. Energy can also flow in through the shield if you need it and draw upon it. Right now, though, you relax. Keep holding our hands; it helps for all of us to be networked right now. Rowan, let's work on your shield."

They strengthened Rowan's mental defenses, making them work unconsciously so Mary couldn't draw on her either; and then Amanda did the same for herself.

Rain slammed against the windows, sounding like hail, or pebbles flung by an immense hand. Other than that, the studio was quiet.

"Where did she go?" Rowan whispered.

"I'm not sure," Amanda said. "Technically, she shouldn't have been able to get out of the circle we created around her when we were talking. One of several things might have happened. She might have gone. She might be low on energy. She might be hiding. She might be—"

One of the windows shattered inward. Chloë shrieked.

"—getting ready to fight," Amanda finished, raising her voice to be heard above the storm.

"She must have been gathering power," Rowan said. "Where is she getting it from? It's not from us, and Bryson's too far away, isn't he? Maybe from James, but that can't be enough." She flinched as another window shattered, closer to them this time.

And then the lights went out, plunging them into darkness.

Rowan felt herself being thrown to the ground. She struggled to take in a breath, but all she could manage was small gasps, as if her lungs had shrunk. Sparks flashed in her vision, and for a moment she feared a detached retina. Only for a moment. That fear was swiftly replaced by terror.

Someone pinned down her arms, kneeling on them so she couldn't move. Knees ground her forearms into the hard earth, the pain so intense she was sure her bones were giving way. Voices—male—but at first she couldn't make out the words over the roaring of adrenaline and dread in her ears. Another pair of hands reached up beneath her skirt to grasp the edge of her tights. She kicked blindly, wildly, and was gratified to hear his grunt of pain. But she was rewarded only with an oath that reeked of whisky before the man straddled her shins and sat on them. The stench reminded her of something, but she couldn't quite remember what.

The man ripped her tights down to her knees, then moved off to pull them farther down. Tangled in the Lycra, Rowan couldn't lash out again. All she could think of to do was press her legs together, keep him out. She was losing feeling in her hands, the blood supply cut off. The throbbing, combined with any attempt to move her arms, caused shooting pain in her wrists.

She thought she might be whimpering. Helpless… She'd tried so hard never to be in this situation again. She couldn't remember, though, how she'd gotten here, or even where "here" was. She only knew that it existed, that three men pinned her down and intended to rape her.

Toby. Something made her think of him then, something about what he'd said about being strong. He'd given her mace to help her, believing she could fight successfully when she needed to. Believing that she wasn't a victim.

It gave her strength. Finally able to breathe in a full complement of air, Rowan screamed. A punch to the side of her head sent a shower of light and pain through her skull.

The man pulled her legs apart; her efforts to keep them closed were laughably useless. Tears of frustration, anger, pain slid down the sides of her head. She hadn't been strong enough after all.

The men on her arms grabbed her legs and held them open, ripping the muscles in her inner thighs, as the third man backed off for a second. In the darkness she could see almost nothing, but she heard him fumbling with his clothes. She tried to scream again, but someone clamped a hand over her mouth, a hand large enough that it pressed against her nostrils as well. She couldn't get in more air, she couldn't breathe. Rowan squirmed, trying to pull in oxygen, but the motion was useless. Terror mounted as she felt herself sinking away…

"Rowan!"

In the distance, she heard a voice call her name. Idly, she wondered about the reality of an afterlife.

"She isn't breathing oh God oh God do something!"

"Rowan, can you hear me? It's Amanda, sweetheart. Listen to me. Listen to my voice. Don't let go of my voice, okay? You have to pull out of this. Try to breathe."

Breathe? How could she do that when her mouth and nose were covered?

"C'mon, sweetie, you've got to try. Try for me, please. Whatever you're…whatever you're seeing or experiencing, it isn't real. Mary's doing it. She's gotten past your defenses. She's causing you to hallucinate."

Pretty real hallucination, Rowan thought. She'd always assumed they were just visual, not physical. She was impressed, in a vague, floaty sort of way.

"Rowan, don't slip away. Hold onto my voice—hold on to what's real. Dammit!"

Something clamped down on her mouth. Which was odd, given that the hand was still there. It felt like lips. Revolted, Rowan tried to turn her head away from them. But the person wasn't kissing her, but blowing air into her mouth.

"Breathe, Rowan, please please please," begged Chloë's voice.

Both Chloë and Amanda were here? Suddenly Rowan realized that she had to warn them about the men. They had to get away before the men got them, too. She couldn't speak, but the pressure was off her arms, and she had enough strength to wave one hand.

If she could get away, if she had the power to do that, she could get Toby, and Toby would help her save them.

"Amanda, she's moving."

The mouth at hers went away.

Rowan took a small breath of clean, rain-scented air, then a bigger one, relishing the feel of it in her lungs. Her head buzzed with the new oxygen.

She tried to speak, and failed; no sound emerged. She cleared her throat, tried again.

"Run," she said. "Get away. Men. Attacked me. Not safe. Go. Call Toby."

"No, sweetheart." Amanda was at her side, holding her hand. Chloë was there, too, with a flashlight that cut through the darkness. Rowan remembered worrying about her eyes; felt relief.

"It's okay," Amanda continued. "There are no men here. It was Mary, in your head, making you see those things."

"It was real," Rowan protested. "I could feel…" She raised one arm and stared at her wrist. No bruising, not even reddening. She turned her arm one way, then another. No pain, either. "They pinned my arms down," she said, still unbelieving. She felt her legs, and her fingers touched smooth, untorn Lycra. "I don't believe it," she said, shaking her head. "It was so real. It wasn't like a dream, or even like a vision. It truly felt like it was happening to me."

"I know, sweetie," Amanda said, smoothing her hair. "Mary's pretty damn strong. How do you think she convinced the boys to attempt suicide?" She and Chloë helped Rowan sit up, propping her against the front of the sofa. "She's gone again for the moment; hopefully she expended too much energy on you and has to rest again. I've tried to strengthen your mental shields, but you've got to help, too."

Rowan closed her eyes, imagining the shields as iron walls. They melted before her eyes. Biting her lip, she tried again. Amanda's support came through, and she clutched it like a proffered hand. This time the walls held, with a hollow metallic clunking as they interlocked.

"Can you help me with Chloë's as well?" Amanda asked. "She'd be Mary's next target."

Rowan did the best she could, unsure if the little bit she could do in her present state of weakness was any help at all. But she saw Chloë's walls go up before she herself sagged back.

"Better," Amanda said. "Rest for a moment. We need to figure this out. Where is she getting power from? Or how?"

Chloë got up and found matches in the kitchen. She began walking around the room, lighting the various candles.

"The building?" Rowan suggested, resting her head against the couch cushions. "This is where she met Edward, where she was forced to sleep with her own father. That's got to raise some pretty twisted energy."

"Perhaps," Amanda said thoughtfully. "Although you'd think the place where she was raped would have even stronger significance for her."

Some of the candles, those too close to the broken windows, wouldn't stay lit, but enough did to dimly illuminate the room. The various statues looked eerily lifelike in the flickering gloom. Rowan gazed at the statue of Boudiccea, at her defiant stance, trying to embody the strength.

"Maybe it's the whole line," Rowan said. "From here to the attack site to her home. Like a ley line."

"No," Chloë said from across the room. They looked up at her. A blackened match dangled from her fingers. "It's this sculpture," she said, pointing to the grouping that re-created the rape. Tears streamed down her cheeks. "It all makes sense now. She compelled me to make it—I didn't know why, I didn't know she was there, but I felt like I had to do it. I was obsessed with it. It was right after I found out I was pregnant; at first I thought I just had more energy because of the baby. The attack—what we thought was the attack on Mary a few weeks ago—happened the night after I finished it."

"You think she's getting her power from the sculpture?" Rowan tried to understand.

"It makes sense," Amanda said slowly. "The building has meaning for her; the sculpture adds to that. She's probably not getting the energy from the sculpture itself, but through it somehow. Channeling the power, focusing it."

Chloë put her hand on the statue, on the back of one of the men. Rowan fought back a wave of disgust and fear. The sculptures illustrated not only what had happened to Mary, but what Rowan had experienced happening to herself.

She watched the play of emotions over Chloë's face, and knew there was a level of difficulty for her, too. As horrible as they were, they were Chloë's work, her art. Rowan didn't entirely understand the depth of the artistic process that Chloë went through; her own website work and occasional Renaissance costuming gave her a thrill when she completed a project she knew was good, but that was all. She didn't understand putting a part of yourself into your art.

"She made me make this," Chloë said, as if in answer to Rowan's unspoken questions. Her voice was hoarse. "It wasn't my idea—it's not something I would ever come up with or choose to do. But it's still my work; I still made it. I hate it, but it's mine." She gave a short, humorless laugh. "Technically, it's pretty good work; there's a lot of emotion in it." Closing her eyes, she rested her head against the stone for a moment, then looked up again. "There's only one thing to do," she said clearly. "Destroy it."

Rowan and Amanda glanced at each other.

"I think she's right," Amanda said. "If we destroy the thing that Mary's channeling her power through, it should weaken her."

Chloë turned her back on the sculpture with clear finality. From her tool chest, she pulled out chisels and hammers. "These are the biggest I have," she said. She grabbed three pairs of goggles as well.

"These will do," Amanda said, taking everything from her and handing Rowan one set. "You—" and she directed these words at Chloë "—should not do any heavy work in your condition." She raised a hand to forestall Chloë's protest. "You still have an important job. We need you to keep an eye out for Mary's return. Because when she does, she's going to be pissed."

Rowan hefted the chisel and mallet in her hands, appreciating their heaviness, their solidness. For the first time in a long while, she felt as though she was about to do something proactive. So much recently had been futile arguments with Mary or a helpless inability to stop what was happening, whether with Mary or her own mind.

Now they were getting somewhere. She didn't even mind—although she'd been aware of it for most of the evening—that Amanda had taken on the dominant role. Rowan appreciated that Amanda knew more about psychic energy, about spiritual matters, and perhaps even about ghosts than she did.

Amanda hugged Chloë. "I know how you feel," she said. "I'd feel the same way about my music. But if I thought my music was hurting somebody…it would have to be stopped, no matter how much it hurt me to lose it."

"That's exactly it," Chloë said. She set her mouth, looking determined. "Have at it, girls."

236

CHAPTER 20

ROWAN TOOK A DEEP BREATH and placed the chisel against the stone. Her first attempt seemed pitiful; her arm weak, her aim poor. What seemed a pathetically small piece of stone was gouged out. Her second attempt wasn't much better, nor her third. She paused, watching Amanda wail away at a different section—the arm of one of the men reaching for the figure of Mary to pin her arms down.

Anger surged inside of her, searing and vitriolic, like lava weakening the earth's crust. With a cry, she slammed the mallet against the chisel, and was gratified to see a larger chunk splinter off. She smashed the sculptures the way she couldn't smash in the heads of the men who'd attacked her, both those in her earlier false vision and the one from college.

"That's right," purred a voice in her mind. "They're evil and bad, all of them. Take your revenge. Seek justice."

"No," she said through gritted teeth. "Not all of them. Just these."

The laughter in her mind grated like nails on a chalkboard. "That's easy to forget, and you know it. One's just like the other."

Rowan let loose a string of expletives as she slammed down a flurry of hammer strokes. She paused briefly for breath, noticing Chloë's shocked expression, but she continued on.

It's not the men, she said to Mary. *It's you. These men were cruel, and I'm using my anger towards them to help me destroy this sculpture. But I'm destroying this sculpture to stop you, because you're cruel as well.*

She heard Mary's rage, saw Chloë stumble back under the force of it.

"Hold on—be strong," she called to her friend. She saw Amanda nodding, her forehead creased in concentration as she no doubt worked to maintain their shields as well as her own.

You see, right there, she said to Mary, continuing to work on the sculpture's demolition. *You're hurting Chloë, who's done nothing to you. Your anger against men has turned you against women as well—against everyone. And we won't let you continue doing that.*

Her efforts so far had created a crack through the back of the figure of the man on which she hammered. She hit the chisel in time with her last words, putting every ounce of strength into her thoughts of sending Mary away. Suddenly the chisel slipped through the crack.

The hammer slammed down on her left hand. Rowan yelled at the wave of excruciating pain. But she'd also been successful: More than half of the statue split off and toppled to the floor. She heard Mary's scream of rage, but it seemed not as loud.

The chisel dropped from her fingers; holding it was no longer possible. She continued smashing at the sculpture with the hammer, almost blindly, but with the same thoughts and desires clear and forefront in her mind.

Move on, Mary, she said. *It's over here for you. There's nothing for you here. Your time is past; the people who hurt you are long gone, and you've had your revenge. The people left are not your attackers. Move on.*

It was, she knew, the message she'd had to learn herself.

Amanda had planned her assault better, and had destroyed the arms of one man and knocked the head off the other. She was about to turn her attentions to the figure of Mary when Rowan shouted, "Stop!"

Both her friends stared at her. Trying to focus her mind past the throbbing pain in her wrist, Rowan said, "Mary's suffered enough. We've destroyed her attackers. Listen…"

"Is she gone?" Chloë asked in a small voice.

"I'm not sure," Amanda said, cocking her head. "Let's try something." She gestured them all to the ruined sculpture grouping, which had been shattered enough that they could stretch their arms around it and hold hands. Rowan flinched and hissed in pain when Chloë took her left hand. Chloë's eyes widened, and she turned her hand palm up so Rowan could simply rest her hand there. The contact was the important thing.

"Move on, Mary," Rowan said, aloud this time. "It's time for you to go. We respect your anger. We are alike, you and I, but we are not the same. You connected with my own fears, the mistrust I'd never been able to let go. But now I have, and you have no hold on me. You no longer have a hold on this world. Your attackers are gone, but your memory will remain. We'll make sure the truth gets told, and that you're not forgotten."

At the edges of her mind she felt resistance, as if Mary were trying to break through, but the effort was weak. "It's okay," Rowan said softly. "We won't forget."

There was a whisper-hush of sound, like the swirl of autumn leaves or the sighing of wings. Rowan thought she saw a spiral of mist rise from Mary's statue and disperse, although she couldn't be sure.

For a moment they stood, silent.

"She's gone," Amanda said finally.

Rowan nodded her agreement. The pressure on her mind—which had been with her constantly but subtly, she realized, for almost two weeks—had definitely lifted. Chloë lifted a hand to her own head, looking stunned but relieved.

"Sorry about the mess, Chloë," Amanda said, looking at the dust and piles of shattered stone, as well as the broken windows.

Chloë snorted, then started to laugh. The laugh proved infectious, and soon they were all howling, alleviating the stress that had built up in all of them for so long.

~

Rowan worried that the legal red-tape would mean the charges wouldn't get dropped against the boys; after all, they couldn't use a ghost as evidence. However, the new information that there had been a previous Mary Cooper who'd been attacked, combined with the fact that no one could find any record of the recent Mary Cooper, proved fairly convincing. The District Attorney admitted that with no hard evidence, no body, and retraction of confessions from the remaining boys, there wasn't much of a case left. Since they were minors, the charge of falsely reporting a crime just got them slapped with some community service, tasks which they all gladly accepted.

Chloë's doctor pronounced her and the baby to be in perfect health, despite the stresses of the night.

"You're definitely over whatever hump you needed to get over," Dr. Melora said. "It should be smooth sailing from here on in."

The gallery in New York City wasn't happy about Chloë postponing her show, but was interested enough in her work to schedule something for the following spring. "Before I'm too huge to actually attend," Chloë said, grinning.

The three sat on the deck, bundled in warm sweaters, gloves, and hats against the chill of a clear day. The slanting sun couldn't give enough warmth, although Rowan was obstinately sure she felt some on her cheeks. She was definitely looking forward to returning to California's mellow weather. This time of year, all she had to worry about was a bit of morning fog.

"I can't thank you two enough," Chloë said. "I don't even know where to begin! Rowan, you...you figured it all out. And you went through hell to do it. What can I say?"

"Stop," Rowan said. "You asked me to help, and I did what I could. I had to work though some shit of my own, and we can't discount Sheriff Candusco's work on the case. And even Mary helped, in her own strange, warped way. Who would've thought to look back almost a hundred years?"

"I've read about ghosts being unable to move on," Amanda said, "but never about one that re-creates their own death in order to blame the perpetrator's descendants. In a way, I'm impressed."

"Although I can't agree with Mary's motives, I have to respect her tenacity," Rowan agreed. "I know what it's like to have that sort of, well, hatred fester."

Chloë squeezed her good hand. "I had no idea you'd been through that in college. I'm sorry we couldn't be there for you."

"I didn't let you be there; it's not your fault at all," Rowan said, trying to reassure her. "I'm really better now. This whole experience has helped me sort things out in my head."

The whole experience had, in fact, changed her, in ways she'd never imagined. Her own attack, years before, hadn't left her so angry at men that she sought revenge on all of them, but it had scarred her emotionally, left her untrusting of men and unwilling to go past a certain level of intimacy. She hadn't even realized how deep that mistrust had gone.

It had gone deep enough to fester. In time, the negative feelings could have twisted and darkened. The night they'd fought and exorcised Mary, something had broken inside her. She'd seen what Mary's rage had done: Not only had she been unable to separate the men who attacked her from men in general, but the anger had warped so much that she didn't care if women were hurt as well. Seeing that, Rowan had realized on some subconscious level that she couldn't accept that, within Mary or within herself. Somehow, that realization had shattered a hardened piece of her, and the shards had melted away, leaving an open, accepting space.

Rowan knew she still had to be careful, alert, aware, just as much as any woman should be. She'd taken self-defense classes, and now it occurred to her that she might be able to share some of her knowledge, not only by teaching similar classes, but in counseling other women through their anger and pain—to, hopefully, keep them from slipping as far and as deep as Mary had.

When Toby invited Rowan out to dinner, she accepted.

She wore her sapphire-blue velvet dress, glad to have an excuse to wear it for a happy occasion, and she let Chloë talk her into having her hair done. She felt indulgent, but Chloë also pointed out that with her hand still bandaged, it wasn't as if she could do much on her own.

She found that she liked the feel of wearing her hair up. For one thing, it allowed her to show off her favorite silver-and-opal earrings.

Exposing the nape of her neck didn't make her feel as vulnerable as she'd expected.

He took her to an Italian restaurant, with deep red curtains and gold wallpaper and tiny fairy lights draped on urns and potted plants.

At first they skirted personal discussion, talking instead about everything else: the upcoming holidays, books, the weather, even the case.

"People were angry at first," Toby said. "But they backed off pretty quickly. It's almost as if they're…forgetting."

"Mary made people believe she existed in this time," Rowan said. "I imagine now that her influence has been removed, their memories will fade."

"Even I'm having trouble remembering all of it," Toby admitted. "But some of it's still clear."

She smiled wryly. "I think those of us who were closely involved will never really forget."

"That's not what I meant." Toby rested a hand over hers. Rowan turned her hand palm up and let her fingers twine with his. "How's your hand?" he asked, nodding his head at her bandaged limb.

"It didn't need a cast, but it'll be a while before I'm back up to full speed," she said. "I'm shipping most of my things home so I don't have to deal with luggage at the airport." She laughed. "Heck, I'm leaving half of it here, since I'll be back so soon. Chloë threatened me with dire consequences if I wasn't back for her show—as if I'd miss it—and of course the baby's due in the spring."

"I'm glad," Toby said. But after he'd helped her on with her coat and they'd gone outside to walk around the green and admire the holiday decorations—the big pine in the center of the green was draped with multicolored lights and every store had a window display—he said, "I wanted to mention something, in case you'd be interested. There's a new women's shelter opening in Tamarack. They're looking for someone to design and maintain their website, handle promotional stuff, as well as work with the women."

Rowan shook her head, unable to keep from smiling. "Chloë already cut out the ad for me. I'm seriously considering applying. In fact..." She caught her breath, realizing she'd just made up her mind, right there. She knew what she wanted to do. "I'm going to call them tomorrow."

"Really?"

"Yeah." She tilted her head up. It was snowing, just barely, a few flakes drifting down to kiss her cheeks. "There are a lot of things I like about California, but coming back east reminded me of what I miss, like seasons. Plus, this way I won't have to keep flying out here for the gallery opening and the baby and...other things."

Through her velvet glove, she could feel the heat of his hand when he squeezed hers gently.

"If you move here, I'd welcome your input on some of my cases," he said. "I could use you on my team."

"I'll be happy to do whatever I can," she said.

"I'd also like the chance to get to know you better," he said, and somehow, she wasn't surprised. Not so much that she'd been expecting it, but...she was glad he said it. Glad he felt it. "You impress the hell out of me, Rowan Everly. I'd like to find out whether there's the possibility of something more with us."

Rowan looked at the gently falling snow, and then she looked at Toby.

"Mary was able to move on, after all those years," she said. "It's time for me to make a few changes, too. So, yes, I'd like that. I'd like that very much."

ACKNOWLEDGMENTS

MY THANKS GO to Colleen Kuehne for her eagle-eyed copyediting skills (any mistakes are entirely mine). Cheerleading emails from Sarah Husch and Teresa Noelle Roberts during the writing of the novel kept me going. Kristine Kathryn Rusch and Dean Wesley Smith continue to offer their wisdom, advice, and friendship, which I humbly and gratefully accept.

And, of course, none of this would be possible without the love and support of my beloved, Ken.

WHAT BECK'NING GHOST
PREVIEW

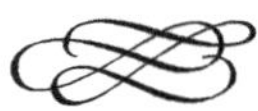

Touch not the cat bot a glove...

The MacPherson family crest above the door gives Rachael de Young, genealogist and psychic, an unexpected chill. She doesn't know that by crossing the threshold, her life will change forever. Because the MacPhersons are a family cursed by jealousy, betrayal, and fire....

Rachael grows closer to the truth even as she grows closer to the ghost of Jordan MacPherson, who died in the tragic fire...and could very well be the person sabotaging her research. But she must trust Jordan's love in order to find the strength to face her own fears, break her one cardinal rule, and stop a madman before he can kill again.

Turn the page for a sample of *What Beck'ning Ghost*, an atmospheric gothic romance from Dayle A. Dermatis.

PROLOGUE

ESPITE HER PRECAUTIONARY SWEATER, Rachael found the cellared chill taking its toll; even as she felt the sneeze building she was scrabbling in the pocket of her worn jeans for a tissue. Tucking her clipboard under her arm, she blew, dislodging an errant spiral of black hair from the ribbon at the nape of her neck. She'd tied her long mane back for convenience, but it never fully responded to her taming attempts. She poised her pen over the clipboard again.

Monsieur LaFayette was gone.

Rachael muttered a minor curse under her breath, not really angry. She was used to the curator's self-absorption when it came to "his treasures."

Part of the Musée des Arts charm was that it was housed in an historic château buried deep in France's wine country. The catacombing wine cellars that ranged beneath served as storage for most of the artifacts not presently on display, walls and floors now carefully sealed to lock out damaging moisture. Fluorescent track lighting provided an unearthly glow. Crates and boxes of assorted sizes, although stacked neatly and efficiently, made each underground room a maze in itself.

"I still should've left a trail of breadcrumbs," she said aloud, propping one ink-stained hand on her hip and leaning against a towering crate marked *Full Suit of Armour, circa 14th Century; one gauntlet dented.*

As if in response, something seemed to rattle within the crate. Rachael gasped and jumped away, imagining the side of the crate swinging open and a metal-covered arm silently dragging her in next to the missing man. Still, she moved closer and peered around it, and spied the half-hidden doorway through which Monsieur LaFayette must have gone. Resisting the urge to make a notation on the wall to help her find her way back, she ducked through the low stone opening. At five-nine, she had swiftly and painfully learned to duck when she went through old doorways.

She found the rotund curator standing before a cabinet, his head barely peeking over the open door, bald skin glinting between the carefully arranged strands of sparse hair. In the cabinet were individual drawers, each labeled in the man's precise handwriting.

"Mademoiselle is not coming down with a cold, one hopes?" he asked, not looking up. His voice reflected the concern he couldn't display while he was intent on his work.

Rachael smiled, ever amused by his formal speech. If it was the last thing she did at the Musée, she was going to get him to address her by her first name.

"I'm fine," she replied honestly. The chill really didn't bother her. Her year-long study in France—and her Master's in French History— completed, she had been ecstatic to get the plum opportunity to be apprenticed to a museum curator. She'd grown to love the small Musée. What it lacked in size, it made up for with some extraordinarily rare and unique pieces of art and artifact.

In the two months she'd been there, with another month and a half to go, she'd learned nearly every facet of directing and running a museum. She felt as if she unearthed buried treasure with every artifact they systematically categorized as they moved through the storage rooms.

Monsieur LaFayette began examining each piece of jewelry in the cabinet to ensure it was undamaged. Rachael dutifully marked them down, adding notations as to what would be done with each object: remain in storage or be put on display, and in the latter case, where it might go.

"This one would go perfectly with the green velvet evening dress," Rachael said, marveling at the intricacy of a delicate silver chain studded with glinting emeralds.

"Oui, mademoiselle—that is a lovely idea," Monsieur LaFayette said, carefully replacing the necklace in its slot. "Please write that down. We will finish here today, and tomorrow we shall begin on the top floor."

The top floor was where the more perishable objects—clothing and documents—were housed. Rachael made the note on her clipboard and returned her attention to the case of jewelry.

"Gold brooch, cross-shaped, set with 4-carat, 36-point topaz," Monsieur LaFayette knelt and read off the next label, the first on the lowest row of drawers.

"That sounds like a royal jewel," Rachael commented, as he jingled his heavy set of small keys until he found the right one.

"We believe, well..." He shrugged. "It was possibly owned by Marie Antoinette," he finished softly, and sighed.

"Possib—*really*?!" Rachael couldn't contain the excitement that leapt in her belly like a frightened hare. "What's wrong?" she asked quickly, as she saw the look on the man's ruddy face.

"We believe it was given to her by a friend just after the Cardinal of Rohan was acquitted of wrongdoing in the Diamond Necklace Affair in Versailles in 1786...but we have no documented proof," he finished sadly. "This could be the piéce de résistance of the Musée's collection, but we will never know."

"May I see it?" Rachael asked softly.

Monsieur LaFayette sat back on his haunches and smiled up at her. "Of course, mademoiselle," he said. "The brooch is quite beautiful. It is still a treasure—no matter who owned it." He slid the drawer open and, almost devoutly, brought out the carefully wrapped pouch. Rachael took it from him with solicitous hands.

As she did, she felt a chill prickle and twitch its way up her spine, a chill not caused by her current underground location. She had seen and touched many a historic object in her studies, but this one affected her differently. Could it have belonged to Marie Antoinette?

Holding her breath, she let the brooch slip from the velvet bag and cradled it in her palm. The curator was right: it *was* beautiful.

It was shaped like a cross, one long piece bisected by a shorter piece, each end flaring out into three scallops. Smaller pieces overlapped, ended in points halfway up the longer pieces. An oval band looped under all four ends, connecting them. Delicate carvings covered each piece's gold surface. The gold and topaz glimmered in the fitful fluorescent light. Rachael reverently traced a fingertip over the design. Around her, the room began to shimmer, fade at the edges.

The woman sat awkwardly in the ornate chair, her swollen belly preventing her from pulling herself close to the small writing table. The room was hot and cloying, the heat from the fireplace making Rachael's face flush. The scent of flowery potpourri was thick, almost overwhelming.

Years of study made Rachael automatically identify the woman's garments as eighteenth-century French court garb. Awed, she realized she recognized the woman from numerous portraits. Even without that, the flowery signature—"Marie Antonia"—gave no question as to the women's identity.

"June 1, 1786," she had written. "Yolande: Come and weep with me, come and console your friend. The judgment that has just been pronounced is an atrocious insult. I am bathed in tears of grief and despair." On the envelope, she carefully printed "Comtesse de Polignac." She stretched uncomfortably across the desk for the sealing wax.

Rachael fought off dizziness.

The scene changed. The woman, her figure now slim, sat very still, holding a small baby on her lap. The brooch clung to the fabric at her throat.

"T'was a gift to cheer me," she said to the painter, who had commented on the pin's beauty. Her lips thinned at the memory of why she had needed to be cheered. She forced a smile. "And to welcome Sophie Hélène Beatrice," she added, juggling the baby, who gurgled appreciatively.

Rachael shuddered, and instinctively closed her hand over the ornate pin. The images intensified.

Now the woman was gaunt, dressed in plain black, no jewels. She tried to remain regal, but her pale blue eyes revealed her fear as she was led to the guillotine. Blood red hazed the view.

Rachael pressed her hand against her mouth, muffling her own screams....

"Mademoiselle? Are you unwell? Mademoiselle de Young? *Rachael!*"

Shaking her head, Rachael pulled herself away from the images, half-reluctant to detach herself from the seductive vision. She clutched the gold-and-topaz brooch in her fist, feeling a desperate need to protect it, hide it. Monsieur LaFayette gently pried her fingers apart and replaced the jeweled pin in its case.

"Mademoiselle?"

"I—I'm fine, Monsieur," she said, staring at her hand. A pinpoint of blood initialed the spot where the pin's clasp had pricked her skin. She curled her hand into a fist again, hiding the crimson dot that reminded her of the wash of blood that had darkened her vision. A vision that had seemed—felt, smelled, sounded—entirely real.

"Monsieur LaFayette, doesn't the Musée have Marie Antoinette's diaries and letters on file?" she asked, remembering what she had seen.

"We have them on microfiche, oui."

"May I look at them?"

"By all means, Mademoiselle."

~

Rachael rubbed the spot at the small of her back that ached interminably. She'd been studying the microfiche of Marie's writings all evening, but had only found the letter Marie had written to Yolande. At first she'd been startled, almost frightened to find something that confirmed her vision. But then she rationalized: surely in her studies she'd come across the letter before, and simply forgotten until her subconscious regurgitated it.

In all the 'fiches, she'd found no mention of the brooch. She'd hallucinated everything, of course. She hadn't eaten much that day; hell, she hadn't eaten much since becoming a starving student in France. Bread and cheese had become her usual sustenance. There was no way she could have seen Marie Antoinette and those events. The thrill of seeing and holding the brooch had sparked an already overactive imagination.

She arched her back, purring with pleasure as her vertebrae untwisted. Her mind, however, remained twisted around what happened, and yet couldn't have happened. The images had seemed so *real*, though; and not just images—all her senses had been violently, acutely involved. She glared at the microfiche reader, wishing she could lay the blame on it for not divulging the information she needed.

She'd started reading the diaries on the day the Cardinal was acquitted of wrongdoing in the Diamond Necklace Affair—a twist of fate that had stunned and angered Marie, Rachael knew—and worked her way forward, day by day. The going was slow; though she knew French well enough to get by during her stay here, the unfamiliar spelling and grammar of the language in the eighteenth century hampered her progress.

There must be some other way…. Rachael snapped off the machine and turned on the small reading lamp that squeezed a place for itself on the desk next to the machine. She flipped open the spiral notebook on her lap. She'd scribbled down everything she could remember about the brooch and her hallucination after she and Monsieur LaFayette had finished the inventory. Almost without thinking, she began to sketch the pin on the opposite page. Her hand seemed to work independently of her brain—a line here, a curve here, delicate shading there to give the illusion of facets in the jewel. The tiny flowers and curves of the etched design blossomed and swirled beneath the tip of her pen….

Rachael stared at the sketch, awed and a little frightened. She'd never been able to draw much more than stick figures, but the brooch seemed to glimmer from its place on the page. Perhaps it was the dim light? She leaned forward, somehow realizing that if she'd kept going,

Marie would have come to life beneath her pen as well, soul flowing out with the ink to stain the paper with sorrow.

Maybe she'd been going about this the wrong way. A slow, tingling realization infused her. Shutting the book, she crossed the hall and stuck her head into the curator's office.

"Monsieur, was there a portrait done of Marie Antoinette to commemorate the birth of her daughter Sophie?"

The small man looked up from his paperwork and frowned thoughtfully, squinting as if to visualize the picture about which she asked.

"There was a small one commissioned when Sophie was three months old, Mademoiselle," he said. "The birth of a daughter was not a momentous occasion, of course, and the portrait is relatively insignificant. I have never seen it, and I am unsure of its exact date. If you think that is the one you mean, try the catalogues from the Musée de France—that is where the portrait of which I am thinking is hung."

Rachael gathered up the heavy catalogues from the bookcase and carried them, pressed possessively to her breast, back to the other room. She set the stack on the floor and settled the first one on her lap, tucking one leg beneath her as she sank into the chair. She leaned forward, trying to make the most of the light from the straining lamp.

Three catalogues to find it. Then, there it was: Marie, skin pale, dress blood-red as if to symbolize the blood that would someday spill. And at her throat, what had to be, despite the size of the reproduction, the brooch. She sat, one hand half-lifted to the jewel, a small smile on her lips, but a haunted, distant look in her eyes that had once been described as "imperial blue."

Rachael gripped the catalogue in suddenly sweat-slick hands, the chill down her back belying the moisture on her palms.

The picture proved nothing. It was too small to conclusively say the brooch was the one tucked away in the cabinet in the wine cellar, a masterpiece of topaz and gold languishing away in anonymity for simple lack of proof. The portrait itself would clinch it, but that was away in Paris, and she had to know now. *Now.*

Then she read the description next to the picture.

Of course. Portraits took more than a few days. She had to look in the diaries four months after Sophie's birth....

"I wore the lovely brooch from Yolande for the portrait sitting today. The painter commented on its beauty. Yolande was a dear to give it to me, but it will always remind me of the Cardinal and his forever unpunished treachery."

Searching back, Rachael found the entry where Marie spoke of receiving a brooch—a topaz-and-gold cross, described exactly like the one in the cellars—from her friend.

So it had really happened. She dropped the catalogue on the floor and drew her legs up into the chair, hugging her knees and rocking, ever so slightly, back and forth. Somehow, when she'd held the brooch, she'd been able to see the past, see directly into moments in its history.

One thought rose above the growing belief, the faint shock-fear and the swirling implications:

Would it happen again?

October, seven years later

"HAVE A NICE VACATION, EH," the cab driver said, and heaved the suitcase over the lip of the trunk.

"Thanks," Rachael said absently, handing him the money, her eyes and thoughts on the grey-and-tan stone house before her. The faintest hint of apprehension trickled down her back, like a single bead of perspiration; then it was gone, swiped away by excitement and curiosity. She wasn't here for pleasure, but for work.

Behind her, the cab kicked into gear and motored off down the driveway that ribboned its way through a row of stately evergreens. And she heard, over the silence of the Adirondack Mountains, only the faint, distant purr of a lawn mower.

Manor MacPherson spread out before her, the late afternoon sun glinting off its many windows. The massive front door, located up a wide flight of low steps, was flanked by two bulging towers. On either side of the towers unfurled the wings of the house; except for the towers, the building was shaped like a capital I, because each wing ended in a front-to-back-facing hall.

Above the front door, in a semi-circle sweep of stained glass, Rachael saw the MacPherson family crest, a cat sejant, proper, and the words "Touch Not The Cat Bot A Glove." She wondered what had prompted the ancient MacPherson clan, far away and long ago in Scotland, to adopt such a warning for their motto: "Don't touch the cat without a glove."

The ominous motto somehow disturbed her, and she reminded herself that this was a job just like any other she'd had in the past few years. Simple genealogical research, back through the MacPherson family tree. She was eager to get started.

Hauling her laptop case and overstuffed suitcase up the steps, she opened the door and maneuvered inside. She stopped. Slowly setting the suitcase back down, she looked around, enchanted.

The front room was as fabulous as the outside of the house promised it would be. On either side, a massive staircase began its ascent; halfway up, each split into two sets of stairs, heading forward and back to connect with walkways along the second floor. Above each staircase was a high skylight allowing a view of the wispy cirrus clouds outside. Hallways led left and right along the front of the house, as well as back beneath the staircases. Straight ahead were two pairs of paneled double doors, one door slightly ajar. A gilt chandelier hanging from the two-story ceiling provided crystalline flashes of light. The room smelled of fresh pine and a light, sweet scent Rachael couldn't identify.

There was no front desk, but a small sign beside a half-open door on the wall to her right said "Manager." Leaving her suitcase and computer inside the front door, Rachael crossed the parquet floor and peered in. A short woman, wearing a pinstriped blue-and-white blouse, khaki skirt, and Docksiders, was sliding a manila folder into a filing cabinet drawer. Rachael knocked lightly, and she looked up.

"Hi! Welcome to Manor MacPherson," the woman said, closing the drawer. Some of the freckles on her face vanished into the grooves of laugh lines around her eyes as she smiled. Rachael guessed her to be in her early thirties. "What can I do for you?"

"I'm Rachael de Young," Rachael said, extending her business card. Embossed in purple on the marbled lavender card were the words "Rachael S. de Young, Genealogical Researcher & Historian," and her contact information.

"You made it," the woman said, sounding pleased. "We've been looking forward to your arrival. Let me go tell Celeste you're here. I'm Karyn Cappricci, hotel manager, by the way." With barely a glance, she plucked a key from a pegboard and swung around the desk, her hip skimming the corner with practiced ease. "I'll be back in a sec—have a seat."

"Thanks," Rachael said, sinking into the indicated chair outside Karyn's office. But she'd been sitting all day—cab to plane to train to cab—and moments after Karyn had hurried off, she was up again, restlessly prowling the front room.

A host of MacPhersons had trod the floor where she walked, and she felt a heavy wave of history undulate beneath her feet. For a fleeting second she had the sensation of standing in the middle of all of them, as they surged and wandered and lived and died around her. Suddenly she felt as though she were no longer alone, and whirled. For the briefest of moments she thought she saw a pair of haunting green eyes, but she was still alone in the hall.

The MacPhersons, she knew, were known for the rich green of their eyes, and yet she couldn't shake the sensation that someone had been with her—not watching her, but being with her.

She was standing before a sweeping oil painting of what could only be the original Manor MacPherson in Scotland when Karyn returned to the front hall and returned Rachael to the present.

"I'm sorry, but Celeste is on an overseas business call," she said. "She'll be half an hour at most. Why don't I take you up to your room?" At Rachael's nod, she swept up the heavy suitcase. "Not only am I the manager, but I'm also the bellhop," she said with a grin as she marched across the polished floor toward the right-hand set of stairs. Though her hips were roundly curved, she wasn't overweight or, obviously, out of shape. Rachael's long-legged stride allowed her to keep up with the energetic woman, and she was only one step behind as they mounted the staircase.

"I was really excited to hear you were coming," Karyn said, her blunt-cut pageboy swinging at her shoulders. "I studied history for a few semesters in college, and I wish I could have taken more classes in it."

"What kind of history did you study?" Rachael asked, now curious.

"Just your basic survey courses. I didn't have many free credits to blow, and history didn't have much to do with my major, Hotel Management. It was a real treat to get the job here—this place is fabulous."

"It is," Rachael agreed admiringly. She wished she could stop and look at every object, picture, and architectural feature that they passed, but she restrained herself, knowing she'd have ample time in the ensuing days.

"This wing, the east wing, is all guest rooms," Karyn explained, leading her down a long, narrow hall. "There are a few in the upper west wing, but most of that is the MacPhersons' private living quarters. We're putting you in one of the business suites, since we figured you'd need some room to spread out your research stuff."

She had stopped about halfway down the hall, and, putting Rachael's suitcase down, inserted the large brass key into the lock. It turned easily, but Karyn had to use a shoulder to help encourage the heavy door to swing in. "Here you go," she said, standing back so Rachael could enter first.

The two-room suite enthralled Rachael, right down to the bowl of fresh flowers on the highboy and the crystal decanter of brandy and two glasses on the night table. She pulled her laptop out and set it on the desk, then slung the case back over her shoulder while Karyn laid her suitcase on the steamer trunk at the foot of the four-poster bed.

"Do you want to freshen up before you meet with Celeste?" the manager asked solicitously. "I know how tiring your trip must have been."

"No, I'm fine," Rachael said quickly. Her curiosity—what had led her to this field of study in the first place—demanded some immediate appeasement. "This is a huge house—how many rooms do you rent to guests?" she asked as she re-locked her door and pocketed the key in the comfortable jeans she'd worn for traveling.

"Twenty. We have eight regular rooms, four honeymoon suites, and six executive suites. We also have two rooms that each have an extra bedroom attached, in case a couple is traveling with a third person. We discourage small children, though—too many delicate antiques lying around."

As Karyn led her back downstairs, she pointed out the frescoes on the stairwell ceiling and the detailed carvings of the wall panels, which she said were exact copies of the originals in Scotland.

"I'm also the tour guide," she joked. "I know as much about this house as Celeste and Ian do."

"What about the family history?" Rachael asked. "Are you an expert on that as well?"

Karyn paused on the landing. "If you're talking about the tragedy, then no. It's not discussed. Since you'll be researching the MacPherson history, I'm sure Celeste will speak to you about it." Her voice wasn't unfriendly, but held a firmness that Rachael knew better than to push. She wondered if Karyn fielded this question often, because of the guide book or simply local gossip. At any rate, Celeste had hired her, so she was the one to question.

"You can wait here, in the parlor," Karyn said, pushing the double doors open further so they could walk through into the room across the front hall. "Celeste will be with you in a jiff. If you need anything, I'll be in my office. Make yourself at home." She smiled and left.

Rachael dropped her attaché case on a settee and walked to the wide bay window. She knelt on the built-in, cushioned bench and looked out at the wide expanse of lawn, smooth as a putting green and dotted with small copses of trees and, Rachael saw with delight, a stone fountain. The lawn sloped away to a thicket of trees. With the afternoon sun upon them, the tops of the trees looked afire, the leaves crackling vermilion, pumpkin, and citron flames. And beyond the trees loomed the mountains that made up the Adirondacks. The majestic peaks ringed her vision, some tree-lined and colorful, others grey with shale and slate; the highest already snow-capped, fading into blue and purple in the distance. Rachael, a Midwestern-born-and-bred flatlander, never ceased to be awed by the presence of mountains, and her attention was only drawn away when she leaned farther into the oriel and saw the edge of a garden peeking out from the right side of the house. She couldn't wait to explore the grounds. But her first priority would be the massive house.

No, she realized ruefully as she slid off the bench, her very first priority would be to find a bathroom. Finding her makeup kit, which was buried in the bottom of her attaché case, which doubled as her purse, she crossed the parlor to the door, and saw that Karyn's office door was shut. Well, she could certainly find a bathroom by herself.

"Pick a direction—any direction," she muttered cheerfully. Well, she'd been in the east wing already; perhaps it was time to explore the West. Karyn had said the family quarters were upstairs, but had given no indications that the lower level was private. She headed down the back corridor, carefully opening doors on both sides. She found two closets, a TV room, a staircase and two generic sitting rooms, and was beginning to give up hope when she discovered a short hall leading right, toward the back of the house. A whining noise caught her attention. That would mean a person, she deduced; she could ask on the whereabouts of the bathroom. She knocked, but no one answered; the whining clatter continued. She opened the door, and, surprised by what she found, she took an involuntary step inside.

Although the paneled walls, stained-glass window edging, hand-woven carpet and heavy dark furnishings definitely belonged to the manor, the rest of the office was thoroughly modernized; so much so that Rachael felt physically jolted. Two computers, each with a large, flat-panel LCD monitor, two printers (one a combo scanner/fax machine), and two telephones completed the high-tech array. The noise was from one of the printers, which was choking helplessly on a piece of paper. Rachael moved to succor the afflicted printer, tucking her makeup case under her arm. She opened the side of the printer, tugged at the paper, and it uncrinkled, revealing several more sheets that had built up in the mechanism.

And then someone grabbed her from behind.

Rachael cried out in surprise, a bright ribbon of fear twisting and knotting itself about her midsection. Her makeup case tumbled to the floor. Heart pulsing frantically, she reached deep for strength and twisted in the powerful grasp, trying to free herself from the vise-like hands that gripped her upper arms.

"Don't turn around," a voice rasped close to her ear. Rachael smelled expensive, subtle aftershave and a hint of smoke—not cigarette, but more carbon-like, as if a match had suddenly flared. She stopped trying to crane her neck around, knowing if she continued, she would only anger her assailant.

"What are you doing in here? Don't you know this is a private office?"

From his words, Rachael realized this was no baseless attacker, but rather, a servant or security guard. She tried to determine why his voice contained the unnatural raspiness, wondering if he were trying to disguise it. His strong fingers bruised her biceps. She gritted her teeth and said, "I was looking for the bathroom. I heard a noise and saw that the printer was jammed."

"The bathroom is down the hall, second door on your left," he said shortly. He released one arm to swipe her makeup case off the floor. He handed it to her, then turned her and propelled her to the door. "Stay out of my office."

As he pushed her out of the room, she caught a glimpse of the hand that held her left arm. It was smothered in a supple black leather glove.

The door shut firmly, with finality; not a slam, but neither a soft click. Trembling, Rachael didn't stop walking until she was in the bathroom. Then she sat down.

By the time she'd finished washing her hands, they'd stopped shaking and she felt calmer. She'd intruded on the man's office, and of course he'd been angry. Yes, he'd been more forceful than the occasion warranted—he'd deliberately tried to frighten her, it seemed—but on the other hand, he'd walked in and seen a stranger messing with his printer. Still, she couldn't fathom why he'd not allowed her to see who he was.

A critical look in the mirror showed her that, as she'd expected, the hours of travel had done little to damage her makeup. Rachael found the stubby end of an eyeliner and brightened the line around her eyes in a cerulean that mirrored and accentuated her eyes. A few quick dabs of powder around her nose and on the slant of her high cheekbones completed her work, and she headed back to the parlor, hoping she hadn't missed Celeste.

Celeste was nowhere in sight, and Karyn's office door was still closed. Too shaken from her encounter with the strange man to sit and stare out the window, Rachael plopped down on the loveseat next to her attaché case and pulled out the heavy, banded folder that held her notes. She wrapped the wide rubber band around her wrist.

Northwoods Press
November 1, 19--

HEATHER MOUNTAIN, N.Y. — Tragedy struck last night at Manor MacPherson when fire ravaged an outbuilding, killing three family members and seriously injuring another.

Killed in the blaze were Jordan MacPherson; his brother, Shane MacPherson; and Shane's wife, Emilie Shaw MacPherson.

Mr. and Mrs. MacPherson's son, Ian, aged 6, is in critical condition at Mercy Hospital with burns on at least 50% of his body, hospital officials said.

Heather Mountain Fire Chief Wayne LeFevre said it is unknown at this time how the fire started in the unused cottage located approximately one-half mile from the manor.

The blaze was first noticed at about midnight by friends leaving the manor after the MacPhersons' annual All Hallows Eve Costume Ball.

By the time firemen put out the fire, the cottage was gutted.

Funeral arrangements for Misters MacPherson and Mrs. MacPherson are incomplete at this time.

No further details were available at press time.

Rachael practically had the words memorized, but the clippings still fascinated her, drawing her back again and again to read the blurred words. She fished in the folder for the next article.

Northwoods Press
November 3, 19--

HEATHER MOUNTAIN, N.Y. — The New York State Police have been called in to investigate the Manor MacPherson tragedy because they have learned two of the deceased were killed not by fire, but by gun shot.

Police have determined that Jordan MacPherson and his sister-in-law, Emilie Shaw MacPherson, were both shot sometime before the fire was started. Shane MacPherson, Mrs. MacPherson's husband and Jordan's brother, was not shot, police said. He was killed by the ensuing fire.

Fire officials continued their investigation today of the Manor MacPherson fire that destroyed an outbuilding on the manor property following the family's annual All Hallows Eve Ball.

"When we learned there had been a shooting as well, we started to look for signs of arson," said Fire Chief Wayne LeFevre. Someone had spilled lamp oil around the building, a cottage located about one-half mile from the manor, he said.

Ian MacPherson, aged 6, remains in critical condition at Mercy Hospital. Dr. Joe Billings said he is unsure whether the boy will survive.

Due back at the manor today from New York City are Celeste MacPherson Jenner and her husband, Arden Jenner. The rest of the immediate family are currently in residence; letters have been dispatched to relatives in Scotland.

A wake will be held at Manor MacPherson on Friday and Saturday.

Burial will be held at 3 P.M. Sunday at the family plot in Heather Mountain.

Rachel spoke into her digital recorder.

"Reminder: see if the State Police will release the investigation records. Also, see if the Heather Mountain Fire Department has records concerning the fire investigation. And see if the chief or any firefighters who fought the fire are still around."

The mysterious fire. In the past few years, Rachael had made a career of solving mysteries—of the genealogical type. She wasn't sure what intrigued her about unraveling family relationships and charting the place of people in history, but she did know she'd chosen a rather limited specialty in the field of history. While most of her colleagues found teaching jobs and worked to get grants for projects, or settled into jobs at museums or universities, Rachael had chosen to create her own niche.

The rest of the *Northwoods Press* articles she'd found contained little information, finally summarizing that police were baffled by the violent crime. The charred remains of a gun had been found in the shell of the cottage; it was believed to have been Shane's, but there was no way to tell who had fired it: whether someone had shot Jordan and Emilie with it or whether Shane tried to defend them. There were no clues pointing towards who might have set the fire. Young Ian, though badly scarred, had survived.

A sheet of heavy, cream-colored paper slipped from the folder as Rachael shuffled through the papers. The letterhead displayed the MacPherson family crest, and along the bottom was a strip of the MacPherson modern dress plaid, black, yellow, maroon and cream. Rachael fingered the fine stationery, looking at the bold strokes making up the signature of Celeste MacPherson Jenner, the person who had commissioned her for this project.

The matriarchal woman sat behind a wide desk topped with black slate, a Mont Blanc fountain pen poised in the act of signing the paper before her, a sheet of ivory stationery. An expensive perfume rose discreetly in the air.

"I've made up my mind," she said. "It needs to be done." Her voice held

conviction, but her eyes were troubled. The person to whom she spoke stood
before her; Rachael could only see his broad-shouldered back, and his hands
where they rested on the edge of the desk—

—his left hand shrouded in a black leather glove.

The man began to turn....

Rachael gasped, the letter fluttering from her fingers. She pressed a trembling hand to her lips.

She hadn't meant for that to happen. She must be more tired than she realized—or more shaken by her confrontation. In the seven years since she'd discovered her psychic ability, she'd learned to control it. Images no longer came unbidden, unwanted, unexpected, when she held an object. But her control had just slipped, and the loss of restraint frightened her.

If she concentrated, Rachael knew she could learn a great deal about Celeste from this simple letter, including things that Celeste probably had no intention of sharing with her. She had already seen Celeste in her office in the act of signing the letter. She'd heard Celeste speak to the mystery man, smelt her perfume. That much, in a few meager seconds, from a single, simple piece of paper—and so much more was possible.

That, Rachael refused to do.

She was glad her talent for psychometry hadn't revealed itself until she was in her early twenties—when she was mature enough to deal with the implications of the power. If she decided to misuse her ability to see images by holding an object, she could delve into the most intimate and private matters a person had. Oh, occasionally the temptation was strong, as it had been when she returned from France to learn of her boyfriend's betrayal. But she'd swiftly decided that, when it came to that situation, what she didn't know wouldn't hurt her. And, she decided soon after, what she *could* know *could* hurt other people.

On the other hand, psychometry could be an extremely valuable tool for an historian. So Rachael had laid down a simple law for herself: Never use her psychometric powers on something that belonged to a living person. Sometimes that wasn't easy, for an object could be passed down through the generations, but, with practice, Rachael had learned how to focus her ability on the time period she was aiming for.

If the object had a particularly powerful event attached to it, however, images of that event might come unbidden, and she would struggle to retain her own identity and control the visions that swept her in. She had worked hard at that control, still knowing it would always be a frightening experience—consciousness snatched away, dropped into a pit where senses sharpened, experiences were unwanted and difficult to escape from. The recent shudder to her nerves had damaged her control as well.

The MacPherson project, she guessed, would be particularly difficult because the potent event had happened a mere forty years ago. The traces of memory of it would be fresh, unblurred by the passage of time, of hundreds of years of later memories pressed on top. Most of the recent history of the families she studied was relatively bland; usually the older events were more exciting. By the time Rachael handled them, the emotional aura on the objects had faded to a manageable level. But there was something about this project that had intrigued her from the moment she received Celeste's first letter.

Intrigued her—and frightened her. Frightened her in the same way that her slip when holding the letter frightened her. That was, Rachael realized, exactly why she had been apprehensive in the first place. The history of the fire hadn't been laid to rest yet, and she would no doubt continue fighting to keep herself from getting tangled in the strands of time.

She squared her shoulders. She was overreacting. She was here to study the entire MacPherson genealogy—the Halloween massacre was only a tiny part of their history, and not what she going to be spending her time on.

Despite everything, she *was* excited about this undertaking, and looked forward to spending some time in the beautiful Adirondack Mountains of upstate New York. Celeste MacPherson had said in the letter that autumn was the best time to visit the Adirondack Park. Rachael knew that the word "park" was a misnomer, bringing to mind tidy, open lands prepared for maximum visitation for city-dwelling vacationers; in reality, much of the alpine land was either privately owned or still in a state of untamed, often dangerous wilderness.

Although she'd never seen the North Country in the other seasons, Rachael had to admit she couldn't imagine a more beautiful setting than the one outside the bay window. Right now, a family of deer placidly munched their way across the lawn near the border of trees.

She shuffled through the papers on her lap, choosing not to reread the relatively unhelpful obituaries of Jordan, Shane, and Emilie, and selected a page she'd photocopied from a guidebook called *Where to Stay in Northern New York*. Pulling the rubber band from her wrist, she twisted it absentmindedly around her fingers as she read.

Manor MacPherson Built in 1850, this majestic hotel is one of the oldest buildings in the North Country. Copied almost to the stone from the historic MacPherson manor in Scotland, the hotel is still home to the MacPherson family. They opened to the public in 1956. Currently, Celeste MacPherson Jenner and her cousin, reclusive businessman Ian MacPherson, jointly run the operation. The MacPhersons also own MacPherson Syrup, Inc., one of the leading providers of maple syrup in the country.

There are few tales of ghosts or spirits at Manor MacPherson, despite a tragedy that the family steadfastly refuses to discuss. In 19--, three members of the family—Ian MacPherson's mother, father, and half-uncle—were killed one night: two by gunshot and the third in a mysterious fire, all in the same cottage on the property. Intense rumor at the time speculated that an illicit affair had been going on between two of the deceased, though no concrete evidence supports this. Some visitors to the manor say the faint notes of a piano are sometimes heard wafting from the music room when no one is inside—but it is doubtful that this romantic notion can be linked to the fire.

As if to divorce itself from that tragic night, the family still holds a gala, full-costume-required Halloween Ball every year, carrying on the family's hundreds-year-old tradition despite the fact that one took place on the night of the 19-- fire.

October is certainly a wonderful month to visit Manor MacPherson, not only for the sumptuous ball but also for the famous spectacle of fall leaves in the Adirondacks as well. Also to be noted is the foliage on Heather Mountain—the area was so named for the Scottish Highlands heather that the MacPhersons transplanted on their land when the manor was built. The hardy plants, blooming with sweet-scented flowers of purple, grey-blue and white, are another special touch that makes a stay at Manor MacPherson unique.

Manor MacPherson has managed to perfectly combine the brilliant architecture of the 1500s with the modern conveniences of the twenty-first century. Open an antique cupboard in your room and you'll find a hotpot, mugs, and a variety of imported teas atop a tiny fridge. Light switches are cleverly disguised to blend almost seamlessly with the surrounding woodwork....

"Rachael de Young?"

An older woman with impeccably coifed short white hair stood in the parlor doorway, smiling.

"Mrs. Jenner?" Rachael moved the overflowing file from her lap to the brocaded loveseat cushion so she could stand.

"Celeste, please," the woman said, coming forward and taking Rachael's hand between hers. "We can't have such formalities when we'll be working so closely together."

Rachael smiled back, feeling the last of her anxieties melt away before the gracious woman. She stuffed the photocopy back in the folder and shoved the whole thing into her attaché case.

"I'm sorry I kept you waiting," Celeste continued as they left the parlor together. "It was a phone call that simply couldn't wait."

"No problem," Rachael said. The woman was several inches shorter than Rachael, and if it weren't for her snowy hair, her erect carriage and slim figure would easily cause her to be mistaken for a woman twenty years younger. Her navy suit and simple, high-necked red silk blouse spoke of both elegance and comfort. Rachael felt grubby in comparison in her jeans and soft grey knit shirt, but Celeste seemed not to notice—or if she did, she didn't mind. "It gave me a chance to look around a bit."

"And what did you think?" Celeste held open a door and allowed Rachael to enter first.

"Everything is beautiful—gorgeous," Rachael said lamely.

"Thank you, dear," Celeste said, and moved around to sit behind her desk.

Her black slate-topped desk.

At Celeste's gesture, Rachael sank into the comfortable burgundy-leather armchair across from her. So. Even unbidden, her visions continued to be accurate to the last detail.

A cluster of framed photos held court at one corner. Rachael tilted her head around to see them. Most were older, sepia-tinted. One, of a dark-haired man, struck her soul; even though the color couldn't be in the picture, she saw him with familiar eyes of green.

"Now, I do want to go over a few things before you get started on your research," Celeste said. "Let me give you a brief overview of the family. Of course, I will always be available to you—I'll give you whatever information I can. The rest of the family is to do the same, not that there are many of us left."

"You said that's the reason you wanted the family history charted," Rachael said. Celeste's office also contained modern computer equipment, but Rachael noted that it was recessed in the back wall and doors could be closed to hide it, better retaining the manor's antique charm.

"That's definitely one of the reasons," Celeste agreed. "Really, Ian and I are the only ones of this line, and we don't seem to be leaving any heirs. I've lost track of all the different groups in Scotland—you'll track most of them down, I'm sure—but I gather they're diminishing as well. Smaller families, fewer marriages, that sort of thing. My main interest, where I'd like you to concentrate, is on our line of the family since we came to America." She leaned forward. "Another reason, Rachael, is that, besides the manor itself, the one thing everyone knows about the MacPhersons is a tragedy we had here a number of years ago. I don't want that to be the only thing everyone remembers."

"The shootings and fire," Rachael supplied.

Celeste's green eyes narrowed. "You know about that?"

"Only because I did some research before I came here," Rachael said quickly, seeing the woman's discomfort. "I'd be a poor historian if I didn't do some preliminary study before I dove into a project."

"That's true," Celeste said, sounding relieved. "So, you know of our tragedy." She breathed in deeply, the sides of her aquiline nose hollowing. "Yes, I'll admit I'm sensitive about the subject—although not nearly as much as Ian is, poor boy." She paused, considering the neat arrangements of objects on her desk: leather blotter, pen holder, closed date book. "I don't want the only thing people remember about us to be that night, and especially not the rumors about it," she said slowly. "But I admit there's a concurrent reason why I hired you."

Rachael waited.

"In the course of your research, if you can, I wonder if you could find out who murdered three members of my family forty years ago."

CHAPTER 2

*E*XCUSE ME?" RACHAEL GASPED. The warning flicker about this assignment that had been lurking in the back of her mind flared to life, Celeste's words like a piece of paper tossed on glowing embers. What, was she getting precognition to go along with the psychometry? What next? Spoon-bending? Reading auras? Astral projection?

"I'm sorry, Rachael, did I startle you?"

"A little," Rachael admitted. "I just don't understand—why do you think I could find anything more than the police did?"

Celeste rose and went to gaze out the window, which overlooked the back lawn that Rachael had been contemplating not long ago. The sun had nearly set, the blue of twilight overtaking the scene. A light in the base of the fountain turned the bubbling water to liquid crystal. The deer had gone.

"Let me tell you a little bit about my family," Celeste said finally. "My mother, Letitia, was twenty years older than her brothers, Jordan and Shane. As a result, I was seven years younger than Jordan and only five years younger than Shane; they were more like brothers to me...."

"We had already left Manor MacPherson that night."

Rachael knew she meant the night of the shooting and fire.

"My husband and I were living in New York City, where he had a business. We had come up for the Halloween Ball, but left on the last train out that night because Arden had an important meeting the next morning. Of course, we came back as soon as we heard the news."

Rachael remembered reading that Celeste's husband had died about a year ago. She wondered if that had sparked Celeste's interest in the family geneology.

Celeste turned and walked back to her desk, sitting and folding her hands before her. Her short, carefully manicured nails shone with a clear polish.

"As the youngest member of the family, and a woman to boot, I wasn't privy to much of what went on in the higher echelons of the household." She laughed shortly, derisively. "I was, however, a good listener. I still am. I heard the rumors, and I heard the whisperings of my family, and I put two and two together." Her eyes, hued the legendary MacPherson green, ensured Rachael's attention. "You've done your homework, so you know what some of the rumors were. I believe my family preferred there not be an intense investigation into the murders. I don't know if they were protecting anyone—perhaps it was simply the family honor."

Celeste smiled, a bit sheepishly, and Rachael nodded for her to continue.

"I thought that since you're already here doing research on the family, you might be able to find some answers," the older woman said. "Oh, I may be being foolish; sentimental and suspicious in my old age. But I truly would like to know what happened that night. Lay the ghosts to rest."

"Do you believe there are ghosts?" Rachael asked, remembering the tour book's offhand comment.

Celeste laughed. "Oh no, my dear, that was a figure of speech. I don't believe in spooks and spirits. I'd like to know more about my ancestors, but I don't expect them to come back themselves to tell me." She sobered. "Rachael, I would appreciate it if you didn't recount our discussion to Ian," she said. "As you must know from your research, he was seriously injured in the fire." At Rachael's nod, she went on. "Apparently he saw someone—his father or mother, probably—head to the cottage, and he snuck away from his nanny to follow. He was caught in the fire, and seriously burned on half of his body. The scars, both physical and mental, can never be erased.

"Because of his disfigurement, Ian has been tutored at home all his life. He even graduated from college with the highest honors through studying at home. Modern technology has allowed him to run his business activities and transactions from his office here in the manor. If a situation demands his presence, he sends a stand-in. He is well-known and well-respected in the business community, but never seen."

Celeste toyed with the black Mont Blanc pen in its holder. "Ian is very self-conscious about the way he looks, of course. But you're a mature woman, Rachael; I don't think you'll have any problem seeing beyond Ian's scars."

"I'm very impressed by what he's accomplished," Rachael said honestly. "It is a true testament to his spirit and drive that he has achieved what he has. I respect hard work and intelligence in anyone."

"Good for you." Celeste rose again. "I don't know how much help Ian will be to you with regard to the fire," she said as she moved around the desk. "He never speaks of it; says he can't remember, which is common in trauma cases like that, I understand. I can't imagine a child going through such an event without experiencing great shock. No matter how long ago it was, it must still bring him great pain."

"Perhaps it would be best if I let him bring up the subject," Rachael said, gathering up her bag. "He knows why I'm here—he may volunteer some information eventually."

"He might," Celeste said as they walked to the door. "We can speak about this some more at a later time. I hope that you'll have dinner with us tonight, Rachael. Guests dine separately, but as you'll be working here, I'd like you to get to know us. Karyn will be dining with us as well—we consider her part of our little family."

"I'd like that," Rachael said.

"Dinner will be at seven o'clock. We don't dress too formally, but you'll want to wear a skirt. We put out a buffet of hors d'œuvres in the parlor at six thirty; you'll be able to meet some of the other guests then."

"That sounds lovely," Rachael said, and they parted ways.

She hadn't realized how travel-grimy she felt until she'd stripped off her clothes. She found her toiletry kit and hair dryer, and carried both into the adjoining bathroom. That room was dominated by a huge, claw-footed white porcelain bathtub. Rachael noted with delight the basket of bath beads, soaps, and powders on a stool near the tub.

The plumbing at the manor was definitely modern. Water cascaded over her, the pounding spray attaining the high temperature she preferred. Lathering up a loofah, she mentally replayed her meeting with Celeste MacPherson Jenner. She found that now, upon reflection, she felt less surprised by the woman's request. She was, after all, a historian, trained in research. If the family had suppressed an investigation into the fire, then she wouldn't have much to go on; then again, with the family pressure turned off, someone might be willing to divulge some long-secret information.

There was another possibility for Celeste's entreaty, however. Biting her lip, Rachael wondered if somehow, impossibly, Celeste knew about her power. If she did, she would certainly believe Rachael was capable of solving the forty-year-old, hushed mystery.

But there was no way Celeste could know, because Rachael had never told anyone of her gift. Whenever she came close, whenever she was tempted to ease the burden by revealing its existence to another, she closed her eyes and visualized the tabloid headlines. She would not, absolutely would *not* allow herself to be known as one of those sleazy psychics who solved murders, tracked down missing children, pointed police in the direction of criminals.

After the surprise of discovering her psychometry had worn off, after she'd returned home from France, Rachael had been woken night after night by dreams of people chasing her, clawing at her, begging her to find their children, their wedding rings, the treasure they were sure their ancestors had hidden: "Touch the handkerchief— oh please, this watch—can you see if you hold these strands of hair —?" They wept, they pleaded, they cajoled, they threatened. They wouldn't stop until she appeased them, and then others would take their places, crying out for the same help; the stories differed, but the desired end was the same. They beat upon her until she acquiesced, and more came and demanded until Rachael dropped of exhaustion. She would wake shivering in her bed, more tired than she had been when she lay down, feeling physically pummeled and sore.

Those nightmares had been interspersed with dreams of cowering as others taunted her as a freak, a crazy, a psycho. Even the gentle faces of her parents would surface, swimming to the forefront, their eyes questioning and fearful.

So Rachael had rented a cabin on Nag's Head for a weekend, and sometime Saturday night, in the dream-suppressing haze of vodka, she had sworn to herself that she would tell no one. She accepted the power, agreed with herself to use it discreetly in her work and never for personal gain.

The dreams never returned.

Rachael wondered if Ian had had such nightmares, or worse, had experienced the taunting, the pity or the fear. He hadn't been born with his scars, they had been thrust upon him as her power had been thrust upon her. But unlike her, he had no way to hide them.

A trail of conditioner tickled down her cheek, breaking Rachael from her reverie. No, there was no way Celeste could know of her psychometry; there was no reason for her to panic. She was tired, and feeling vulnerable; that was all.

After her shower, she put on her favorite dress, a comfortable turtleneck that hugged her upper figure and flared out at the waist. She knew the teal blue brought out her eyes and the form-fitting cotton knit accentuated her slim waist. She worked hard at her figure, having inherited her mother's bountiful bosom and thus the tendency to gain weight, despite slim hips gained from her father's side of the family. Rachael was unable to resist a twirl before the mirror, flaring the calf-length skirt nearly to her stocking-tops…but in mid-twirl her ankle twisted and she nearly fell, catching the wall just in time.

"Damn heels," she muttered as she eased into the chair in front of the floral-skirted dressing table. She crossed one leg over the other and glared at the black, spike-heeled pump. She grasped the heel, and it wiggled obligingly. "Damn," she repeated. She made mental note to take it in to a shoe repair shop in town, and leaned forward to apply her makeup. A silver Victorian-inspired necklace and matching heart-shaped earrings, a jingling cluster of bangle bracelets at her left wrist, and her grandmother's silver-and-diamond ring on her right hand, and she was ready.

She didn't hurry downstairs; instead, she lingered, admiring the manor and all its intricacies: the ornate carvings, the surprises of tiny portraits and landscapes tucked in unusual nooks, the occasional well-placed antique chair or table. An object propped on a built-in shelf caught her eye, and she paused to examine it. It was an old cloak pin: a crest badge, and a MacPherson one at that; Rachael could just make out the faint letters of the motto on the curve of the gold circle. After a brief hesitation, she picked it up. She needed to find out whether she was back in control of her power.

Cupping the cloak pin in her palms, Rachael stared at it until she had its curves and clasp memorized. Closing her eyes, she pictured the pin, and hefted its weight in her hands, the metal heavy and cool. Then, carefully, she blanked her mind of all thoughts and opened herself to whatever might come.

The room smelled of tallow and peat, of unwashed bodies—and of death. By the fire it was warm, but the rest of the room felt cold and damp. The fire provided the only illumination, for it was twilight outside the small, unshaded window.

A man lay on a pallet, eyes shut, unmoving. A woman gently unfastened the cloak pin from his woolen wrap and straightened, turning to face a young boy of no more than fifteen, his face pale beneath his shock of red hair. He stood, back straight, as his mother pinned the badge to his cloak with trembling fingers.

"You're the eldest, now, Ewen," she said, her eyes bright with unshed tears. Rachael had to struggle to understand her words, garbled by her thick brogue. "You're the laird of our house. We'll send word to th'MacPherson in the morn."

Rachael let out a whoosh of air and opened her eyes, blinking to reorient herself in the brighter-lit hallway, and the present. She gently replaced the pin on the shelf. She longed to retreat to her room, find the art pad and colored pencils as yet unpacked, and dust the fine freckles on the boy's cheeks. Though she had no real talent for art most times, after she used her power she found she could render the scene in exquisite precision, often revealing details she hadn't noticed.

Realizing she was now late, Rachael hurried the rest of the way down the hall to the staircase. Halfway down the stairs, she paused on the landing, listening. Subtle music drifted out of the parlor between the open double doors; she identified the faint droning wail of bagpipes. From this angle she couldn't see inside, but she heard the murmur of voices as well. She quickly started down the last flight of stairs.

And then the heel of her shoe snapped. Rachael felt herself pitching forward and grabbed frantically for the banister, her stomach lurching. Her fingers skidded along the finely polished wood, unable to gain purchase. She cried out.

A firm hand grasped her elbow, stopping her fall, hauling her upright. She clutched at the banister again, and this time, steadied, she managed to grab hold of it. Gasping, she gripped the sturdy wood with both hands, and turned to thank her savior.

No one was there. She could see both flights of stairs after they split, and there was no way someone could have gotten down one of the hallways before she turned. She slowly sat down.

"Rachael, are you all right?"

The voice was Celeste's. The woman had emerged from the parlor. Several other faces peered from the room in consternation.

"I'm fine—my heel broke, and I stumbled," Rachael said, willing her heart to slow its incessant drumming. She held up the offending shoe; the heel dangled. She took a deep breath. "I'm fine."

The other faces receded politely. As she approached the doors, Celeste asked, "You're sure you're fine?"

Rachael nodded. "I need to go get another pair of shoes."

"No, you rest for a moment. Maria?"

The black-and-white clad servant paused in the doorway to the parlor, looking up at them.

"Could you run an errand for me, please?" Celeste asked. Maria passed her tray of shrimp cocktail to another maid in the parlor and came up the stairs to where they were. Rachael described the shoes she wanted, and gave Maria her room key and the pumps.

"You're still pale," Celeste said. "Would you care for a drink?"

Rachael requested a whisky sour, and when Maria returned, Celeste passed the order on to her. The servant, her reddish-brown hair caught in a neat hairnet, smiled and hurried off.

"How many people do you have working here?" Rachael asked, slipping on the lower-heeled burgundy pumps.

"Nancy Rabideau is in charge of the staff, as well as being our full-time cook," Celeste answered as they walked down the stairs and across the front hall. "Her husband, George, is the groundskeeper. You've already met Karyn, of course. We hire out for daily maids and other servants."

As they entered the parlor, Maria arrived with her drink. Rachael smiled and thanked her.

"Now, let me introduce you to the other guests," Celeste said.

Rachael made brief small talk with all the people currently staying at Manor MacPherson. Doug and Ally, the honeymooners, giggled and said hello and went back to their contented murmuring at one another. Businessmen Brian, David, and Kevin each shook her hand gravely and then delved back into their quiet, earnest discussion; and William and Janet, a couple from nearby Plattsburgh who were celebrating their twenty-fifth anniversary, welcomed her to upstate New York.

"A couple from Alabama will be arriving Sunday," Celeste added after they had made the rounds. "Then there'll be a brief lull before the All Hallows Eve Ball crowd."

Rachael sipped her drink, feeling the alcohol warm and relax her. "You keep busy," she commented.

"We try," the older woman said, surveying the group. "Guests are the lifeblood of a hotelier, of course."

They chatted for a few minutes, and then dinner was announced. The guests filed into the formal dining room, and Celeste led Rachael to where the family would be having their supper.

If this is the small *dining room....* Rachael thought, gazing around the expansive room. The white vaulted ceiling was crossed with dark beams, and a dark, carved wooden screen half-hid a door on the side wall that probably led to the kitchen area. A tapestry on the back wall depicted, appropriately, a medieval feast scene. A long heavy table dominated the room, a drape of milky lace upon it. The table was set with Bird of Paradise china and a delicate crystal that glittered in the light provided by an overhead chandelier, carefully dimmed, and candles on the sideboards and dining table.

Rachael was several steps into the room before she realized there was someone already seated at the rectangular table; at the long end, away from the door. His profile was to the women as they entered, the candles causing his silhouette to flicker. He was studying something on his lap, pausing only to type some figures into the calculator that sat on the table next to him; his plate had been pushed aside to accommodate the small machine.

"Ian," Celeste said affectionately as they walked toward him, "Can't you set aside your work long enough for dinner?"

"I was just going over a few figures before everyone else showed up," he said, his fingers swiftly tapping. He examined the calculator's display out of the corner of his eye, made a notation on the paper on his lap, then flicked off the machine. He slid something, which seemed to be a book of matches, off the table and into his jacket pocket.

"Ian, this is Rachael de Young, the historian I hired."

"Ms. de Young." Ian stood, and, smiling, extended his right hand.

Rachael was glad Celeste had prepared her for Ian's looks. She could imagine how it must hurt him when people unwittingly flinched at the sight of the shiny, puckered skin on the left side of his face. He had grown his hair longer and combed it down to cover the burned area on the side of his scalp where no hair now grew. No left eyebrow remained, and the scars tugged up at the left corner of his mouth. The burn scars continued down his neck until they disappeared into the starched collar of his shirt. His left hand was shrouded in a black leather glove.

"Good evening, Mr. MacPherson," Rachael said calmly, returning his firm grip, remembering how his hands had painfully gripped her arms and shoved her from his study.

"I'd like to apologize for my actions earlier this evening," he went on. "I didn't realize who you were."

"That's quite all right," Rachael replied. "I can imagine how it must have looked to you, finding me fiddling with your printer."

"I hadn't realized you two had met," Celeste said, looking from one to the other.

"We ran into each other earlier, briefly, when I was waiting for you," Rachael said quickly, not wanting to embarrass Ian by relating the whole story. Before she could continue, however, another voice called out,

"Oh, dearie me, I'm not late, am I?"

Rachael turned to see a petite, elderly woman enter the dining room. She walked with a cane, but seemed to be using the instrument not as crutch, but as a way to propel herself faster toward them.

"No, Felicity, you're not late," Celeste said warmly. "Come and meet Rachael."

"Rachael!" The woman took one of Rachael's hands between hers. Rachael expected frail hands, but instead felt wiry strength beneath the papery, cool skin. The woman's green eyes were bright and seemed to regard her—and the rest of the world—with bemused contentment. Paint, bright orange, smudged her cheek. "How good of you to come! I'm Felicity MacPherson. You must call me Felicity— don't be stuffy just because I'm old; I won't stand for it."

"Thank you, Felicity."

"Felicity is my aunt—she and my mother were twins—and Ian's half-aunt," Celeste explained. "She's an artist."

"So I gathered," Rachael said.

"Whoops!" Felicity looked down at the paint-spattered smock she still wore. Leaning her cane against a chair, she reached behind and untied the apron. She looked around thoughtfully, then opened the credenza along the side wall, wadded up the smock and tossed it inside. Shutting the door, she leaned against the credenza with an innocent smile that was negated by the wicked twinkle in her eyes.

Celeste cleared her throat. "Felicity is quite well known in the Adirondack area, as well as central New York and Vermont. She had several shows in New York City that were rather successful."

"You might want to include some of Felicity's work in the volume of family history," Rachael suggested, delighted by the whole interchange.

"That's a lovely idea," Celeste agreed. "I had been considering a gorgeous oil she did of the manor."

Maria slipped into the room through a back door and informed Celeste that the guests had been served.

"Please tell Nancy we'll wait a few more minutes," Celeste told her. "Karyn hasn't arrived yet."

"Rachael, may I refresh your drink?" Ian asked. At her nod, he took her empty glass to the row of crystal decanters on the far sideboard. She noticed that he walked with a slight limp, as if the left side of his body were stiff. When he returned, she sipped the cold, sour drink and asked him about the business of running a hotel. He was describing their different forms of advertising when Karyn hurried into the room.

"I'm sorry I'm late," she said breathlessly. "Brett's sitter cancelled at the last moment, and I had to drive him to a friend's house in town. Brett's my son," she added for Rachael's benefit. "I'm also a mother," she said with a grin, continuing her earlier listing of her duties.

"You don't live in town?" Rachael asked.

"Karyn and Brett, as well as Nancy and George, live in cottages on the grounds," Celeste supplied. Seeing Maria peering into the room, she nodded at the servant's unspoken question. "Why don't we sit down?"

They clustered at one end of the long table, Ian at the head, Celeste on his left and Felicity to his right. Ian poured everyone wine as Maria and a plump, middle-aged woman, who was introduced to Rachael as Nancy Rabideau, brought in the first course, a crisp green salad with bright cherry tomatoes and Roquefort dressing.

The conversation flowed with the wine, enhancing each course of the meal. Karyn asked Rachael about her work, and so Rachael found herself at the center of attention during most of supper. Everyone seemed honestly interested in her career, although she noticed that Ian grew quiet when she discussed the family studies she had done.

"It seems to me," he said finally, "that the past is the past. What do we really gain by spending so much time and energy studying it? Isn't it better to look to the future, work toward it?"

He didn't speak antagonistically, and Rachael wasn't offended by his questions. He brought up a debate in which even historians took sides.

"Some say we can learn about the future from studying history," she said, dabbing cream sauce from the corner of her mouth with her napkin. "You know the old idea: that we must learn from our mistakes or forever repeat them."

He set his fork gently onto the china dinner plate. "But isn't it better to learn from our own mistakes, instead of trying to interpret someone else's?"

"You've got a point," Rachael said, warming to the debate. "The farther we go back in history, the harder it is to learn exactly what happened. The outcomes are easy to see, but it's harder to determine what caused them."

"Let the past be the past—let it rest," he said.

"Ian," Celeste said.

"'The circumstances are in a great measure new. We have hardly any landmarks from the wisdom of our ancestors to guide us,'"

Felicity quoted. "Edmund Burke," she added as they all looked at her, and popped an asparagus tip into her mouth.

"Felicity," Celeste said in the same tone of voice she had directed at Ian.

"Oh no, that's okay," Rachael said quickly. "I've had this sort of discussion many times before. Many people feel the way Ian does. Unfortunately, sometimes those are the people holding the grant money."

Karyn and Felicity chuckled, and even Celeste had to smile.

"Well, what Rachael does is different," she said. "Researching a family's genealogy is a way to make the past relevant."

"I don't agree," Ian said. "In fact, I see less of a point in finding out that, oh, one's ancestor owned twenty head of cattle or fought in the Battle of Hastings."

Rachael chewed a piece of chicken, savoring the creamy wine sauce. "Some people simply find it interesting," she said. "For others, it's a matter of pride to be able to say their great-great-great-whoever came over on the *Mayflower*."

"I've always felt our ancestors helped shape who we are today," Karyn spoke up.

"What a lovely way of phrasing it!" Celeste said. "That's exactly what I was thinking—I've just never been able to put it into words."

"I like to believe I've shaped myself." Ian looked up. He rolled his knife between his fingers; candlelight glinted off the blade. The scars on the left side of his face seemed to pulse a deeper red. "I am who I am because I've worked, and struggled, and learned—and yes, failed, and learned from my own mistakes. My great-great-great-whoever had very little to do with it."

"'People will not look forward to posterity, who never look backward to their ancestors,'" Felicity said complacently. "Also Burke."

"Then you're not in accordance with Celeste on this project?" Rachael asked Ian.

He set down the knife carefully, the end of the blade resting on his plate. "Celeste and I discussed the matter at length before you were hired," he said finally. "While I may not be in total agreement on the necessity or value of this research, I will give you my full cooperation." He smiled slightly. "I was overruled, but that doesn't mean I'm not a graceful loser. Please don't hesitate to come to me with questions, Rachael. I do want to help you."

"Thank you," she said. The strained atmosphere escaped out the door as Nancy and Marie brought in the dessert, a fresh fruit sorbet and slices of spongy, light pound cake.

~

After supper they retired to one of the sitting rooms Rachael had found on her quest for the bathroom. Large mirrors on the walls, gilt-framed, made the room seem larger without reducing its intimacy. The fireplace held a careful placement of birch logs, a fire unnecessary this early in the season.

Finally feeling the effects of her day of traveling, Rachael declined an after-dinner crème de menthe and chose another cup of coffee instead. The French vanilla aroma was rich and comforting.

Celeste asked Rachael where she would be starting her research.

"I'd like to interview each one of you," she answered. "You'll all have different memories, have heard different stories about the past. I'd also like to go through whatever family papers are available. After that, I'll see about getting whatever certificates—birth, marriage, death—and other official documents. My first goal is to put together as complete a family tree as I can, and then work on details from there."

"I know there's a family Bible in the library," Celeste mused. "I'll see what else I can find."

"Why don't I give you the full tour of the manor on Sunday?" Karyn suggested. "I should have the afternoon free after the Alabama couple check in. They're due at one, I think."

"Didn't Grandfather have a file of papers in his office that were related to the family?" Ian spoke up.

"I think you're right," Celeste said. "Can you find that?"

"I'll try. You know how Grandfather's study is."

Celeste turned to Rachael. "The man had a truly unique filing system," she said.

"If you don't mind, I'd love to look through his files myself," Rachael said. "There's no telling what may crop up. No offence, but you might not know if something was important or not," she said to Ian. "I've learned the hard way that anything can be useful: a receipt, a scribbled note, a ticket stub...."

"No offence taken," Ian said. "I'll look for that particular file, and you can go through the study later, at your leisure."

Rachael felt a yawn coming on, and her coffee cup clinked in the saucer as she hastily set it down and covered her mouth. "Well," she said with a laugh, "if I'm going to get any work done tomorrow, I'd best get myself to bed."

"I'll walk you to your room," Ian offered, and she accepted. She said goodnight to the others, and they left.

"I want to apologize for my actions this afternoon," he said. "I had no idea who you were."

"It was my fault as well," Rachael said. "I shouldn't have gone into your office uninvited."

"I overreacted," he said. "We should just agree to forget it happened."

"Good plan."

They lapsed into silence, Ian so silent that Rachael thought he was brooding. She noticed that he made a point of walking at her left, so his unscarred side was presented to her.

"I hope I didn't offend you with my remarks at dinner," he said suddenly. "I was in no way trying to demean your work."

"I wasn't offended," she assured him. "You presented some valid points. I'd rather debate with you than to argue with some pig-headed fool who doesn't even listen to what I'm saying."

He smiled. "I meant what I said—I'll help you in any way I can. Though I don't think I'll be much of a source for you."

"You might be surprised," Rachael said. "If you spent any time with your grandparents, you might remember some of the stories they told you."

They began the ascent of the stairs, Rachael discreetly slowing down so Ian wouldn't overextend himself.

"I won't be much help to you with regard to the night of the fire," he said suddenly. "I remember nothing."

"Celeste told me," Rachael admitted.

"I know that you will have to include that night in your research, because it is a part of our history," he said. She could hear the tension in his voice, saw the way his shoulders tightened beneath his suit jacket. "But I ask you not to dwell upon it." They were nearly to her room, and Rachael was already reaching into her small handbag for her key when he swung to face her, placing his hands lightly on her arms. "That part of the past is very painful for me—for the whole family. There is no need for you to do more than mention it in the book. That night did not shape me: I shaped myself from what remained of me after the incident. And there is nothing to be learned from the past."

"I understand," Rachael said. It was best not to argue with him, nor to agree and have him challenge her work later. "My job here is research. While I intend to produce as complete a history of your family as I can, I don't want to hurt anyone."

His shoulders dropped slightly, and he let her go. "Thank you. Good night, Rachael."

She put her shoulder to the door and bumped it open. "Good night, Ian."

The room was dark; but then, neither man needed light to know the other was there. One could sense the other's presence, and the other needed no light to see.

"She has power," one said. "Strong power."

"I know," the other said. He stared out the window. Soft fingers of clouds lovingly caressed the cold half-circle of the moon.

"You will not harm her," the first man said evenly. His words nonetheless conveyed a subtle threat.

"I will not let her learn the truth," the second man said. There was the barest hint of desperation in his voice. His fist clenched. "I *cannot*."

"But you will not harm her," the first man repeated, his words a cold presence. "I will not allow that."

END OF PREVIEW

What Beck'ning Ghost is available in print or ebook from all your favorite retailers.

ABOUT THE AUTHOR

Dayle A. Dermatis is the author or coauthor of many novels (including snarky urban fantasy *Ghosted* and YA lesbian romance *Beautiful Beast*) and more than a hundred short stories in multiple genres, appearing in such venues as *Fiction River, Alfred Hitchcock's Mystery Magazine,* and DAW Books.

Called the mastermind behind the Uncollected Anthology project, she also edits anthologies, and her own short fiction has been lauded in many year's best anthologies in erotica, mystery, and horror.

She lives in a historic English-style cottage with a tangled and fae back garden, in the wild greenscapes of the Pacific Northwest. In her spare time she follows Styx around the country and travels the world, which inspires her writing.

She'd love to have you over for a virtual cup of tea or glass of wine at DayleDermatis.com, where you can also sign up for her newsletter and support her on Patreon.

~

I value honest feedback, and would love to hear your opinion in a review, if you're so inclined, on your favorite book retailer's site.

~

For more information:
www.dayledermatis.com

BE THE FIRST TO KNOW!

Sign up for Dayle A. Dermatis's newsletter for *free* fiction, plus the latest news, releases, and more.

Sign up at DayleDermatis.com.

For more in-depth conversations and special sneak peeks, you can also support her continued work by joining her community of patrons out Dayle's Patreon.

Patreon.com/Dayle

9 781946 462084